Castaway Cottage

ALSO BY JOANNE DEMAIO

The Seaside Saga
Blue Jeans and Coffee Beans
The Denim Blue Sea
Beach Blues
Beach Breeze
The Beach Inn
Beach Bliss
Castaway Cottage
Night Beach
Little Beach Bungalow
Every Summer
—And More Seaside Saga Books—

Summer Standalone Novels
True Blend
Whole Latte Life

Winter Novels
Eighteen Winters
First Flurries
Cardinal Cabin
Snow Deer and Cocoa Cheer
Snowflakes and Coffee Cakes

castaway cottage

A NOVEL

JOANNE DEMAIO

This is a work of fiction. Names, characters, places, and incidents are either the product of the author's imagination or are used fictitiously. Any resemblance to actual persons, living or dead, events, or locales is entirely coincidental.

No part of this book may be reproduced, or stored in a retrieval system, or transmitted in any form or by any means, electronic, mechanical, photocopying, recording, or otherwise, now known or hereinafter invented, without express written permission of the copyright owner.

Copyright © 2018 Joanne DeMaio
All rights reserved.

ISBN: 1717066216
ISBN-13: 978-1717066213

www.joannedemaio.com

Title Page Photograph:
National Oceanic and Atmospheric Administration/Dept. of Commerce
Photographer: American Red Cross

To the last-standing cottage on the beach

A storybook in the sand.

one

THE BEACH IS EMPTY TONIGHT. Beneath a heavy rising moon, all Jason Barlow sees are shadows. From the boardwalk, he looks out at the water to the idle swim raft. If he squints just right, can't he picture vacationers drying off there after a cooling swim earlier in the day? It's still so warm, it wouldn't surprise him if someone were on the raft even now.

Still in his suit pants, Jason long ago shed the jacket and wears his dress shirt unbuttoned and untucked over a tee. He steps off the boardwalk onto the sand. The distant rocky ledge at the far end of the beach is merely a dark silhouette against the moonlit water. Near the rocks, he can make out the last-standing cottage on the sand. Pale lamplight fills a few of its windows, the light casting illumination on the wraparound deck, on the surrounding scrubby dune grass.

He crosses the beach to walk down near the water. After a long day, the hard-packed sand below the tideline soothes his gait. His dog runs ahead, sniffing the salt air and nosing the dry seaweed on the beach. Walking alone in the summer hush, all Jason hears are leftover echoes of the christening celebration earlier that evening. Voices laughing and talking, silverware clinking on plates, glasses ringing in toasts.

One thing the night beach is good for is this: It keeps him company. There's always a memory stirred, or the voice of his brother's spirit drifting in on a sea breeze, or in a wave breaking on the beach, or in the boats creaking against pilings in the marina.

How many miles has he clocked walking along the water's edge at Stony Point? It's a thought that strikes Jason tonight. His mind drifts then ... much like the line of seaweed snaking down the beach.

There were the countless times as a kid, crossing the sand with his father and brother. Loaded down with crabbing gear, together they headed toward the rocks. Those days, the walks were all quiet talk, and life lessons his father gave them with his 'Nam stories or sea lore.

Later, there were the times when Jason acclimated to his prosthetic leg, relearning *how* to walk. That was when he discovered the best place on this blessed earth to cradle his gait, his thoughts, his torment, was on this very stretch of sand.

But more recently, Jason found himself storming off down that beach. Three years have passed since he kept his best friend, Kyle, from meeting a clumsy, drunken death. It happened in a near-fall off the boardwalk and onto the concrete walkway of the boat basin below. Jason saved him with one last-second yank. But Kyle's callousness with his own life that night infuriated Jason. He worked that emotion off walking down the dark beach alone afterward. It was the first time Maddy ran after him, the German shepherd sensing his distress. She still does.

Hardest to believe is that it's been over two years since he and Maris walked the winter beach on Christmas Eve. They headed toward the snow-dusted boardwalk, where potted fir trees twinkled at either end. That's the night when Jason took her hand in his and proposed to her.

Which led to his wedding reception right on the beach two summers ago. That evening, strolling the water's edge with his bride, Jason finally felt like a very fortunate man.

Still did last summer, when Sal caught him deep in private thought—talking to his brother's spirit in the night. After explaining himself, he and Sal walked the high tide line to the boat basin. There, they boarded Sal's rowboat and drifted out on the Sound ... their words drifting, too, talking about Jason's brother Neil, and about Sal's life growing up in Italy.

During all those seaside walks, there was one constant, one beacon in the night: the last-standing cottage far down the beach, near the rocks and patch of woods beyond. The cottage rose there on the sand, sometimes illuminated, sometimes in dark shadow against the even darker night.

Tonight? A few lights are on in the rambling beach house, so someone is definitely there.

Jason continues walking along the high tide line. Waves lap at the shore, but no breeze lifts off the water. With each step, that one cottage looms closer. The slight illumination of lamplight spills onto the deck. Seeing the cottage in years past, the sight used to be a comfort.

Now? The sight of that grande dame of the beach feels bittersweet. The cottage is showing signs of deterioration, revealing hints of summer stories to share. How he itches to sign it on for his new cottage-renovation TV show. But after leaving a voicemail with the owners days ago, no one ever called him back. They must not be interested.

Even his brother, Neil, was fascinated by that one cottage. He set his manuscript there—the manuscript Jason's beautiful wife, Maris, has now taken on in her commitment to finish Neil's story. So the house remains a special place, indeed ... alone on the beach but so out of Jason's reach.

While the waves gently roll onto the sand, the low moan of a distant foghorn carries in the still night air. Close to that lone cottage now, he can better see its details in the dim moonlight: the elevated white deck; the big windows facing Long Island Sound; the dune grass growing wild behind it.

Suddenly, there's a harsh noise. A slider screen, rusty in its tracks, abruptly opens—as though the person pushing it open is agitated, or annoyed. In a moment, a woman walks outside and leans her arms on the deck railing. She's looking out on the dark beach.

Looking, actually, directly *at* Jason. What alarms him then is her serious tone of voice when, not taking her eyes from him, she begins talking.

"You're late," she says.

two

"STRIKE ONE, MR. BARLOW." STILL leaning on the deck railing, the woman squints through the darkness at him. "Already you're wasting my time."

"Excuse me?" Jason looks back down the beach, then turns and points to himself. "I am?"

"Didn't you get my message?"

"Message?"

"Text message. You were supposed to be here by eight o'clock."

Frantically, Jason pulls his cell phone from his pocket, all while explaining. "I was at a get-together. There was no service there."

"A party?" the woman asks. "Seriously?"

"No." Jason's scrolling through his messages and doesn't find any from this annoyed woman watching him. "I mean, a *christening*. I was the godfather." He returns his phone to his pants pocket, then lifts his arms to show his dress shirt—loose and unbuttoned now—as he walks closer to the cottage-on-stilts. At the same time, he's also trying to size up this woman standing on the deck. "I'm sorry, I never got your message."

"If you didn't get my message," she instantly tosses down at him, "what are you doing outside my home?"

"What?" Okay, so she wastes no time, minces no words, and thinks fast. Unlike he's doing, caught totally off guard. "I was just ... *walking*. I live here, over on the bluff. On Sea View Road? I walk the beach with my dog."

"Why don't I believe you?"

He hooks his fingers in his mouth and gives a sharp whistle. When his German shepherd lopes out of the shadows to his side, he orders her, "Maddy, sit." Then he motions his hand to the dog while watching this defensive woman on the deck.

"Well, it doesn't matter now," she states.

Still the woman doesn't move. She simply squints into the darkness as though trying to decipher some details, or see his expression. Something. But he's standing in shadow on the sand. Then, as suddenly as she had slid open that rusting slider, she abruptly turns and heads back inside.

"Wait!" Jason looks over his shoulder, then at her again. "It's late, but I can get my papers and come right back."

She glances at her wristwatch. "I was closing up for the night, Mr. Barlow. Don't need to hear a sales pitch. You're not looking to buy this cottage, are you? Because it's not for sale."

"Absolutely not, Carol. It's Carol, right?" When she pauses near the slider, lamplight from inside falls on her. So he can make out that her hair is bobbed in a blunt cut above her shoulders. Long bangs sweep her eyes. She wears a tight black tank top with fitted jeans. A faded red sweatshirt is slung around her waist so that the fabric hangs down her backside, with the sweatshirt's sleeves knotted in front. "I'm a local architect," Jason quickly adds. "This cottage here is perfect for a new venture I'm part of." Now he stands at the bottom of the deck stairs. "Do you own this place?"

"I'm the owner's daughter," she tells him, still standing half inside, half outside.

"I'm really looking for the owner. Can you put me in touch?"

"I can." Now she turns to face him directly. "But you have to get through *me*, first. And I was about to call it a night."

"I'm really sorry I didn't get your message." He grabs onto Maddy's collar when the dog tries to climb the steps. "Five minutes," he insists. "If you can give me five minutes."

"You had your chance." As though out of patience, Carol waves him off and turns to the door once more. She slides it along its rusted, squeaking tracks.

All Jason remembers now is his wife's aunt, Elsa, recently reminding him how persuasive he can be. Because let's face it, he convinced her—stubborn and decisive in her grief—to *not* sell her inn, and to complete its renovation.

But the problem tonight isn't Elsa, who he *knew* well enough to badger.

It's Carol. She's a tough nut to crack, and he's not sure *what* one-liner might sway her. Because it's obvious he has time for only one stinkin' line. She's so done with him, brushing him off like a bothersome gnat.

And he's seconds away from her slamming that slider shut.

"When my brother was alive," he calls out as he climbs a few steps, "he'd say that every cottage tells a story." He hopes it works, bringing Neil into the mix. Hell, Carol looks like a beach girl. With that tousled sun-bleached hair and those casual clothes, plenty of her life's stories must've happened right in this cottage.

Then there's her attitude, too. Damn, even that has some beach-girl edge.

"And I'd like to help tell *this* cottage's story, right here," Jason persists.

Once more she does it. This Carol-with-an-attitude turns and slightly bends as she squints through the misty darkness. What little illumination falling from the cottage windows doesn't reach him, though.

"Have a seat at the patio table." As she says it, she moves to a few deck lanterns and begins lighting them. "You have fifteen minutes to make your case."

At the end of a long and hectic day, it feels so good to be in comfy clothes. Wearing her turquoise chiffon caftan, Elsa crosses the kitchen and puts a knitted cosy on her teapot. After shouldering open the side door, she carefully steps outside and carries the covered teapot across the dewy lawn to Celia's guest cottage.

Halfway there, Elsa stops and looks out toward the distant beach. A heavy moon rises over Long Island Sound, and in the still air, she hears the small waves lapping. The beach is dark, though, except for the lone cottage on the sand. Surprisingly, a few of its windows are illuminated tonight, and some lanterns are flickering on the deck. After considering it a moment longer and wondering if Jason knows someone is there, she continues on to Celia's. There, she sets the teapot on a porch table and knocks on the screen door. "Yoo-hoo!" she quietly calls in.

"Elsa?" Celia asks, hurrying closer from the other side of the screen. "What are you doing here?"

"I saw your lights on. Have a tea with me?" Elsa motions her arm to the waiting teapot. "Chat about this love-filled day?"

"Of course! Come on inside."

"Wonderful, because the tea is just about steeped." Carrying in the warm teapot, Elsa follows behind Celia. Lamplight casts a golden glow on the white board-and-batten living room walls. "You put Aria to bed?" Elsa asks.

"She's sound asleep," Celia answers over her shoulder. "Completely worn out after being outside in that salt air all afternoon. Sleeping just like her father used to, so deeply."

At the kitchen counter, Elsa pours two cups of tea. Behind her, Celia sets out placemats on her painted kitchen table. "The caterers cleaned up everything already," Elsa tells her. "They did such a nice job with the party." She sets the teacups on the distressed white table as Celia arranges a plate of raspberry pastries. They sit then, add cream to their tea and make small talk.

"It was such a beautiful day," Celia says while stirring a spoon in her cup. "And Aria wearing the same christening gown that Maris and Eva wore, well, it made the day all the more special."

Elsa sips her tea. "Your daughter stole the show today."

"I want to have another look at those necklaces you gave us." Celia reaches over and brushes through christening gifts on the end of the table. She finds her star pendant and clasps it behind her neck. "This is just gorgeous," she whispers.

Elsa, meanwhile, lifts the shining brass ring out of Aria's happiness jar. "Jason finds such meaning in the simplest things. I mean, a carousel brass ring!" She holds up the soft ribbon and the dangling polished ring glimmers. "He made this as precious as the finest gold. Which is why he's so good at what he does—restoring run-down beach cottages. He makes them shine again." Elsa glances around the kitchen at the dried flower bunches hanging from exposed ceiling beams; at the vases of sea glass and heather on a pine wall shelf. "Look at what he did with this old guest house!"

"I know." Celia reaches across the table and squeezes Elsa's hand. "Hey, what are we doing tomorrow? It's Monday, after all, a workday. *And* the last week of July already. Should we finish stocking the inn's gift shop?"

Elsa shakes her head.

"No?" Celia asks, sitting back and sipping her tea.

"No. Tomorrow will be a perfect summer day, sunny and dry. We'll put Aria's new playpen on the beach, under the umbrella. And we'll have a nice, quiet time after today's busyness. Because, as I've mentioned to you," Elsa says, her voice dropping, "before the inn opens, I want to savor some of these summer days."

Celia hesitates, then a slow smile comes. "Okay," she whispers in the hushed kitchen. Outside the open windows, a cricket lazily chirps in the night. "Just the three of us, sitting beside the sea."

It feels like a wave's breaking right on him. Seawater pelts his face, his arms, his whole body—drenching him instantly. Standing outside in the brunt of the hurricane, it's like he is standing on the deck of a boat on a stormy sea, its crashing waves washing over it.

But he isn't. He quickly closes the slider behind him, then bends nearly in half against that wind as he crosses the cottage deck to the railing, holds on tightly, then lifts his face to the sea spray. Of course, it's not a wave hitting him, though the storm surge is so high, it wouldn't surprise him.

Instead, it's simply the category-four winds carrying that much water, whipping his hair and face, dousing him but good. Doesn't matter. Because anything feels better than being inside that cottage right now. He'll take this as long as he can.

Or at least until he feels her touch. Feels her drape a blanket over his shoulders and turn him around as she huddles beneath the blanket with him.

Maris, lying in bed with manuscript pages scattered on the sheet, can so picture this visual. Which is why she likes to review

Neil's manuscript before she goes to sleep. In the morning, she often wakes up with an idea of where to take a scene, a chapter, a paragraph even. To help the muse now, a hurricane lantern shimmers on the nightstand.

When Jason walks into the room, though, she looks up from the pages.

"What a night," he says as he heads to his dresser. He stands there and empties his pockets, putting coins and his keys on his dresser top, then takes off his button-down shirt.

"Have a nice walk?" Maris asks from the bed, then resumes reading.

"Well. An interesting one, anyway."

Okay, so now he has her attention. She sets her papers beneath a brass ship-wheel paperweight on the nightstand as Jason walks to his bedside chair.

"You won't believe it," he tells her while hanging his shirt on the chair back, then sitting. He bends and lifts the loose fabric of his suit pants to remove his prosthetic limb. As he pulls it off, his father's dog-tag chain slips from his tee's collar. "Man, I was caught *so* off guard."

"Really?" Maris sits up straighter and props her pillow behind her. "What happened?"

Jason looks over as he sets the prosthesis aside, then peels the silicone liner off his stump. "Carol Fenwick is what happened."

"No way! The lady from the cottage? I thought she was ignoring you."

"I thought so, too." No sooner does he say it than his cell phone dings. Three times. So he pulls his phone from his pants pocket. "Yup. There they are," he tells Maris, flicking his phone screen. "The text messages I *never* got at Elsa's tonight, when we were sitting outside with everyone. No cell service there." He tosses the phone on the bed for her to see, then puts the silicone liner on a small table near the chair.

"Oh my God," Maris says before setting the phone on her nightstand. "So you *met* her?"

After explaining how he finagled a few minutes from this Carol and talked on her deck, he tells Maris the rest.

"She's got a real wall up, but I broke through and somehow passed the first round with her." Jason pauses as he lifts himself on one leg, takes off his pants, then sits again and pulls on his navy drawstring pajama shorts. "Now comes the hard part. I need her father's approval—and if he's anything like his daughter, it won't be an easy feat."

"They're not thrilled with the opportunity? You know, to have a pro come in and restore their cottage to its former glory?"

"Not *this* family. They've had lots of bogus offers from folks who *want* that coveted property. You know, it's the crème de la crème of Stony Point. So those Fenwicks are *really* standoffish, and suspicious—almost to an extreme—of *anyone* who comes knocking."

"But you said you passed round one with Carol. So what's next?"

Jason maneuvers himself to the bed and settles beneath the sheet. "Wednesday's round two. Like I said, I'm meeting with her father, who actually owns the place. The cottage has been in the family for generations, and my worry is that he'll be far more protective of it than his daughter."

"But that's good, right? I mean ... that you'll at least *have* a round two. You'll talk to him, and try to convince him?" Maris reaches over and touches Jason's whiskered face, dragging a finger along his jaw. Though she's hopeful, what she doesn't say is that he looks tired tonight—more fatigued than the christening and beach meeting should've left him. "So maybe round two won't be so bad?" she whispers.

"We'll see." He plumps the pillow beneath his head and sighs as he settles into it. "All I know is that it's been one helluva day."

three

For Kyle Bradford, every morning starts the same way in their house on the bay. He opens a moving box. It's not much, but his box-a-day routine helps get the dwindling mountain of cartons emptied and tossed. And one thing's for sure: You never realize how much stuff you have until you move.

Well, *two* things are for sure. The second being that nothing—no way, no how—stops Kyle from getting his single daily box unpacked. He's put away linens; photo albums; toys; tools. You name it, he's inventoried it and stashed it in its new rightful place on a shelf, in the garage, in the kids' rooms. His mission is to have his new home fully lived in by summer's end, without a carton, box, or container of any kind left in sight.

Which is why, every morning, out comes his box cutter as he slices open a taped-and-sealed cardboard carton. Without fail. Even if he's running late. Even if he unpacked *two* the previous morning. Even if they're shorthanded at the diner and Lauren has to waitress, and her parents are watching the kids. Like on this Monday morning.

But it's early still. And he's wearing his work clothes—black pants and black tee. This way, when he gets to the diner, all that's left to do is put on a freshly pressed chef apron.

So he has enough time to sit at the small mahogany desk in his living room alcove, with today's opened box on the floor beside him. It's paperwork and family-documents day, apparently. Each banking form, each birth certificate, each medical record gets filed into the right folder, in the right drawer. Methodically, but quickly.

"A place for everything and everything in its place," Kyle whispers when he drops in the declarations page of his homeowners insurance policy.

Slowly but surely, the house is getting fully unpacked. Routine is returning to his family.

And it's all good. Especially after Aria's christening yesterday, when life felt sublime, as sweet as it's supposed to feel. That one day beneath the sun, beside the sea, made *everything* worthwhile. Even this unpacking.

Almost done with the day's box, Kyle reaches for the last few papers. On top is his and Lauren's marriage certificate. He reads it, running his hand over the details—particularly the date.

"Wow, look at that," he says to himself. "Wait. How many years?" He looks again. "A milestone! Ten years." Throwing a glance over his shoulder, he calls out, "Ell! Ell, come here."

"What?" Lauren hurries into the living room while towel-drying a breakfast dish. She wears a yellow Dockside Diner tee with black capris, ready to waitress.

"Check this out." Kyle holds up the certificate.

Without giving even a glance, Lauren pats his shoulder. "You get too distracted going through this stuff. Just finish up, because we really have to get to the diner. It's late."

"No, hang on." Kyle grabs her hand. "Seriously. How long do you think we've been married?"

"Nine years? Wait, is it ten?"

"Yep. Look at this." He hands her the paper. "Ten years."

"No kidding." Her eyes scan it quickly before she drops it on the desk. "We must've lost track after that crazy summer last year. You know, with Sal here ... and then gone so suddenly."

Kyle lifts the marriage certificate again. "Unbelievable," he murmurs. "Ten years, Ell. Best years of my life."

"Aw, honey." Lauren kisses the top of his head. "That's so nice. We should frame that." She nods to the paper still in his hands.

The paper he suddenly can't stop looking at. "Hang on."

"What now?" Lauren asks, still dragging her towel over a plate.

Kyle squints to make out the certificate details, then holds it up. "Look at that."

Lauren takes the certificate and reads it aloud. "Kyle Bradford—"

"No, no. Read it again." Kyle watches her from his seat. "*Carefully.*"

After a deep breath, Lauren tosses her dishtowel over her shoulder and reads again. "Kyle Bradford and Lauren Smith were lawfully married the twenty-third day of September."

Kyle grabs the certificate. "No. Don't you see? Klye Bradford. It says *Klye*. K-L-Y-E. Did you marry Klye?"

"No. I married Kyle. That's just a typo."

"Just a typo?" He gives the certificate a shake. "This is a sacred document, Ell. It represents so much about our relationship, and our commitment to each other."

"Kyle." She yanks the towel off her shoulder and swats his arm with it. "You're being ridiculous. We're married, and that piece of paper sitting in a file for ten years doesn't change things."

"It doesn't? But maybe that typo means we're *not* really married. Maybe ... maybe we've been shacking up for the past decade, in the eyes of God. Maybe we're living in sin."

As if to prove it, the sin part, Lauren bends low, tips up his chin and plants a deep kiss on his mouth. "Boy, did we live in *sin*, then. Remember that time we fooled around in the outdoor shower cabana? And skinny-dipping at Little Beach? *Scandalous* ..."

"Oh, no." Kyle pushes his chair back to distance himself from some painful new truth. "That's all one thing, those shenanigans, if we're husband and wife." He stretches forward, lifts the marriage certificate and quickly drops it again when he reads his misspelled name. "Now all those memories are tainted."

It's obvious Lauren doesn't buy that, not with the way she swats him again before racing Hailey and Evan to the front door to let in her parents. So Kyle drops the few remaining legal papers in the desk.

One box every day. Monday's? Done.

This document box is emptied, and so is his heart.

He picks up the marriage certificate one more time, unable to takes his eyes off his misspelled name. Can anything *else* go wrong in his life?

Forty minutes later, Lauren's day shifts into overdrive. After standing at the mirror in Kyle's diner office and putting her hair up in a topknot, it begins. First she fills a few napkin dispensers on the diner counter and adds salt to various saltshakers. It's all prep work: stacking diner T-shirts for patrons to purchase, putting out new driftwood art she brought along in a shopping bag, dusting the fishing floats hanging in the windows. As she does, the little boutiques across the street catch her eye. One, with a striped awning, sells children's clothing. Maybe she'll stop in on her lunch break and pick up back-to-school tees for the kids.

When she finally ties on her white half-apron, Jerry arrives jangling his keys and whistling a tune—ready to cook with Kyle.

"Pitching in today?" Jerry asks Lauren. He drops a few newspapers on the diner counter, complimentary for their customers.

"All week," Lauren tells him. "Covering for the head waitress."

"Stacy's off?"

"Vacation." Lauren grabs an order pad off the counter and drops it in her apron pocket. "So you've got me instead this last week of July."

"Kyle," Jerry calls out as he heads to the kitchen. "Look how nice your wife is, lending a hand here."

"My wife?" Kyle steps away from the big stove, where he'd been arranging the morning's utensils. "Let me ask you something, Jerry."

"Lay it on me." Jerry stacks a tower of clean white plates on a shelf above his stove.

It's obvious what's coming. Because Kyle hasn't stopped fretting about that darn typo since he discovered it. So—partly fussing with the coffeemaker, partly eavesdropping—Lauren hovers behind him and Jerry.

"Do you think certificates matter?" Kyle asks. "You know ... birth certificates, death certificates. That sort of thing."

"Sure. You've got to have records. Like the certificate of ownership I signed over to you a few years back, when you took over this old diner. Certificates *validate* your life."

"Yeah, well. Hold that thought, guy." Kyle trots to his office and is back at the stoves, pronto, with a piece of paper in his hand. "Check this out."

"Kyle!" Lauren stands there, coffeepot in one hand, her other hand on her hip. "You brought that *with* you? I thought you filed it away at home."

Kyle gives the certificate to Jerry, then hurries to the domed pastry case on the counter. He pulls out a sugar-coated cruller and sets it on a plate. "I want opinions about this error." Leaning low, he scans the parking lot through the diner window. "Where's Jason already? He's usually here for his coffee by now." With his apron fabric, Kyle wipes a few sugar grains off his fingers. "He'll know."

"Know what?" Jerry asks. Marriage certificate in hand, he walks around the counter and sits on a red-cushioned stool.

"What to make of that." Kyle hitches his head toward the certificate, then walks to Jerry and points out his misspelled name. "It's all wrong, just like my life. Shit, it's like I'm always *almost* there, but not quite."

Lauren notices the day's first customers walking up the few stairs to the diner entrance. Beyond them, down the street a bit, sunlight glints on the blue harbor waters. White masts of sailboats dot the view. "I thought you were happy!" she exclaims to Kyle while tucking a pencil behind her ear. "I mean, come on. You get to cook behind your beloved stove all day. And you're a block away from that pretty harbor, where you can take a walk on breaks."

"At the very least, Kyle," Jerry says on his way back to the stoves. Pausing to lift a chef apron off a wall hook, he manages to toss a wink at Lauren. "Sure is nice of your *girlfriend* to pitch in today."

⁓

For Jason Barlow, the best part of Monday mornings is this: fresh coffee and a warm cruller straight from The Dockside's pastry dome. Because after lazy weekends with his wife, Monday mornings are rough—so a little diner comfort goes a long way.

But when he walks into the diner, it's so mobbed, he gives his watch a double take to check if he's behind schedule. He's not. So apparently a lot of folks need that Monday diner comfort, especially on these hot July mornings. Jason grabs his regular stool at the counter, where a cruller waits on a plate beside a steaming cup of coffee.

"Hey, Bradford," Jason says when Kyle, wiping his hands on a towel, walks out from the kitchen. "How about packing this up to-go today?" Jason nudges the coffee mug across the counter.

"What?" Kyle tosses the towel over his shoulder, then nudges the cup back. "Sit and stay awhile."

Jason shakes his head and checks his watch again. "Busy as hell, no can do. Driving into Hartford to meet with Trent and some of the producers at CT-TV. Everyone's in panic mode to secure the next reno project. Either filming has to begin right away with the cottage on the beach, or we need plan B if this project falls through."

"Can't your producers step in? Convince those cottage owners—Fenwicks, is it?—that being on your show is a good thing?"

"Not really. I'm actually meeting with the owner Wednesday morning. Trent can sweeten the pot with offers of discounted work. It might help lock things down, but I'm thinking it's more on me."

Kyle nudges the pastry dish closer to Jason. "Yeah, well a cruller takes three minutes. You sit there and keep your blood pressure down, would you?"

"Fine, Doc." Jason bites into the soft, doughy pastry. "Always monitoring my health," he says around the food.

"Somebody has to."

"So." Jason shifts on the stool, raises the cruller and pauses before another bite. "Sup with you, Bradford?"

"What's up?" Kyle steps closer and squints at Jason. "I'll tell you what's up. Look at this." He pulls a piece of paper from his apron pocket and slides it across the counter.

"What am I looking at?"

"Well, you're pretty new to the rules and regulations of love. Married what, two years now?"

"Last I checked." Jason sips his coffee while reading the paper. "What's this? Your marriage certificate?" He slides the paper back to Kyle. "Your name is spelled wrong."

Kyle snatches up the certificate. "No shit, and I knew you'd notice, too. Did some unpacking before work and came across this."

"You didn't check it back then, when you got married? Because this signifies the most important day of your life. Imagine what Sal would say about it, man."

"Hey, Jason," Lauren says while pressing past Kyle to pick up a customer order at the stoves. "Kyle on your case, too? I told him to let it go. That certificate is just a formality," she adds over her shoulder.

"Formality? Or *legality*?" Kyle calls after her. "Maybe we're not married, Ell. That certificate might never hold up in a court of law."

"Ask the judge," Jason tells him.

"The judge?"

"Commissioner Raines. Cliff. Former State of Connecticut family court judge prior to being Stony Point's beach commissioner."

"Good idea." Kyle folds the paper in half and fans his face with it. "But in the meantime, I'm not really sure me and Ell are legally married. So I've got to fix this, quick."

Lauren approaches again, this time carrying an empty tray after delivering her table's breakfast dishes. She sets the tray on the counter, wraps her arms around Kyle from behind and gives him a playful squeeze.

"Lauren," Jason says. "Just a thought. But maybe you don't want to fix it, you know what I mean?"

"Fix what?" she asks, patting Kyle's backside before collecting her tray.

"Your marriage."

It's funny how the idea stops her right in her tracks. She sets the tray down on the counter and adjusts the pencil tucked behind her ear. "Hmm. Interesting. Because let's face it," she suggests to Jason with a wink, "marriage gets pretty staid and predictable."

"What?" Kyle takes her arm and turns her toward him. "Seriously? That's how you feel?"

"Just saying." She tugs herself out of his hold and picks up her empty tray. "Same two faces every day," she vaguely continues, as though the thought has been on her mind lately.

And suddenly, Jason feels like he's at a tennis match, the way his head turns to watch these two go at it. It's *so* obvious Lauren is teasing her husband, but Kyle's too wound up to realize it.

"You don't find comfort in familiarity?" Kyle asks. When she shrugs nonchalantly, he starts to say something, stops, then starts again. "If you feel that way ..." He slides off his wedding band and gives it to Jason.

"What am I doing with this?" Jason joggles the ring.

"Hold on to it," Kyle orders him. He leans an elbow on the counter and talks quietly, just inches away from Jason's face. "You're the designated keeper of my ring, until this is resolved. Because I *don't* think I'm technically married."

Lauren looks from Jason to Kyle. "Well," she huffs before setting down her tray once more.

Sitting at the counter, Jason drops his chin into his open hand and rubs his jaw—all while waiting for Lauren's next move.

And she doesn't disappoint.

No, instead Lauren pulls off her wedding rings and hands them to Jason, too. "If you're not married, Kyle ... then neither am I!"

four

WHILE SITTING ON EVA'S KITCHEN window seat Tuesday morning, sunshine and the scent of the sea drift in through the screen. With these weekly coffee visits, Maris couldn't be more present in Eva's life. It's the main reason she left behind her big city, denim-design career—to be present in the lives of her friends and family. Like her cousin Sal was.

As Maris tips back her coffee cup to finish the last delicious drops, her sister jumps up from her seat at the old mahogany pedestal table.

"Let's go outside," Eva insists while pushing in her gray-cushioned chair. "Walk off this blueberry muffin before we both have to get to work."

And so, their time together being as fluid as the waves, in minutes they are stepping off the front porch and crossing the lawn. Their flip-flops snap along; a robin sings in the shade of a maple tree. Maris stops in front of Eva's new realty sign. It's large and hanging by hooks from a wooden post.

"I just love the new name, Eva. *By the Sea Realty*. But what made you change it from *Gallagher Realty*? That's your last name, after all."

"Listen. This past year, everyone got a new start. You, with your work now that you're becoming a *novelist*. And Jason's career is growing with his TV show. Elsa's opening her inn. Celia had a baby. Then Kyle and Lauren moved to a new house. And what did I do? I got a haircut."

"And it's beautiful!" Maris touches the side-swept bangs of Eva's blonde-streaked auburn hair.

"But it's not enough. I'm thirty-five and haven't made a change since God knows when. So I decided to spruce up the business."

"Well, with a name like *By the Sea Realty*, who wouldn't check out your cottage listings?"

"That's what I'm hoping. I've been tinkering with my website, too. Because Tay will be going to college soon, and I need to bring in more business to help pay her tuition bills." Eva brushes her hand over the hanging sign before walking to the sandy beach road. "I'll be uploading new cottage photos on the website later today. Which is where we're headed, to grab an outside shot of my new listing. Come on, sis."

"Where is it?" Maris asks with one last glance back at Eva's new realty sign.

"Champion Road. Right behind the beach."

In no time, they walk that narrow dead-end street, which is lined with a sandy slope topped with swaying dune grasses on one side, and weathered cottages on the other. Most of those cottages have upper-level decks, from which to see the sweeping seaside view beyond those dune grasses. By the turnaround at the far end, the marsh spreads out in more green grasses and winding inlets of seawater.

The road is so familiar, Maris could walk it blindfolded. It's a street that triggers so many memories. Like the times, growing up, she walked with Eva toward the patch of woods near the marsh.

There, they'd find the secluded dirt path twisting through the trees. The path curved this way past brush, that way past low-hanging branches, until it opened onto ragged Little Beach. And often, decades ago, onto some random teen party around a campfire.

Then there was the golf cart race held on Champion Road two summers ago. That contest decided who'd be Jason's best man at their wedding—as if anyone stood a chance competing with Kyle for the honor.

And now, this. First, a quick stop taking photographs of Eva's new listing: a two-story, silver-shingled bungalow with a sandy front yard, the marsh in the back. It's a summer home custom-made for strolls across the street to the beach, or for lazy rowboat rides through the lagoon.

Afterward, she and Eva continue to the end of the street, where that lone cottage Jason's been eyeing rises from the sand. The sight of it taunts him lately, the way he can't make headway in securing its reno. Maris feels the same seeing it now.

"Let's go back along the water," Eva says as she slips off her sandals before climbing the few granite steps leading to the sandy beach. "We'll walk near the waves. It'll be cooler there."

Then, just for fun, Maris swats her sister as she trots past her in the sand. "Race you!" she calls back over her shoulder.

Quite honestly, Cliff's getting sick and tired of seeing this. Tired of seeing it, and tired that no one's doing anything about it. There's a reason, after all, that the beach association has landscaped certain areas near stone walls, or at the ends of streets to guide traffic through turns. It's to give a pretty summertime visual to the vacationers here. And those tended, bordered areas have always been filled with black-eyed Susans. The golden yellow flowers grow tall and hardy throughout the entire season.

Until now.

It's annoying that whoever approved a change from the much-loved black-eyed Susans to white Shasta daisies did it the year *before* Cliff became commissioner. If the issue were brought up during his reign, he'd have vetoed the whole absurd idea.

Because here it is, a nice hot summer nearing *only* the end of July—and many of those daisies are already dead. Spent and withered on their stalks. The white petals are drooping and fading. And the flowers' yellow centers? Brown.

It bothers him enough that he pulls his security car over to the curb, gets out and snaps off a couple of the dried-out blossoms, scrutinizes them, then tosses them back among the sagging, faded flowers. At the very least, there's one person who will know exactly how to advise him. So he lifts his cell phone, takes a picture of the pathetic border plantings and texts it to his son with the message: *Why are these dead already?* As a landscape architect, Denny will understand what's going on with these daisy duds.

In less than a minute, Cliff's phone rings.

"Ran their course," his son says when Cliff answers. No *Hi, Pop*. No greeting. Just matter-of-fact Denny getting to the point, as usual.

"So they're not coming back?" Cliff asks while walking around the flowerbed.

"From what's in the picture you just sent me? Nope, they're dead and gone."

"But the flowerbeds aren't cleaned out until after Labor Day. Are you saying that folks here have to look at *dead* daisies for another month now?"

"Guess so." Denny pauses, as though he's scrutinizing the photo on his phone. "Weren't black-eyed Susans planted in the borders other years?"

"They were."

"What nitwit changed it to daisies? The daisies don't even look beachy like the Susans do. Not to mention, the Susans can be cut back after flowering, so another round of blossoms grows. Don't you have a landscaper taking care of things there?"

"Yes. And that landscaper convinced the Board of Governors it was time for a floral change."

"*I'd* convince the Board it's time for a new landscaper. Because, seriously. Daisies? They belong in a mountain meadow, not at the beach. You know, I always tell my clients that black-eyed Susans look like the sun in a flower. Their golden petals are soft rays of sunshine, custom-made for summertime at the shore."

"Oh, I like that." Giving the spent daisies a look of disdain, Cliff walks back to his cruiser and gets in again, lightly hitting his steering wheel and muttering *rays of sunshine*. "Hey, Denny ..."

"What's up, Pop?"

"We still on for Cruise Night next week? We can hit the one at Ocean Beach, they're supposed to have lots of classics."

"Sure, sounds good. But I'm busy at work now. Call you on the weekend."

After hanging up with his son, but before starting the car engine, Cliff does one more thing. Well, two if you count the glare he first tosses again at those pathetic daisies.

Then he types a note into his phone's reminder app. Just a few words are enough. *Next BOG meeting. Ditch the daisies.*

They'd run barefoot across the sand and raced to the water's edge.

"I'll be working in the old shack today," Maris, breathless now, tells her sister. "Tapping into Neil's presence."

"Where are you at in the book?"

A gentle wave breaks at Maris' feet and cools her off after their run across the sand. "Inputting margin notes Neil planned to insert into the story. Then I'm drafting concepts for the ending."

Eva lightly taps Maris' arm. "Run the plot by me again?"

"Okay. There's this group of beach friends, gathered for a summer reunion. They're holed up in a cottage when a hurricane hits. Right there." As she says it, Maris hitches her head toward the gray cottage rising on stilts on the beach. "Lots of tensions flare, with a little pairing up, a little romance," Maris adds with a wink. "But an argument changes things, bringing on some petty jealousy, which then leads to *serious* drama." She sloshes through another breaking wave. "Sound familiar?" she asks.

"I'll say. Story of our lives?"

Maris shrugs.

"But Neil really didn't write the ending?" Eva asks.

"No. He didn't get that far before he died. So I'm not sure where he wanted to take the story. But boy, would I love to honor his vision."

The cottage on the beach is right beside them then. "Wait!" Eva quietly says as she grabs Maris' arm, then calls out to a woman sweeping the cottage deck. "Carol?"

The woman leans on her broom and shields her eyes against the sun. "Eva? Is that you?"

"Yes!" Eva steps out of the shallows and heads toward the cottage-on-stilts. "Nice to see your place opened up again. You staying for the summer?"

Carol walks to the railing and leans her arms on it. "Not sure yet. Just airing it out today."

"It's a good morning for it," Eva says while motioning to the blue sky, where clouds are gathering on the distant horizon. "Might get a shower later on."

Maris watches the woman on the deck closely, knowing it's the same woman who reluctantly talked to Jason on Sunday night. She appears to be in her early thirties, with a somewhat offhand attitude.

Carol takes a deep breath of the salt air while checking out the sky. "Looks it. We could use some rain," she says, then turns to Eva. "Listen. I've got a pitcher of fresh lemonade. You ladies like to join me on the deck?"

"Yes!" Eva tells her while grabbing Maris' arm again. "That'll be wonderful!"

Maybe for Eva, but Maris begs to differ. The last thing she needs is to mess up Jason's chance to secure this cottage for his next renovation. So … she does it. Right as they climb the deck stairs once Carol goes inside for the drinks.

Yes, Maris gives her sister a good swift kick in the leg, whispering, "*Eva!*"

"Ouch. Why'd you kick me?" Eva asks over her shoulder.

Maris stops climbing and hesitates on a low step. "Why'd you say *yes?*"

"Why not?" Eva turns around from a higher step and eyes her. "It'll be good book inspiration for you. Didn't you say Neil's story takes place right here?"

"Well, yes. But Jason's coming here *tomorrow.*" Maris walks up one step closer to Eva. "To talk to Carol's father? I told you before, remember?"

"Oh, right. So this is good!" Eva climbs the remaining steps, then motions for Maris to hurry up behind her. "We can put Carol at ease about his project pitch."

"Or ruin the whole thing." Maris steps onto the deck, already taking in the architectural details. From a distance, she'd always noticed the jutting angles of the outside walls. Jason told her the cottage was designed that way with storms in mind. The angular corners deflect powerful winds away from the structure. But she'd never seen the cottage this close up, and notices now the wear and tear inflicted by the sea. The windows' white shutters are dingy with streaks of mold; fading paint peels from the white trim beneath the eaves. And the cedar shingles? Some are nearly black with sea damp and age. She grabs Eva's tank top fabric, then, and pulls her close. "I *hate* to meddle in Jason's business."

"Shh, be quiet!" Eva glances at the rusted slider—opening as they speak. "Here she comes."

In that instant, Eva's expression changes. She walks over to the deck table, smiling and already helping to set out glasses and napkins.

"One for you," Carol says as she hands Eva a tall glass. "And one for your friend."

"Oh, she's not my friend." Eva opens the patio umbrella. "This is my sister, Maris."

"Maris." Carol extends a firm handshake. "So nice to meet you."

When Carol sits and lifts the lemonade pitcher, Eva gets right to it. "Whatever happened this spring?" she asks as she sits, too. "You were going to rent out the cottage? I thought for sure you'd come back." Eva tips her head toward the shabby gray-shingled beach home. "You *know* I would screen any potential renters. And I can assure you, you'd be booked for the summer with this prime location. Right on the sand, with panoramic water views ... This cottage is king of the beach!"

"What *happened* is my father," Carol explains.

Which gets Maris' attention. Any information she can gather today might help Jason tomorrow. Might help him sway this family to sign on for a cottage reno—one televised, no less.

So she sizes up this Carol, with her blonde hair styled in a blunt angled cut above her shoulders. Long bangs sweep her eyes, keeping them somewhat concealed and making it hard to read her expression. And her clothes? Pure beach: faded denim cutoffs with a stark white, fitted midriff top. Simple, easy, no fuss. Two thin gold chains loop around her neck.

"Your *father* happened?" Eva asks. "What do you mean?"

Carol tips her chair back and stretches her arm to snag a pair of sunglasses from the deck railing. "Dad put his ironclad fist down. *No outsiders allowed in the cottage*," she explains while putting on the round circle sunglasses with a dark green tint. "No one much has been here at all since my mother died. This has been her family's cottage *forever*, it seems. They've owned it for decades. And you know how the old-timers are. They never let go of *anything*, especially property, passing it through the generations." Carol tosses a casual glance at the seaworn cottage. "I actually talked with a local architect proposing a modest renovation. He mentioned something about featuring the project on a TV show, too, which *would* be an interesting way to tell this old gal's story."

Maris quickly sets down her lemonade and leans a little closer to Carol. "And I can vouch for that architect."

Carol says nothing. Only her barely visible eyebrows seem to rise, giving Maris a glimpse of that mistrust Jason tuned right into.

"Jason Barlow's my husband," Maris explains then. "And he wants to tell your cottage's story for a lot of reasons. As for that TV program? It's a new cottage-reno show he's hosting on public television."

"I'll be damned!" Carol gives a short laugh. "You're married to that dude? I met him the other night and we talked a little. Well, I snapped at him is more like it. Seemed like he had some bullshit up his sleeve."

"Oh, no. Let me assure you, if anyone can tell a cottage's story," Eva interrupts, "it's Jason. He's the best around. Actually won a big award—Connecticut Coastal Architect of the Year."

"Is that right ..." Carol sits back. But she does more, too. She lifts her sunglasses to the top of that suspicious head of hers and squints at Maris. "This throws a new light on Mr. Barlow, if *you're* his better half. Because I *like* you." Carol stands up then, walks to the deck railing, leans her hands on it and takes in the blue view before turning. Then she leans back on the railing and crosses her arms. "It would be something if your guy could get these walls to talk, for real."

When Carol glances up at the second-level windows, Maris has the feeling they're being watched. *And* that Carol's being careful about what she says, as though the mystery-person inside is closely eavesdropping.

Actually, Maris has no doubt when Carol lowers her voice after returning to her seat. "Because seriously?" Carol asks. "These damn walls hold some Stony Point secrets that fade more and more with each passing year. It'd be a shame to lose them to time, and neglect."

Maybe Maris is interfering, maybe not. But it seems that putting distance between Carol and whoever is behind those upstairs windows might help. If Maris can talk to her somewhere *else*, she might make progress. Because, heck. Secrets in the walls? Like whispered stories in the sea breeze, this is *right* up Jason's alley.

So Maris does it. Something tells her she's got to be as abrupt with Carol as Carol is with them. Without hesitating, she leans across the table and clasps Carol's arm—just above the worn leather bracelet strapped round and round her wrist.

"Can you come to dinner, Carol?" Maris asks. "Tonight?"

five

By EARLY EVENING, EVERYTHING'S ABOUT ready. Maris scoops a few loose coins off the kitchen counter and drops them in a brass dish there. Beside it, the multi-device charger juices up their cell phones, as well as Jason's tablet. She doesn't know if he might need it while talking to Carol. The tablet holds some digital cottage designs he may want to show her.

With no time to spare before Carol arrives, Maris pulls the roasted rosemary potatoes from her fickle oven—which she's been checking every ten minutes to be sure the temperature hasn't spiked. Or quit on her. She slides out the tray of nicely browned potatoes, adds a drizzle of olive oil and returns the pan to the oven. When she does, the oven door slips from her grip and slams shut.

"Jason!" Maris calls out. She hears him coming down the stairs, with the dog apparently racing him from the sound of that jangling collar. "Can't you put *this* kitchen on your show? I'm making do, but these antiques of yours are awful."

"We're livin' the dream, sweetheart." Jason stops in the arched kitchen doorway. "You're writing a novel, I'm filming a TV show. No time left for ourselves. Or the house."

"Oh!" Maris grabs a dishtowel and turns to him standing there in khaki cargo shorts, olive-green tee, brown belt and leather-band watch. On his feet? Boat shoes. Taking a step closer then, she swats his backside with the towel. "Go heat up the grill!"

By the time he crosses the kitchen to the slider, Madison is already there, pacing at the glass door. "It's starting to rain," Jason announces while looking out.

"Put on your poncho." Maris glances back at him, then unwraps rib-eye steaks from the fridge and sets them on a platter. "Mmm. These look so good. They from Maritime Market?"

"Absolutely," Jason says as he lifts his rain poncho from a nearby wall hook. "Butcher cut them fresh for me."

While he's outside getting the grill going, Maris slices zucchini, giving only one nervous glance to her erratic oven keeping the potatoes warm. When Jason comes back in with the dog, Maddy paces the kitchen again.

"Jason," Maris says, mid-zucchini-slice. "Give the dog some kibble so she's got a full belly and settles down."

When he's in the pantry filling the dog's bowl, Maris calls out, "Did you get wine?"

"Lambrusco." He sets down the dog bowl and stands beside Maris then.

"Good. It'll pair nicely with the steaks." She turns and squints at his disheveled, wavy hair. "You need a haircut, mister."

He says nothing. Instead he gets another platter from the cabinet and lays out the zucchini strips for grilling.

"And remember," Maris says. "Be nice tonight."

He slightly rolls his eyes. "That Carol. She's a piece of work."

"And *you've* never been?" Maris wipes her damp fingers on the dishtowel, then presses a few wrinkles out of her striped tank maxi dress. "So, *sorridi*. Smile, okay? Force yourself," she adds while grabbing Jason's hand to check the time on his watch. "Because she was *fine* with me and Eva this morning," Maris explains while lifting a jean jacket from the chair back. Putting it on as she sits, she cuffs the jacket sleeves, bends then and lastly slips on her leather sandals. "Carol was probably just suspicious of you. *And picking up on your tension.*"

As if to prove it, Jason slightly jumps when the doorbell rings.

"There she is now," he says. And that's it. He does nothing else except to follow the dog rushing down their paneled hallway.

Shaking her head and watching from the kitchen chair, Maris hears the dog's nails clicking on the wood floor, hears rain spattering the dark windows, hears Jason opening the front door.

⁓

"My mother named me after Hurricane Carol."

As Jason walks through the kitchen, their guest talks to Maris in the dining room. There, the black lantern-chandelier casts golden light on the painted farm table, where vintage blue-and-white china plates are anchored by crystal goblets. Platters of roasted potatoes and grilled zucchini sit between pillar candles flickering atop silver-metallic pedestals. Marsh grasses and wildflowers spill from a ceramic vase on the antique sideboard.

Carrying in the grilled rib-eye steaks, Jason knows. He can clearly see that Maris is doing everything she can to help him secure this renovation. Even the way she dims the lantern-chandelier now, as they sit down to eat, sets an intimate atmosphere.

"There used to be several cottages right on the sand," Carol explains while swirling the Lambrusco in her wineglass. "Then after a few hurricanes way back in the day, only one cottage was left—ours. Mom was just a little girl when her parents actually bought it in the sixties, *well after* Hurricane Carol. But her family always felt that their lone cottage on the beach was a sign of strength, the sole survivor. *Especially* of Carol, a category-three hurricane which took plenty of the old places out to sea. So when I was born years later and Mom wanted to give me a strong name, it was that one. Carol."

It surprises Jason, the way she opens up so early with that name story. He sees the difference his wife makes in relaxing this Carol—with her white rolled-cuff shorts, crochet sweater loose over a cropped chambray top, and, seriously? Laced leather ankle boots on her feet? But all the huff and bluff in her style fades with Maris setting her right at ease.

Of course. Maris has that knack, and did it to him, too. When she returned to Stony Point three years ago, Jason was pretty much living with a stern expression on his face and his arms folded across his chest. Didn't take long for Maris to unknot *him*, either, that's for damn sure.

"You have a meaningful name then, which I totally get," Maris says across the table. Candlelight flickers between the two women. "My name, Maris, is Latin for *of the sea*."

"Nice." Carol raises her glass. "Seems like our mothers would've been friends."

"What'd you say your mother's name was?" Jason asks when he sets down the steaks and takes a seat beside Maris.

But Carol cuts *him* no slack. "I didn't." Her words are matter-of-fact. After a quick glance to Maris, though, she continues. "But it's Kate. Kate Fenwick."

"I'm sure she would be so proud the cottage is still in your family," Maris softly says.

"Definitely." Turning to Jason, Carol explains, "But she's been gone five years now. So the cottage belongs to my father. It's the *family* cottage, he says. For me, and my brother, too."

"Will your brother be at our meeting tomorrow?" Jason asks.

"No," Carol tells him. "He's out in the Pacific Northwest doing his own thing and not much interested in our Connecticut beach home."

"Maybe he'll have a change of heart someday," Maris suggests.

"I hope so." When Maris nudges the steak dish her way, Carol lifts a grilled rib-eye onto her plate, then adds a heaping scoop of the roasted rosemary potatoes. "And that's something my mother always said our cottage had, too. *Hope.* Which her family *really* needed later on."

"Hope? Why?" Jason asks while shaking salt on his steak, then cutting a piece.

Carol stabs a few potatoes and lifts the fork to her mouth, all while watching Jason from beneath her too-long bangs. "Her father—which would be *my* grandfather—died in a hurricane the year they bought the place. He was taken out to sea, right here."

"Really. At Stony Point?" Listening closely, Jason reaches for his wine goblet.

Carol nods. "You've lived in this old cottage for years, Jason. You never heard the story?"

"It happened in the sixties? No, that's before my family's time. When my father finally returned from 'Nam, he bought our place a few years later, in the seventies. After all that fighting in the jungles, he sought the kind of peace that comes with living by the sea."

"Ah, yes," Carol agrees while slicing a hunk of steak. "Something we always return to."

"But how *did* your grandfather die, Carol?" Maris asks. "You said it was during a hurricane?"

"Well, I *say* died," she manages around a mouthful of steak, "but that's the tricky part. We don't really know with absolute certainty," she says while jabbing her fork at the air, "that he actually *died*. The story began when my grandparents bought the cottage in the early sixties, springtime. My mother was only a little girl then. She and her mother—my grandmother—moved in when school let out in June. Her father commuted to work from here and counted down the days until August, when he'd be on vacation. How proud he was that he'd scrimped and saved to afford his family a beach home. He was only in his thirties and dreamed of spending *every* summer at his cottage on the beach. But he didn't get even one." When Jason lifts the wine bottle, Carol nods to her glass and he refills it. "Oh, I still hear my mother's voice, dropped low on summer evenings on the deck, telling me and my brother the story …"

six

It was the year an unexpected hurricane barreled up the coast. Nobody really thought it would come this far north to Connecticut. Except for Mom's father, Carol tells them now. Rain taps at the window, and candlelight flickers on the dining room table. *His name was Gordon,* Carol says, *and he would've been my grandfather. According to my mother, he knew the storm would hit Stony Point by gauging the humidity, and utter stillness, the days before.*

Then the winds finally came, and the swells rolled across the beach. Oh, Mom—she was only nine years old that summer—but she remembered how fiercely those waves came so far up on the sand. It happened fast, my mom told us, and by the time folks knew the storm would hit full force, there was hardly time to prepare. First thing a lot of people did was move their small boats out of the boat basin behind the boardwalk. Get them to dry land. Meanwhile, others were shuttering their windows or hammering plywood over them.

Which is what my mom's family did—her mom and dad. They'd been covering the cottage windows. Mom's mother closed the shutters against the whistling wind, and her dad hammered. They were working their way around the deck when they saw Sailor out on the nearby rocks. Sailor was a neighborhood boy whose family rented a cottage back on Champion Road. This was their second summer vacationing at Stony Point, and the friendly little boy always wore a sailor's cap on the beach. Always! So everyone called him Sailor. They'd give him a salute when he passed by, heading to the rocks with his sand pail and crabbing gear. He was about seven the year that surprise hurricane hit.

So my mother's father, Gordon, was high on a stepladder when he noticed Sailor that day. The boy was on the rocks near shore, but waves were rolling in dangerously close. Gordon yelled to Sailor, but his voice was lost in the wind. Mom was little, yet she remembered watching at the window. Her mother and father both began yelling together then. Finally, Sailor looked over and they motioned him off the rocks. "Right away!" they called out. "Get home, Sailor!" When he collected his pail and started climbing toward the beach, Mom's parents finished shuttering the windows and got safely inside the cottage right as the hurricane was hitting.

Minutes later, just minutes, there was a pounding at the door. My mother said she'd never heard anything like it, the sound was so urgent. It was Sailor's mother, looking for her boy. Sailor'd been pleading to get his crabbing tackle box he'd left behind on the rocks. But they could hear the crashing waves from their cottage, so his mother forbid it. It wasn't safe. Apparently he'd slipped out, though, while she was getting the clothes off the line. When she came back inside, Sailor was gone. Well, she was panicked in the storm—her hair was drenched and windblown, her face distraught. The thing is, my mother's parents said they saw Sailor, but couldn't actually vouch that he left the rocks. They'd been busy hammering against the hurricane. So, if Sailor wasn't home, could he have gotten confused? Afraid? He was only seven! Mom's father wondered if maybe the boy scrambled over the rocks the other way around the outcropping, to safety on Little Beach. Because he was nowhere to be found—not at his cottage, not on the main beach, and not on the rocks on this side of the point.

"That tackle box is his pride and joy. All he wanted was to bring it back to the cottage. But he knows the rules," Sailor's mother insisted. "He knows the rules! And Sailor always follows them. Bad weather? You get home, get off the rocks!"

Castaway Cottage

It got quiet then, Mom said. Her father, Gordon, went out on the deck in all that wind and considered the waves. Then he ventured below the cottage. Just like now, she tells Jason and Maris, *the cottage was raised up on stilts, and they kept a wooden rowboat beneath it. Sometimes they'd go paddling in calm seas. And that day, ours was the only boat available.*

Gordon decided he'd make one quick trip around the point to Little Beach on the other side. Said it would be faster this way than walking through the path in the woods to get there. Everyone argued, but with a glance at the churning sky, Gordon insisted there was still time. It was a solid boat, and he thought it would hold up. He'd look quickly and come right back. Because the boy could be right around the point!

Well, you can imagine, Carol explains now, taking a sip of the red wine before continuing. Darkness presses against the dining room windows this rainy evening; but inside, the china and silverware glimmer beneath the candlelight. *My grandfather must've been a strapping young man at the time. In his thirties and full of vim and vigor. So folks must've believed he could do this. Mom's uncle was with them, Gordon's brother. He helped Gordon get the boat in the water, but Gordon wouldn't let him come along, just in case.*

So with the sea spray blowing, Mom's dad valiantly paddled. Everyone watched that rowboat rise and fall on the swells, and Gordon did good! He kept going, his strong young arms pulling on those oars and staying away from the rocks. He made it out farther and farther.

But Mom would tear up every time she told the story, when she remembered how her dad waved to them, right before he turned the boat to round the stony point, looking for the neighbor's boy. For little Sailor.

~

"And no one has seen my grandfather since then."

"They didn't find any evidence?" Jason asks. "Something from the boat? A paddle, or life vest? Or even the rowboat itself, beached somewhere?"

"Nothing." Carol's shaking her head. "The authorities searched, but they never located his body, or the vessel."

"Oh my God," Maris says. "And what about the boy?"

"Did anyone ever find Sailor?" Jason asks.

"That's the twist of it all." Carol lifts her napkin and pats her mouth. "He got off the rocks, but on the way back to his cottage, a neighbor pulled him inside to safety. She said the wind was practically blowing him away. She tried calling Sailor's parents, but with tree branches snapping, the phone lines were already down. And by the time the woman's husband made his way to Sailor's cottage to report that their son was safe, it was too late."

"No," Jason nearly whispers, shaking his head.

Carol nods, then sips her wine again. "My grandfather, Gordon, had already gone out in the boat. As for Sailor and his family? Their rented cottage sustained some damage from that storm, mostly from the lagoon surge. So afterward, Sailor's family packed their things and left. But I think it was mostly because they couldn't stay there anymore, feeling responsible for Gordon's disappearance. And the people who actually *owned* the cottage? They patched it up and sold it not long after that. A new family moved in the next year. Fixed up the place and you'd never know what happened that one summer."

"What was the boy's name?" Jason asks now. "This Sailor?"

Carol shrugs and moves aside her empty dinner plate. "My mother never knew. Sailor's family rented here for barely two summers. In and out. No one ever saw the boy again after that hurricane, and Sailor's story turned into local folklore. Not to mention that anyone around here who knew my *grandfather* has either moved away or passed on. And so the tale turns into hearsay. You know, how much is truth? How much is spinning a yarn?"

"What a *tragic* story, though," Maris says as she begins collecting their plates. "But fascinating, at the same time."

"It is." Now Carol looks directly at Jason. "And one I'd love to preserve in that old cottage's walls. Because even though Gordon never returned from that rowboat ride, our cottage withstood all the storm and its wrath. And stood strong against every hurricane since ... Gloria, Sandy. The problem you'll have is that with all that cottage history, my father doesn't want to change much."

"Neither do I," Jason assures her. "It's an architectural feat, your cottage blueprint. Those wall angles are designed to withstand hurricane winds and sea surges. The angular structure deflects it all, and apparently deflects it well."

"That's true, but there's always a storm that can do it. That can take something down." Carol glances to the rain-spattered windows then. "And if that happens, if my family's cottage is ever wiped out, nothing can go up in its place. Because no insurance company will cover a new building there, not right on the sand like that, at the water's edge. Nor would zoning allow a rebuild. Which makes my cottage even *more* valuable. It's actually irreplaceable."

Maris stands behind Jason and sets a hand on his shoulder. "Why don't you take Carol to your studio? Show her what you've drawn up," she quietly says.

"Oh, no." Carol quickly stands and backs up a step. "I should probably get going." She looks around, as though unsure which direction leads to the door. "I don't want to be any trouble."

"It's okay." Jason finishes his wine and stands then, too. "My studio is right here, out back. I have some sketches I was going to run by your father tomorrow. But after hearing Sailor's story, I'd love to hear *your* thoughts on them now."

⁓

Maris turned on the outside spotlights to illuminate the backyard. Across the wet lawn, the barn studio looks like a hulking shadow. Weathered fishing buoys hang randomly on its brown rough-hewn walls.

While hurrying beneath a large black umbrella, Jason explains to Carol how he converted his father's old mason workshop into his and Maris' studio. When he opens the double slider, there's a faint whiff of wood dust and tools inside. The salty sea damp on rainy days like this draws that lingering scent from the walls.

As Carol steps in, he takes the wet umbrella from her and sets it aside. Already, she's walking further into the studio. Raindrops spatter the skylights, which Carol glances up at as she heads closer to a wall of photographs. The massive framed images depict Jason's redesigned beach cottages and seaside homes.

"Your work?" Carol asks as she turns to face him.

"It is." Standing at his drafting table, Jason switches on the swing lamp there. "Have a seat," he tells her while motioning to a wheeled stool at the table.

Carol settles on the stool and browses the sketches laid out in front of her—the penciled images are unmistakably new design possibilities for her cottage. Displayed beside them are faded postcards showing her family's beach home from a bygone time before the hurricanes hit.

"What are these?" Carol asks, lifting one.

"That cottage-reno show I'm hosting?" Jason adjusts the swing lamp so the light shines on the cards. "It's for CT-TV, and the whole team there would love to bring you on board for the next project. So the director of research at the station got ahold of those. They're copies of original Stony Point postcards from a collection at the Boston Public Library."

"Seriously?" Carol lifts another and scrutinizes the timeworn images of several cottages lined across the beach. A low seawall, now long gone, had been erected in front of many of the beach homes.

"Look closely at this one," Jason says while handing her a card giving a clear view of *her* family's cottage. "These postcards date back to the fifties and sixties. You can see that your cottage apparently had a blue-and-white striped awning over part of the deck. It's a detail that could be brought back in a redesign."

Carol sets down the image as Jason next points out design possibilities on his sketches. Moving from one drawing to another, he talks about extensive deck work, and siding options, and window choices. Carol is silent as he does so. She simply takes it all in, as though she never saw beyond her family cottage's existing structure—neither to its historical past, nor possible future.

But what surprises Jason is that this attitude-prone woman *remains* silent, even as he finishes presenting his design options. There is no retort from her; no arguing that her family can't change what her mother loved; no questions demanding who does he think he is with his highfalutin design ideas; no counterpoint that the cottage is to remain as-is to honor Gordon—forever lost at sea.

There is only silence as she spins around on the stool and glances again at the huge framed photos of his finished jobs. Then she turns back to his raw sketches of her family cottage.

"Everything okay?" Jason asks when her silence continues.

"This is some den of creativity." She says it, but looks only at the sketches and postcards on his drafting table.

At first, Jason can't tell if her words are sarcastic or not. So he says nothing. Instead, arms crossed, he leans on his big work desk and waits for her to continue.

"I'm actually awed," she admits. "You certainly honor the integrity of these seaside structures." As she talks, she spins around on the stool again and looks at his mounted photographs. Finally, she walks over to them for a closer look at the grand shingle-style New England cottages, and tiny painted bungalows, and gabled summer homes he's renovated. "I'm sure CT-TV is glad to have you. Their local viewers will eat this up."

Okay, so he was wrong. There was no sarcasm. But her mannerisms still hint at a mistrust. Of *everything*. So he waits, thinking her mistrust might simply come from the way her grandfather lost his life by being so giving—so trusting—and look what it got him. Her family apparently hasn't let its guard down since.

Yet this Carol—with her blonde bangs falling over her eyes, and her leather-booted feet scuffing along his studio's wood-planked floor—is proving to be a contradiction. Her slouchy ankle boots, cuffed white shorts and cropped denim top might have a devil-may-care vibe on this steamy July evening. But her pauses and sudden quiet hint at something more. It's as though she's torn from both sides and is unsure of which direction to bring her family cottage, and her family itself.

Jason notices how she's drawn to the shelf of Neil's seaworn leather journals. It doesn't surprise him; most people who enter his studio end up in that same spot. Carol picks up the framed photograph of Neil from beside the journals. In the picture, Neil is in his twenties, hair overgrown. He wears jeans and a tee as he's bent over a clamp while working on a wood project in this very barn.

"You?" Carol asks with a casual glance back.

Jason shakes his head. "No. My brother." Jason walks over to the shelf and pulls off a journal, which he opens and hands to Carol. "Neil died ten years ago. These are all his," he says, motioning to the assorted journals and scrapbooks spilling from the shelf.

"So you were close," Carol remarks while lifting a seagull-feather bookmark, then turning a salty page.

"We were. Neil's the one who told me that every cottage tells a story, and these journals are filled with his observations, notes, photos, drawings." Jason steps back as she thumbs through more pages. Over her shoulder, he can see the slant of his brother's cursive, the pencil lines of his rudimentary design sketches. "It's why I keep his things here. Neil's work is a *huge* part of all my designs."

"I can get that." Carol sets the journal back on the shelf and returns to the drafting table. On her way across the floor, she looks up at Maris' loft, the wood stairs, the mounted moose head. "So Neil's this building's ghost."

"Pardon me?"

"Ghost. That's what these old buildings hold onto, more than anything else. Some lingering ghost." With a sad smile, she sits on the stool again. "Don't forget. My family's lived with Gordon's ghost in that old cottage. For decades now."

"You kind of spooked me for a second. Because there's actually a passage in one of those journals where Neil wrote the very same thing ... That old buildings are all about ghosts."

"Then we're on the same wavelength, Mr. Barlow," Carol says as she lifts one of his sketches beneath the swing lamp. "Can I take these with me? I'd like to show them to my father before he talks with you. I'll give them back tomorrow, at our meeting."

Jason agrees and rolls up the sketches. As he slides them into an architectural tube, his cell phone dings with a text message.

"It's Maris," he tells Carol. "I hope you can stay for sea-salt caramel brownies and coffee?"

"Oh, Maris bakes?"

Jason could laugh, thinking about the dried-out pastries Maris has served him over the past few years.

But he doesn't. "Bakes?" he asks instead. "No." Shaking his head, he walks Carol out through the double slider. Then he shuts off the studio lights, locks up and they cross the wet lawn toward the house, its paned windows aglow. "In life," he explains, "it's important to either master some things, or have connections. When it comes to baking, Maris has connections."

seven

"Hey, Marty," Kyle says as the barber pumps his chair up. "How's things?"

"Good, Kyle. What do you want today?" Marty pats the side of Kyle's head. "The usual Wednesday morning trim?"

"No, let's change it up in this heat." Kyle tips his head to the side while considering his reflection in the large wall mirror. He draws his hand down his cheek and across the soul patch on his chin. "Give me a buzz cut, would you?"

"Seriously?" Jason asks from the black-padded, chrome-trimmed seat beside him.

"Yeah, guy. I need the air to hit my skin, cool me down some." Kyle looks out Coastal Cuts' windows toward a marina across the street. The sun shines bright this early, glaring on cars passing by the barbershop, and on white sails bobbing in the distant bay. "It's been so hot, I'm trying to feel that damn sea breeze everyone *says* blows off the water." He turns to his reflection while touching the side of his head. "But buzz it up the sides, only to the top," he tells Marty, who's moved to the counter and is sorting through neatly aligned combs and clippers. "Okay? Keep it a little longer there."

"And how about you, Jason?" The shop's other barber, Max, stands behind Jason. "You're looking overdue, man."

"He is," Kyle tells Max.

"So what brings you in today?" Max asks as he flips open a black cutting cape and attaches it around Jason's neck.

"I'll tell you what brought him in," Kyle says. "It's amazing how much sway a *wife* has."

"Nice try, Kyle." Jason slowly drags the back of his hand along the side of his face. "No cut today, Max. But how about a shave?"

"A shave?" Kyle asks as Marty lifts a comb to his hair. "Oh, man. Maris is going to kill you, Barlow. Doesn't she want you looking polished?"

Jason shrugs. "Well, Max?"

"How long since you last picked up a razor?"

"Don't know. Five, six days?"

"Yeah, I'll clean you up. Come on over to the sink while I get a hot towel."

Jason switches seats to one closer to a sink. Within minutes, his chair is reclined, whiskers softened and Max is ready to brush shaving cream on his face.

"What's that scent I'm smelling?" Kyle asks while Marty buzzes clippers up the back of his head.

"Sandalwood oil," Max tells him from the sink, where he's lifting the hot towel off Jason's face. "I put a few drops on the towel before heating it."

"Nice. I like that." Kyle tips his head to the side as Marty continues clipping and trimming, his scissors snipping and smoothing off random strands. Miniature tall ship replicas line a wall-to-wall shelf above the mirrors. In the mirror's reflection, a news anchor gives the headlines on a mounted television, and the far wall is covered with a collection of assorted wall clocks.

"You still *unmarried?*" Jason asks while getting his face lathered.

"As far as I know, I could be," Kyle answers over his shoulder. "Haven't seen Cliff around lately to have him look at my marriage certificate."

"What?" Marty asks while drawing the clippers along the other side of Kyle's head. "You're getting divorced, after you and the Mrs. just bought that house?"

"No. No, guy. Just have a problem with my marriage certificate," Kyle explains. "Come to find out, there's a typo in my name."

Once the barbers give Kyle a good ribbing, insinuating his marriage is null and void, Jason stretches over from his reclined chair and hits Kyle's arm. "Hey," Jason says. "So when do you want your rings back? Because I don't like holding onto that merchandise."

"Not yet. If Lauren knows I got them back, she'll forget about the whole typo thing and let it go." Kyle pauses as Marty uses a spray bottle to wet down the top of his head before trimming there. "And I need to fix it. That certificate represents my marriage, man."

"Watch it, though," Max warns him while drawing a straight razor down Jason's face. "Without a ring, the pretty lady might get used to being single *and* ready to mingle."

"Our friend Max here has a point, Kyle," Jason tells him when Max maneuvers the razor carefully around the scar on his jawline.

"Eh." Kyle checks out Jason just as Max finishes up the shave, drawing the razor along Jason's neck. "Hey, looking sharp, bro," Kyle tells him. "You sure you don't want a cut, too? Don't you have that meeting today? At the cottage on the beach?"

"I do," Jason says as Max pats down his face with another hot towel.

"Clean up with a haircut and maybe it'll help you lock down that reno for the show," Kyle insists.

"Get off my case, Bradford. Because we're not leaving here with matching haircuts," Jason tosses back while considering his freshly shaven face in the mirror. "Don't know how well reno talks will go over with the old man, anyway. He's a rigid New Englander, set in his ways."

"An old-timer, huh? They don't like change, that's for sure." Kyle watches Max apply a balm to Jason's face, patting it on his skin briskly.

"You're all set here, Kyle," Marty says as he grabs the clippers to clean up around Kyle's sideburns, then works a dollop of gel into his new cut.

"Hey, douse me with that, would you?" Kyle asks, hitching his head to Jason getting his face balmed. Max raises Jason's chair from its recline position, then gives his face a light slap before removing his cape.

"The cooling balm?" Marty asks. "What about those whiskers on your chin?"

"My soul patch?" Kyle rubs his fingertips across it. "Yeah, take it off. I'm over it."

"Shit, there goes your soul, Kyle," Jason says, hitting his shoulder when he passes behind him.

Kyle eyes his chin, lifting his head and scrutinizing his face. "Makes a mess in the sink keeping it trimmed. Off with it."

"Let me clean up your neck, first. Head down," Marty says before running the straight razor down the back of Kyle's neck.

As he does, Kyle's cell phone dings. He pulls it from his pocket and reads the text message. "It's Lauren," he calls over to Jason at the register. "In a panic."

"What now?" Jason asks while pulling a few bills from his wallet.

"She's stripping wallpaper, and wanted to finish a wall when her scraper broke. The handle snapped right off." Kyle puts away his phone. "Needs me to stop at the hardware store on the way back."

"I'm really pressed for time, Kyle." Jason looks over at all those ticking wall clocks. "Got to get things ready for my appointment. Why don't you swing by Elsa's? She must have some scrapers hanging around from the inn renovation."

"Perfect," Kyle says as Marty cleans up his face, balms it, then brushes off his shoulders with a soft-bristle brush after removing his cutting cape. Feeling like a new man, Kyle gets up from his chair and walks across the checkerboard-patterned floor. "There's always someone at the beach who has whatever you need."

After dropping Jason off at home, Kyle cruises along Sea View Road. The sight of water there always lowers his blood pressure, especially as he fills his lungs with that salt air. Finally he swings a right toward the Ocean Star Inn, parks his truck out front and gives a wave to Celia spraying the hydrangeas along the side of the building.

When he knocks at the inn's door, Elsa answers. She wears a tie-front blouse with capris, her leopard-print reading glasses perched low on her nose.

"Kyle! What a nice surprise. Come on in!" She sweeps the door open.

Ever the hostess, within minutes Elsa's got him planted in her kitchen, seated at her brand-new massive center island. An equally huge vase of fresh-cut hydrangeas sits on the marble countertop. Kyle has a coffee in one hand, a vanilla-drizzled cranberry-orange biscotti in the other.

"I saw Celia watering the flower gardens when I came in," he says around a mouthful of biscotti.

Elsa slides some books and papers off to the side of the island. "She has Aria outside in the playpen, now that the humidity has broken. The baby's getting some fresh air while Celia tends the gardens." Elsa sits then, with her own coffee, and lifts her reading glasses to the top of her head. "Now, to what do I owe this visit? Everything okay at the Bradford house?"

Kyle nods as he dunks his biscotti into his coffee. "I'm just in a bind. Lauren's removing wallpaper and her scraper broke before she could finish the job. She asked me to get her one after my haircut."

"Oh." Elsa considers his hair. "And I like that look."

Kyle, running his hand across his trimmed hair, tells her, "I went shorter for the summer. It's been so darn hot."

"Where'd you get it done? Because Clifton could use a new style, something like that modern look of yours."

"Coastal Cuts. Tell the commish to ask for Marty. He does a great job, and finishes up with a nice straight razor down the neck."

"Will do." Elsa jots down the barber's name. "And listen, you came to the right place for a scraper."

"Good. Jason thought you might have one."

"Jason?"

"He was at the barber's with me. Got himself a shave."

"Well, he's right. He built me a storage closet for the inn, with a space for *everything*." She heads to the hall closet and returns with a basket. "There are *two* scrapers in here, so you can help your wife," she says with a wink. "Plus razor blades to trim edges, and a wallpaper scoring tool, and long rubber gloves. Lauren will be all set." Elsa puts the basket near Kyle. "Bring her a couple of biscotti, too. For energy."

Castaway Cottage

"Excellent," Kyle says as he presses the last of *his* biscotti into his mouth. From where he sits, he has a grand view of the turret down the hallway. "Great sightlines in here, Elsa. What a job Jason did."

"He's the best." She sips her coffee while gazing around the kitchen, but lowers her reading glasses to her face when she considers Kyle. "*You* look a little tired, though. Are you taking the day off, spending some time away from the stoves?"

"No way. I'm going in after lunch. This is just my Wednesday haircut morning. Which also means my honey-do morning."

"Honeydew? You mean, the fruit?"

"No," Kyle laughs. "More like, *Honey, do this. Honey, do that.* Lauren's got an endless list of things for me to do around the house." He pauses then and sips his coffee.

"Kyle, you are also quieter than usual today. You sure everything is okay?" Elsa reaches across the island and gives his hand a brief squeeze.

"Actually, I do have something on my mind." He pulls out a copy of his marriage certificate that he's kept secretly tucked into his wallet, then slides the paper across the island.

Elsa adjusts her leopard-print glasses while reading. "Oh! Your marriage certificate. And you've been married ten years, too!"

"Wait." Kyle motions to the paper. "Look closer."

"Kyle Bradford and Lauren Smith were lawfully married the twenty-third day of September."

"No, back it up."

Elsa peers at Kyle over the rim of her reading glasses, and he motions for her to look again at the paper. So she does, lowering her glasses a bit. "Klye. *Klye!* Oh, well that's just a teeny-tiny mistake."

"Mistake? Or fate?" Kyle stands and paces her kitchen. He

walks past the garden window, where her miniature red pots spill with fresh herbs. "Am I *really* married, after all?"

Elsa looks at the certificate once more. "Kyle, you know that marriage is so much more than what's on a piece of paper."

"Doesn't it start there, though?"

"Well." Her eyes drop to the document again. "I suppose. So you can do one of two things. Get my bottle of whiteout in the drawer over there and we'll work a little fix."

"No, no. Not on a legal document. And that's only a copy, anyway. But I'm not tampering with the law." Kyle takes the certificate copy from her and folds it up again. "What's my second option?"

Now Elsa takes off her leopard-print glasses and sets them on the marble-top island. Then she looks him straight on. "A vow renewal ceremony. That'll correct *everything*."

"A what?"

"Vow renewal ceremony," she repeats. "You know that I'm now a Justice of the Peace. So you and Lauren can be my *very* first couple married here." Elsa sweeps her arm toward a new kitchen window, this one facing a distant view of the water. "Officiated by me ... right here at the sea!"

Which doesn't help Kyle's nerves one bit. In fact, it would take *several* rides down Sea View Road to get his blood pressure out of the danger zone.

Because, *a wedding!* Well, sort of. But again?

Shit, he hasn't stopped sweating with Elsa's bombshell—not since dropping off her wallpaper basket to Lauren at home. And now, even with the truck's windows rolled down and the wind blowing in from all sides, he still sweats while driving to work. It's bad enough that the first thing he does at the diner is go into his office and change into a new black tee. Even then, he looks helplessly around the room—at his work desk, at the chef aprons hanging on wall hooks, at the framed photograph of his diner. *Anything* to orient himself, his *life*, and not feel panicked at the thought of a vow renewal.

He finally sits at his desk, breathes in and breathes out, then again, before getting an idea. Okay, so one group text message to the guys should do it. They'll be able to bail him out of this predicament. Somehow, some way.

Sand Bar tonight. Big dilemma. Help me!

eight

THE ONE PLACE JASON DOESN'T need a clock is on the beach. Walking the driftline Wednesday afternoon, he can tell the time without a glance at his wristwatch.

Yes, it's four o'clock, obvious by the mass exodus. Families, packing up their umbrellas and tubes and towels, are leaving the beach like a retreating wave. All that's left behind are stragglers, sitting in low chairs at the water's edge, the waves lapping at their feet, a few white seagulls patrolling the sand. On a hot summer day like this, most of the departing families will probably end up on some restaurant patio overlooking Long Island Sound. For dinner, they'll eat fried clams, fish and chips, and lobster rolls. He thinks that sounds good, and might have the lobster special tonight at The Sand Bar, when all the guys show up for whatever catastrophe prompted Kyle's text message.

But as Jason gets closer to the lone cottage on the end of the beach, food is the furthest thing from his mind. Even as the late-afternoon sun casts its golden rays on the cottage, its silvery shingles are still shadowed with black. And even from here, it's apparent that the graying wooden shutters are actually white, but dingy with years of neglect in the salty sea damp.

Castaway Cottage

"This is the job I need," Jason quietly says before he's too close to the cottage.

When a Jet Ski approaches, he turns his head, listening. Silver plumes of water spray up from beneath the vessel as it screams past. *Don't blow it,* Jason thinks he hears. Either it's Neil's spirit, or else it's the Jet Ski slapping the water as it propels forward.

"Thanks, guy," he whispers with the slightest salute before climbing the steps to the cottage's upper deck.

"Mr. Barlow."

He looks up the stairs to see Carol leaning her arms, hands clasped, on the deck railing. She nods to him, and wears a loose cropped tee over ripped skinny jeans. Today, thankfully, she doesn't look as annoyed as every other time he met with her. Though with those round wire-framed sunglasses covering much of her face, it's hard to be certain what's going on beneath them.

"Come on up," she says. "I'd like you to meet my father."

Jason obliges, lifting his own sunglasses to the top of his head once he gets to the deck. Her father—a man in his late fifties, maybe—stands beyond Carol. A beat-up, safari-style brimmed hat tops his wavy hair; his short-sleeve button-down and khakis are casual; he drags a hand across his goatee while waiting.

Then, in a surprising contradiction to his daughter's cautiousness, this man abruptly steps forward, hand firmly outstretched. "Jason, good to meet you. I'm Mitch Fenwick."

Jason shakes his hand. "Thanks for having me, Mitch."

"Dad, this is Jason Barlow," Carol begins, "who is also the host of that new cottage-renovation show on public TV."

"We actually premiered the show right here on the beach a few weeks ago. Used the movie screen on the sand," Jason says. "First reno was Foley's old place."

"Sorry I missed it," Mitch tells him. "I hear you had a big turnout."

As Mitch talks, Jason sees his scrutiny, though. Mitch's head is slightly upturned, and from beneath his sun-faded hat, he squints closely at Jason. So it's there, the suspicion his daughter also doesn't *fully* shake. Mitch is just better at camouflaging it.

"We hadn't opened up the cottage for the summer yet," Mitch is explaining. "Been here only about a week now." He waves for Jason to follow him to the deck table, where its umbrella is open and drinks and pastries are set out. "Trying to freshen up the rooms for another season."

Jason sits at the table as Carol lifts a pitcher. The ice in it clinks as she fills their glasses with a fruity-looking, cool drink. "I've shown Dad your sketches," she says.

"They're rough ideas, Mitch. I did some research, studied old postcards depicting the cottage in its early days. I like to tap into that history in my work. It all speaks to the original structure and its intent."

Mitch *seems* interested, as far as Jason can tell. They talk more, sitting in the shade. Jason shares ideas he'd like to bring to the project, including wrapping the deck around the cottage, and possibly bringing an observation deck to the roof. He asks what Mitch and Carol envision in a renovation. They loosen up with that one, tossing out ideas for their beloved cottage. That it's beloved becomes more apparent, the more they talk. Mitch quiets again, though, when Jason mentions the TV show. He slowly removes his canvas brimmed hat, drags a hand through his fading blond, grown-out hair, and sits back to eye Jason.

Again, there it is. That suspicion.

Drawing a hand over his goatee now, Mitch asks, "Does this CT-TV cover the renovation expenses?"

"Unfortunately, no," Jason explains. "That's typically not how these shows work. The costs are actually paid by the homeowner.

But," Jason adds when Mitch waves his hand and scoffs at him. "Hear me out. Lots of local companies discount or donate their products and services, just to get valuable exposure on the show. Which translates into new business for them and hefty savings for you. My fees, for the architectural designing and blueprints, would be discounted in this case as well."

Still, Mitch has withdrawn. Jason lost him with mention of *television statio*n and *cameras* and *production team*. Mitch looks out at the beach, then back at his own cottage walls. "You've renovated many places here?"

"Dad, I told you about the cottage photographs in his studio," Carol reminds him. "You'd really like his vision."

Jason props his elbows on the table and rests his chin on his clasped hands. "I've done lots of work right at Stony Point, as well as up and down the Connecticut coast."

"My daughter says you actually have roots here?" Mitch asks.

"I own a cottage on the bluff." Jason motions across the beach. "On the other side, looking east. It was my father's. He bought it after coming home from the Vietnam War."

Mitch nods, but says nothing. He's closed right up again; something switched his demeanor.

"I moved in permanently a couple years ago," Jason continues. "Got myself married. There's a barn out back that my father used for his masonry work. I converted it into my studio and do most of my designing right there."

Mitch lifts his hat from the table, fusses with the beat-up brim, and puts it on again. Then he sits back and looks out at Jason from beneath it. "But why *my* place for your show? There are plenty of properties that could use your attention, so I don't really get it. Your choosing this one," he says, waving his hand to his old dame of a cottage, "makes me really wary. I've had plenty of developers wanting to get their hands on this last-standing beach cottage. It can never be replaced, you know, should it ever go down."

"I'm aware of that." Jason says no more.

"And in the ridiculous offers that have come my way, I've always sensed some greed." Mitch tips his head, still scrutinizing Jason. "So I'm trying to find yours."

"Jeez, Dad. Lighten up." Carol looks from her father to Jason. "Like I've said, it's a very coveted building," she softly adds.

"Well, I have no ulterior financial motive. And you're right, Mitch. There are *lots* of properties here that need work. CT-TV's website has been screening applicants that meet certain criteria. But the show's chosen reno project also needs a *story*, or an interesting history that would transfer well to the episodes. Of course, yours fits the bill." From the table on this elevated deck, Jason takes in the coastal view then. Frothy waves lap along the tideline on the nearly empty beach—a beach once lined with grand shingled cottages built right on the sand. Now, in the late-afternoon sunlight, only a few vacationers stroll seaside. They're oblivious to Stony Point's history, and to the fading memories of what once stood where they walk. "Location is paramount, too. And for filming purposes, yours nails it—right onshore."

"Mom would've *loved* it, being a part of the show," Carol says to her father. "Especially since her family history is so ingrained here, the way she lost her father."

"And that's a private matter, Carol," Mitch counters. "Family business. Not sure I want that broadcast across the state."

"But maybe it could give some sort of closure to the story," Carol presses on. "How many times did Mom talk about that day? She never got over it, really."

"Those personal stories are what draw people in, Mitch," Jason argues. "They give a unique dimension to the cottage. And I'm happy to honor your wife, not only in the reno, but in the episodes, too. You know ... with pictures, home movie clips ..."

Mitch squints long at Jason. "Much as I like your suggestions for the place from the drawings my daughter showed me, I'm still not sure it'd be worth my while." Again, a silent pause. "I'll make it easy for you and cut to the chase, Jason. A renovation here would be a *hell* of a lot of aggravation, zoning red tape, time—*and* cash. For what? What's really in it for me?"

Jason tosses up his hands and sits back. "A few things, Mitch. Preservation, which my designs incorporate. But ..." When Mitch nods slightly, Jason hesitates before continuing. Because he could go on with the usual spiel.

Except so far, that spiel has gotten him nowhere. Mitch Fenwick is as resistant as ever to a renovation—if not even *more* so. So Jason does it; he tries a different angle. "I have personal reasons for wanting this reno, Mitch. A personal reason, more than *anything* else."

"Okay, I figured as much, so now we're talking. Hotshot architect like you? You could practically nail down any cottage here. Which is why I still *don't* really trust you. But here's your last chance. Explain your personal reason. And make it good." With that, Mitch leans back in his patio chair, lifts a sandaled foot to his knee and crosses his arms over his chest.

Jason glances out at the Sound. Someone's swimming lazily past; a couple of kids are crabbing on the nearby rocks. Then he turns to Mitch. "My brother was fascinated with this place."

"*This* place?" Carol asks.

Jason nods. "He started writing a novel back in the day, and it's loosely set at this very cottage."

"Wait." Mitch suddenly sits up and pulls his chair in close to the table. "Your brother. Let me think a second," he says while holding up a hand signaling for silence. "Nelson. No … no. *Neil*." He looks silently at Jason. "My God, it's Neil, isn't it?"

"You knew him?" Jason asks.

"I did. Son of a gun, our paths crossed. Oh, it's been years, but he's the kind of guy, well, I just never forgot him. Met him one day when I was up on a ladder, scraping some peeling window trim on this place. And I noticed him hanging around, down near the water." Mitch hitches his head toward where the waves are lapping at the shore. "Watching. Just watching me."

He was there when I hauled out the wooden ladder from beneath the cottage, Mitch begins. *It was a cloudy day, and when I was dragging the ladder over to the side, he caught my eye. He was walking, barefoot. Wading in the shallows, coming down the beach. Didn't give him another thought until later, after I propped that old rickety ladder up against the shingles. Climbing up it, the damn thing jostled with each step. Thought for sure I'd set my foot on one rung and go right through it, then drop two stories.*

When I looked down to gauge how safely I could climb, that's when I noticed him still there, this guy hanging around near the water. Had a pencil behind his ear, his hand looped around some journal or pad. Again, I didn't think much of it and got to work scraping the window trim.

But he was on my mind, now. So I looked back once or twice and, shit, he was still there. Looked almost like a college student, the way he was dressed casual in those cuffed jeans, his hair long and kind of wavy in the sea breeze. Thought maybe he was taking notes for some paper or project, so I gave a yell to feel him out. Find out what he was up to.

"Want to see inside?" I called down.

"Seriously?" With no hesitation, he walked out of the shallows and crossed the sand.

I looked over my shoulder at him, and he seemed all right. Figured I'd question him more before giving him a little tour. Funny thing is, right away I liked him, when he kept walking across the sand straight to the ladder. Without me saying a single word, he steadied that shaky ladder like an old pro as I came down, like he knew it wasn't really safe to be shifting my weight on that thing with all its dry rot from being under the cottage. Something about that gesture of his had me trust him.

So when we walked around to the deck, he was commenting on the silver shingles, and asked if I minded if he took notes.

"For what?" I asked. "You a college fellow? Or just casing out the joint?"

"No," he said with a laugh. "The name's Neil. I do a little construction, in business with my brother. Been working on a novel on the side." When he said it, he raised his journal as if to prove it.

So he came inside, looked around. Commented on the paneled walls. Picked up a trinket or two. And you know, I'd never met anyone writing a book before. So I was interested in his process. He made everything sound so fascinating, talking about the old windows here, looking out toward the rocky ledge. Noticing the way the sea spray would hit the glass panes. Seemed hung up on the view of the sky, from this higher vantage point. With the cottage being on stilts and all.

I don't know. There was something about him. He had a way of seeing things—the sea, the beach—that made me feel, right away, like a part of that story he was writing.

~

"I saw him a few times after that, that one summer. He was a good-looking kid. Laid-back. Always in jeans and a tee, I remember he'd fiddle with a couple of dog tags on a chain around his neck—mostly when he was thinking, working something out."

"Shit. That's my brother all right," Jason says. "And I'm just about floored to hear this, Mitch. It's pretty amazing."

"Did Mom meet him?" Carol asks as she sets her sunglasses on the table.

"She did," Mitch says while nodding. "I brought Neil inside a couple times after that so he could take a look around, jot notes for that book of his. He'd write the locations of certain rooms. Sketch views from windows, that kind of thing."

"Unbelievable." Jason looks up at the cottage windows, then back at Mitch. "I actually *have* those notes, but I always thought they were purely fiction. Details Neil made up. *Never* realized he'd been inside here."

"He was!" Mitch sits back, shaking his head. "Damn, what a coincidence. Thing is, though, we lost touch after that summer. My wife, Carol's mother, got sick. Kate's been gone five years now, and I haven't been back here much since then. But seriously, bring your brother by sometime. It'd be great to catch up with him—"

"Oh, Dad," Carol interrupts, grasping her father's arm. "I forgot to mention ..." She hesitates and throws Jason an apologetic look.

If he's not mistaken, this is the first time Carol's at a loss for words, curt or not, defensive or not. "That's okay," he tells her, then turns to Mitch again. "My brother died in a crash. A terrible bike wreck. We were on his Harley, and, well I lost my leg that day, too." As he says it, Jason nods to his prosthetic limb. "It's been ten years now. Probably would've been right after you met him."

"Well I'll be goddamned." Mitch actually stands, then, walks around the table and reaches for Jason's arm so that Jason stands, too. When he does, Mitch steps closer and simply clasps Jason's shoulder. "I am so sorry."

Jason only nods.

"That is a terrible shame, losing your brother like that."

"It was a tough time, Mitch."

"So whatever happened to that novel of his?" Mitch asks. "Because I've often thought about it, wondering how he'd spun that story."

Jason walks to the deck railing and leans back against it. "He never finished it. Neil wrote a lot of it, and then, well, there was the accident," he explains. "But you know? Life works in mysterious ways, Mitch. Because my wife's actually finishing up his book now."

"*Maris?*" Carol asks. She turns up her hands in disbelief. "She never said a word!"

"Well, she's private about it. You know how that is. Like the family matters you mentioned before, Mitch. We keep things close."

"But Maris? That's incredible," Carol admits.

"It is, watching her work with Neil's story," Jason agrees. "But she doesn't like to say much until she sees how it all goes."

Mitch walks over to the deck railing then, too. Beside Jason, he leans against it, raises the brim of his hat and eyes his shabby seaside cottage. He's quiet for a few moments, rubbing his hand along his goatee. "She's not a bad old place," he finally says.

"And hell, you know what they say," Carol insists, moving beside her father and eyeing their tired family cottage. "A change is as good as a rest, Dad. So maybe it's time now."

Mitch, abruptly again, walks to that rusty slider door, scrapes it open, then turns to Jason. "Why don't you come inside? Have a look around."

"Seriously?" Jason asks, and don't they all hear the irony of his one word—the same word Neil first said to Mitch ten long years ago.

"Please. And you know ... I think I might even have a picture of your brother somewhere around here."

Mitch holds the door open and Carol goes inside first.

But Jason still leans against the deck railing, silent. He can see a little bit inside, past the open slider, to some furniture—an old lobster trap used as an end table, looks like. Damn, this last-standing cottage on the beach holds more stories than he ever could have imagined.

Again, Mitch brusquely waves for Jason to follow him inside.

Jason simply nods and does just that.

nine

Even though the Sand Bar has air-conditioning, Patrick's got one particular quirk about managing the place. On warm summer evenings, the a/c is turned off and the doors stay propped open to the night. He tells anyone who complains that the sea breeze coming in sets the bar's mood.

It's true, Kyle knows that. Pungent salt air drifts into the dark bar while the jukebox plays some honky-tonk tune, and it all has you feel like a fisherman just off the boat after a long day at sea. Kyle drags a finger around his T-shirt collar and thinks that you also get used to it this way, with no a/c. The heat doesn't feel all that bad, especially once you stop, sit, and nurse a cold drink. He looks around the shadowy room, where Patrick keeps the fisherman vibe going. Decorative wood pilings of varying heights, tied with nautical rope, stand on either end of the long bar.

"So what's up with this meeting, Kyle?" Cliff asks from across the table. "Family okay?"

Kyle pulls a basket of pretzels across the tacky tabletop, nodding as he scoops up a handful.

Nick, sitting beside him in their regular booth, lifts the pitcher and pours himself a beer. "Diner probs?"

"Nah," Kyle tells him around his mouthful of salty pretzels.

"Got that new house of yours insured for hurricane season?" Matt asks.

"It's not that. All's good with my humble abode," Kyle says while tossing back another handful of pretzels.

Cliff takes a long sip from his glass of beer. "So what's your dilemma?"

"I'm waiting for Barlow to get here," Kyle admits with an impatient glance toward that open entrance door. "Don't feel like telling the story three times. Where the hell is he?"

"He's always late," Nick remarks.

"No, more like he's always *busy*." Kyle props his elbows on the table and eyes Nick beside him. "Unlike you, Nicholas. Tooling around in your new Whaler at night. Shootin' the breeze with folks all day on the beach. *You* might call it patrolling, but, hell, let's get real."

"Didn't you get your degree?" Matt asks. "You had a big party at Elsa's inn this spring. When are you going to get a real job, for Christ's sake?"

Cliff jumps in and answers for Nick. "After Labor Day. I need you patrolling full-time this summer."

After putzing around with bullshit and small talk, Kyle figures now's as good a time as any to at least get *started* with his predicament. So he pulls his folded marriage certificate copy from his wallet and flattens it on the tabletop. "Judge. You worked in family court for decades," Kyle says as his fingers press the wrinkles out of the paper. "So I have a question for you." He hands Cliff the marriage certificate. "See that error in my name? In a court of law, would that hold up?"

Cliff lifts the paper and pulls it closer to his face, then moves it farther away. "Sheesh, I could use Elsa's reading glasses right about now." He looks over the paper to Kyle. "Anyway, what are you getting at with this?"

Kyle shrugs. "Want to be sure me and Lauren are legally married."

Cliff looks at the copy again, squinting to see it clearly. "Never encountered something like this. Not in my whole career presiding over domestic cases. I'd have to research its validity."

"All I know," Matt says while lifting the beer pitcher and topping off his glass, "is that you and Lauren had one emotional wedding. Especially coming so soon after Neil's funeral. Then Jason arriving at your nuptials with one leg ... being brought in sitting in a wheelchair, no less? Still banged up from the accident? Damn."

As he says it, Kyle's clearly aware of how silent their usually unruly booth has gotten.

"It was tough," Matt's saying. "So much went down in that one month. One thing after the other."

"I don't know, Bradford. You could be opening a can of worms, revisiting the past with your marriage certificate. Maybe just let it go and move on," Nick suggests.

"Yeah, maybe." Kyle drags his hand back through his newly cut hair with another glance to the bar's propped-open door. "The whole Stony Point wedding track record isn't too good. Starting way back with Matt and Eva's shotgun wedding when she was pregnant at eighteen, then my sad wedding."

"Sad?" Cliff asks. "But maybe your wedding was a *good* thing everyone needed at the time, no?"

"Not quite," Kyle says with a long breath. That one stinkin' typo has him doubting everything now. "That bike wreck changed a lot of things, Judge, after Jason's brother died. It was bad, really bad. But I mean, we couldn't very well cancel our *wedding*, so when it rolled around a few weeks later, we all pretty much went through the motions."

"Everyone was shot that year," Matt remembers.

"Definitely," Kyle agrees. "And then? Then there was Jason and Maris' wedding two summers ago," Kyle reminds them. "A beach gala to beat *all* others. No one can ever top Barlow's event ... just like his monster pinball score no one can ever match." Kyle looks to the doorway when a motion catches his eye. "And hey, there's the man now."

When Kyle whistles and waves him over, Jason first stops at the bar and has Patrick pour a pitcher of beer, which he brings to the booth. He sets it down, grabs a chair from a nearby empty table and drags it over.

"Celebrating is in order," Jason announces while lifting the pitcher and filling a glass for himself, then topping off the others.

"Really. What's going on, guy?" Matt asks.

Jason eyes them all—Matt and Cliff, Nick and Kyle—before revealing his coup. "Just came from the Fenwick place. After a *lot* of back and forth, finally got the reno job locked down."

"No shit!" Kyle leans over and high-fives Jason. "Yeah, man. That's the one to snag."

"Sounds like it wasn't easy," Cliff remarks. "They give you a tough time?"

"You have no idea. It was damn hard getting through to them. That family's dogged resistance is tied up in a *boatload* of personal history there, but it's a long story. One you'll see on the show, when it airs," Jason says, raising his glass to theirs before taking a long swallow of his brew. "Because I finally convinced them to sign on. Wait'll you see the episodes. Lots of good stuff to cover. Only thing hanging now is an official name for the show."

"Still nothing?" Kyle asks.

"Nope." Jason tips back his chair and has another swig of beer. "*CT-TV Cottage Redo* was just a placeholder for the pilot episode."

"Not even a close second? Some catchy rhyme?" Kyle asks.

Jason shakes his head. "Nothing that captures what the show *really* does. So we're under serious pressure to come up with a title."

The waitress approaches then, her order pad in hand. "Well, boys. What'll it be tonight?"

"I've been in the mood for lobster all day, but don't feel much like working for it. So give me a lobster roll," Jason says.

"Hot or cold?"

"Hot." Jason turns up his hands. "Who eats lobster rolls cold?"

"Whoa," Cliff says. "Touchy subject, plenty of people eat them cold. But not me." He motions to the waitress. "I'll take one, too. Hot, extra butter."

"And hot for me," Kyle puts in. "With a side of slaw." As he downs a pretzel, he goes off on a lobster-roll tangent. "Northern New England actually gets *offended* by hot lobster rolls. They serve them cold up north, with mayo."

"Even though I'll take mine hot, with corn on the cob on the side, northern New England should know," Matt says. "Maine is synonymous with lobster. So wouldn't they be right?"

"Hold your lobster claws, Officer," Kyle counters. "Connecticut *officially* made the very *first* lobster roll. In 1929, in Milford. It's in the record books. And they made it *hot*, with drawn butter." With those words, Kyle kisses his fingertips. "There's no other way."

"Well," Nick says, leaning over from beside Kyle and talking to their patient waitress standing there with pencil poised. "I'll shake things up and try a *cold* lobster roll. Extra mayo, too. And French fries, for the table."

"Hot, cold. What's the big deal?" Matt asks when the waitress leaves. "I mean, we're talking a friggin' hot-dog bun stuffed with lobster meat."

Jason nearly gags on a mouthful of beer. "You kidding me?" he asks. "What's the big deal? It's ownership, man ... claiming the authentic title. You know, like I did as Aria's godfather. Ain't nothing like holding the title."

"True. Kind of like that marriage certificate issue, making you wonder if you've legally claimed the *husband* title," Cliff adds with a nod to Kyle across the table.

Jason sees it, the way there's a twinkle in Cliff's eye, but *nothing* will lighten the load for Kyle. "You still effing around with that?" Jason asks.

"Oh, man." With his two words, Kyle simply deflates. He pulls his fingers across his chin, as though seeking that soul patch he had shaved off earlier today. "What am I going to do?"

"You've got ten minutes, till the food gets here, to tell us your probs." Jason reaches over and slaps Kyle's shoulder. "Because all talking stops once those lobster rolls arrive."

"Ten minutes to fix my life." Kyle drops his head into his hand. "Ay yai yai."

"This is about more than a typo, Kyle," Cliff says. He leans forward, elbows on the table. "You're too distraught. You going to spill it, or what?"

Now it's Kyle's turn to eye them all, one at a time. "Think I want to get married again. I *think*. Even though it scares the hell out of me."

"Married?" Nick asks beside him. "To who?"

"Who do you think, asshole?" As he asks, Kyle gets Nick in a headlock and gives him a brisk noogie, rubbing his folded knuckles roughly over Nick's head. "To my *wife*."

Nick twists out of Kyle's ironclad grip and gives him a shove. "What? You're *marrying* your *wife?*"

"I have to right what's wrong," Kyle explains. "Change Klye to Kyle. Getting married again was Elsa's idea," he adds, tipping his glass to Cliff. "She suggested a vow renewal ceremony to fix things. Her idea was to either do that, or get some whiteout and eliminate the typo that way."

Cliff downs a handful of pretzels. "News flash. Elsa *could* just be bullying you into a vow renewal. She's mighty desperate to put that JP feather in her cap. You'd be her first ceremony."

"Wait." Jason pulls his chair in closer. "Are you talking the whole shebang? Tuxes, gown, flowers?"

"Well, yeah ... but casual. But that's not even the real problem. Which would be getting Lauren on board." Kyle grabs his cell phone and flashes a photo on it, one showing his half-stripped dining room walls. "She couldn't care less about that certificate. Stripping wallpaper's her latest obsession."

Cliff takes the phone and gives the picture a look. "Did you propose, first time around?"

"Sure I did, ten years ago," Kyle says, taking his phone back. "I guess."

"You're telling us you got down on one knee?" Matt asks as he swipes Kyle's phone and considers the partially stripped wallpaper.

"One knee?" Kyle shrugs. "Well, no. It just kind of happened. We'd been going out for years, since we were teens. Next thing you know, we thought we should get married."

"Not on one knee?" This time, Jason lightly slaps Kyle's face. "Salvatore would *kill* you if he knew that. He was all about the *love*, man."

"Oh, right." Kyle slaps Jason back, landing a blow on his

shoulder. "Like you proposed to Maris on one knee."

"Damn straight I did. On the boardwalk, on Christmas *Eve*."

"All right. Barlow really can't be beat, Bradford." Nick gives Kyle another light slap, so that Kyle's getting it from all around now.

"I even decorated the boardwalk first," Jason tells them. "Strung those twinkly lights under the pavilion, had Christmas trees lit up on either end. Made sure there was a dusting of snow. You know the way women like that kind of thing."

"I'm screwed. The most I can come up with is to scrape the words *Marry me again?* in our never-ending wallpaper." Kyle looks at the pathetic dining room photo on his cell phone, then puts the phone back in his pocket. "Judge," he says then. "I need all the help I can get. You got that lucky domino on you?"

"Always." Cliff pulls a scuffed-and-faded domino from his pocket and flips it over a couple of times. "So you're looking for a way to win over Lauren? To actually propose? That's why you summoned us?"

When Kyle snaps his fingers, Cliff tosses him the domino. "Yeah," Kyle relents, his thumb already rubbing over the dotted black square.

Matt looks out toward the open doorway, where across the street and past some scrubby dune grass, seawater laps at shore in a small inlet. "How about something like a message in a bottle. You know," he says to Kyle now, "act like it washed up on the sand."

"Or what about a ring in a shell?" Jason asks. "I gave Maris a conch shell off the beach a couple years ago, and she *still* has it."

Nick, rubbing the vague goatee he tries to sneak in during the summer, argues. "No way. You'll put a diamond ring in a shell. And ... and one of those rogue seagulls will grab the shell, smash it on the rocks and see what they can eat inside it. This time—your bling!"

Before Kyle can decide, the waitress returns carrying a large platter. It's spilling with plates of lobster rolls and red baskets of French fries and paper cups of coleslaw and bags of onion rings, with extra sides of melted butter. She distributes it all, saving the last lobster roll for Nick.

"All hot, except for this one." She sets the mayo'd lobster roll in front of him. "Enjoy, fellas."

Wasting no time, they all start in on Nick.

"Rip me off a piece, Nicholas," Cliff says first.

While handing Cliff a small hunk, Nick slaps away Kyle's hand.

"But I need a sample, too," Kyle insists as he manages to fork off a slab of Nick's lobster. "If I'm going to serve these at the diner, it'll be my summer poll. Hot or cold? I'll put up my ballot box and customers can fill out tally slips." As Kyle chews the cold lobster, he trots over to the bar. A minute later, he's back with a pen and rips a napkin into five parts. After marking H or C on each piece, he gives one to everybody at the table. "These will be my first tallies. To get the count started."

He passes around the pen at the same time that Jason stands and reaches over for Nick's cold lobster roll. He evenly knifes into it, divvying it up among them. By the time he's done cutting, a smidgeon is left for Nick—which Jason slides down the table in Nick's direction.

Nick turns up his hands, asking, *"What the?"*

Problem is, no one's listening. They're all too busy squeezing lemon wedges over the meat before biting into their chunks of Nick's lobster roll. In a moment, it starts—serious deliberation of the merits of hot versus cold, butter versus mayonnaise. A couple of the guys change their tally vote and tell Kyle they need a new napkin ballot. At the same time, any remaining cold lobster pieces are being considered on their discerning palates, then compared to the hot lobster they dig into next.

As the hot-cold argument continues, a voice calls out to the waitress. Jason can't be sure if it was Nick—desperate to salvage a meal—or someone else having a shred of sympathy for the now lobsterless dude. But the voice rings out from their corner, the words carrying across the room to where the waitress stands at the bar talking to Patrick.

"Another cold lobster roll here, please!"

⁓

When the meals are done, when every last morsel's been dipped, dunked, salted, buttered, ketchuped and eaten, when the dishes are pushed away and the last sips of beer downed, Jason stands.

"Let's blow this joint," he says, then lifts his napkin and wipes his mouth. "I need a nightcap after that lobster roll."

"Nightcap?" Kyle asks, leaning back and stretching his arms to the side. "You're in the right place, right *here*, guy."

"No, no," Jason admits with a laugh. "In *my* house, nightcap means ice cream. Maris wants me to bring her home something from Scoop Shop. My treat tonight, guys. It's on me."

"Scoop Shop. You mean the little place on Shore Road, before the train trestle?" Nick asks as he shoves Kyle out of his seat.

"That's the one." Jason tosses up his key ring and grabs it, jangling, midair. "*Andiamo.* Let's go."

ten

To CLIFF, IT'S ALL MUSIC to his ears. He often sneaks a visit to that little ice-cream parlor late at night, getting a treat to-go and settling back in at his trailer-apartment ... a Dino album spinning on the turntable, the trailer windows slid open to the night air as he relishes each cool mouthful of some sinful flavor. Those ice-cream stops have been his summer secret. But still, he's game to go there now to top off the lobster grub.

And so, twenty minutes later, not only are they still deliberating Kyle's wedding proposal ideas. They're also standing inside the Scoop Shop, lined up at the glass case while deliberating tubs of ice cream beneath it. The way they toss around opinions on sundaes, cups or cones; frozen yogurt or dairy free; black-raspberry chip, strawberry or coffee toffee; granola, hot fudge or sprinkle toppings, it's a wonder they ever get out of there.

And at times, they almost don't.

"Do you give samples?" Nick asks the teen working behind the counter.

"Are you *kidding*?" Kyle glares at Nick. "Just make a decision."

"Yeah." Matt steps closer to the glass case. "Be a man."

"I don't see *you* ordering," Nick throws back at them.

When the same clerk asks Cliff if he wants his usual, with extra hot fudge, all the guys turn to him with upturned brows—which Cliff blows off while muttering he's still thinking. And somehow—between that, and the taste-testing and, yep, that's right, the small-medium-large size consideration—by the good grace of God, five flavors are doled out in heaping cups and cones, and Jason manages to pay at the register.

"Wait." Jason turns back before they all get through the door. He snatches the buy-ten-get-one-free card from Nick's hand. Five holes have been punched in it.

"Hey," Nick says.

"I *paid*, man. These are working toward *my* free." Jason puts the card in his back pocket, then heads outside.

"Like you need it," Nick says behind him.

"Just get out of here." Jason holds the door open and motions for them all to go through. "Because that was actually embarrassing."

"What was?" Matt asks while lifting a heaping spoonful of cookie dough ice cream doused with rainbow sprinkles.

"Didn't you see those kids behind us?" Jason asks him. "Rolling their eyes like we've never seen ice cream before? Shit."

Outdoors again, they walk beside the low-slung brick building. Red-and-white striped awnings extend above silver benches. Separating each bench is a tiny black bistro table for two. Kyle sits at one of those, alone, while the others sit side by side on two benches. The sun has gone down, traffic on Shore Road is light, the sky lavender. The railroad tracks run directly behind the building, and a freight train rumbles past as they dig in.

Cliff has to smile, though, when between heaping ice-cream scoops, the guys get Kyle fretting again with their goading, their questions.

You getting new rings?

No way, my bank account's tapped out, Kyle explains. *Barlow, I'll swing by your place and pick up my rings, in case I ever think of how to propose.*

How about at a sporting event? On the big-screen at that new minor league stadium in Hartford?

What about an airplane banner?

Until finally, Kyle waves them all off. "I've got to class it up," he says, lifting a spoonful of melting sundae dripping with whipped cream and hot fudge. "Because this is my second chance to get married. And remember what Sal always said about second chances? They're *molto speciale*. Very special." He takes another taste of ice cream. "Man, I miss the Italian."

"Well, listen," Jason suggests. "Maybe you're overthinking it. Keep things simple, Kyle. That's what DeLuca would've done. Just write your proposal in the sand, or something like that."

Kyle leans back in his little bistro chair and stretches out his legs. "That's actually not a bad idea, Barlow, especially since I do live at the beach now."

"Be sure to write it high enough so the waves don't wash it away," Nick advises. "You'll be walking along the water, thinking you're proposing, and the question will be out to sea."

"So you want to propose on the beach?" Cliff asks. He scrapes his spoon along any fudge remnants in his cup. "Hmm. I actually have an idea." It all comes together then, especially when he thinks of Elsa. Recently, she's been busy assembling happiness jars for her inn's opening. The ingredients are usually spread out on her kitchen island: shells, sand, sea glass, polished stones, dried flowers. Cliff spoons up the last dregs of his ice cream.

"Whaddya got, Judge?" Matt asks.

"Okay, listen closely." Cliff gets up and tosses his plastic cup and spoon in a nearby trash can. "Here's how we'll put Operation

Get Kyle Hitched into motion." Cliff paces in front of them as they polish off their monster ice-cream scoops. "Nick, you'll need my camera. Matt, see if Eva has any decorations left from Taylor's birthday party. And you?" he asks, stopping in front of Jason. "Have Maris shine up those rings real nice for Kyle."

And so it is that an hour later, Operation Get Kyle Hitched is a go. Cliff once again sits in a booth, this time in the back room of the Ocean Star Inn. The windows are open and the jukebox plays a melancholy tune about having a fling, and leaving one last time.

"Now *what* is so important that it couldn't wait until morning, Clifton?" Elsa slowly twirls a spoon in her cup of tea.

"Do you hear that man singing on the jukebox? Talking about the look in someone's eyes, when you just know that love is gone?"

Elsa sips her tea, then carefully sets the cup in its saucer. "Is this about us?" she asks, motioning her hand between them. "Are you breaking up with me?"

"How can I break things off if we've never formally declared what we are to each other? So, no. No, this is about Kyle and Lauren's love," Cliff insists. "Because from the tormented look in Kyle's eyes tonight, they need that vow renewal ceremony more than anyone realizes."

"Seriously?"

Cliff nods. "So here's the plan. First, I need you to send a group text to everyone."

"Now?"

"Now. Where's your cell phone?"

"Right here." Elsa pulls it from her robe pocket. "I keep it with me in case Celia needs anything for the baby."

"Okay, good. So you can send a text. Lauren will never suspect a thing with it coming from you. You know, with the way you're always calling group boardwalk meetings and dinner gatherings. Because we've *got* to get poor Kyle hitched, once and for all."

"And what's the second thing?"

"A little creativity that needs your DeLuca magic touch."

"Oh my gosh, Cliff. What's gotten into you?"

"Love." He slides out of the booth and goes to the jukebox thinking of Kyle distressed about his marriage. So Cliff selects an old Sinatra song about love lost to the summer winds. "That's what's gotten into me. *Amore*, pure and simple," Cliff adds when he sits again, reaches across the table and takes Elsa's hand in his. "Kyle's got it bad for Lauren. And he's afraid this marriage certificate thing will snowball into some out-of-control situation where he'll somehow lose her."

"Well, that's just *crazy*."

"I know that, and you know that. But Kyle needs our help, regardless."

"Okay." Elsa slides her cell phone close and sets up a group text. "But we've got to craft this just right." She pauses and looks up at Cliff. "Ooh, I'm so excited ... This will be my first official inn ceremony!" she says with a little clap before stretching over the table and giving Cliff a quick kiss.

"Let's do this," Cliff tells her quietly. "Everyone but Lauren will know it's a proposal setup."

When Elsa nods, he sits back and watches her diligently type.

PLEASE COME: Emergency Meeting
WHEN: Tomorrow morning
TIME: 7 AM
WHERE: Stony Point Boardwalk, beneath shade pavilion
WHY: Good news to share!

eleven

"NO ONE'S HERE YET," LAUREN says, stepping onto the boardwalk. "That's strange." She shields her eyes from the bright sunshine and squints down the length of the beach.

"It's early," Kyle tells her. "They'll show up."

"But Elsa called an emergency meeting. I thought she'd at least be setting up a table, or a coffee station." When they get beneath the shade canopy, Lauren sits on the boardwalk bench. After this meeting, she's headed to the diner with Kyle to cover for another vacationing waitress. But for now, Lauren leans back and breathes that salt air. *Cures what ails you*, she thinks. It's not too often that she gets to sit here this early and take in all the seaside quiet. A seagull swoops low over the sand, its lone cry piercing. Beyond, those ocean stars sparkle on the morning's blue water.

She glances at Kyle then, who is standing still and looking out at the lazy lapping waves.

"Let's walk," he says, suddenly turning to her.

"Now? What about Elsa's meeting?"

"Eh," he says while dabbing his forehead with the back of his hand. "They'll all be here when we get back."

"But we're in our work clothes."

"It'll just be a little walk on the beach, Ell. You and me."

After another glimpse down the empty boardwalk, Lauren kicks off her sandals and steps barefoot onto the sand. Kyle takes her hand and together they walk to the water. The sand is soft on her feet, the sun warm on her skin. At the water's edge, Lauren tips her face to the sky right as Kyle splashes a handful of water on his face, then runs his wet hands back through his buzz-cut hair.

"You okay?" Lauren asks.

"Me? Yeah, why?"

"You're awfully quiet, and seem tense, too."

He checks his watch. "Have to get to the breakfast crowd. Jerry will be busy manning the stoves alone."

Lauren throws a worried look back to the still-empty boardwalk.

"Come on," Kyle says over his shoulder as he walks ahead along the high tide line. When she catches up, he points to the lone cottage on the beach. "Barlow's so pumped. The family there agreed to a reno for his show."

Lauren considers the cottage rising from the sand like a beach sentry, but all she sees is a memory. Damn beach. Does *every* walk down it have to bring up the past? The cottage ahead is raised on stilts, and her sudden memory comes from one long-ago dreary day. During their affair, she and Neil once got caught in a rain shower and ducked beneath that cottage. They huddled there until the rain let up enough for them to make a run to the boardwalk pavilion. It's all clear: the sight of her that day in a cropped denim jacket over a white eyelet blouse; Neil in cuffed jeans, a black sweatshirt; both of them drenched. So much so that Neil slipped off his dog-tag chain to keep it dry, and tucked it into the leather journal he'd been carrying.

"Last night at The Sand Bar?" Kyle is saying. "It was all Jason talked about. Said that cottage has some surprising history he'll explore on the show."

"I'll bet," Lauren murmurs beside him.

"They're still tied up in knots, though, about the right name for the show. He and the producers. Can't seem to nail it, I guess."

"Hmm." Lauren eyes the cottage. "Maybe they need to take a poll, like you do at the diner."

They keep walking, slowly, because it's that kind of sunny morning with blue skies, no clouds. Kyle occasionally skims a stone, and as Lauren collects a few shells for their daughter, Hailey, she points ahead to something in the sand. "What's that?"

"Where?"

"There. In the sand, near that seaweed. Looks like a bottle. Maybe something washed ashore."

Kyle takes her hand again and quickens his pace. "Let's check it out."

~

"Wait!" Cliff orders in a hushed whisper. "Stay back," he says as his outstretched arm keeps the others behind him. Slowly, they all climb the boardwalk steps.

"Do you see them?" Elsa asks over his shoulder as she presses into him. She can't help it, really, with the way everyone else is pressing into *her*, trying to steal a glimpse of Kyle and Lauren.

"Shh!" Cliff says. And when he does, he puts his finger to his mouth. Which gives everyone else the opportunity to surge forward, now that his restraining arm has moved out of the way.

"Look! There they are." Maris points down the beach.

"Okay, bend low," Eva says after Matt lifts Elsa's lemonade

cart onto the boardwalk. Eva takes hold of its handles and, half bent over, quickly wheels the cart toward the shade pavilion.

Meanwhile, Jason and Matt now carry a folding table and get that set up in the shade. From where Elsa directs them all at the boardwalk steps, she watches. It's a sea of ducking heads and hushed laughter. There are bobbing balloons, and covered pastry platters, a tablecloth and carafe of hot coffee.

Oh, Elsa loves it all. A seaside proposal! She lifts her sunglasses and checks that everything is being set in the right place. And, what's this? Does she really have butterflies in her stomach? Because what this day will lead to is her very first formal event at the Ocean Star Inn.

"Everything okay?" Jason asks when he comes up the steps behind her again. This time, he carries a box of paper cups, and plates, and napkins hauled from Elsa's golf cart.

"Just feeling a little anxious for poor Kyle." Elsa walks with Jason toward everyone clustered beneath the pavilion. "Oh, I almost forgot. Did you clear all the sand off the boardwalk this morning?"

"At five o'clock. Had my leaf blower. Watched the sunrise as I blew every grain off every plank." He stops her, briefly holding her arm. "You see a speck?"

"Of course not." Elsa keeps walking then. "Come on. We have to get this done, and fast!" Way down the beach, she catches sight of Lauren and Kyle as they lift her jar from the sand. So Elsa trots to the others to quickly delegate tasks.

"Jason and Matt? Hang these streamers with the tacks I brought. Maris," Elsa says, turning to her niece. "Tie balloons onto the boardwalk posts. And Cliff—"

"I know," he answers, resettling his COMMISSIONER cap on his head. "I'm on it." He begins hanging paper lanterns from hooks beneath the framework of the shade pavilion.

Like a fine-tuned machine, Elsa's beach party is all coming together for Lauren and Kyle. Celia is tying streamers on Aria's baby stroller. Eva is setting out pastries on the folding table, prompting Matt to sneak a cinnamon twist drizzled with vanilla frosting and give half to Jason.

Lastly, Elsa pulls a whisk broom from her tote and brushes off the boardwalk bench so that everything for the happy couple will be just ... perfect.

⸺

"That's odd," Lauren says. She hurries over while lifting her sunglasses to the top of her head. "It looks like one of Elsa's happiness jars." With that, she picks up the jar filled with sand, seashells, a twig of driftwood and, yes, her diamond ring. "Kyle?" Lauren asks, turning to him.

Kyle looks at the love of his life. He gives a small smile, then glances away. A bead of perspiration trickles down his face. "Okay." Another smile, and quick breath too. "So what I'm trying to say, Ell."

"Wait, *you* put this here?"

"I had a little help." Kyle glances over his shoulder, but sees no one. He's also hoping all else is going as planned on the boardwalk. "But yes. It's from me."

Lauren holds the jar with two hands, looking from it to Kyle. "I don't get it."

Kyle steps closer. Beneath the bright morning sun, Lauren's hair is pure blonde; her face lightly sun-freckled; her smile tentative. "Listen," he begins. "Our first time around getting married, well, it was a wreck." When she starts to argue, he holds up a hand. "No. We both know it. It's just the truth, with what went down with Neil, and then the way he died ... and Jason being messed up. We had a real rough time getting started."

"Kyle," she whispers.

He shakes his head, so she stops. "And then, Ell," he explains, "well, seeing my name botched on that marriage certificate after all these years, it just seemed wrong. Because it reminded me of all that *went wrong* ten summers ago." He takes the Mason jar from her and looks at the ring set inside. "And what we have now is so right that I want to *do right* by you and our marriage. For the kids, too."

"Kyle."

He can see it, how she can't help the few tears that slip along her cheek. And he knows damn well what those tears are about. There's no denying that their marriage started on unstable ground. But they *made* it; they're still together and in love more than ever. So for a moment, he's at a loss for words.

"Kyle, what are you saying?" Lauren persists.

Shaking his head again, this time he clears his throat, too. Then he reaches out and lightly touches her arm. He's not just a kid this time—in his twenties and ignorant to the ways of life. To the way that stone bluff—real or not—is sometimes steps away, and anything in his days might sweep him off it. Everything's tenuous, always, if you think about it. So he looks out at Long Island Sound, vast and unfurling beside them. Another trickle of perspiration runs down his face, which he quickly wipes away. When Lauren steps even closer, he does what he set out to do.

He opens the Mason jar.

Then he removes her diamond ring from the stick of driftwood inside it, before setting the jar in the sand. Straightening, he smiles again and touches a strand of her hair.

"Kyle? Now I'm worried. Because you're *really* quiet. Is everything okay with you?"

He shrugs. "I hope so. Because what I'm saying is ..." He drops to his knee and takes her hand in his. "Ell. *Lauren*. Here's the deal. I'm asking you if you'd *ever* consider marrying me. *Again*, I mean. Give me a chance to do right by you, and become my wife in a ceremony right here at the Ocean Star Inn. In a vow renewal, officiated by Elsa."

"Elsa would do that?" Lauren whispers again, not taking her eyes off Kyle—still on one knee.

"She would. And I'd make *damn* sure that every single moment is just perfect. For you." Like he knew would happen—he just didn't know when—it does.

Now.

He chokes up and has to look away. To *not* see the emotion and—well, if he had to name it—the love ... pooling in Lauren's gentle grey eyes. But it's only a moment before he looks at her again. "That is, if you'll have me as your husband."

Surprising him then, Lauren drops to her knees. She's smiling, and she brushes her fingers across Kyle's face. She's also nodding. Nodding and leaning close, and kissing him. Right there ... on her knees, in the sand.

Somehow, he never saw this coming.

Never imagined her taking his proposal *so* seriously.

Never expected the tenderness she brings to the moment.

His hands rise to her neck and cradle her face as, with sheer relief, he deepens the kiss. As he does, slowly, his smile returns. When he can't hold back, he stands and quickly scoops Lauren up, still kissing her as he wades ankle-deep into the salt water. That kiss is shorter, though, because he can't stop himself from yelling out a *Whoop!* as he spins around with her in his arms, the water splashing at his feet. When he sets her down, she's still quiet, which quiets *him*. But she stretches on her tiptoes and kisses him once more, her lips soft, her touch insistent, in the most romantic seaside kiss that—well, damn it—that anyone's ever had. That kiss is as light as the summer breeze, sweet as the salt air, and stirring as the rippling waves of the sea.

To cool themselves down before getting carried away, Kyle drifts a little deeper into the water with her. "You're sure, then?" he eventually asks, pressing back a wisp of her hair, touching her face. "You'll marry me again with a vow renewal?"

"Oh, I can't *wait*! I can picture it already." As though suddenly afraid she'll lose her vow-renewal happiness jar, Lauren runs out of the water and clutches it close.

Kyle follows behind her. "Until then—until we say *I do* again," he adds, "Elsa's orders, Ell. We have to fill that jar with happy mementoes reminding us of this day."

So Lauren begins.

As Kyle loops his arm around her shoulders and they wander in the direction of the boardwalk, she drops a white seashell into the jar ... in between kisses that they can't hold back. Even with Nick sneaking around behind the dune grasses on the berm, and ducking near the bench, they go at it. Nick's got Cliff's camera in hand, and snaps picture after picture as though he's a professional photographer.

Finally, it's all good. As they cross the warm sand, Lauren's hand in Kyle's now as she leans close; as the waves lap easy at their feet; as applause and whistles break out from the boardwalk; as he sees the CONGRATULATIONS banner strung across the shade pavilion; as the whole gang runs onto the sand amidst hugs and back slaps; as Nick sets off a bottle rocket at the water's edge, Kyle knows.

He knows already that *this* time, Bradford wedding 2.0 is a go.

It's been years.

Yes, *years* since Lauren's had a day like this one. A day when the happy surprises continue from morning till night. And she hasn't stopped smiling, not for one second.

Her day started with such a simple thing: a pretty glass happiness jar. Oh, if she could bottle her smile, wouldn't it be tucked in that jar, too. Instead, the jar will *elicit* a smile, no matter the hour, the year, the moment she might gaze upon it. Her happiness jar will always have her think of all today's sweet surprises.

Like the mini party on the boardwalk after she accepted Kyle's vow renewal proposal. The food, and coffee, and bottle rockets and smiles. The tune Celia strummed on her guitar as Kyle danced with Lauren on the sand while a breeze lifted off the water.

Yes, she'll always remember that celebration with merely a glance at her glass jar.

Then there was the diner. When she and Kyle finally drove to The Dockside, the first thing she said to the cook, Jerry, was, "Guess what? I'm engaged!" Which prompted Jerry to pop a bottle of chilled champagne, with toasts all around.

After which, Kyle took a piece of chalk and wrote on the Specials Board: *Just Engaged*. Beneath the words, he tacked up a photograph of the two of them on the beach.

So of course, congratulations came all day from customers, new and old.

Oh, the day's been happy, happy, happy.

Then, once they arrived home late afternoon, Lauren's parents and children had made a romantic pasta dinner. They served her and Kyle alone, outside on the picnic table. Hailey-the-hostess showed them to their seats; Evan-the-waiter with a white towel draped over his arm, took their order. Tiki torches were lit, soft music played.

Now, finally, is the quiet moment Lauren's been especially waiting for. It's nighttime. Kyle's sitting alone on the living room sofa in their bungalow on the bay. In their new home, sweet home. Leo Sterling is on the TV screen, giving a summery weather forecast for more blue skies.

A forecast that suits Lauren's life today. All blue skies, as far as she can see. Everything's good. The kids are in bed. A train goes by.

It's just the right time for the day's last surprise, this one at Lauren's hand.

This one while wearing a sexy nightie—a very sheer sleeveless navy top with a matching G-string panty.

She approaches Kyle from behind and rubs his neck, then leans low and wraps her hands around him. Kyle takes her hand in his, kisses it, then does a double take when he notices her revealing lingerie.

"Let's celebrate," Lauren murmurs into his ear.

He looks over his shoulder as she tugs his hand, but then pulls free from her hold and turns back to the television.

"Come on, hon." Lauren bends and kisses the side of his rough face, covered with whiskers at day's end.

"Well, the thing is, Ell ..." Kyle says, leaning forward, then looking back at her. "We're getting married again. And I thought it'd be nice to make our wedding night *memorably* special."

Lauren smiles, and her fingers toy with the lacy fabric of her babydoll top. "What do you mean?"

"I mean, the night of our vow renewal needs to be ... pure." He props his elbows on his knees and tosses her another look.

His eyes drop from her face, down the length of that sheer nightie, along every visible curve of her body beneath it—from the plunging neckline to her lace-covered hips—then back to her face. "We need to save ourselves for marriage."

"No way." She hurries around the sofa and takes his hand, giving another tug.

"Not tonight, Ell." Kyle pulls free again and crosses his arms over his chest. "I'm good here. This way, by abstaining now, we *really* have something to look forward to."

"Are you *serious*?"

"Never more."

Lauren bends close and touches the side of his face. "We have to *wait* now?" she whispers.

"It's just a month or so." Kyle looks from the TV screen to her, but only for a second. Only long enough to once more take in the sight of her breasts spilling from her top, of the lace fabric glancing her hips—all while shaking his head slowly as though it's *all* he can do to resist. "Every day without sex will make our wedding night all the more beautiful. With you."

Lauren settles beside him on the sofa, pressing her body close before moving to straddle his lap, all while purring, "I'm not so sure about this. Let me change your mind?"

"Nope." He gently pushes her away. "Goodnight, now."

"For real?"

"For real. You'll see."

"Kyle!" She stands in front of him, utterly not believing that the Kyle Bradford *she* knows can possibly say no to what she *and* her see-through nightie are offering. "If I knew that our vow renewal ceremony meant taking a vow of *celibacy* first—"

"You're *so* worth the wait," he quietly tells her. "And I'll be up later. *After* you're asleep."

What those words do to Lauren, well, they land the day's final surprise.

Kyle intends to *save* himself for marriage.

It's so shocking, this unexpected final surprise of the day—so startling—that Lauren simply, but slowly, walks toward the staircase. It's really impossible to believe this turn of events. She climbs the stairs one at a time, pausing to lure Kyle with another sultry look over her shoulder—only to see him settling on the couch, getting comfortable for a chaste night ... alone.

twelve

IT'S BEEN A WHILE SINCE this has happened. Maris isn't sure when she's last been so frustrated with writer's block at the keyboard. The words of Neil's novel just won't flow, and none of her usual tricks are working. Nothing helps—not tinkering with prior passages; not inputting Neil's margin notes; not reviewing early chapters; not even lighting the wick on one of Neil's dusty old hurricane lanterns for atmosphere.

So on Friday, she tries one more tactic: flipping Jason's pewter hourglass and setting her sandy one-hour deadline. Some people work better under pressure, and she's one of them. All that matters is beating the clock now. Well, beating the sand grains. They motivate her enough so that with much concentration, her fingers eke out a line of text. But when Maris looks at the computer screen again, she winces, then holds her finger on the DELETE key to remove the entire sentence.

One thing's for certain. When this type of writer's block settles in, *anything* becomes an excuse to walk away from the keyboard. Like now, when she picks up a rag and dusts off the shack's rough-hewn shelves. But maybe moving the rag around Neil's leather journals, and conch shells, and baskets of beach stones will inspire an idea.

A glimmer of hope returns when one of those journals gets her attention. On its pages, she skims Neil's slanted cursive, his words detailing rooms in the last-standing cottage on the beach. It's still hard to believe that he actually *toured* that cottage, just for his novel. So when he writes about the white-paneled ceiling, or the lobster-trap end tables, his notes are utterly authentic.

Of course. How else would Neil create *anything*?

No wonder his manuscript reads so vividly. Its details couldn't be made up; they're that genuine. Even Mitch Fenwick saw that honest scrutiny in Neil. Maris remembers what Jason told her after meeting with Mitch.

When Neil walked through the Fenwick cottage, Mitch said my brother made him feel like he was a part of the story he was writing, just by the detailed way he noticed things. The sea, the beach outside the windows.

"The hell with dusting," Maris says as she moseys back to her desk. Sitting again, she flips through manuscript pages filled with Neil's work. "Darn it, why don't *I* write this good?"

It's a question that plants all types of doubt and sets the tone for today's writing session.

If you'd call it that.

If you'd call now rearranging some of Neil's things on *another* shelf ... writing. Carved duck decoys, and old coffee mugs all get moved around, nudged, touched.

Which sparks an idea that has her hightail it to her laptop, where she types a few more lines, sits back and studies the words. "Nah," she whispers while deleting yet again.

A minute later, she's standing at the shack's window, watching the wind rustle the leaves. "Well, I'm *thinking*, too," she exclaims under her breath.

But not coming up with anything. Or ... let's get real. Not coming up with where to take the story. At least, not until the leaves rustle again, which gives her one last idea.

So she listens intently.

Just like Jason does. She's caught him many times—standing at a window, or an open door—listening, listening. Okay, so if it works for him, can it work for her, too?

"Neil? Are you *really* there?" she quietly asks. "Help me out."

The leaves still whisper, the breeze sighs. But words? A *message*? Maris looks up toward the summer sky, and waits.

Suddenly her cell phone rings, which gets her rushing to her desk where she scoops up the phone … and hesitates. Because it's a bit unnerving, the way the phone seemed to ring in response to her plea to Neil. Quickly, then, she looks at the caller ID.

"Aunt Elsa?" Maris asks with some relief.

As Elsa talks, Maris listens closely, nodding as she does, before disconnecting with a happy *Yes!*

***

When Jason stops in the shack's open doorway early that afternoon, he sees Maris packing: laptop to tote; Neil's journals next; favorite pen slipped in tote pocket; pages of notes into folder.

"You're not leaving me, are you?" Jason asks from where he leans on the doorjamb.

"As a matter of fact," Maris answers over her shoulder, "I am." She doesn't stop moving as she talks. Doesn't stop tidying her work area, turning down the wick on the old hurricane lamp to extinguish its flame. "Somebody else has caught my loving attention, Mr. Barlow."

"So you're out of here, then?"

"Yes. While you've been so busy, someone else swooped in and stole my lonely heart."

Jason still merely watches her. Well, watches and smiles as he crosses his arms.

"It's someone *very* special," Maris continues while tapping a handful of manuscript pages on the table. "We don't even talk much. Our love is such that it's enough to simply gaze at each other." She hoists her tote strap onto her shoulder and throws him a smile, too. "It's your godchild, Aria Gray," she says while walking to the doorway and giving him only a hint of a kiss as she squeezes past. "Elsa just called. She and Celia have last-minute inn shopping to do, and they need a babysitter for the afternoon." Maris walks outside and talks over her shoulder now. "Maybe I'll get some writing done while Aria naps. I'll be gone for the rest of the day."

"Me, too," Jason calls to her. "Over at the Fenwick place with Trent, some of the crew. All afternoon," he shouts while shielding his eyes from the sun and watching Maris head to her golf cart. "Paperwork to get signed, camera work to map out."

Maris turns around and walks backward. "No name for the show yet?"

"Not yet. But the pressure's seriously on, now that we signed the project and are ready to film a promo teaser."

With a wave, Maris turns again and tosses her things in the golf cart, then climbs in and starts it up. "I probably won't be back in time to make dinner."

"That's all right." Jason walks to the driveway. "Friday fishing tonight. Kyle's got supper covered at the diner."

"Bring me back a plate of something?" Maris asks as she pulls her golf cart alongside him. "On your way fishing?"

"Will do."

After a quick kiss, it happens then, the way life often does. Everything goes quiet—even quieter than it was a few minutes before. Something about the whirlwind of Maris breezing out leaves a silent void in its wake.

Jason turns and, stepping on a few dried twigs, heads back to the shack to lock it up. Once in the doorway, though, he instead wanders inside. It's not too often that he gets a quiet moment alone among his brother's things. He stands in the center of the room, as though merely a guest. As though he's just visiting.

Or intruding.

This space was that deeply personal to Neil. So much so that he kept it secret from Jason, ten years ago. Everything—from the seaworn buoys hung on the shack's outside shingled walls, to the candles covered with dribbles of hardened wax, to the fishing rods mounted on the back wall, to the two-burner camping stove. To the journals and papers and typewriter. It's all the framework of his brother's private life.

Jason walks to Maris' desk and picks up a handful of manuscript pages there. As he starts to set them down, a passage catches his eye. Something about it hooks him. So he takes the pages to the doorway, where sunlight shines on the words. In the day's stillness, he can almost hear Neil's voice saying them aloud, as though reading Jason this passage from the novel.

Castaways. That's what they all look like. Drenched and tired from trying to survive the storm. In the kitchen, the lights flicker off, then come back on. Everyone's gathered there, heating clambake leftovers before the power goes out for good. After bringing in the deck furniture and shuttering the last of the windows, some of the guys fling wet jackets over chair backs. A couple of the women towel-dry their hair. Dishes clatter; someone laughs as they gradually settle in at the table. But from where she stands in the kitchen doorway, there's a noise behind her. She turns to see him coming in through the front door. Coming in with a sheet of rain and wind. His waterlogged clothes cling to his body; his hair is slicked back; raindrops cover his tired face. Their eyes meet, and she smiles. Slightly.

Castaways, without a doubt. Each of them stranded in this big old cottage on this long summer weekend.

"Wait a sec," Jason says as he backtracks and rereads the passage. Still holding the manuscript pages, he then pulls his cell phone from his pocket and makes a quick call.

"Hey, Trent," he says when his producer answers. "I think we've got a name for the show."

―⁓―

Maris holds Aria against her shoulder and gently rubs the baby's back.

"So you're all set?" Celia asks. She reaches over and touches Aria's silky dark hair. "You have my cell number, right?"

"I do. I'll call you with any questions." Maris gives the baby a slight bounce. "And to check in, too."

"She just had her bottle, and I changed her diaper. So she's comfortable." Celia hovers close. She walks to the side of Maris to get a look at Aria's face. "Oh, before I forget … If you lightly shake the seashell wind chime near her crib … at naptime, well …"

Whispering that it's time to go, Elsa comes up behind Celia and takes her arm. Maris isn't sure Celia would *ever* leave without Elsa's prodding. Still holding Aria, Maris walks to the front porch of Celia's guest cottage and waves goodbye.

The problem is, this baby thing isn't as easy as she thought it would be. Aria whimpers, so Maris goes back inside and sets her in the bouncy baby seat in the living room. When Maris then opens her laptop on a small table there, she talks out the novel's latest plot point to Aria. Softly.

"*The storm has just struck. Everyone's settling in the kitchen, of course.*

The power's not out yet, so they're cooking, and eating. And anxious, too, with the way the wind and rain are hitting the windows."

But still, the baby fusses.

So Maris picks her up and holds her close, humming as she walks past a mini wire lobster trap on the end table. Beside it, dried marsh grasses spill from a seashell-encrusted vase. Celia's living room has a nautical look to it, with its white board-and-batten walls and coastal touches. Circling it while gently rocking Aria, Maris finally ends up where she started ... at her laptop. There, she bends to read an open document. Her typed notes play with a castaway theme she'd read about while in the shack. That thought of the book's friends being tossed adrift like castaways and not only landing in the same cottage—but surviving there, too—intrigues her.

Wait. *If* they do survive.

Another idea comes suddenly, so she sets Aria in her baby seat again, then sits at the table and starts rapidly typing.

After a few minutes, Maris stops and tips her head. Her fingers pause above the keyboard. No longer is she hearing Aria whimper and fuss. No. Instead, along with the noise of her clicking computer keys, Aria is ... cooing! So Maris looks over to see the baby pumping her tiny fists in her bouncy seat.

And *smiling*!

"Aria!" Maris quietly exclaims as she reaches over and strokes the baby's soft cheek. "Aren't you my good luck charm!"

A work pattern sets in, then. When Maris types a little more, the baby coos. When she stops, Aria whimpers. Thinking it all a coincidence, Maris tests her clickety-clack theory—typing another paragraph to the baby's cooing accompaniment, then stopping.

In mere seconds, Aria fusses.

"Well, I'll be," Maris whispers with another look at Aria in her bouncy seat. So Maris raises her hands above the laptop keyboard and types the next paragraph.

And yes, it's true!

Type … coo.

Stop typing … fuss.

Looking at the full manuscript page she's just written, Maris gives a little cheer.

With that, she has no choice but to get on a writing roll—if only to keep little Aria happy. Throwing a warm smile to the baby beside her, Maris madly types away.

thirteen

KYLE HAD DIMMED THE CEILING lights before Jason arrived. The low lighting signals to customers that the diner's closed, and saves him from turning away folks at the door. The lighting does something else, too: It creates an optical illusion. Kyle remembers what he said years ago when Jerry owned the place. *From outside, the glowing lanterns make the windows look like portholes, and the silver diner could be a ship coming in from sea.* That's precisely when Jerry changed the diner's name to The Dockside, as though his big silver ship was docked right there, roadside. Timers switch on those window lanterns now, right when Kyle passes behind Jason sitting at the counter.

"What the hell's in this delicacy?" Jason asks, raising a soft roll spilling with scraps of meat and onions.

Kyle looks back from where he's flipping the CLOSED sign in the door. "Pulled pork sandwich? Shredded pork loin with lots of the good stuff. Barbecue sauce, onions, ketchup, chili powder, brown sugar. The works," he says when he walks behind the counter. "Topped with lettuce and plenty of sauce drippings."

"This is amazing," Jason says around a mouthful. "I'm beat, and haven't had a decent meal in a long time."

Kyle sits on a red-cushioned stool at the end of the counter. "What'd you do all day?"

"For one thing, locked down a name for the show."

"No shit. Let me guess. Something like ... *Barlow's Bangin' Bungalows?*"

"Good one," Jason says with a laugh. "But no, man. It's actually pretty sweet." Jason pauses for a mouthful of soda. "Got the idea from Neil's manuscript. It's a riff on one of his passages. I just reworked a few words." He spins toward Kyle to announce it. "*Castaway Cottage.*"

"Nice! *Really* nice. Has a ring to it, and hits all the title requirements. It's short, mnemonic, catchy."

"Trent was on board with it right away," Jason says while lifting a forkful of coleslaw. "He liked how it suggests a neglected cottage, just the kind I fix up. And the title alone, *Castaway Cottage*, draws you right in with the suggestion of some story."

Kyle gets a damp rag from behind the counter and starts wiping things down. "It's like a sign from your brother, finding a name that way. You know, in his book." When he looks over, Jason's so intent on devouring that pulled pork sandwich, all he can manage is a nod. So Kyle finishes wiping off the countertop, then tosses the day's newspapers in the trash.

"How's the vow renewal coming along? Making plans?" Jason asks. He's also dragging half his sandwich roll through drippings on his plate.

"Not yet. Only got as far as a celibacy commitment."

"A *what?*" Jason sputters between bites.

"You heard me. I convinced Lauren to take a vow of celibacy with me. We're saving ourselves for our wedding night. So, no fooling around for a while." Kyle sits again, this time to refill napkin dispensers. "It's *really* annoying Lauren, though. Practically had to wear two pajama pants to keep her away from me. But I don't know. It seems important this second time, to make that wedding night mean something."

"Come on, Kyle," Jason says as he lifts a French fry dripping in ketchup. "Where do you come up with this shit?"

"The Italian."

"Sal? I don't think so."

"Absolutely. He was all about things being *molto speciale,* especially second chances. So I want my wedding-redo night to be very special. Hell, it's the only time I'll get a second chance at it."

"If you say so," Jason tells him while pressing the last hunk of his pulled pork sandwich into his mouth.

"It's funny, too," Kyle says as he picks up a pile of napkins, "the way this abstaining's driving Lauren crazy. Now that she can't have me, I'm, like, irresistible."

"I'll bet. And what about you, dude? You're talking a solid month of cold showers."

"Eh, no prob. Because I'm having too much fun watching Ell try to wear me down."

"Set a date for this epic ceremony yet?"

"We're meeting with Elsa tomorrow to iron out the details. One of which ..." Kyle says while leaning over from his napkin-filling and giving Jason's shoulder a shove. "You're still my best man, right? Just like first time around."

"Wouldn't have it any other way." He extends his hand to Kyle.

Kyle obliges, clasping Jason's hand in both of his. It's kind of ironic, the way he does that. Because it's the first thing Kyle did ten years ago upon seeing Jason's father bring him into the church in a wheelchair the day of Kyle's wedding. Kyle hurried over and took Jason's hand the same way, before leaning down and embracing him, too.

"Hey," he says, slapping Jason's hand before letting go. "Let's get a move on. It's late."

"I have to gas up the car on the way."

"What? On a Friday? Bad timing."

"Why?" Jason grabs a napkin and wipes his mouth.

"I get my gas on Wednesdays. Everyone knows that gas stations raise their prices on Thursdays to cash in on weekend driving trips."

"Yeah? I'll keep that in mind next week." Jason stands and stretches then, taking in the sight of the dimmed diner. "When are you trading in that old gas-guzzler anyway?"

"Let me get settled in at the house first. For crying out loud, I'm still unpacking random boxes every day." Kyle takes Jason's dirty plate and brings it to the sink around back. "Then I guess I'm getting married again," he calls over the running water. "So … a new truck's after that."

"Listen, make up one of those sandwiches for my wife, would you? Put it in the cooler and we'll drop it off on our way to the rocks."

"Already done. I figured no cooking was happening at the Barlow homestead." Kyle rounds the corner from the back and heads to the pastry dome, where he pulls out a few fudge brownies. "I'll sneak a couple for us, too. We'll have them on a fishing break."

Jason pats his stomach. "I'll be packing on the pounds if you keep feeding me this way."

"Nah, you're lean and mean from all that TV show stress." Kyle heads with his bags to the door. "And hell, we'll skip the golf cart and *walk* to the rocks from your place. Burns more calories that way." After turning his key in the locks and pulling on the door handle twice, he catches up with Jason in the parking lot. "I read that walking on sand uses two-and-a-half times more energy than walking on hard surfaces."

⁓

There's something else beach walks are good for, too. Storytelling. That slow pace across the sand—when you're meandering along with the high tide line, the waves lapping at your feet—somehow gets stories to unfold.

The same happens now.

With fishing poles slung over their shoulders, Jason and Kyle walk down the footpath to the beach. Jason has his tackle box; Kyle carries an insulated bag of food.

But it's once they hit the sand, with the low moon rising over the water, that the storytelling begins. Seeing that distant cottage-on-stilts, Jason can't help but imagine that long-ago stormy day when waves crashed on the beach and the wind rattled the windows. Everyone in the beach cottage would have been panicked, fearing the worst for a neighborhood boy who charmed the community with his sailor cap and ever-ready crabbing gear.

Telling Sailor's story to Kyle tonight, Jason leaves nothing out. As they pass the boardwalk, he talks about the boy's endearing sailor cap—which got everyone to salute him. *He always had it on. Always. Over his head of blond hair.* When they pass the distant swim raft, Jason tells Kyle about Sailor's penchant for crabbing on the rocks. *He was only seven, but he took right to it. Kind of like we did, growing up.* And once they cross the beach and the imposing Fenwick cottage rises before them, Jason tells about the last fateful time Sailor ventured to those rocks beyond. *It happened just as a hurricane hit the Connecticut coast, back in the sixties. The family was shuttering the windows right there on the deck when they spotted Sailor alone on the rocks.*

Across the blowing wind, they yelled over to him, telling him to get home, fast.

And by the time Jason and Kyle bait their lines and cast off, Jason's told Gordon's story, too. *He was the reluctant hero who went looking for the boy when his worried mother couldn't find him. Gordon hauled out his rowboat from under the cottage—and ended up lost at sea during the hurricane. I'm telling you, it's the stuff of seafaring tales.*

"Damn. Poor guy. And what about the kid? He make out okay?" Kyle asks as he tugs at a nibble on his fishing line, his rod bending with a persistent bite.

"Sailor." Jason nods toward the Fenwick cottage. "He did. After all that drama with his panicked mother, so desperate to find him. And then Gordon doing the heroic thing for the sake of the child? It was all for nothing. Because the whole time? Sailor was at a neighbor's place, safe and sound. The neighbor saw him and was afraid he'd get hurt by a tree limb, or downed power lines. So she hauled him inside as the kid was making his way home to his own cottage."

"Shit, man. What a tragedy."

"Definitely. Sad part is that Gordon, Carol's grandfather, was never seen again. He was only in his thirties, probably our age. His biggest dream was to spend every summer at his new cottage there, right on the beach."

"Don't tell me. He never got even one, did he?"

"Nope." Jason studies the cottage. In the pale moonlight, the sight could be from fifty years ago during that one unfortunate summer. A few windows glow with lamplight. Shadows fall on the deck. You could just imagine the grief inside those walls then, the wrenching realization once Gordon's rowboat never rounded this rocky ledge again.

"Think this Gordon dude somehow made it, though?" Kyle asks as his fishing line goes limp. He reels it in while musing. "You know, like maybe he hit his head in the storm and lived a new life somewhere down the coast, but with amnesia? You're talking the 1960s ... Hell, he *could* still be alive, in his eighties now."

"Bradford, *you* could write a book, with a yarn like that one."

"Fate, man. You never know." Kyle sets down his fishing rod and gets two cans of beer from the tote. "Just trying to do the right thing for some kid and *poof.* Gone." He snaps open the cans and gives one to Jason.

"See how folklore happens?" Jason takes a long swig of his beer. "That one story turns Gordon into a bona fide hero."

"And what became of little Sailor? If he was only seven, he probably never even knew what actually went down."

"From what Mitch and Carol told me, his family left after the storm. It was their second summer renting a place back on Champion Road, there." Jason hitches his head in the direction of the street running behind the beach, on the other side of the dune grasses. "No one blamed them, of course. But it must've been too much to live with, thinking someone lost his *life* on account of their boy."

"Who was it? Did you get Sailor's real name? Was the family familiar to you?"

"Nobody knows his identity. Anyone who *might've* known is gone now, dead or moved away. Including the owners of the cottage Sailor's family rented. They sold their place a year later, and, you know, who kept records of renters back then? There were no formal contracts, nothing. So the boy's grown into a mythic figure now, the kid with the blue-and-white sailor cap. Only seven years old, just a little guy with sun-bleached blond hair. The boy everyone saluted when he walked across the beach carrying his pail and tackle box."

Kyle looks toward the cottage on the beach and raises his beer can in a toast to the sad tale.

"And the guy, Gordon?" Jason asks. "He's a hero washed out to sea." In the misty darkness, the Gull Island Lighthouse beam sweeps across the water. Jason imagines the many nights when Carol's family must have stood on that cottage deck and watched for any sign of Gordon out on the water. A drifting rowboat. One of its paddles, even. A life jacket. Something. "No one ever saw him or his boat again. The authorities searched *everywhere* and came up empty."

"I can't believe Gordon disappeared right here." Kyle looks out at the night water, too. "Around the point we fish off of every week?"

Jason nods. "It's like the damn sea swallowed him up whole."

fourteen

JASON KNOWS THE DRILL. PROMOTIONS can never start too early; buzz can't begin too soon. Saturday morning, he's standing in front of the CT-TV camera much the same way he did when promoting Elsa's renovation. This time, though, rather than the Ocean Star Inn, it's the rambling gray cottage on the beach rising behind him. The sky is the exact blue his producer seeks; the late-July sun perfectly casts its summer rays; heat wavers in the air; dragonflies hover above the sweeping dune grasses.

As the show's host, not only could Jason use a shave, but he stands in the sand wearing a black short-sleeve top over gray camo work shorts—leaving his prosthesis on full display, too. Once the renovation begins, he'll be in long pants; but for now, it's important to capture the feel of summer beside this historic cottage. And to stick to his guns about not changing his appearance for the network—what you see is what you get.

"To check out the first *official* castaway cottage," Jason announces as he perches his sunglasses on top of his head, "look no further than over my shoulder."

His cameraman raises a hand to stop him. "There's a glare. Could you move to the left?"

As he does, Nick hurries over and positions a light-reflector stand to block the glare from the morning sun.

"Okay. Take two," the cameraman says as he steps behind the viewfinder.

Jason adjusts his mic and gives his promo spiel again. Right in the middle of taping, a family approaches and it's Nick to the rescue once more. Patrolling the beach on guard duty, he's proved invaluable as the station's taping began. Switching from on-camera assistant to patrol mode, Nick quickly retrieves two half-rotten wooden sawhorses from beneath the stilted cottage and uses them as a beach barricade. This way, meandering families can't interrupt the filming.

"Off-limits," Nick says to the curious onlookers. "Filming in progress. Stay back, please."

With another nod from his cameraman, Jason finishes taping. "This last-standing cottage on the beach," he says, "has withstood every hurricane to ever roll up on these shores. The cottage is a local pillar of strength, a true beacon on the sand. Holds lots of secrets in its walls, too." He tosses another glance at the gray building-on-stilts, with its fading shutters and weathered deck. "So join us on our first season of *Castaway Cottage* ... as we transform this big old beach house in the little town of Stony Point," he concludes as the camera pans out. "Coming soon to CT-TV."

Once the film crew takes off, Jason sits on the cottage deck with Carol and Mitch. After setting more vintage postcards on the patio table, he points out the awning on the cottage's original design.

"Before my renovation work can even begin, we'll be seeking

variances to elevate the existing house in compliance with FEMA flood regulations," Jason explains.

"A variance? Why's that necessary?" Mitch asks.

"Zoning restricts the building height to twenty-four feet, but we'll be proposing a little over thirty. Your cottage sustained some damage in Super Storm Sandy, and to repair it, it's necessary to raise it. Also critical in our petition is that the area *below* the elevated cottage *not* be considered a story. There won't be quite six feet of head room beneath the building, and without a slab either, it can't be considered living space."

"That will cover the zoning requirements?" Carol asks.

"A few other things need to be addressed. Realigning the deck stairs, for one. I'll have a full list for you. But today? Today I'd rather hear *your* vision for this place." Jason looks to Carol, then Mitch. "Both of yours."

"Our vision?" Mitch repeats, adjusting the battered safari hat on his head. "Mine doesn't waver too much from what's already here."

"Come on. You must have something you'd like to see," Jason insists. "Lay it out for me. You know," he motions to the cottage, "in your wildest dreams."

"Okay, then. First and foremost, I'd like it to remain shingled. The way it was when it weathered all those storms," Mitch begins. "I'm sure there are more practical options for a home sitting on the edge of Long Island Sound. But that seaworn look ... Well, it speaks to me."

"Yeah," Carol agrees. Wearing a tight black tank tucked into seriously shredded jeans, along with a braided black leather necklace, she lifts her dark sunglasses and looks directly at Jason. "But it would be cool if somehow the *sacrifice* my grandfather made can also be communicated."

"Gordon was a hero, actually," Mitch adds. "Even if a forgotten one. So we'd like to keep the memory of his sacrifice alive. To acknowledge his attempt to rescue the little boy in the blue-and-white sailor's cap. Sailor." Mitch tips up his own hat and looks out toward the rocky point, to the last place Gordon was ever seen as he paddled his rowboat through stormy waves.

"I've got an idea." Jason sits back, hands turned up as though saying ... *Of course!* He reaches for one of the vintage postcards then. "Without being pretentious, this design detail *could* do the trick. It'll fit with the cottage aesthetics, *and* its history, while at the same time recognizing the Sailor story." Jason points out the original awning that appeared over the long deck. "Its striped colors? Blue-and-white, the same as Sailor's cap," he says.

"Jason." Carol's eyes actually tear up at the sight of that awning. "My mother would've loved being here for all this. Right, Dad?"

Mitch nods. "I could just picture Kate sitting with a book beneath the shade of that awning. It'll be our tip of the hat ... to the little sailor boy her father tried to save."

"I'm on it, man." Jason picks up the postcards and tucks them into his leather messenger bag. "You two really don't have anything else on this kid? With Gordon losing his life for him, it feels like there should be more. No one even got a *name*?" Jason looks to both of them. "Nothing?"

"Not that I know of." Carols stands then. "It's hot. Let me get us something to drink while we piece together any details. But my mother was probably the *very* last person left who was actually there that day. Who really knew the boy. *And* who had any memory of the event that took her father's life." As she slides the gritty slider open, Carol says over her shoulder, "And she's gone, too."

Jason pulls his sunglasses down from his head and puts them on. "It's just that the more I know about the history of a place, Mitch, the more meaning I can bring to a renovation." Jason picks up his pen and jots a note or two on his pad. "Nothing you can remember your wife saying? A last name? Even Sailor's first name, with a physical description?"

"Well." Mitch stands and walks to the deck railing. He looks down at the sandy beach below. The tide is out, so there's a long stretch of flat, smooth sand right in front of the cottage. "Actually," he says, running a hand along his goatee. "There is one more thing."

***

Mitch motions for Jason to follow him down the deck stairs. They stand on the hard-packed sand, right below the high tide line. As far as Jason's concerned, it's the one place on earth that beats all others for walking—and thinking. There, silver flecks of mica shimmer beneath the sunlight. A few strands of dried seaweed and random shells and stones dot the beach close to the cottage.

Mitch walks a few slow steps, clearly thinking. Or *remembering*... It's as though his memory is actually taking shape right as he says the words.

"Sailor's family vacationed here at Stony Point for only two summers. So his time here was brief. But sometimes that's all you need, a brief appearance in someone's life, to make a lasting impression. Now my wife, Kate, she was a year or two older than Sailor, but ..." Here, Mitch stops, tips up his safari hat and looks at Jason beside him. "Kate was a bit of a tomboy. Kind of like our daughter is, too. Carol. Carol reminds me a lot of Kate when she was younger. Anyway, being a tomboy, my wife was friends with

Sailor. Growing up, she'd hang with the boys, no problem, and keep right up with them, too."

Mitch returns to the deck stairs and sits on one of the lower steps, elbows on his knees as he looks at the flat, smooth expanse of packed sand at his feet. Jason leans on the staircase handrail, waiting.

"I remember Kate saying that when Sailor *wasn't* out on the rocks, he had the best set of Matchbox cars around. On some days, he'd bring around a couple cases—one case of those little metal cars and one a pop-up town to drive them on. They'd set up on a blanket right here, on the flat sand at low tide. It was the perfect spot. That pop-up case would open up wide, and there'd be a whole community. Neighborhood streets, buildings. You know, there'd be a school, church. A hospital. Gas stations and houses. A post office ... and grocery store. The beach kids would hunker around for hours, making up stories as they zipped those cars along the pretend roads."

Mitch is quiet for a long moment as he pictures his wife being just a little girl, playing here on the sand. "I imagine she'd be on her knees, leaning on her elbows, maybe, scooting some mini vehicle around town, talking out an imagined story." With a quick breath then, he stands and shuffles one of his leather-sandaled feet in that smooth sand.

"That's all I remember her saying about the boy, Jason. The way he'd go out on the rocks crabbing, or bring over his car collection and that readymade play-town—roads and all. And *always* in his blue-and-white sailor hat." Mitch takes off his own battered hat and fiddles with it before squinting back at Jason, still standing at the railing. "There's no other record of Sailor. Not even a photograph. Trust me, I've looked, Jason. But there's none. Just my secondhand memory."

When Mitch starts walking toward the rocky outcropping beyond the cottage, Jason catches up with him. They walk silently for a little ways. For some reason, Mitch's memories have quieted him.

"You know," Jason begins. "My father had those cars as a kid, too. Years later, he stored them in a big old wooden trunk. The cars, a few spinning tops, model airplanes. That kind of thing. But it was that case of metal cars Neil and I liked best. We'd play with them on rainy days in the cottage. I remember a blue pickup truck, a sheriff's car with a siren on top. A little station wagon, a yellow taxicab. Had a blast driving those cars up and down the living room floor. My father had quite a few cars collected."

"Exactly." Mitch stops at the rocks and looks out toward the point, then back at Jason. "So the funny thing is, Sailor could fit the bill of *any* of a generation of boys back then. Which makes him all the more forever this great mystery."

fifteen

IF THERE'S ONE SOUND KYLE Bradford wouldn't mind never hearing again, it's the one he's hearing this Saturday morning: the scraping and ripping of wallpaper as he and Lauren strip their dining room walls. They're in a time crunch, with Lauren wanting to redo this room before their vow renewal. Which is fine by Kyle—especially since they'll be able to *finally* investigate that old water stain as sheets and scraps of old vinyl wallpaper peel off the wall in a soggy mess.

Well, they'll get to it *if* Lauren can focus and stop trying to be provocative.

Kyle's vow of celibacy has become somewhat of a challenge for her; that's plainly obvious. Kyle sneaks a look over his shoulder to see her stripping wallpaper behind him. She wears, seriously, a tight cropped tee over short-shorts? Her hair is in a topknot and, wait. Is she really wearing sparkly pink lip gloss while perforating and peeling stinking wallpaper? Kyle smiles to himself, then resumes pulling a nearly full wallpaper sheet straight off the wall.

Until two enticing hands reach around his waist from behind. It's a good thing Evan and Hailey are outside in their pop-up teepee. Last he looked, Hailey was coloring, and Evan was cleaning his crabbing gear.

Because in the quiet house now, Lauren's arms pull him close. She stands on tiptoe and presses into him while whispering in his ear, "Finish the back wall for me? I want a better look at that stain behind the wallpaper, but I can't reach that high." As she kisses his neck, he feels every inch and curve of her body against his backside. "But my strapping six-foot-two *fiancé* can reach it ..."

"Right now?" Kyle asks as wallpaper removal solution drips off his sponge and trickles down his arm.

Lauren doesn't miss a trick, grabbing a rag and softly stroking his skin, moving all the way to his shoulder.

"Oh no." Kyle pulls away. "You keep your hands to yourself." When he glares at Lauren, she simply bats her, yes, her heavily *mascara'd* eyes. Having none of that, Kyle slides a stepstool closer to the back wall and starts on the paper there. Being busy doesn't stop Lauren, though. As he's standing on the stool, he feels her two hands massaging his back, moving in a soft circle as she tries to wear him down.

The problem is, seduction wilts when you have two kids—one of them yelling in through the window now. "Mommy," Hailey calls from outside. "Can we get a dog?"

"Isn't Taylor babysitting them so we can wedding-plan with Elsa?" Kyle asks as he works on the wallpaper strip right over the persistent water stain.

"Oh, shoot," Lauren whispers as she rushes to the kitchen window. "No dog, sweetie. But maybe we can visit Maddy soon. You two pack up your backpacks to go to Taylor's now. Hailey, remember to bring your bubble wand. Tay's making a bucket of soapy bubble water. And don't forget your crabbing things, Ev. You can crab off the dock, in the marsh there."

"Can I go *in* the water?" Evan calls from outside. "So I can walk along the banks and look for blue crabs?"

Lauren actually lifts the screen and leans out to give her answer, accompanied by her pointing finger. "No!"

It's a clash Lauren's been fighting all summer as Evan tests her resolve. In between peeling off sheets of wallpaper, Kyle listens first to her, yelling: *No. Hailey would want to go in, too. And there are currents there!* Then to Evan pleading: *But I want to look for blue crabs in the mud.* To Lauren warning: *You crab from the dock, young man. Or else Taylor can watch you guys right here.*

But when Kyle pulls at the next tacky sheet of wallpaper—slowly peeling it off the wall—his long, low whistle gets Lauren rushing back to the dining room. She stops behind him as he then moves to the next sheet of wallpaper and pulls that one off the wall, too. By the time he gets to the third sheet covering that massive water stain, he hears Lauren gasp.

And when he pulls that last full sheet off the wall and steps down off the stool, Lauren's got her hand clasped to her horrified face as she backs toward the doorway—far, far away from the stripped wall.

"Oh my God, Kyle. That's just ... *awful.*"

He looks from the black-splotched wall, to Lauren, whose eyes are riveted to the full width and length of finally exposed drywall. When he steps back and takes in the disgusting sight, Kyle has to agree. "*Gesù, Santa Maria,*" he whispers.

Lauren comes up behind him, with absolutely no horsing around this time. The thought of seducing him has obviously been spooked right out of her.

"Is that what I *think* it is?" she asks.

"We have to cancel," Lauren's been telling Kyle during the entire golf cart ride to the Ocean Star Inn—*after* he made her put on a light blouse over her too-tight tee and too-short shorts. "Because this is serious."

"What?" Kyle asks in disbelief, finally skidding to a stop at her insistence. "After I proposed to you on the beach? And the whole gang helped us commit to this vow renewal?"

"Elsa will understand," Lauren says as Kyle parks the cart. "You'll see," she calls over her shoulder while rushing to Elsa's door and rapidly knocking.

"Elsa!" Lauren says right as the door opens. "Bad news. I'm not sure about having the ceremony anymore."

"*What?*" Elsa looks past her, as though checking to be sure Kyle's there, too. "Come on in, both of you. We'll talk over lunch. My chicken wraps are all ready."

"I don't have too much of an appetite," Lauren tells her as she walks down the hallway toward the kitchen.

Elsa veers into her dining room, where new floor-to-ceiling windows face the distant beach. She pulls out one of her navy French-country chairs at the wood-planked table. Even at lunchtime, candlesticks flicker. And large seashells are set randomly among them. "What's wrong?" she asks, motioning for Lauren to sit.

"We've bought the worst cottage at the beach." Lauren drops onto the waiting chair. "Oh, Elsa. It needs *sooo* much work."

"All homes do," Elsa says, untying a half-apron before sitting too. "When you first move in, there's always a lot of work."

"Not like our house," Lauren argues. "First there was an ant problem. Then there's the train going by at night, which Kyle calls *white* noise."

"Helps me sleep," Kyle says with a shrug as he pulls out the painted chair beside Lauren.

"But when *I* hear it," Lauren tells him while fighting burning tears, "that metal grinding sound on the tracks has my eyes pop *wide* open!"

Elsa reaches over and pats Lauren's arm. "You just have to get used to things. Give yourselves time to adjust. It'll be okay."

Nothing helps, though. Lauren can only shake her head and continue with her rant. "Then there's the bathroom's banging pipes, which I thought might be contributing to a *huge*—I mean, *massive*—water stain on our dining room wall."

"Ell," Kyle whispers harshly. "Stay positive! That's three negatives in a row. If you keep talking about our new house that way, you'll *never* like it!"

"But it gets worse!" Lauren insists while turning back her blouse cuffs.

"Worse?" Elsa's eyes drop closed. "Oh, no."

"Guys?" another voice asks. "What's happening?"

When Lauren spins around, Maris is standing in the doorway to the kitchen. She wears a white sleeveless top with frayed white shorts and has a pen tucked behind her ear.

"Maris? What are you doing here?" Lauren asks with a sudden sob.

"Is Jason around?" Kyle interrupts as he puts an arm around Lauren. "I texted him, but I really need to talk more."

"Oh, Kyle. He's so busy, the station's got him booked. I think they're taping a promo clip for the show." Maris approaches the table and sits across from Lauren. "Lauren? Why are you crying?"

"It's just that everything in my life's been so hard. I mean, we move here, and Kyle throws out his back. We get settled in the house? And I notice a horrible water stain on the dining room wall." She presses her fingers to her eyes to stem the tears *and* the runny mascara. "So today we *finally* take down the wallpaper over the stain and see that it's *not* a stain, after all."

"It's black mold," Kyle tells them.

"*What?* Then that's what you've been smelling!" Elsa pulls her chair in closer. "Lauren, how are the kids? You can get *very* sick from mold."

"That's why I texted Jason," Kyle explains. "He called in a favor from a mold specialist, and the guy's coming over at three. But I'd like to talk to Jason in person, get the lowdown from him."

"Don't jump the gun, guys. Jason tells me he sees mold on his job sites. It's so damp at the beach, it grows easily. And sometimes it can be quickly remedied," Maris offers. "If it's not *too* bad, you can just replace the drywall, use a lot of bleach to clean it up—"

"But sometimes it *is* very serious, Maris." Lauren dabs her eyes with a napkin. "I don't want Evan and Hailey getting sick, and Hailey *has* been sniffling. Oh," she says around another sob, "I knew something was wrong with that stinking smell. I don't even want to go back there."

"Where are the kids?" Maris asks.

"Eva's," Kyle tells her. "Taylor is babysitting."

"Okay, good. Because if it *is* serious," Maris quietly says, "a mold-remediation crew will have to seal off the area, and you won't be able to live in the house while the damage is being repaired."

"And you will stay here," Elsa insists. "I have empty rooms, and the inn's not open yet."

Lauren gives Elsa a weepy smile. "No, Elsa. It's enough that you're hosting our vow renewal ceremony. And you're so busy preparing for your grand opening in September. I can't impose."

"We'll be all right." Kyle kisses the side of Lauren's head. "Maybe our homeowners insurance will cover a hotel stay."

Lauren nods, figuring that's probably their only option.

Until Maris bolts to her feet. "I have a *great* idea!" she says. But that's not all Maris does. She also runs around the table, crouches beside Lauren and clasps her hand. "If you have to leave your home, you'll stay with me and Jason. We have *plenty* of empty bedrooms in that big old house!"

With a long, worried breath, Kyle sits back. "I don't know, Maris. You better check with Jason first. He's very regimented with his routine. Plus he's so busy these days, not to mention a little tense. He, well, he might not like us being there."

"Nonsense!" Maris still crouches beside Lauren, but looks to Kyle. "You two were each other's best man! I will *not* take no for an answer."

"But what about your writing?" Lauren asks. "Don't you need a quiet house?"

"No. I write in the shack, out back. Neil's old shack." She stands and turns to Elsa then, giving her a quick hug. "*And* I write in the turret. Here. Elsa set up a writing nook for me." Then, it's back to Lauren. "And don't forget, life experiences *enrich* storytelling—so your family staying with us will be good for me. And, well, Jason will get over it."

"Nothing's definite yet, so we won't rush to conclusions. When Jason's mold pro looks at the situation, we'll know better," Kyle says, then pauses to check his watch. "In a few hours."

Inching toward the doorway now, Maris still assures them. "Okay. I'm going back to my writing nook. But in the meantime, you two are *not* cancelling your vow renewal because of this. You pick a date with Elsa. And just know," she says as she leans into the dining room to remind them. "Our house is *your* house."

"We'll see." Kyle waves her off. "Maybe it's just the one wall that's got mold, and we can bleach the spores, replace that nasty drywall and not have to leave."

Lauren looks over her shoulder to Maris. "Fingers crossed," she says, raising her own tightly crossed fingers.

"If not," Maris insists, "Jason and I've got you covered."

In the meantime, Elsa begins serving lunch. "And remember, Lauren. Kyle." She gets two glass goblets from her chipped-paint cupboard, then scoops up two chicken wraps dripping with lettuce, tomato chunks and Caesar dressing. "Do not argue with what we call in Italy ... *signora della casa*. The woman of the house. Maris is the woman of the *Barlow* house, and so everything's settled. You'll go there."

"That's right," Maris says as she heads down the hall to get back to her writing.

There's a little more, too, that Lauren makes out as Elsa sets a wrap on her plate. She barely hears Maris' last words tossed over her shoulder, echoing back to the dining room.

"*That's what friends are for!*"

sixteen

"THAT'S WHAT FRIENDS ARE FOR?" Jason asks. "Maris, that's what *phones* are for."

Doesn't she get it? The last thing he needs is company. He's tired, it's Saturday—the end of a long-ass day, the end of a bitchin'-busy week. It's one of those days when the *very* first thing he does when the door closes behind him once he's finally home is this: land in his upholstered chair in the living room and remove his prosthesis, first. Second? Give his leg a rubdown before sitting back in the chair with one God damn long sigh. Seriously, he could've dozed right off with his head dropped back in the chair like that.

Instead, he reached for his forearm crutches and got himself into the kitchen, where he's sitting now—crutches leaning against the table, Maris hauling in bags of groceries for the apparently full house they're about to have. Madison lies beside the slider while Maris comes in and out. The dog normally would be sniffing around her overloaded grocery bags, but Maris bought the German shepherd a rawhide chew bone to keep her otherwise occupied.

When the last of the umpteen bags are brought in and Maris

closes the door behind her, Jason looks over his shoulder. "If you'd *called* me—"

"I couldn't call you," Maris interrupts. "The mold is that bad, they had to pack and leave ... *ASAP!*"

"But I could've had Eva find them a cottage rental. There must be some place around here sitting vacant."

"They can't afford that," Maris informs him as she drops the last heavy brown bag on the counter. "Between fixing up their house and vow renewal expenses, they don't need an overpriced cottage rental, too." She reaches into one of the multitude of bags and pulls out colorful packages and cans, which she loads onto cabinet shelves. "And remember, Jason," she says while maneuvering a jumbo box of cereal, "sometimes you have to let *love* in!"

Meanwhile, Maris doesn't stop crisscrossing the kitchen. She moves from the mountain of brown grocery bags on the counter, to the refrigerator, back to the bags ... before heading to the pantry, then back to the bags once more. This time she sets some of the groceries right on the table before deciding where to stock them. Jason checks out her haul, astonished at what the Bradford family is in for here: frozen pizzas, dippin' cookies, yogurt with gourmet chocolate chips, organic maple syrup, string cheese. He reaches for a yogurt container, peels off the top and asks Maris for a spoon. When she gives him one from the dish rack, he mixes in the chocolate chips and samples the yogurt.

"You only buy the good stuff when we have company," he says around a mouthful.

"Jason! That's for the kids. Do you know how much money this all cost? Three hundred dollars!"

"Three *hundred?*" He scoops another mouthful of creamy yogurt. "Maris, we're only living on one income now."

Still, she doesn't stop moving. It's absolutely incredible how much food and paper products are crammed into these bags. Packages of instant stuffing, potato chips, hot dogs and hamburgers. Paper towels and tinfoil. Frozen waffles and loaves of bread. When each bag is empty, she hands it to him to nicely fold into a neat square.

But yup, Maris heard his one-income comment, loud and clear. And won't let it go ignored, either. "So you're saying you don't want me to write?" she asks while stacking cans of French-style beans. "Is that it?"

"No." He folds another bag and sets it with the others to store in the pantry bag rack. "You're just not making a regular income. Yet. *Yet*, I mean." When he glances at her standing at the open cabinet, she's looking over her shoulder at him. Silently. "Never mind," he tells her. "What do you want me to do here?"

"Help me make some beds."

He reaches for his crutches and stands there, leaning into them. "I'll put my leg back on and meet you upstairs." Halfway to his living room chair—the one where twenty minutes ago, he swears he momentarily dozed—he calls back, "Who's going where?"

It's obvious by Maris' muffled and distracted voice that she's bent into the refrigerator when she answers. "I'll figure that out when I get up there."

She wouldn't have to figure it out at all if she'd just called him. If they'd just found somewhere else for the Bradford family of four to crash while their house is rid of mold.

Anywhere.

Elsa's inn. The little motel over on Shore Road. With Lauren's parents.

Because hell, *that's what friends are for?* More like, the quickest way to *end* a friendship is to live together. Because how does the saying go? Oh, yes. Familiarity breeds contempt.

By the time Jason gets his liner, sock and prosthesis on again, then heads upstairs with the dog at his heels, Maris is about done in the kitchen. He hears her coming up behind him when he's standing at the linen closet.

"I guess we have to put Kyle and Lauren next to us. It's the only room with a double bed." She brings an armful of sheets to that room. "Oh boy," she calls out then. "I hope they don't think they're on some sort of vacation here and start up with their hanky-panky."

"Don't worry," Jason says as he walks into the room. He picks up the fitted sheet and flips it open over the bed. "Kyle took a vow of celibacy."

"A what?"

"He's not having any sex until after their vow renewal."

"Are you kidding me?" Maris asks from across the bed, where she's tucking the sheet corner under the mattress.

"Nope. He wants their wedding night to be special. Said he'll double up his pajama bottoms to keep Lauren away, if he has to."

"Seriously?"

Jason flips open the top sheet and together they center and tuck it on the bed. "I guess Lauren is trying to wear down his resolve, being provocative, trying to seduce him and all."

"Oh great." Maris tosses a look at the thin wall separating this bedroom from theirs. "Please, not here."

"Let me remind you, sweetheart," Jason tells her while fluffing a pillow. "This *was* your idea."

As he says it, the doorbell rings, prompting the dog to fly down the stairs with a low growl. Jason gets it; he's growling too—complaining under his breath as he downs the stairs and heads to the front door.

Until Maris yanks his arm from behind. "Jason!" She turns him toward her. "Take a breath." When he pulls out of her hold, she insists. "Like your father taught you!"

Of course, his beautiful wife knows *just* the right words to say to get her way. So he stops and fills his lungs, twice.

"And smile," she whispers while hurrying past him.

Jason steps back, holding the dog by her collar as Maris opens the door.

And there they are, the whole Bradford clan, standing ragtag in his doorway. Evan's got his snorkel strapped on his head; Hailey holds a bag of plastic farm animals; Lauren's got an armful of clothes on hangers draped over her arm; Kyle carries a big brown carton.

"We packed some stuff, and tried to plan ahead," Lauren says, almost apologetically. "But after the mold crew assessed the situation, they wanted us out of there to start containment right away," Lauren cries. "Kyle managed to grab a box of wedding mementoes—as if we can even think straight to review them for our vow renewal. *And* we brought some of the kids' things, to keep them busy." She looks back at Kyle, then to Jason and Maris. "You sure you have room?"

"Of course!" Maris takes the clothes from her arms and gives them to Jason. "Hon, why don't you and Kyle put the boxes in the dining room?" she asks him while taking prancing-and-excited Maddy by the collar. "Near the wedding gifts we didn't get to yet."

"I really hope it's no trouble, guys. Because they said the entire mold-remediation process could take days," Lauren tells them. Just then, Hailey squeezes past her, pats the dog's head and laughs when Maddy licks her face. "But thankfully it was so much easier packing and coming *here*," Lauren continues. "It's a long drive to my parents' place, and this way we can keep tabs on things at our house."

"Sit," Evan whispers when he steps into the foyer and stops beside Maddy. "Sit, girl."

While bending to hold onto the now-sitting dog whose tail doesn't stop sweeping the floor, Maris reaches out her free arm—grabbing Lauren and pulling her inside. "No trouble at all."

"You sure, guy?" Kyle steps over the threshold and stops in the dark foyer.

Jason takes the carton from his arms, throwing a quick look to Maris at the same time. "No prob," he tells Kyle. "That's what friends are for."

seventeen

PARADISE.

Since marrying Maris, Jason Barlow's version of paradise has not wavered. For him, paradise is lingering in bed with his wife on lazy Sunday mornings. Seagulls caw out on the bluff. The sound of breaking waves carries on the sea breeze. The morning sun paints the water gold. Nothing else compares to that bliss.

Problem is? This Sunday, his paradise is nowhere to be found.

"Maris." He looks over at her beside him. She's lying on her side, facing away from him. "Are you up?" he asks with a gentle nudge.

"I've been up for hours," she quietly answers without moving.

He touches her long brown hair. "Please, sweetheart. Please tell me that somewhere in those hundreds of grocery bags you unloaded yesterday there was a box of breathe strips. That snoring drove me crazy all night."

"Me, too. Why didn't you hit the wall? They're right on the other side."

"And that's a little too close for me." Jason sits and maneuvers himself to his bedside chair. "I'm getting up."

"So am I."

When she tosses the sheet back, Jason glances over at her right as she stretches before getting out of bed. She's wearing her black satin-and-lace cami and shorts. What he wouldn't give to touch that soft, cool fabric. To feel it beneath his hands as they glide over her. To lift that cami off, like he would on any other summer Sunday morning.

Instead he hooks on his crutches and walks to his dresser, where he opens the drawers and grabs a clean change of clothes.

"I'll make the bed." As she says it, Maris straightens and folds back the sheets. "Maybe Kyle's snoring will ease up once they settle in here."

"Maybe. Maybe not." After tucking the day's outfit—cargo shorts and tee—into a cloth bag hanging from his crutch handle, Jason walks to the bed and lightly leaves a kiss on Maris' cheek. "But don't forget," he whispers. "We're letting love in." It isn't until he gets to the doorway that he turns back and gives her a wink. "That's what friends are for, darling."

So far, so good. It seems he'll have first dibs on the bathroom. Quietly, he heads out into the hallway, safe until Kyle opens *his* bedroom door right as Jason passes it.

"Hey, Jason," Kyle says. He steps into the hallway and stands there shirtless, with only a pair of light summer pajama pants on. "Fine morning. Windows open, salt air coming in from the bluff ... so pungent! I slept really deep here."

"Good morning, Kyle," Jason answers as he tries to maneuver around him in the hallway.

"After you, bro," Kyle quickly backs up into his bedroom. "I'll grab my robe and go downstairs to get the griddle going. See what I can cook up on that stove of yours."

"The left rear burner is a little touchy. New stove's on my to-do list," Jason says as he goes into the bathroom, closes the door and stops in front of the porthole mirror there. Leaning on one crutch, he runs his hand over his face to gauge the necessity of a shave. But that's not all he does. He also drops his eyes closed for a long moment at the sound of clattering pots coming from down in the kitchen.

Remembering to breathe then, he hangs his clothes on a wall hook outside the tub, sets up his shower stool and turns on the spigot to drown out, well, to drown out just about everything else.

―――

By the time Jason's showered and dressed, the dog is sitting outside the bathroom door, apparently waiting for him. And apparently unaccustomed to the commotion coming from downstairs, where the house is in full Bradford swing. So Jason makes his way down the stairs on his crutches—with Maddy nipping at them the whole way. She even manages to twist herself around and walk down the stairs backward while snapping at the crutch tips. Once he makes it safely to the bottom, Jason notices Evan sitting on the living room couch watching the whole dog spectacle.

"What's up, Evan?" Jason asks while walking into the room. "Your dad cooking us some grub before he goes to the diner?"

"Yeah."

While walking past Evan toward the upholstered chair in the corner—where his prosthetic leg leans—Jason hears snatches of talk coming from the kitchen.

First, Kyle. *Crumble some cheese in these eggs, Hay.*

Then Lauren, to Maris. *Where are you at in the book?*

Maris, answering. *Last part. Except I'm a little stuck.*

Lauren, while setting dishes on the table. *Come with me and the kids on the beach today. We'll set up at the water and hash things out.*

The whole time, dishes clatter; silverware clinks; the refrigerator opens and closes; food sizzles on the stovetop.

"You're missing all the action, Ev," Jason tells him as he sits in his chair.

Evan merely shrugs, all while keeping his eye on the dog pacing near Jason. When Jason unhooks his crutches and reaches for his prosthesis, he looks over at Evan again. "Hey, buddy. Why don't you go out in the kitchen, near the slider, and grab Maddy's lobster chew toy?"

"Really?"

"Sure. She'd like that."

As soon as Evan rounds the corner, Jason begins with his leg, carefully rolling on the silicone liner first, then adding a sock. He aligns them just so before smoothing them onto his thigh, then reaching for the prosthetic limb.

"I can't find her toy," Evan says when he barrels back into the living room. But he stops short when he sees Jason lining up the prosthetic limb with his stump.

Jason looks up at him and motions for him to sit on the sofa. "It's okay, Evan. I'll help you look in a second. This is just what I do in the morning, with my leg and all. But I'm all right." As he says it, he stands and tests the fit, putting some pressure on the prosthesis. Then he crosses the room and casually musses Evan's moppy hair.

Of course Evan has no way of knowing, but Jason's also doing that with a little disbelief. Today, more than ever, he's taken aback at how much Evan looks like Neil did at that age. Maybe it has something to do with Evan being right *here*—in the very house where Neil grew up.

"Come on," Jason tells the boy. "We'll find Maddy's toy now."

Somehow they make it through the kitchen: weaving around pulled-out chairs, and Kyle hovering around the stove, and Maris reaching into the cabinets. "Over there," Jason says, bending low and putting his hand on Evan's shoulder. He turns him toward the pantry. "Right there, near her dog mat."

Evan hurries to the big chew toy and tosses it in the air for Maddy.

"Breakfast!" Kyle calls out then. "Yo, Barlow. Eggs are getting cold."

Well, one thing's for certain. Jason seriously could get used to what he's seeing on the table: freshly scrambled eggs, crisp bacon, whole-wheat toast. While eyeing Kyle's breakfast spread, he wanders over to his chair—a chair occupied by one little girl swinging and kicking her legs while waiting for her food.

"Babe!" Maris calls across the room. "Pull up a chair from the dining room."

When he does, he nearly trips on the dog prancing around while her clamping jaw squeaks her red lobster. She's obviously delighted to have a new playmate who'll toss the toy in the air in a game of catch. Meanwhile, kitchen chairs scrape; Lauren doles out food for her kids; and Maris, sitting at the far end of the table, gives him a small wave across the distance.

But it's Kyle who surprises him when he comes over holding a frying pan and personally doling out breakfast on Jason's plate.

"*Really* appreciate this," Jason tells him. "But don't you have a diner to run?"

"This is the least I can do for you and your wife. Feed you guys. And Jerry's opening up the diner, so I can go in a little later."

"What's happening with the mold issue?" Maris asks while sprinkling salt on her eggs.

"I'm headed over there in a while to talk to my contractor,"

Jason says. "They need to get their gear in there and start sealing the house." As his fork presses through the eggs, Jason sees the melted cheese and tiny tomato pieces and dash of pepper. He lifts a hunk of egg with the orange-and-yellow cheese oozing off his fork, and motions to it while looking at Kyle.

"You like that?" Kyle asks as he tosses a towel over his shoulder and returns the now-empty pan to the stove. "Blended Cheddar-Monterey Jack cheese."

Jason shakes his head and lifts his fork to his mouth. "Take notes," he tells Maris across the table. "Please."

"I can leave you the recipe," Kyle says as he finally sits between his kids. As he does, Evan tugs at his arm and whispers a question in his ear. On his other side, Hailey's asking him for more cheese on her eggs. When Kyle reaches to the center of the table and lifts the plate of bacon, Lauren stretches over and snatches a piece for herself. Kyle holds the plate aloft for her and catches Jason's eye, too. "Welcome to family life, Barlow."

⚬

Later that morning, Maris sits beneath the beach umbrella beside Lauren. Towels and sand pails are scattered around them. Little Hailey floats past wearing her ladybug tube; Evan dons his swim mask and snorkel as he wades waist-deep, looking for a spot to explore beneath the rippling Sound. Another family sets up their beach gear beside them—totes dropped on towels, sand chairs snapping open, umbrella flipped up. Near the water's edge, joggers move past; a father and son play catch out deeper in the water—falling with a splash each time they catch the ball.

"Think, Lauren." Maris tips up her straw cowboy hat. "*Think.*"

Lauren sits straight and clasps her arms around her bent knees.

"I'm trying, but it's been ten years now. I used to read pieces of the story, but mostly I'd paint driftwood while Neil wrote in the shack." She looks further down the beach to the lone cottage on the sand. "It's amazing that Jason clinched that cottage for his show. You know, with it being the exact same one Neil brought to the novel. I remember Neil even talked to the owner and finagled a tour of the inside."

"He did," Maris tells her. "Mitch showed Jason a photograph he took of Neil."

"Seriously?" Lauren whispers, her head tipped as she looks at Maris.

Maris merely nods. "Neil put his heart and soul into this manuscript."

"Mom!" Evan calls as he walks out deeper. "Can I swim to the raft?"

Lauren shields her eyes, then stands and walks in ankle-deep. "Aw, I don't think so, Ev," she answers. "I know you like to, but not without Dad here. That's deep enough," she tells him, then returns to her seat and leans close to Maris. "He's just like Neil," she says. "In his own world with the sea, and the salt air. It's uncanny sometimes."

Maris watches Evan while reaching over and briefly clasping Lauren's hand.

"I think Neil was drawing upon all of *us* in his novel. The whole gang," Lauren tells her then.

"Me, too. And what's eerie is the way he predicted so much in that storyline. One of the characters even reminds me of Kyle's brother."

"Really!"

Maris nods. "Has Kyle *ever* spoken to him, in all these years?"

"No," Lauren admits with a long sigh. "No contact at all. The book is closed on *that* chapter of Kyle's life. Believe me."

"I can totally get that." Maris sits back and looks out at Long Island Sound. Morning sunshine drops tiny stars on the water's ripples, the ocean stars twinkling gently. She pulls her cowboy hat lower, then grabs a pen and journal from her tote. "So Neil never talked about the ending of his book? Because I'm *still* stumped on where to take the story."

"What I remember is the way he'd mention the hurricane parallels with the friends that summer."

Maris writes a few lines in the journal. "So, where would it end, compared to a hurricane …"

"Right, but don't overthink it. I'm sure Neil was trying to predict how *we* would all end up. You know, after the storms we'd weathered." Lauren looks at Maris and shrugs. "Ironic, no? The storm of Neil, Kyle and me?"

"I see that triangle in his story."

Maris glances down the length of the crescent-moon-shaped beach to the lone cottage on the sand. Beyond it, the coastline curves around a rocky outcropping and patch of woods, which form a natural barrier protecting this little stretch of beach. Beyond that stone jetty, though, where the beaches are more untamed, that's where Neil kept his secret shack—which Jason had towed on a barge. He wanted to bring that part of Neil's life home, safe and sound. Jason knew that any big storm coming up the coast would've taken the shack out to sea, once and for all.

That's what storms do, after all. In their wake, they change the landscape. They wash things away. They leave behind debris, take things down, alter sightlines. We seek the familiar once storms pass, once the waters have calmed and the winds subsided, only to be startled at the changes.

That night, Lauren walks into her bedroom at the Barlow house. She quietly closes the door behind her and in the dim lamplight, sees Kyle lying on his side in the bed. On her nightstand, a large piece of white coral is propped against a miniature painted lighthouse. Something about the still moment has her feeling relief. They *made* it through the first day of imposing on their good friends. Hopefully, they'll get through the upcoming days just as smoothly.

"Kids are finally asleep," she says as she takes off her robe and drops it on the foot of the mattress. Admiring a framed needlepoint scene hanging on the wall, Lauren reaches up and touches the tiny stitches making up the little sailboat and blue sky. "I said goodnight to Maris and Jason. They're downstairs watching TV," she whispers while turning to Kyle and brushing her hand across his shoulder.

"I'm beat." Kyle settles in the old bed and the mattress squeaks as he does.

Lauren gets in on her side of the bed. "Oh, look! Our hosts left us a note on the pillow." She picks it up and opens it. "Isn't that sweet?"

"What's it say?" Kyle asks over his shoulder.

"Let me see. It looks like it's from Jason, actually."

"To you?"

"Mm-hmm. It says *Dear Lauren*." She pauses with a quick laugh.

"What?" Kyle glances over his shoulder again.

"Okay, get ready for this. *It might not be the train keeping you up at night at your new house. It could be your husband's snoring. Try these.*" She holds up a few breathe strips.

"I don't snore." Kyle pulls the sheet up over his shoulder.

"Sorry to say, but sometimes you do, honey. Lately, more so. Maybe it's from stress." She unpeels a breathe strip and holds it out for him. "Just try one. There's no shame, no judgment."

Kyle reaches back over his shoulder and grabs the breathe strip. He presses it across his nose and sniffs deeply.

"See? That's not so bad." Lauren settles beneath the sheet, too, then stretches to shut off the bedside lamp. "Goodnight, now."

"What? No kiss?"

"Not with that thing on your face."

"*No shame, no judgment* ... Yeah, right," Kyle whispers as he presses his pillow beneath his head.

⁓

The nice surprise is that Lauren sleeps soundly on this bed in an old cottage on the bluff. So soundly that what happens next frightens her. When she wakes up very early in the morning, she *believes* it's a morning from ten years ago ... when she woke up beside Neil in this very bed, in the midst of their secret affair.

Out on the bluff, seagulls are crying as they swoop over the rocks on their early feeding frenzy. Lauren listens with her eyes still closed. Warm air drifts in from the paned window overlooking Long Island Sound. She lies on her side, facing the doorway. In a moment, Neil's hands come up from behind her and glide over her skin, along her arm, up to her shoulder. When he leans close to kiss that shoulder, then her neck, the mattress squeaks. His hands pull her close as she murmurs his name.

Suddenly her eyes open and she orients herself. The room is dim at this early dawn hour. On the old dark dresser, she makes out a wooden lantern filled with seashells instead of a candle. Seashells she remembers collecting ten summers ago with Neil,

CASTAWAY COTTAGE

then bringing the shells here ... to this very room.

So was it Neil's hands she felt just now while dozing, or simply that gentle air dropping on her, touching her skin?

In a moment, she closes her eyes once more and believes it's true. Somehow, in that salt air—*Cures what ails you*, he'd whisper—it was Neil.

It's his spirit, forever haunting her in sad seaside moments like this, when nothing more than a stirring breeze brings him completely back to her again.

eighteen

SHE'S NOT SURE WHY, BUT lately Elsa's noticed a sudden urgency in her days. If it's not one thing, it's another. From Kyle and Lauren's mold issue, to Jason securing a renovation for his TV show, to, well, to even Celia on this fine Tuesday morning.

With little Aria strapped to her chest in one of those ergonomically correct infant carriers, Celia's pacing Elsa's kitchen. Not only is her baby strapped to her chest, her phone is also pressed to her ear. After Celia asks someone on the phone about arranging a ribbon-cutting ceremony at the inn, she stamps her foot and looks over at Elsa. "She put me on hold. *Again!*"

Elsa gives her a patient smile before turning to her big calendar planner opened up on the kitchen island. "Hmm," she muses to herself as her pencil hovers above the month of August. So much to plan! She's thinking the vow renewal could work on one of the last two Saturdays. "Kyle and Lauren," she whispers, considering their seaside nuptials. "I'll talk more with them tomorrow," she half says to a pacing Celia. "They're coming over again, after our last visit was cut short with their mold problem."

Still pacing, Celia only nods. So Elsa turns the page of her planner, stopped suddenly by a loud knocking at the inn's front door.

"Can you get that, Elsa?" Celia curtly asks, lightly bouncing to keep Aria happy. Multitasking has become routine for her lately. "Because I'm *still* on hold."

"Are we expecting anybody?" Elsa sets down her pencil.

"I'm not."

Whipping off her reading glasses, Elsa heads to the door. "Maybe it's Cliff. I haven't seen him around … He's so busy with the summer crowd and getting his agenda ready for a jam-packed Board of Governors meeting tomorrow."

Another knock comes, and the door swings open right as she gets to it, causing her to back up a step when Jason sweeps in. He wears khaki cargo shorts with a half-tucked polo shirt, and his face looks unshaven, possibly for days now.

"Jason!" Elsa says. "Nice to see you."

Carrying his black work duffel, he walks straight past her—there it is *again*, that sense of urgency. But he's *also* holding one of those white take-out bags Elsa so dearly loves. And … once he drops it on the kitchen island, he *does* give Elsa a quick hug before backing up and eyeing her closely.

"Elsa," he pleads. "Help me."

⁓

If he had to say so, yes, Jason would admit to believing in magic.

Because whenever he walks into the Ocean Star Inn carrying one of those magic white bags, it works its trick on Elsa. As soon as he lifts out the two egg sandwiches and still-warm cinnamon crullers, that white bag usually sways her to his side.

"You've got to get me out of there, Elsa," he says around

tearing open a ketchup packet with his teeth. "I'm telling you, I can't focus in my own home this week. Can't hear myself *think*. Please. Give me a quiet room here."

"Jason!" she says in a loud whisper, with a glance over at Celia still pacing *and* rubbing Aria's back—all while on the phone. "Is it Maris?" Elsa asks. "If you're having marital problems, I can help."

"No. It's not that." He swirls ketchup on his steaming cheesy-egg sandwich, which prompts Elsa to do the same to hers. "It's the Bradfords. I love them, seriously. But that's a lot of people under one roof over at my place."

As he talks, Celia begins talking on the phone, too. She looks over at Jason and Elsa, then quickly goes into the dining room to conduct her phone conversation.

"That's right …" Elsa lifts her sandwich, but pauses when it's midway to her mouth. "Maris offered them *your* house."

Okay, Elsa's obviously playing Jason now, because he can't miss the damn twinkle in her eye as she says that, right before she sinks her teeth into her sandwich.

But he's no fool, and came prepared. So to get his way, he casts another magic spell—this time with a little paper bag of golden, crispy, perfectly peppered, slightly greasy hash browns. He slides the bag across the marble island before pleading his case. "You *must* have a room with a desk. Just a tucked-away corner to make some phone calls, do a little designing? The station's under a time crunch, and I've *got* to move forward with the blueprints for the cottage on the beach."

"Hmm." Elsa discreetly pulls his hash browns closer to her side of the island, and her fingers then gently lift one out. "What about your barn studio—with your big drafting table, and the skylights letting in the sunshine? Can't you work there?"

"The problem is," Jason says while peeling the lid off his take-out coffee, "there's no air-conditioning in the barn. So the windows are open ... to the sound of a zoo! The dog's running around in the yard with the kids. Hailey's splashing in Maddy's kiddie pool. Evan's shooting his cap gun, then gets the dog running after a Frisbee."

"Oh." Elsa gingerly dips her hash brown into ketchup. "Well, that's *family*, Jason. Bustling with *love*! I'm so happy to see you opening your home and heart to them," she says, pressing the entire hash brown into her mouth before continuing her thought. "And to the possibility of more family in your *own* life?"

"Stuff it, Elsa." He ups the ante by reaching into the bag for a sugar-and-cinnamon flecked cruller—which he sets on a napkin and slides her way, too. And he's blunt about it, no less. "Here. You can have this, and *in exchange* I'll pick a room upstairs. It's only Tuesday," he says with a glance at her giant planner shoved aside for their junk-food breakfast. "So I'll need the room for two or three days, until the mold remediation is complete at the Bradford house. By the end of the week, at the very longest."

Elsa wavers between hash browns; the sweet, twisted cruller; and the gooey, ketchup-dripping egg sandwich ... which she decides upon. As she bites into it, yup, her eyes flutter closed while she waves off Jason.

He'll take that as his cue, thank you very much, and quickly stands. His bag of magic tricks wore her down. "Oh, and one more thing," he warns his aunt-through-marriage. "Keep it a secret, would you?"

Elsa merely nods while chewing.

"No." Jason sits again, sets his arms on the island top and leans close to her. "No, I mean, for *real*. I *don't* need to be found out here and lose my quiet time."

Still chewing while nodding with gusto this time, Elsa asks,

"Will you be spending the night, too?"

"No. Just the days. Everyone will think I'm on job sites, or at the TV studio. They'll *never* suspect I'm right here."

"Jason!" Celia breezes into the room and, okay, Elsa's influence must be rubbing off on her. Because the very first thing she does is pick up the second cinnamon cruller and bite into it. "Say hi to your godchild!" she says while wiping sugar crumbs from her chin.

Jason stands, pushes in his stool and turns to Celia and the baby strapped to her chest. "Oh, Aria," he says while squeezing her tiny hand. "You are so lucky to be clueless." With that, he grabs his duffel and coffee before heading down the hallway in the direction of the staircase—intent on finding an empty room upstairs.

But that's not all he's doing. He's also listening to the two women left behind in the kitchen.

"So, Elsa!" Celia says while dragging out a stool. He can just picture her sitting there, eyes wide, silently pointing in Jason's direction. "What's going on? Give me the scoop."

"Just between you and me," Elsa begins, then pauses.

Jason's sure she's leaning to the side to see if he's out of earshot, which he isn't.

"You can't tell anyone, though," Elsa orders Celia. "It's a secret!"

That's all he hears, because now he's putting one foot in front of the other on Elsa's mural-covered stairs, leading to the quiet solace of some third-floor room. There, he drops his duffel on a bed, sits at a distressed-white beachy desk meant for guests penning thoughts, or jotting postcard messages.

Finally, in a moment hard-fought to win—in the far-removed, third-floor quiet—he looks out the window and sighs.

Castaway Cottage

~

By Wednesday morning, Jason wonders why he even bothered. Apparently the secluded spots of Stony Point, like the sanctuary of Elsa's inn, are getting more and more crowded.

He spent the morning in his private, secret room there. Sitting at the white table at the window, he drew several initial sketches of the cottage on the beach, all while seeing it from his third-floor vantage point. Beyond the distant cottage, sea and sky soar.

Don't forget the sky, he remembers his brother always telling him. So Jason's initial sketches include dramatic views of that skyscape. After a couple hours, he leans back in the desk chair and feels good. He's making progress. But he also needs to stretch his legs and grab a bottled water from the kitchen. First, he slides his phone close and texts Maris, who he assumes is home in Neil's shack, writing away.

"On job site," Jason whispers as he types his text message. "*On my way out. Do you need anything for later?*"

In a second, his phone dings with her response, which he also quietly reads aloud: "*No. Busy writing. All set.*"

Good enough for him, Jason signs off and heads quickly downstairs for a water. Halfway down, though, he hears a voice asking, "Jason?" So he stops and turns to see Maris at her designated writing nook in the turret. Her papers are spread out, her laptop opened. *Damn it*, he thinks. His bluff is about to be blown.

"What are *you* doing here?" she asks, standing and walking to the banister. "I thought you were at a job site."

Jason glances back up the stairs to his oh-so-sweet, quiet, once-secret room that he never should've left, then looks back at her. "I thought you were writing in the shack?"

"What about you? Why aren't you working in your studio?"

Jason simply shakes his head. "I'm getting some water. Be right back, sweetheart."

He hurries down the stairs, hoping that by the time he returns to his desk, Maris will be so engrossed in her writing again that he can pass her alcove unnoticed.

"Jason?" he hears again, this time prompting him to back up with a glance into the dining room. There, Kyle, Lauren and Elsa sit together at the long wood-planked table. Elsa's trusted planner lays open before them. "What are *you* doing here?" Kyle asks.

"What are *you* doing here?" Jason tosses back to him.

"Planning our vow renewal."

"No work today?" Jason asks then.

"It's Wednesday. I took my half-day off this morning."

Jason leans in, looks at them for a second longer, then rushes to the kitchen while calling over his shoulder, "I'll grab a drink and get right out of your way."

As he's opening the refrigerator, Maris walks into the room. "Jason. I cannot believe you have an entire office upstairs. It's like you're leading some secret life!"

"An office *here*?" Lauren calls from the dining room. "What about your barn studio? Are the kids bothering you at home? I can ask Taylor to babysit them at her house, instead of at yours, if that helps."

"No." Jason opens his bottled water while standing in the dining room doorway again. "It's not that—"

"Listen, bro." Kyle waves him over to Elsa's blocked-and-numbered calendar planner. "What do you think of a date for my vow renewal? Our ten-year anniversary is in September, but we want to have the shindig before the kids go back to school. So," he says, pointing to the August page, "we're thinking maybe the third *or* last Saturday of August. Got an opinion?"

It's obvious Jason has no choice but to get involved in this project. There's no escaping it, not with the way every face is lifted and watching his. So he walks into the dining room and stands beside Elsa. When he looks to the squared dates spread out on the table, everyone else does, too. "The third Saturday is too close to my own wedding anniversary, when Maris and I usually go away. Any chance you can bump it up earlier in the month?"

"If it works for you, guy? We'll keep it in the running." Kyle nods to Elsa, before reaching up to shake Jason's hand. "That's what friends are for."

nineteen

SOME DAYS CALL FOR A certain attitude. A certain *je ne sais quoi*. Especially when the day will include visiting with a special someone.

So as Cliff walks through his trailer-apartment while folding a small blanket beneath his arm, he stops to first, put on a light jacket. And second? To pick up the lucky domino from his metal tanker desk. He joggles the domino and flips it spinning like a coin, then snatches it out of the air and sets it on his desk once again. Feeling carefree, he heads outside to his golf cart, makes a quick stop at the convenience store past the railroad trestle, then whistles a tune on his way to Elsa's.

When she opens the door, it's obvious that she's starting her Thursday by reading in bed. She wears a silky robe over her pajamas, and her leopard-print reading glasses are perched atop her sleep-mussed hair.

"Cliff?" She looks past him, then steps back to let him by. "Come in. Is everything okay?"

"Yes. All's good. But I need you to come with me, actually."

"Now? I'm reviewing my JP wedding vows." She glances down at her wrinkled sleep clothes. "And I'm not dressed. Just come in and I'll go out with you later. For crying out loud, it's only five-thirty in the morning."

"Precisely." He reaches for her hand and hitches his head toward his golf cart. "I insist, you have to come with me."

Of course, she resists his *insist*. "Who goes out in their pajamas? Only hobos do. One of my neighbors here did that the other day. She skulked around in her baggy robe and scuff slippers, yanking weeds beside her garage. Oh, it was a pathetic sight, I'm telling you." Elsa pulls out of his hold. "A woman outside in her pajamas in the daytime is a woman who's all done. So please, Clifton, at least let me get dressed!"

"Well, make it fast." Cliff follows her inside and waits at the kitchen island, where he sits and taps his fingers on its marble top.

"How'd the Board of Governors meeting go last night?" Elsa calls out from some dark recess of her room.

"Fine." While waiting, Cliff turns her elaborate planner and reads different events and chores jotted in the squares. From Elsa's muffled questions, he figures she must be pulling on a shirt right about now. So he shrugs, picks up a marker from the island and moves the planner close. *Spend morning with Cliff Raines* he writes in today's block.

And just in time. Right as he drops the marker, Elsa turns the corner dressed casually in leggings and a shoulder-baring tunic, over which she wears a silk neckerchief. Sometimes he can't believe this transplanted beauty from Milan even gives him the time of day. After she grabs her keys from the counter and they walk outside, he helps her into his golf cart.

"Here." Cliff reaches into the backseat, then sets a tray with a bag and two take-out coffees in her lap. "Hold this."

"Whatever are you up to?"

"A sunrise drive, okay?"

"What?"

Settling into the driver's seat, he nods to the eastern sky. "It's a beautiful morning, so I'm taking you for a sunrise drive. And for a picnic on the path." With that, he burns out of her stone driveway, making his golf cart's wheels spin while spewing the small rocks.

"Cliff! You really don't have to *woo* me anymore. You got what you wanted, didn't you? I'm staying on here at the inn."

"Well," he tells her with a quick glance at her honey-highlighted hair, her brown eyes. "Maybe I *like* to woo. At my age, it's nice. Keeps me on my romantic toes. Anyway … Jason was the one who suggested I try this wooing last fall—and I've found that it's something I really like to do. Woo."

With her hands holding the tray steady, Elsa turns to face him. "You're serious, aren't you?"

"Never more so." Cliff rounds a gradual curve and steers the golf cart onto Sea View Road, where the sun is just rising to the east, over Long Island Sound. The sky is streaked violet-red at the horizon, with that yellow sun hovering low. "Some of the best moments I've lived here have been with you by my side."

"Okay." Elsa straightens in her seat and can't help but take in the sunrise view. "Now that's very sweet, Clifton," she vaguely says.

"Not to mention," Cliff adds while maneuvering the bumpy beach road, "you've been so busy with inn prep and being a new grandmother. I totally get that, but it's been difficult locking down times when you're available." He reaches over and squeezes her wrist. "To be wooed. So I'm trying the dawn hour now."

It happens, then. It's one of the rare instances when Elsa stops prattling on about one thing or another. Whether it's the scenery that does it, or the thought of being wooed, who knows? But he steals a glimpse of her smile, too, as he drives along, passing sleepy cottages still cast in dawn's shadows. The cottages, and the swaying beach grasses nestled alongside them, are mere silhouettes against the golden sunrise. Finally, Cliff parks at a curb where a public pathway leads to a scenic lookout area. In all of Stony Point, there's no place with a better view at this hour.

After getting out of the golf cart, he carefully leads Elsa along a narrow stone pathway beside dewy grass. The path winds in a gentle curve, sloping downward toward a rocky shore. Once there, Cliff spreads his blanket on top of a wooden bench and motions for her to sit. As she gets comfortable, he opens a napkin on her lap and hands her a take-out coffee, along with one of those sweet crullers she favors.

"Look," she says as she dips her cruller into the coffee, then lifts it to her mouth for a soggy bite. "It's like the sun is rising straight out of the water."

Sitting beside her, Cliff bites into his blueberry muffin while taking in the sight of the brilliant sun climbing above the horizon. "It's majestic, actually. Don't you think?" Cliff asks. There's really no other word for what they're seeing: The light of the sun reflecting on the water makes it look like the sun itself is painting the sea gold. The beauty of those golden streaks rippling on the water leaves them speechless as the day unfolds before them.

Murmuring how nice this is, Elsa bites into her cruller and sips her coffee.

"Okay," Cliff says when he abruptly stands, then turns and gives Elsa a quick kiss. "Sun's up. That's it."

"That's *it*? Just like that?" she asks while plucking her sugary fingers from her mouth.

"Yes. I saw that itinerary at your place. And I have my own, too." He reaches into his pocket for his key. "I have a full workday today and have to stick to my schedule."

Though she starts to argue, Cliff keeps after Elsa. He sweeps off their crumbs and packages up their wrappings so he can whisk her back to the inn. There's really no point in lingering, anyway.

The sun has risen; the memory's made; the day's begun.

Leaving Elsa at her doorstep minutes later, Cliff zips back to his trailer. A few other early birds are out, some jogging, one watering their shrubs—all waving hello when he drives by. Finally pulling up to the Stony Point Beach Association's white, flat-roofed modular trailer, even he's surprised that he still calls it *home*.

Secretly, but it's home.

Home because this darn place and its demanding residents keep him plenty busy maintaining order, leaving him no time to house-hunt.

Not that he minds. Something about this metal trailer—with its sliding windows and steel entry door—has grown on him. There's a rigidity to it that's well-suited to a beach commissioner who has to keep the coastal community's rules enforced. He props open that steel door now to let fresh summer air into the stuffy interior, and heads straight to his tanker desk where he'll resume keeping order.

Breakfast done; sun up; time to work.

First order of business as he sits there is, yes, one more flip of his lucky domino. This time, with gratitude that his sunrise outing with Elsa went exactly as planned.

Now, on to the day's business. Next up? Finalizing the minutes from last night's BOG meeting. A few lines, dates and typed summaries later, the minutes are ready to print and post on the community bulletin board. It's Cliff's way of keeping Stony Point residents informed of developments that might affect them. He decides to take the long way to the bulletin board by cruising down Sea View Road again. This way he might relive his sunrise memory.

But instead? Nothing. The sun is higher in the sky now, and already his crack-of-dawn date with Elsa feels like a misty daydream.

Peeling out around a curve and leaving that memory behind, he eventually parks at the end of the boardwalk, where he sits in his golf cart and reviews each item on the printed meeting minutes.

Shasta daisies got the shaft, he reads. *The Board voted unanimously for next year's return of black-eyed Susans—in their full summer splendor.* "No more daisy duds," Cliff mutters.

Next? *Numerous mosquito complaints indicate a pesky population explosion*, he skims. *Targeted spraying has been approved.*

The final item, though, leaves Cliff frustrated: *Barlow Architecture's request for a two-week exemption to the Hammer Law was denied.* Of course, Cliff's was actually the deciding negative vote. Even though he likes Jason, and even though it was made clear that the exemption was intended solely to allow filming to begin for *Castaway Cottage*, Cliff felt he *had* to hold firm.

Before posting the meeting's minutes, he gives a long look to that last order of Barlow business and regrets that he had to let Jason down.

"But ... The rules are the rules," he whispers while stepping out of the golf cart. "For a damn good reason."

twenty

ONE THING JASON STILL HASN'T gotten used to is this: turning into his kitchen early in the morning and seeing Kyle Bradford sitting at the table. Even though it's Thursday—meaning it's day five of the Bradford takeover of his home—and even though Kyle is as quiet and as unobtrusive as he can be while sipping a coffee before going to work at the diner, Jason's still surprised when he comes upon him there. Maybe it's the way Kyle's so *unnaturally* quiet, and alone, in those moments.

"Hey, guy," Jason says on his way to the refrigerator. He pulls out leftover chicken cutlets Elsa sent him home with yesterday and begins making a breakfast sandwich.

"Good morning," Kyle says. "Sleep well?"

"Not particularly," Jason answers over his shoulder. When his bread pops in the toaster, he drops on a few thin cutlets, fresh tomato slices, cheese and a slathering of mayo.

"What's wrong?"

"Cliff Raines is what's wrong. At last night's Board of Governors meeting, he would not *budge* on my request for a Hammer Law exemption for the cottage on the beach. I'd petitioned for it so that demo work could at least begin *before*

Labor Day. Trent even took the floor and said a few words."

"Are you kidding me? Cliff wouldn't grant it? Not even for CT-TV, which would bring good buzz to this beach?"

"Nope." Jason slices his sandwich in half. "So I guess we'll have to film other things first. You know, some outdoor clips, local lore segments. It'll just have to be a quick September demo to meet the show's deadline." After setting his plate on the table, he turns to pour himself a coffee.

"That's nothing new, I guess, the gig with the judge. Cliff's pretty set in his ways." Kyle sips his coffee while looking at something on the table. "*The rules are the rules,*" he vaguely says. "But jeez, would it kill him to bend some for you?"

With a shrug, Jason walks over. "What do you have there?"

"My wedding album. Lauren and I thought we could get some ideas for our renewal ceremony." Kyle turns a page.

"Now that's a blast from the past," Jason says as he sits, too. He lifts a sandwich half and bites in while leaning over to see the old pictures. "Looking pretty sharp in that tux, Bradford."

"Not sure what I'll wear this time around." Kyle squints at another picture. "Something more casual. Keepin' it chill, you know?"

"Sure." Jason sips his hot coffee. "Especially with that vow of celibacy. Talk about chill. More like *icy.*"

"Yeah, no kidding." Kyle turns another page, and this time slides the photo album across the table to Jason. "Check it out, man."

The image Jason sees unnerves him, actually. Mostly because he has no memory of the picture being taken—even though it's *him* looking right at the camera and posing for the shot. He's sitting in his wheelchair at the altar, just weeks after losing half his leg. The picture was apparently taken after Jason's father wheeled him beside Kyle, and before the bride came down the aisle. Jason and his father are in suits, but Jason's left pant leg had been cut and hemmed at the knee to accommodate his newly amputated leg. And to keep the swelling down, that leg is raised and prone on an amputee board attached to the wheelchair. His father stands behind him and is holding the wheelchair's handgrips.

Still, it's not *that* sight of himself that unnerves him. It's more his father that does it ... Seeing him, Jason can't help wishing he were still alive.

The day of Kyle's wedding was a difficult one, probably more so for Jason than anyone else. But he insisted on being there. Jason knew that somehow, someway, they all had to start healing after the horrific motorcycle crash that also took Neil's life. Kyle and Lauren's wedding, a few weeks later, was a way to start. To somehow move forward.

So Jason's father agreed to wheel him into the church and reception hall. Throughout the ceremony and dinner afterward, he stayed close by. Whenever Jason even *looked* at him, his father responded. He would bend to hear Jason's words, or step behind the chair to transport his son off the altar area and down the aisle, out of the church—where Jason took his place in Kyle and Lauren's receiving line. Sitting outside in his wheelchair, Jason shook hands and took hugs from so many friends who were glad to finally see him again. There was no avoiding the tears of happiness—and of loss, too. He felt those ones in the hugs that lasted too long; in the handshakes that wouldn't let go.

In Kyle relinquishing his groom greetings to stand beside Jason, to clasp his shoulder at the right emotional times.

"Shit," Jason says now. "Seeing these pictures, you realize how hard the day really was. For everyone. I *get* that now ... more than when I was there, living it."

"Yeah." Kyle moves his chair and leans over to see the photograph of Jason's father pushing the wheelchair to the head table at the reception. "We get through what we have to sometimes."

"It's hard to believe I was such a wreck. Damn, it's all over my face. Losing my brother. Not having my prosthesis yet. Feeling utterly lost, I guess."

"You've come a helluva long way, bro," Kyle says as he lifts his coffee cup in a toast.

Jason obliges the toast before looking closer at the image of his father—dressed to the nines in a black suit and standing in perfect military posture. Something about this particular picture surprisingly breaks his heart. Maybe it's the round pin he can't miss on his father's lapel. The pin is gold, engraved with the head of an eagle, and outlined with stars. Around the blue edge, the words read *Vietnam War Veteran.*

"To this day," Kyle is saying, "I'm amazed that you showed up to be my best man. It must have taken every ounce of strength to be there like that."

"From the looks of these pictures, I'd say so. I don't know *where* I found that strength, when I'm sure I just wanted to curl up alone in a dark room somewhere."

"Well, listen. I'm glad I brought out this wedding album, and that you're seeing it." Kyle carries his coffee cup to the sink, rinses it and puts it in the dishwasher. "Because now I have to ask you something."

"Shoot."

"Okay." Kyle leans against the counter, arms crossed, as he nods toward the pictures of Jason at the wedding. "I know you already agreed, but you sure you're up to doing that again? Being my best man? Because I totally understand if it brings back too much pain. Especially since it's the ten-year anniversary of *everything*—my wedding, the bike accident, and Neil's death. No prob if you change your mind."

Jason looks at the pictures once more. He flips back a page to the shot of his father wheeling him down the church aisle after the ceremony. But whether it's the memories choking him up, or if it's Kyle *still* being the truest person Jason's ever encountered, he can't be sure.

Behind him, Kyle is still talking. He's saying something about if it'll dredge up too much emotion, surely Nick or Matt would step in as best man this time around. Everyone would get it.

"It's your call, Barlow. Think about it. And hey, no hard feelings either way. You just let me know." With that, Kyle Bradford gives him a small salute, jangles his key ring and heads out the door.

It doesn't take Jason long—just a second or two.

"Hey, hey! *Wait*," he calls just as Kyle's closing the slider behind him. Kyle stops though, and looks inside to Jason—who's turning in his seat and giving a thumbs-up. "I'm in, Kyle. Once a best man, always a best man."

In the minutes after Kyle leaves for The Dockside, Jason turns the pages of the wedding album again. Sitting alone in the quiet kitchen, he can't stop himself, actually. Very few photographs were taken during that time after the motorcycle accident, and seeing these is like seeing someone he forgot about over the years.

But it *is* him, *and* his life—broken as it was.

So he looks a little longer at Kyle's old wedding images.

Looks at the receiving line where bridesmaids and their tuxedoed groomsmen stand in the sunshine outside the church.

At Kyle and Lauren's first dance later, the two of them clinging close beneath a solo spotlight in the darkened room.

At the guests being served dinner during the reception, glass hurricane lantern centerpieces glimmering on each round table draped in white linens.

But mostly, he looks for photographs where his father might appear, even in the background.

As Jason browses, no one else in the house has gotten up yet. The kitchen is still; the morning quiet. It's a morning oddly similar to the September morning of Kyle's wedding ten years ago. Jason remembers sitting in this very room with his father early that day, having coffee together. Not much has changed in this kitchen since then—not the appliances, the table and chairs, the countertops—so it's easy to picture the memory. Waiting to head out to Kyle's wedding, Jason and his father talked little. A phrase here and there. A question, a brief answer. There was only the clink of coffee cups being set on the table, and their sparse, low voices.

He closes the photo album now and sets it on the kitchen counter. Instead of getting ready for work, though, Jason opens the slider and takes his coffee cup out to the stone bench on the bluff.

His father's bench. A bench he made after the war so he'd have his own private place to sit with his thoughts.

All these years later, it's Jason who sits there now. Sits facing the same sea his father did. Sits taking in the vast view of blue, with an orange sun breaking the misty horizon—where a few seagulls swoop low over the salty Sound. Sits imagining his father's eyes taking in the very same, unchanged sight.

Sits missing the man, for all he's worth. So much so that Jason's not sure what's worse: that darn lump in his throat, or the ache in his heart.

Because Kyle's photographs revealed something to Jason that he never really saw before.

Not until today.

For all his father's war stories from Vietnam, for all the life lessons those stories imparted on Jason and his brother, today's might be the strongest. It's kind of incredible that his father is still telling war stories—even after he's gone.

Because what Jason just saw in those photographs spoke of the kind of soldier his father truly was.

Oh, yes. It was there, written all over his father's face as he hovered behind his broken-down son at Kyle's wedding.

That image said it all to Jason, today. Said what type of soldier his father was in 'Nam.

His father's close presence that wedding day must've been the same as when a comrade, or a friend, or some poor guy in his unit came out of a war battle bloodied or beaten down. Some parched, dying man, whose head his father would lift to give a sip of water from a tin cup.

Or someone whose arm his father would sling over his shoulder as he hauled him out of the jungle to a medevac chopper.

Or some wounded and immobile guy whose lips his father might hold a lit cigarette to, giving the soldier another drag or two—both men tired and dirty and hanging on.

His father *never* backed away, looked away, walked away. Not from a soldier. Not from his son.

Jason knows it now. Without a doubt.

Because in those pictures in Kyle's photo album, Jason *was* that beaten-down soldier that his father wouldn't ever let fall.

twenty-one

THAT AFTERNOON, JASON CAN SEE that Mitch Fenwick is leery at the sight of a cameraman following Jason up the deck stairs. Okay, so getting Mitch to sign on for the renovation was one thing; getting him smoothly through the project might be another. Lesson learned? Don't allow for any surprises with the Fenwicks.

"I thought this was more a walk-through," Mitch says once Jason's on the deck. "To give *you* a feel for the original structure."

"It absolutely is. But your reno is also a kind of documentary. So we need to *document* your cottage beforehand, to give viewers a visual before-and-after. No way to do that without filming now."

Mitch looks from Jason to the cameraman, then turns when Carol pushes open the slider, gritty in its tracks. "Hey, Mr. Barlow," she says, fiddling with a thin black choker on her neck.

"Carol." Jason steps closer. "I was just explaining to your father that we need to get some footage of your cottage in its *before* condition, as part of the show. Inside and out."

"Oh, man. Already?"

Jason simply nods, with a slight motion to his cameraman.

"Dad?" Carol crosses her arms and comes up beside her father.

"Just feels a little awkward being on camera," Mitch admits. "Figured *Jason* would lead the tour and handle this part."

"But Dad, don't you remember?" Carol asks. "The personal angle is what draws the viewer in. And—like it or not, ready or not—that personal angle would be you and me."

"Yeah, I know. Just thought I'd be watching from the sidelines while Jason did his thing. Wasn't really expecting I'd be filmed much."

"Totally get that, Mitch. But as I'd mentioned in our previous talks," Jason explains, "the show is unscripted, to keep it real. And the more things roll here, the easier it'll get. You'll see."

Mitch lifts off his safari hat, tosses it on the deck table and nods at Jason. "One thing."

"Sure, what's that?" Jason asks.

"Any advice?" Mitch motions to the camera. "Feeling a little stage fright all of a sudden."

"No problem. Do some stretching, and shake out any knots," Jason suggests. "It helps. Other than that, be yourself and talk to me like you always do. About anything. The cottage, your family living in it. Pretend the camera's not even there."

"Easier said than done." But Mitch tries, stretching his arms straight in front of him, then to the side.

Jason squints at him while mulling over something. What the hell, it can't hurt. "Listen. My wife's aunt, Elsa DeLuca, just went through this whole shebang with her beach inn. It was our pilot episode. From nuts to bolts, start to finish, she was a real trooper throughout her renovation." Jason pats down his pockets. "Do you have a pen and paper? I'll give you her number so you can talk to her. It'll be worth your time. Because believe me, she'll share all the lowdown on the process, and then some."

Meanwhile, Carol's pulled her cell phone from her pocket.

CASTAWAY COTTAGE

"Elsa DeLuca," she says while typing. "What's the number? I'll put her on my phone and Dad can call her later."

Jason obliges, and thankfully, even that seems to have helped Mitch. He tags along on the tour, and though he lets Carol do much of the talking, he tosses in a tidbit every now and then.

They leave the deck and walk around the cottage perimeter first, noting how the building's multi-squared shape reduces wind pressure on the structure. From the sand, the camera crew also films the view of the nearby rocky ledge, where a few boys stand with their crabbing lines dropped into tidal pools. The camera pans to the beach, too. Beneath the midday sun, striped and colorful umbrellas line the shore, and vacationers wade leisurely into the cool water. As Jason and the crew round the Fenwicks' stilted cottage and climb the stairs to the deck again, Carol points out the hurricane shutters used by her grandparents decades ago, and still used as recently as during Super Storm Sandy.

But it's once they're filming indoors that Mitch mentions a phenomenon attributed to the many windows, as well as to the cottage's high elevation. "Because the structure is raised on stilts," he begins, "from inside, the elevated sightline takes in only the expanse of water. So you get that sense of being high up, like on a ship."

Carol walks to a large, double sliding window. Beyond it, there is only blue, as far as the eye can see. Jason steps aside so that the cameraman can capture this boating sensation.

"My mother used to tell me that on some days, she got slightly seasick." Carol sets her hand on the windowsill, as though steadying herself on a ship. "The motion of the water through the windows made her feel as though she were on a swaying boat. It's happened to me, too. And if I didn't hear my mother say it, I'd wonder if I'm going crazy. I mean, how can you get seasick *in* a cottage?"

Perfect, Jason thinks. Perfect, and fascinating. He'd had some doubts if Carol would come through for him. Especially with the antagonistic attitude she unleashed at the get-go, when they'd awkwardly met on her deck the night of Aria's christening. But she knows when to dial that brashness down for the benefit of the camera, *and* for this beach house—which apparently means more to her than she'd first let on.

Once the filming's done, Jason thanks Mitch and Carol for being good sports and opening up. As he waits on the deck for the film crew to pack their gear, he turns to Mitch again. "Seriously, you give Elsa a call. I'll let her know you'll be in touch. I'm sure she'd be down with talking to you guys about her experience with the show."

"Absolutely," Mitch says. "Nothing like hearing stories straight from the trenches."

"Okay, Jason," the cameraman calls from behind him. "That's a wrap for today. Ready to go?"

"Wait!" Carol interrupts.

When he turns back, Jason sees Carol giving her father a questioning look, to which he slightly nods.

Carol steps closer. "If you have a few minutes, Jason. *Privately*," she adds with an apologetic smile.

"Right now?" Jason checks his watch.

Carol nods. "Before you leave, my dad has something he wants to give you."

The cameraman comes up behind Jason and clasps his shoulder. "I'm good, man," he says. "I'll get this back to the studio and see what we've got to work with." He points to a plane flying low over the blue water. Behind the plane, a wavering sky-ad banner advertises a local seafood joint's clam-roll special. "Might stop there on my way for a snack."

CASTAWAY COTTAGE

"Excellent. Should be great chow. I'll check in with you later, guy." Jason waves him off, then gets back to the Fenwicks. "Mitch? What's up?"

"Sit," Mitch says, nodding to the patio table.

Okay, so there's something about his tone that Jason doesn't question. He sits, looks at Mitch and turns up his hands.

Just then, Carol hurries over and cranks open the patio umbrella against the bright afternoon sun. "The thing is, we found something when we went through some stuff here," she says while snapping the umbrella in place. "You know, to get ready for all this filming. And, well, this might hold a lot of meaning for you."

She sits across from Jason and looks up at her father, who is still standing. So Jason looks, too. When he does, Mitch gives him an envelope.

"What is it?" Jason asks as he flips the envelope over in his hands.

Mitch sits then. He sets his arms on the table and looks from the envelope to Jason. "It's a letter," he explains. "A letter from your brother, Neil."

twenty-two

OKAY, SO IF KYLE KNOWS the whereabouts of the Barlows' cooking utensils better than Maris does, he can figure not too much cooking happens in this antiquated kitchen.

"Wait till Jason sees this," Maris says from where she stands at the stove. Her hair is in a low ponytail and she wears an apron tied around her waist. With a fork, she lifts the edge of her seasoned and flour-dredged cube steaks.

"Fry them another minute," Kyle says just as his cell phone dings. He pulls it from *his* apron pocket and reads the text message from Lauren. *Back to school shopping early b/c of vow renewal. Got two backpacks.* "Sweet," he whispers as he types the word back to her.

"You should give cooking lessons, Kyle," Maris is saying. "You make it so easy, people would line up for this!"

"That's not a bad idea. Adult Ed at the high school has classes like that. I'd call mine, let's see ... Dockside Delights, favorite meals direct from the diner."

"I always get overwhelmed with recipes, and never know where to begin."

Kyle walks to the stove and checks the steaks, then motions for her to set them on a platter. "Always go step by step, Maris.

And keep it simple." He watches how hesitant she is even with moving the breaded cube steaks. "If a recipe has a ton of ingredients, skip it."

"Okay," Maris nods, as though struggling to take this all in. She also flips a second plate on top of the cooked steaks to keep them warm.

Meanwhile, Kyle's poured most of the skillet's grease into a bowl. "Let's get things ready for the gravy." He shows her how to whisk flour into the pan's remaining grease, saying it needs to be golden brown.

"Hmm." Maris whisks the flour mixture. "It's a little lumpy."

So Kyle takes a look, then tells her to add more grease from the bowl. And as she then adds milk, salt and pepper, more milk, and *whisks, whisks, whisks,* they do what Kyle loves about cooking.

They talk.

"I really appreciate this, Kyle," Maris says over her shoulder. "When I had my denim career, there was no time to cook in the kitchen. So when I quit last year to dabble in other things, I'd hoped cooking would be one of them." She lightly laughs then. "I'm sure Jason hoped so, too."

Leaning against the counter, Kyle's keeping an eye on her gravy while jotting down recipe steps. "This chicken-fried steak is a nice hearty recipe. It'll keep your husband happy. I feed him this in the winter when we start up Friday night card games, and he loves it."

Adding a dash more pepper to her gravy, then whisking again, Maris asks about Kyle's vow renewal. "Does Lauren have a dress yet?"

"She's looking around for something that needs no tailoring. No time for that."

"I got my gown at Wedding Wishes, back in Addison. Celia's

friend Amy actually owns it. Maybe Lauren could try there?"

"I'll tell her, thanks." Kyle forks a steaming green bean from a pot on the back burner.

"And what are *you* wearing?" Maris asks. "You and the guys?"

While eating one bean, he snags another and lets it cool on his fork. "I want to keep it casual. I'm no fool, Maris, and know damn well that a lot of emotions are tied up in this ten-year anniversary. Especially for your husband. He lost his brother *and* his leg that year, too. Which is why I asked Jason about being my best man again early this morning, before I went in to work."

"He's okay with it?" Maris asks while tipping the gravy pan his way.

"Seems to be." Kyle leans over to check her gravy-cooking. "Looks good, let it simmer now."

"Oh! And I have an idea for your outfits," Maris says when she turns to the mashed potato pot and gives those a whisk. "How about a formal suit for the guys, but lose the jacket? You know, just wear vests over a crisp-white shirt and tie. The vest keeps the look formal, while casual, without the jacket."

Kyle's moved to the sink, where he fills the dishpan with hot, soapy water. "You know something? I'm liking the sound of that style."

"Then," Maris says while peeking at her gravy again, "to really have fun, how about leather flip-flops for the guys? It's a *beach* shindig, after all."

"Totally rad idea. Really appreciate the advice." Kyle begins soaping off their prep bowls and dishes. "And here's some more *cooking* advice, while we're at it. Always clean as you go. Clean everything!"

When he looks over his shoulder at the table covered with potato-peel scraps and snapped-off green bean tips, Maris does, too. As if on cue, she brings the soiled bowls and spoons to the sink where he's washing.

"Don't ever cook in a mess," Kyle says. "It'll result in a meal that doesn't impress."

Something's different. As Jason walks to the back slider from his SUV, he senses it, but can't tell what it is. Not until he steps onto the deck and catches the aroma of some amazing dinner cooking—a rarity in his house. He opens the slider and walks in to see Kyle standing in an apron at the stove.

"Hi, honey. I'm *home*," Jason calls out, dropping his duffel on the counter.

Kyle looks back at him while scooping beans onto a platter. "Hi, sugar," he says in a high-pitched voice. "Want a taste?" He holds up a slotted serving spoon.

Jason can't resist, and so walks over as Kyle spears a few beans on a fork. Jason takes the fork and devours the sample in one mouthful. "Damn, Kyle," he manages around the food. "Never thought I'd say this, but I think I'll really miss you when you're gone."

"You like?" Kyle asks as he cups his hand beneath the fork and waits for another response.

"Amazing." Jason reaches over and strokes Kyle's face. "You're the best, toots."

"Eh." Kyle swats Jason's butt with a dishtowel before turning back to his bean-ladling. "Extend any compliments to your wife. She cooked all this. Maris definitely has it in her to whip up a lil' home cookin'."

Some things you have to see to believe, so Jason leans into the dining room where Maris is setting the table. He raises an eyebrow at her. "Going to hold you to it, darling."

"Yes, Jason." She gives a little finger-wave while setting down forks and knives. "I'm *full* of surprises."

Okay, so some things you might have to see to believe ... but some things you can't resist. Like now, he can't resist giving his aproned wife a kiss, whispering in her ear, "I've got a surprise for you, too."

"What is it?"

"Something to show you." He hitches his head back toward the kitchen, where Lauren and her kids are coming in and swarming Kyle at the stove. "But later." After giving her another kiss, he returns to the kitchen chock-full of talk and dog-patting and hand-washing. While unpacking his work duffel and rinsing his coffee thermos, Jason thinks maybe he was too hard on the Bradfords staying here, after all. It hasn't been a *bad* week. As he walks past Kyle at the stove, he slaps his shoulder. There's a reason Kyle was his best man, and it shines through.

And these dining room dinners? Heck, each one feels like a holiday feast. After Kyle and Maris set down platters of chicken-fried steak, and mashed potatoes, and gravy, the festivities begin. Hailey swings her legs in a chair as Lauren fills her daughter's plate.

"How'd filming go, bro?" Kyle asks when he unties his apron and takes a seat.

Jason turns on the black lantern-chandelier over the painted farm table, then sits across from Kyle. "Not bad. A little tough on Carol and Mitch, this first day on camera. But they'll get used to it." Jason sets two steaks on his dish. "TV crew will be *here* tomorrow to do some filming out in the barn studio."

"Hey, speaking of tomorrow," Kyle says as he lifts a forkful of mashed potatoes. "Good news. Got the all-clear from your mold-remediation team. New drywall's up, furniture's been thoroughly cleaned. We can go back home tomorrow afternoon."

Jason high-fives Kyle across the table. "So I heard. My guy sent me a text. Not one spore was to be found after the cleanup. His crew went above and beyond removing that mold, so you can breathe easy now. Literally."

"I am *so* relieved!" Lauren says as she cuts into her steak.

"I hope you're feeling better about your house now?" Maris asks.

"Definitely." Lauren digs into her gravy-covered piece of meat.

"I sometimes see mold at places here, from all that sea damp," Jason assures them. "And I guess your previous owner let a big plumbing leak go, too. So if you ever have any plumbing issues, you'll want to take care of it right away."

"Will do." Kyle swigs from his glass of water. "I'm also taking a pass on fishing night tomorrow, to get the fam settled back in."

Just then, Evan asks his father to scoop him more potatoes. And Maris dashes salt on her beans; and Hailey needs her meat cut; and Jason, well, he finally gets something. He *gets* Elsa's taste-testing gauge of how quiet the room goes while her guests chow down.

Because his own dining room goes quiet, too, as buttered flaky biscuits are dragged across gravy-spattered dishes, and potatoes are swirled in with beans, and forks and knives clink.

"Dad," Evan whispers when he's done eating. "It's movie night on the beach. Can we go?"

"You bet," Kyle says.

"I want popcorn!" Hailey adds.

"For you, princess? Anything." Kyle gives her a wink as he says it.

"That's good," Lauren tells Kyle. "You take the kids to the movie and I'll start packing things up here."

※

It isn't until after the kids are sent in the other room to watch TV for a while that the talk returns to the Fenwick job Jason's taken on.

"Too bad you'll miss fishing tomorrow, Kyle," Jason says as Maris pours wine for the four of them. "Nick's taking us out in his boat to fish on the water. Cliff, too."

Kyle laces his hands around his wine goblet. "Let me know what's biting."

"We're dropping anchor near Little Beach, right where Carol's grandfather went missing over fifty years ago now." Jason sips his wine. "Man, what a story," he says.

"What?" Lauren looks from Jason to Kyle. "What story?"

So as often happens with folklore, the story is told once again. This time, as they pick at remnants of their chicken-fried steak and mashed potatoes, Gordon's tale is shared, and the hurricane's force is described. It's over their second glass of wine that poor Sailor's mother comes to life again as Jason tells how she desperately went to the Fenwicks' place looking for her son.

"Little Sailor was found, safe and sound, but at a *different* cottage. *And* ... it was too late. Gordon had already gone out in his rowboat for the boy," Jason explains. "The sad twist is that Carol's family never saw Gordon, or that wooden rowboat, ever again. Not a trace of them."

"They must've looked everywhere," Kyle muses.

"Carol told me the search and rescue soon changed to a search and recovery," Jason goes on. "But even that failed. They could find no sign of Gordon *or* the boat, its paddles, a life jacket. It all must've washed out to sea."

"Jason." Lauren sets down her fork and looks right at him. "Stop right there. I've been thinking—and this could be a complete coincidence, guys—but years ago, when I was about sixteen, I'd sometimes hike up to Little Beach alone. One time, it was the day I painted my very first driftwood painting—so I've never forgotten it."

"Okay ..." Jason says, waiting to hear more.

"The thing is," Lauren continues as she leans her arms on the table, "the painting was of a beached *rowboat* I saw there. It was around the bend and set way, *way* back in the dune grasses. And really? When I think about it? The only thing that could've planted that boat there is some big storm surge."

"Really." Jason tips his head. "Do you remember where, *exactly?*"

"Sort of." Lauren hesitates. "At the very least, Eva's still got that painting, sitting on her desk. Want to go see it?"

Jason wastes no time and is already wiping his face with his napkin. "When?" he asks, pushing back his chair.

"Go!" Maris tells them. "You two go now! I'll text Eva that you're coming, and will clean up here."

"Kyle?" Lauren asks, standing and pushing in her chair. "You'll get the kids to the movies? Bring the blankets, and a chair for yourself?"

"I'm on it." With a grand sweep of his hands, he waves them out. "Take off, you two."

───⁓───

Within minutes, the Fenwicks' mythic story comes fully to life—all in the palm of Jason Barlow's hand.

Standing on Eva's front porch, he holds the piece of painted driftwood that Lauren had once given to Eva. The long-ago light touch of Lauren's paintbrush lets the natural grain of the driftwood show through the colors she painted.

Seeing that wood grain now, fifty years after Gordon's rowboat disappeared, makes the story all the more real. Gordon's fate all the more sad.

The lone boat lays abandoned in sea-grass among small rocks. The hull's aged wood shows through its white paint and brick-red bottom. Lauren's paint dabs of green and yellow and brown fill in blades of sea-grasses and stones that apparently moored the lost boat.

Looking at the driftwood painting, can't Jason just see a young Gordon fiercely paddling this vessel through the storm waves? Jason can almost hear the oars creaking against the oarlocks; hear the waves splashing over the hull; feel the salty sea spray drenching Gordon's face, his hair, as he rounded the stony point in this wooden boat, searching for little lost Sailor.

twenty-three

STANDING IN HIS BARN STUDIO, Jason pulls a worn leather journal off the bookshelf. He's got most of Neil's old journals and scrapbooks memorized. "This thick brown leather one?" he explains as a cameraman moves closer. "Waves. The olive canvas scrapbook? Vintage cottages. The black leather one tied shut with a string of rawhide? The Connecticut coast. And the list goes on." As he pulls each from the shelf, it amazes Jason how his brother's legacy is a part of his TV show. "Some journals still have a salty grit to them from their time left in an old fishing shack," Jason continues. "And pages of others hold onto grains of beach sand."

Slowly, Jason flips through a few sandy pages. "Though Neil's gone now, something of my brother—some thought or idea or design detail—gets pulled from these pages and makes it into every renovation I complete." Bookmarking a journal page with an old seagull feather, Jason walks across the studio's rough-hewn wood floors toward his drafting table. The camera pans the space as he crosses the room. "We've got a jam-packed first season of *Castaway Cottage*, but surprisingly it all begins right here, with my brother's archives."

When Jason settles on the stool at his drafting table, he hears the jangle of Maddy's collar as she scrambles up the stairs to Maris' loft. The dog lies on the floor above him, keeping her muzzle resting just beneath the railing. Jason hitches his head toward her lookout spot. "My assistant will lay on the guilt when it's time for a walking break on the beach."

With his brother's journal open before him now, Jason adjusts his swing lamp and overlays a blank sheet of tracing paper over a rough sketch of the first two floors of the Fenwick place. Recent photographs of the cottage are also clipped to the top of his drawing board.

"It would be easy to scan these photos into my computer and engage my design software to rework potential drawings. But I prefer starting a project the old-school way—by sketching. Sketching keeps me in *physical* touch with the emerging design."

When the camera swings around to film from the side, Jason explains his task beginning the Fenwick renovation. "The structure's parameters still keep the cottage's reworked third story very small—less than fifty percent of the total area of the floor beneath it. Which forces me to get creative with the space."

At the drawing board, his pencil moves in lines and angles across the tracing paper to work out a sketched concept. With a glance at Neil's detailed lighthouse drawing in the open journal, Jason does it. Borrowing from his brother's sketch, Jason's own hand completes the top half-floor of the Fenwick cottage.

"In my proposed renovation, that third-floor room's walls will be comprised mostly of long windows—to mimic the lantern room of a lighthouse." While sketching the multipaned windows now, his pencil delineates the frames mimicking the look of astragals around a lighthouse's actual storm panes. When the sketch is complete, he sits back as the camera comes in close to capture the image. "A large lantern hanging in there will bring that lighthouse feel to the space," he says. "And tune in next time to find out *why* this cottage is the beacon of the beach."

"Okay, that's a wrap for today," Trent says then from where he stands at the barn studio's double slider.

Jason drops his pencil on the sketch, takes a deep breath and rolls away from the drafting table. Spinning on the stool, he looks over at his producer. "A wrap for you, but not for me." He holds up the tracing-paper sketch. "I have to finish *designing* this now. Which will take a heck of a lot longer than five minutes of footage." He sets down his sketch and shuts off the swing lamp. "Oh, and I also have a new lead for something we *might* be able to bring to the show." But he doesn't mention that he and Lauren are hiking to Little Beach Saturday on the off chance they can locate that old rowboat she'd painted on driftwood. If it *is* Gordon's, Jason will have struck pay dirt. "I'll tell you more if it pans out," he only adds.

"I'll be waiting," Trent says. "But for today, we got really solid material to incorporate into an early episode. Once it's edited in, we might need some voiceover work, explaining your studio, what you're doing here. The drafting process, your tools."

"Got it."

"You know the gig, Barlow. And keep in mind, too, we need to film an intro for the show. One that will open all the *Castaway Cottage* episodes. It has to include a little about who *you* are, what you do. It'll be brief, but pack a punch. I'd like to film soon so it'll be a summer shot—all blue skies and white sands—which always sells it to the viewers." Trent walks over to the cameraman and gives him a hand carrying the equipment. "Everyone wants the beach," Trent says over his shoulder.

Jason opens up the doors for them, shakes their hands as they carry their filming gear out to a CT-TV van, then waves them off. Once back at his drafting table, he hears Maris outside chatting with Trent. While waiting for her, he turns on his cell phone to a series of dings as emails and voicemails come rolling in—which is precisely why the phone was off during taping.

He scrolls through the messages now: a voicemail from the owner of Beach Box with a question; another voicemail with a new project inquiry; an email from his contractor at the Sea Spray job; and the zoning office seeking a clarification on the Fenwick project.

But they can all wait when Maris walks in, which gets Madison rushing down the stairs. Her paws dance around Maris, her tail wags as the German shepherd follows her over to Jason's drafting table.

"How'd it go?" Maris asks.

"Good. Really good." Jason wheels back on his stool. "Especially how all this," he says with a grand sweep of his hand, "all Neil's journals and influence, are actually incorporated into the show."

She gives his shoulder a squeeze, then brushes through his sketches. "You must be so happy. Because your brother would've loved seeing where you've taken the business."

"I miss him on days like today."

"I'll bet." She bends and gives him a hug while he still sits. "What a crazy day it's been, no? Bradfords packing and leaving. Then your filming."

"Definitely," Jason says as he files away his initial sketches.

"While you were filming here, I actually set up sand chairs and the umbrella on the beach. Want to go? Get an ice cream off the truck and relax for an hour?" She hitches her head toward the door. "Unwind before your fishing tonight?"

"Sounds perfect, sweetheart." Jason opens the slider and motions for her to go through. Of course, Maddy follows at their heels. "Because I've been waiting for a few minutes alone with you. There's something really important you have to see."

twenty-four

J ASON HASN'T DONE THIS IN a long time. Too long—if he had to say so—since he's sat beside Maris beneath an umbrella on the beach. But he really needs this quiet time with his wife. What he has to show her is *that* important.

Long Island Sound's a little choppy as the tide comes in and the waves break close by. Their splashing sound is rhythmic, and familiar, and it does get him to finally unwind.

Well, either the waves get him to relax, or it's the ice-cream bar he holds. Hasn't done that in a while, either—sit back in a sand chair, with his *only* immediate plan being to enjoy an ice cream. Looking down the length of the beach, he's apparently not the only one with this plan. The view is mobbed with families, couples, retirees—everybody with somebody, nobody alone. Actually, it seems all of Stony Point is on the beach, or standing knee-deep in the water, on this warm Friday afternoon.

"I can't *wait* to hear this," Maris says as she finishes her strawberry-crunch bar in the shade of their umbrella. "What on earth do you have for me?"

"What I have," Jason says as she stands to toss their ice-cream wrappings in the trash can, "is the key to unlocking Neil's manuscript ending."

Maris wastes no time grabbing off her straw cowboy hat and swatting him with it. "Don't tease me!"

"No joke," he calls after her as she trots across the hot sand to the trash. When she returns a minute later, he picks right up talking. "Mitch and Carol gave this to me yesterday. They found it while cleaning up their cottage before the filming began." He pulls an envelope out of Maris' tote, where he'd secretly slipped it earlier. Running his hand along the envelope, then turning it over, Jason explains. "Mitch received this ten years ago, but forgot all about it. His wife had since died. Not to mention so much time passed since Neil had been at the cottage."

"So you're saying this is something of Neil's?"

"It is. I mentioned it to you yesterday, and was waiting for the right time to show you."

"But what is it?" Maris asks when he gives her the envelope.

"A letter from Neil to the Fenwicks. A thank-you note, actually, for letting him tour their cottage. And to show how much he appreciated that they talked to him."

Maris opens the envelope and unfolds the paper inside it. Jason watches as her eyes drop to that familiar cursive she's grown so accustomed to seeing while working on Neil's manuscript. Her words come softly when she begins reading the letter, but suddenly she stops. When she looks over at Jason, her eyes are filled with tears.

"Oh, Jason," she whispers. "When I read these lines he wrote, it's like he never even died ... and he's right here." She holds out the letter. "Will you read it to me? Please?"

Jason nods and takes the letter. After a moment when he glances out at Long Island Sound before him, he begins.

Joanne Demaio

~

Dear Mitch and Kate,

Opening your home to me as I write my novel is a deeply personal and gracious gesture. It means more than you can ever know. So I felt it important for you to know something now. To know the part your very cottage will play in my story. The best way to tell you is to ask you a question ...

Have you ever walked along the high tide line? Within this tangle of seaweed running the length of the beach lie seashells, stones, driftwood, and various gifts from the sea. The driftline, which is also the title of the novel I'm working on, invites scrutiny.

Maris closes her eyes then. Doing so makes this chance discovery all the more intimate. Because hearing only the voice reading beside her—with gentle waves lapping at her feet and a salty breeze touching her face—that voice could just as well be Neil's as Jason's.

A beach's driftline parallels the underlying theme of my story. Ten years later, a small group of friends who spent their childhood summers at the same beach are reunited. Gathering in a weather-beaten cottage, they are each drawn back to the emotional harbor of their cherished Stony Point, seeking shelter from life's seas.

At the same time this handful of thirty-somethings grasps for stability, and roots from which to flourish, a hurricane barrels up the Connecticut coast. Its havoc leaves them stranded in that lone cottage on the beach—and leaves their journey fraught with tears, laughter, pain, wisdom and growth. Their journey is the DRIFTLINE, *and their tears, laughter, wisdom and pain are the seashells, stones and driftwood that make up the chapters.*

Now, Maris opens her eyes. She wraps her arms around her bent legs and looks out at Long Island Sound. With Jason reading the words, Neil's story comes to life just like it did a decade ago to Mitch and Kate. She can picture Neil sitting in his tiny shingled shack, his hand pressed to this very paper to pen the words capturing his saga of friendship, and of the sea. When she looks down the beach toward that lone cottage on the sand, if she squints just right in the glare of the afternoon sunlight, can't she just see a shadow of a young man, free as the sea breeze, walking along the tideline? The wind billowing his loose denim shirt; his jeans cuffed as he wades into the water; his hand folded around a leather journal; his thick brown hair lifting in the breeze.

As the hurricane recedes, Jason continues beside her, *the DRIFTLINE wanders and meanders through their lives, holding, at first glance, seaweed. But upon closer look, it holds much more; for some a treasure ... if they look deep enough within themselves.*

A few silent moments pass, moments when Maris still sees that shadow meandering the beach, slipping behind one family, weaving around a sandcastle.

Until finally, a hand touches her arm.

"Jason," Maris says as she covers his hand with hers. "That is so beautiful. Neil explained this same concept to me years ago. I never forgot it, the way he told me about the driftline on Eva's wedding day."

"It must have really meant something to him," Jason says with a regretful shake of his head.

"And his title! *Driftline*, babe. *That's* the title. I never knew he had one. But of course it would be *Driftline*. The word embodies everything your brother was about—his curiosity, his searching, his love of the sea and coastline—all of it somehow entwined. And it's how he was to all of us, just completely wrapped up within our lives."

"Will this help you?" Jason asks.

Maris takes the letter from him. "With everything," she says while skimming it. "It gives me a framework to the story I didn't know was there before. And to think that if you never got this project with the Fenwicks, I'd never have this."

Jason stands up and drags a hand back through his overgrown hair. "Shit. Even now, everything's still connected," he says with a nod to the letter.

Maris stands, too. "Come on. Let's walk it. The driftline." She bends to cuff her faded jeans. "*Neil's* driftline."

They do, and damn if Maris doesn't catch glimpses of that vague shadow ahead, all while walking, while lifting a strand of seaweed to find a piece of sea glass beneath it. Waves lap along the beach, and a seagull caws as it swoops low. After hearing Neil's personal words, she can just imagine *him* on a day like this, taking the same late-afternoon walk along the water's edge.

As they move down the beach, Maris reaches for Jason's hand, linking their fingers, connected, and so utterly inspired by the special letter that quietly washed ashore in their lives.

twenty-five

"IT'S GOOD TO BE HOME." Kyle opens the old glass-paned door and steps onto the front porch. "Ah, back on the bay." He sits on a wicker chair and sips from a tall glass of ice water.

"It was really nice of Jason and Maris to let us stay with them," Lauren says while she switches on the twinkly lights around the porch windows. "But there's nothing like our own space. I don't even care that we have to do a little fixing up. Painting, redecorating."

"Me neither."

They're quiet then, as Lauren rocks on a porch swing and the night settles around them. Kyle shuffles through a handful of envelopes.

"Is that the mail? Anything interesting?" Lauren asks.

"A questionnaire."

"From the mold people? Because they did do a great job. Didn't leave a mess behind, either."

"No, it's from Elsa. A questionnaire about our vow renewal."

"Oh, she must've dropped it off." Lauren gets a pen and moves to the chair beside Kyle. "Let's answer some now."

Kyle takes the pen and shifts the paper so she can see, too.

"First question. Time of event?" He glances at Lauren, who is leaning her arm on his chair.

"Easy. Six o'clock. That'd be a perfect time, going right into the evening sunset."

"Décor?"

"Beach chic, just like Maris did at her wedding."

Kyle jots that down and reads the next question. "Attire? Oh, man, I've got this one. Maris gave me some great ideas. Formal suits for the guys, but with no jacket. Just a vest over the button-downs. Casual, but the vest punches it up."

"Nice," Lauren murmurs while stroking his arm. "I like that."

"What about you? You need a dress."

She grabs her cell phone from a small painted table. "Wow, I'm running out of time. This vow renewal is fast approaching." She begins typing on her phone. "Let me text the ladies," she says, whispering their names as she pulls them up. "*Maris, Eva, Celia, Elsa.*"

"Maris knows a place in Addison," Kyle says. "I guess Celia's friend owns it? A wedding shop?"

"Right." Lauren still types. "I remember Celia mentioning it."

"When will you go?"

"Tomorrow." Her phone dings with instant responses. "It looks like a good day for everyone. But it'll have to be after lunch," she vaguely says while typing again, "because I have plans in the morning."

"Doing what?"

"I'm going with Jason to Little Beach to look for that old rowboat."

"Too bad I have to work. But Saturdays are mobbed at the diner," Kyle says as he sets the questionnaire on that same painted table and takes a drink of his ice water. "I'd like to have seen this significant historic vessel."

"*If* we even find it. Believe me, it'll be so buried. Jason will probably need a crew to dredge it out. But first he wants to check if it's even still there at all."

"Be careful on that path through the woods. There's lots of brush with ticks. And the Connecticut shore *is* the birthplace of Lyme disease, transmitted *by* those very ticks."

"Kyle, aren't you overreacting?"

"What? No way. Don't need you coming down with fever and arthritic symptoms. I read that one of the best preventive measures is to cover up. So be sure to wear jeans and long sleeves."

"Will do, don't worry. At least Cliff had the sense to remove that dead tree blocking the path. It was such an eyesore, *and* a safety issue." Lauren finishes sending her text messages, then sets her phone aside. "Well, Kyle. It's our first night back home." Her voice drops to a whisper, then. "And since you skipped Friday night fishing with the guys …" She leans close and snuggles against him. "*And* since the kids are asleep …"

"Oh, no." Kyle glances down at her before picking up the wedding questionnaire again.

"Come on," Lauren purrs. "Let's go upstairs?"

"I mean it, Ell. No to your nuzzling."

"Hmm. I'm not so sure about this new Kyle I'm about to remarry." She draws a finger along his arm.

"The old Kyle's still around." He takes his questionnaire and water glass to the little sofa further down the porch. "You'll see him again on your wedding night," he explains. "And what a night it'll be. Our first time around at the altar got *so* messed up, and now we have this second chance to do everything *right*. A second chance, which is *molto speciale*, as Sal liked to say. Remember?"

"I *know* I can sway you to change your mind," Lauren says

when she crouches beside him and drags a finger along his *leg* this time.

All that does is get Kyle to instantly stand up and back away. After opening a couple more porch windows to cool himself off, he does something else, too. He hitches his thumb for Lauren to get away from the couch.

"Fine," she mutters while squeezing past him, her body suggestively grazing his in all the right places.

When Kyle settles on the couch again and folds his arms across his chest, Lauren doesn't quit. Yup, she looks back. *Longingly!*

Oh, Lauren and her wiles. After touching his frosty water glass to his warm face, he breathes in that sweet salt air lifting off the bay. *Anything* to distract him from what he's passing up with her.

"Okay, you win. But you definitely didn't *score*," she says while waving him off and heading inside. "Goodnight," she calls over her shoulder in a singsong voice, one intended to convey that she can handle this celibacy thing just fine, thank you. "And sleep tight out there, all by your lonesome!"

Kyle looks over toward the porch doorway, but doesn't move from his little couch. Instead he feels the lightest sea breeze drifting in through the open porch windows. The house is dark now, with only Lauren's twinkly lights casting a soft glow in the night. There's a sound, too, and he listens closely. It's surprising to hear the distant, gentle breaking waves out on the bay across the street. That sound carries to him on the still night.

Lapping, lapping at the sandy shore, over and over again.

⁓

In the darkness, Nick's little Boston Whaler putters along. It's a calm night, and the boat moves smoothly over the water. When they pass the big rock just behind the floating swim raft, Jason reaches over and lets his fingers drag through the black water. Up above, only a thin sliver of moon shines, leaving the night as dark as it is still.

"Drop anchor out at the end of the point," he tells Nick.

Nick lets up on the throttle. "Why there? You don't want to go out into deeper water?"

"No." Jason's sitting on the seat in the boat's bow. "I want a good look at both sides of the point—Little Beach side and Stony Point side. Want to see how a boat might get beached in either place."

Cliff looks on from a newly varnished wood seat in the stern. "That's easy enough to figure, Jason," he says while motioning out toward the rocky ledge at the end of the beach. "If a vessel washed up on the Stony Point side, it would land on the rocks there. Or else get beached up on the sand. Little Beach is more untamed, with lots of boulders. It would be hard for a boat of *any* kind to get past them to the beach."

"In a storm surge, it's possible, though," Jason counters as Nick steers and slows before rounding the point. "One *could* wash right through the spaces between some of those boulders."

"Why?" Nick asks when he kills the engine. His Whaler simply floats then, gently rising and falling on the rippling Sound. "Who beached a boat? Don't tell me it was you and your brother, back in the day." As Nick talks, he drops anchor so they don't drift, all while scoping out the rocky point.

"Shit, no," Jason tells them. "Neil was meticulous. Our boat was his pride and joy. As soon as he'd dock in the marina slip, he'd wipe down the interior, spray off the fiberglass hull and keep that boat shipshape, never mind beach it."

"Wait." Nick picks up his fishing pole and baits his hook. "You had a slip in the boat basin? Do you *still*? Because name your price and I'll buy it off you."

"Sorry, kid. I let go of that a long time ago. The only one with a boat slip now is Elsa, for that old Foley's rowboat of hers."

Cliff casts his line and it whistles out over the water. "So where *are* you docking this fine vessel, Nicholas?"

"On its trailer, on the side of my parents' driveway." Nick sets down his fishing rod and grabs a can of beer from a cooler on the floor. "It's looking like a junkyard there with my boat parked like that. It would be so much easier if I could drop it in the sweet little boat basin here." He hands Cliff the cold beer. "Boss, can't you bump me up on the waiting list?"

Cliff snaps open the can and takes a long drink. "Now you know that the rules are the rules. Got to wait your turn. What number are you on the list, anyway?"

"I don't know." Nick hands Jason a beer, too. "Something like twenty-three."

Jason lets out a low whistle as he sets down his can and opens a bag of chips.

"So whose boat beached, then?" Nick asks as he casts his line out beyond the rocky point.

"Someone from my latest reno job. The Fenwicks. Happened a long time ago, though."

"Really." Cliff sits stock-still waiting for a nibble on his line. "What happened?" he quietly asks.

This time, while being on the very water where Gordon tragically died, Jason tells the story again. As gentle waves slosh against the boat's hull, the heroic effort of a man in search of a lost boy comes to life. With barely a slice of moon in the sky tonight, Gordon must've felt the same sense of darkness when storm waves washed over his boat and took him to sea. Jason repeats everything to Cliff and Nick: from little Sailor being on the rocks, to Gordon and his wife waving him home as a hurricane hit, to the panicked pounding on their cottage door a half hour later when Sailor's mother could not find her son.

"This happened right there?" Nick asks, motioning to the Fenwick cottage on the beach. Lamplight spills from its windows. "In that cottage?"

"Sure did." Jason points out how the family stored an old rowboat beneath the stilted cottage. "Gordon and his brother got the boat into the water. This way, Gordon could just round the point to look for Sailor and come right back."

"Now let me get this straight. Gordon was *related* to the Fenwicks?" Nick asks.

"Yeah. Gordon's daughter, who was about eight or nine when Gordon died, was actually Carol Fenwick's *mother*. Kate, her name was. So Gordon would've been Carol's grandfather. It's probably why Gordon went after the boy, too. Because Sailor was a beach friend of his daughter's."

"And who was the little kid? You get a name?" Cliff asks while tugging on his limp fishing line.

"No name. Everyone just knew him as Sailor." Jason squints into the darkness, scoping out the far side of the rocky ledge. "A little boy around seven, who always wore a blue-and-white sailor's hat. He loved to crab on the rocks, *and* play with his Matchbox car collection. Guess he had one of those pop-up towns to go with it, too. You know the kind ... You open a plastic case and up pops stores and schools and a police station, houses and all winding neighborhood roads. A whole town. Word has it Sailor and the beach kids would set up on a big blanket on the sand and zip those cars on the play-roads in front of that cottage. Until after the hurricane, anyway, when Sailor's parents packed everything and hightailed it out of here, apparently devastated at the tragedy that happened on account of their son."

"Damn," Nick says. He talks while finding the ham and cheese sandwiches that Maris packed. After unwrapping one for himself, he presses the tinfoil flat on his seat and uses it as his plate. "That would really be something if you could find that little boy. Sailor. He was just being a kid, you know? Who could blame him, going out on the rocks and getting his tackle box out of the storm? We probably would've done the same thing. If you could get him on your show, it would really tug the viewers' heartstrings."

Cliff reels in his line and helps himself to a sandwich, too. "Can you do a search, Jason? It's been a long time, but maybe there are records?"

"CT-TV's research department did a preliminary look around. But there are no news reports with the boy's actual name, or his family's either. Maybe because Sailor was a minor—only a child at the time? Whatever the reason, the accounts just refer to Carol's grandfather trying to save a *neighbor's* young son."

"So if he was a neighbor, someone *must* know the family name," Nick insists.

"Unfortunately not. It was only the second summer Sailor's family was here, and they were *renting* a cottage. To make matters worse, the trail really goes cold when the next year, the owners of the cottage they rented? Up and sold it. They patched some storm damage and put it on the market. It's one of those cottages sitting farther back off the road, over on Champion. So with the change of hands and no rental records, the family's name was lost."

"Wow." Nick tips up his beer can to finish it off. "Sailor would tear everyone's heart out."

"He would," Jason agrees. "And the thing is? Mitch and Carol don't blame Sailor. Instead they've wondered what *became* of the boy. Carol even thought it would make Gordon proud to know if Sailor went on to live a good life."

"To know *something* good came out of the day, well, it would be nice," Cliff quietly adds.

Sitting in Nick's little Boston Whaler, Jason looks out at the rocky point. He feels the boat rise and fall with the sway of the sea, only imagining the violence of a *hurricane* sea.

"For now," Jason tells them, "all I've got is Lauren's tip about an abandoned rowboat off Little Beach. She saw it twenty years ago and painted it on a piece of driftwood. So could it be Gordon's? There might be something there, might not. I have a photograph of the original rowboat to compare it to. Me and Lauren are going there tomorrow. If we can match something on the photo to what might even be left of the old boat, it could give the Fenwick family some sort of closure."

"Those damn hurricanes," Cliff says. "They're so dangerous. You can't take any chances when they blow in. I mean, look what happened to that family! That's why I updated the hurricane protocol here in the Stony Point handbook. This is supposed to be a happy family vacation place."

"Still," Nick muses as he casts off again. His fishing line unfurls beneath the dark, nearly moonless sky, over the just-as-dark water. "It sure would be nice to hear Sailor's side of the story, all these years later. See how he turned out."

The passing beam of the Gull Island Lighthouse sweeps over the Sound, then returns it to darkness once more. It's so vast tonight, the dark sea and sky, leaving nothing in sight to get your bearings. Jason looks out at it all warily. Like happiness, he's learned to never fully trust the water.

Because that same dark water can take anyone out with it, all at the sea's whim.

twenty-six

As DARK AS THE NIGHT was the day before, Saturday morning is as light. The hot August sun pulses; the beach simmers. On their way to search for the long-lost boat, Jason wears a backpack filled with hand tools, a shovel, gloves and rags. Lauren has a tote with a snack and bottled waters. Small relief comes to them only when they get to the end of the beach. There, they pick up a shaded path in the patch of woods separating Stony Point's main beach from Little Beach. The dirt path winds through scrubby pines and old oak trees. But it's the flicker of sunshine breaking through pockets of deep shade that plays with Jason's view, and his memories. This overgrown path rutted with tree roots and wild brush hasn't changed much.

As a matter of fact, the day could be straight out of a summer from thirty years ago, when he and his brother were just young boys ...

Something about the woodsy path insulated them. All beach sounds behind them—motorboats, and families' laughter, and splashing races into the water—were gone. *Not muffled, but purely gone as Jason and his kid brother traversed the winding path. Now they heard only the rustle of gently blowing leaves, the whistle of birdsong, the buzz of cicadas and a lazy passing bee. They felt as far from the sea as you could be, and instead were traipsing the pretend jungles of 'Nam. He and Neil wore their camping vests, the pockets stuffed with jackknives and flashlights and small stones intended as grenades.*

Many times, their mission in the jungle was specific: to make shelter so they could pick off any Viet Cong unnoticed, and survive another day at war. Neil, wearing their father's tiger-striped boonie hat pulled low over his moppy hair, kept lookout with a pair of binoculars, while Jason held his rat-a-tat toy rifle at the ready.

"Snake!" Neil warned, stopping in his tracks and pointing to a low-hanging tree limb.

Jason rushed up beside him, took aim and pulled his gun's trigger. An imaginary spray of bullets fired off with the electronic whirring of his gun.

"It's a good spot, Jay," Neil whispered while glancing around for the enemy. "Right there." He nodded his head toward the broken tree limb leaning from the tree to the ground.

"Radio our location in to camp," Jason whispered back.

So Neil did; he walked off-trail, circled around the broken limb that would serve as their shelter's foundation, then pulled his walkie-talkie from a vest pocket. The unit squawked first before he left a muffled, coded message for their superiors.

That done, the work began. Off-trail, they scoured the forest floor for thin, fallen branches. Climbing atop mossy rocks and over massive tree roots, they filled their arms with sticks. These became the roof support propped against their fallen limb. Next they searched for jungle ferns. Traipsing through low valleys, the lush ground cover provided ample supply. Only the largest fern leaves would do as they laid them one at a time over their stick roof to conceal their shelter. If it was morning, often the green leaves were still covered with dewy drops of water.

One big, swaying leaf at a time, they silently got the job done. When they finished laying the leaves across their entire stick framework, their Vietnam lean-to was invisible to the naked eye. It blended seamlessly into the surrounding forest brush, and just in time. Footsteps approached, snapping twigs beneath each one. In a panic, Jason and Neil scooted beneath the fern leaves and hunkered down in their jungle shelter. They froze, peeking out through the dewy green fronds to watch sandaled feet pass them by, unaware of their presence.

Safe at last, Neil opened his canteen and Jason unwrapped combat rations—a sandwich, crackers and some candy. And that's where they remained for much of the day, hiding from the enemy. Beneath those ferns, ants became scorpions to be smashed; leaf caterpillars became leeches to be plucked off their skin.

When they finally received word on their walkie-talkie that it was time to move on, all evidence had to be destroyed. So from a safe distance, the two fatigued soldiers emptied the stone grenades from their pockets and pelted their shelter to oblivion—before running pell-mell down the path, tripping on dips, being slapped in the face by overhanging vines, all while swatting at hovering dragonflies. Out of breath, they soon rounded a sharp turn in the path that opened onto a vast and wild beach to the safety of their base camp, where their unit waited. And where they collapsed with relief on the silver mica-dotted sand.

―

"Look," Lauren says now when they round the last corner of the wooded path and turn onto Little Beach. She points out campfire remnants closer to the water. "Some things never change."

"Still partying up here." Leaving his childhood memory behind, Jason lightly kicks an empty can into the charred debris as they continue on across the sunny beach.

"I remember that day I came up here to paint, and I picked up sticks of driftwood as I walked the beach." While explaining, Lauren stops, turns and looks behind her, then ahead to the curve in the beach. "I'm trying to place where I finally set out my things." She walks further, stops again, then continues. "I'd hauled myself up onto a large boulder."

They keep walking, passing another boulder someone long-ago painted to look like a dinosaur's head, a sight since becoming a landmark here. The sun beats strong at this early morning hour, and sandpipers run along the shore, keeping pace with the two of them. Jason shields his eyes and scopes out the more remote terrain beyond the sandy beach.

"I think it was over there where I set up." Lauren stops and points left to a spot back among the rocks and not easy to get to. Then she pulls Eva's driftwood painting from her tote and tries to better gauge the angle she painted it from. "Is your leg okay?" she asks, looking back at Jason. "Can we walk more?"

"Absolutely. I put a protective sleeve on it to keep the sand off, so I'm good."

"But it's rough going. Very rocky."

"I'm fine, Lauren." Jason figures she might have seen him favor his prosthetic leg while hiking the trail. He catches up to her and talks more. "It's not the terrain bothering me. Sometimes my leg acts up a little, which it *has* been doing lately."

"Really. How so?"

"Nothing serious. It's just that I'm *aware* of it, which I shouldn't be. Usually happens when I'm stressed. Or tired."

"Makes sense," Lauren says as she pauses before maneuvering the rocky ground ahead. "Because you've got so much going on with the new show, no? Not to mention, it *is* the ten-year anniversary of ... Well, you know. Since Neil died." She reaches over and clasps Jason's hand. "Did you tell Maris your leg's been bothering you?"

He shakes his head. "I don't want to worry her right now as she's finishing up Neil's manuscript." When Lauren hands him a bottled water, he uncaps it and takes a long swallow. The water feels so cool going down beneath the hot sun, he quaffs half the bottle. "I actually gave Maris something that's helping her with the ending."

When he starts to tell Lauren about the letter from Mitch Fenwick, it doesn't escape him how she has to sit. How the emotion of a story about Neil from ten years ago—which happened right in the thick of Lauren's *affair* with Neil—takes hold of her. She rests on a large, flat boulder, her arms drawing up her knees, her eyes watching Jason.

"I guess Neil wanted to share what he was writing with the Fenwicks. Especially since they were generous enough to let him tour the cottage he set the story in. His letter summarizes the whole novel, and gives Maris a sense of direction for the ending."

"Oh, Jason." Lauren gives him a sad smile. "That's incredible."

"Definitely. It means a lot to have it," he tells her, before finishing his water and putting the bottle in his backpack.

"Okay." Lauren stands then, and glances past the nearby rocks again. "So, you ready to locate that boat?"

"Let's do this."

—

Lauren leads the way, pointing out a couple of areas where she thinks the boat might have washed up. The rocky landscape is difficult to cover, but there are also pockets of sandy beach dotted with wild dune grasses. They wander among the boulders, cross the sand, and look for any sign of that old rowboat among the green swaying grasses. Stones are overturned, clumps of tall grass pushed aside, sand brushed away.

When they find nothing, they backtrack through the sand and rocks to search again.

"Darn, I had such high hopes!" Lauren says while lifting her sunglasses to the top of her head. "I thought for sure that old boat would still be here."

"This part of the beach is really overgrown. And any storm surf could've washed up and taken the boat right back out to sea."

Turning to the west, Lauren rounds a bend where the ragged beach opens up. "Let's look more," she says over her shoulder. "Because if *I* feel the sadness of that little missing boat, I can only imagine the sadness that family felt about old Gordon."

"That's the kicker, though. He was a young guy when it happened. A young father, actually, just helping a neighbor find their son. Sailor."

"Sheesh, the story keeps getting sadder." Lauren trips in the sand, then regains her footing and keeps walking. "I was only sixteen that summer I was up here painting, but I remember climbing on a boulder beside smaller rocks, and lots of dune grass grew in the sand between them." She pauses and turns around to eye the spot where she'd tripped moments before. "Wait." Quickly backtracking, she digs her sneakered foot into the sand. "Hmm. Jason," she calls when he veers to the left. "*Wait!*"

Something about the urgent tone in her voice has him hurry over. "Did you find something?"

"Look! I think it's right here, the boat." Using her foot, she pushes sand away. "It *is*. It's completely covered now. But my foot hooked the top edge of it before, when I tripped."

"Holy smokes. Some storm just about buried it forever."

Jason pulls the small shovel from his backpack and digs sand away from the wooden hull. The rowboat is tipped to the side—and completely covered. Sparse blades of dune grass grow from the sand anchoring the boat in place. But Jason's able to reveal some of the wooden framework. It's graying and rotten in spots. But it's also surprisingly intact, from what little they can get at. It's as though the sand acted as a protective layer, preserving the rowboat as a sort of fossil.

Perspiring now, he looks over his shoulder to see Lauren standing beside him holding her driftwood painting. "Is this the same boat?" Jason asks while pressing his arm to his sweating forehead.

She nods. That's all, just nods as she drops to her knees. "I think so. Look," she says while holding her painting close to the exposed hull. "See? It was white ... with a brick-red bottom. And I can make out some white, beneath all this gray." She looks at Jason. "Could this *really* be Gordon's rowboat, too, after all these years?"

"Don't know." Jason bends to shovel away more of the sand, removing some from the boat's interior now. "It *could* be, but it's in really rough shape." He sets down the shovel and pulls out his cell phone to grab a few photographs. Which is precisely when he notices one small detail. "Well, I'll be goddamned." He points to the telltale, faded words painted on the stern of the boat.

Lauren, pressing back her hair, squints closer. "Oh my God. That's it!"

twenty-seven

A FEW HOURS LATER, LAUREN finds herself saying those very same words again—*That's it!* It happens while gown shopping at Wedding Wishes in the countryside town of Addison. Wearing a white satin robe, she's sitting on a padded bench in the dressing room. The storeowner, Amy, stepped out to the storage room for a dress she thought was custom-made for Lauren. And though Lauren can't see them on the other side of the dressing room curtain, Maris, Eva, Taylor, Elsa and Celia are working on Lauren's unfinished vow-renewal questionnaire.

But when they suddenly go quiet, Lauren knows Amy is returning with her top pick.

"No peeking, ladies," Amy warns them all on the other side of the pleated curtain.

"Just a little?" the women beg.

"Nope. Remember when you bought your dress here, Maris? We wouldn't let Eva see it until it was on you," Amy says. She brings the covered dress into the dressing room and swings the curtain closed. "Lauren gets the first look."

"Oh, I'm *so* excited." Lauren quickly stands to watch Amy unzip the white garment bag and remove the gown.

"Wait." Amy turns to her. "Close your eyes until I say so."

Lauren nods, then tightly closes her eyes. She hears Amy fussing with the hanger and the dress fabric. When Amy whispers *Okay*, Lauren looks. If ever there was a perfect moment in all this vow renewal planning, this is it.

Right now.

Her eyes drink in the two-piece, white lace wedding dress. The high-neck sleeveless top is cropped, with a scalloped hem that'll show a hint of her midriff. And the bottom is a fitted, ankle-length lace skirt with a small train. There's something so casual, and bohemian, and beachy to the dress that, yes, Lauren says those same two disbelieving words she said this morning upon finding Gordon's rowboat.

"*That's it!*" she whispers to Amy.

"I knew it." Amy gives her a quick hug. "And I think it's just your size."

While Amy unclips the long skirt from its hanger, Lauren unties her robe—but also listens to the women outside the dressing room digging into her questionnaire.

"Date?" Maris asks.

"Elsa," Lauren calls from behind the dressing room curtain. "At first I was thinking sometime at the end of the month. But … would you be able to pull this off next weekend?"

"Oh my gosh! In one *week*?" Elsa's voice asks in return. "Are you *sure*? Because we could do the end of the month, no problem."

"No," Lauren calls back while Amy helps her step into the most divine long skirt she's *ever* laid eyes on. "Kyle and I want this to be a simple summer party. And I don't want to overthink things, either. If the ceremony's next week, I'll just fly through the preparations and the day will be here, pronto."

"Well, how about if we have it next *month*?" Celia asks. "That'll give us lots of time to plan and decorate for the event."

"But we really don't want a big to-do," Lauren says when Amy holds aside the robe fabric and pulls up the skirt's zipper. "It's just an intimate affair with family and, well, basically with all of *you*." Lauren's hands touch the skirt's long, lacy front.

She can't mistake it then, when Elsa decides. Lauren can tell by the way Elsa rattles that questionnaire paper. "The Ocean Star Inn is *always* accommodating, so next weekend ... it is!" Elsa insists, right as Lauren removes her robe and hangs it on a wall hook so she can try on the dress' top. "And Celia? We're going to be busy, busy, busy!"

Amidst the hoots and cheers celebrating the date, Amy quietly helps Lauren into the lace midriff top.

"What time do you want to have the ceremony?" Eva calls out.

"Evening," Lauren says, turning to see her reflection in the wall mirror. The lace top is perfectly fitted to her every curve. "So the beach is cleared out. How about six o'clock, before the sun sets? I think I marked that on the form. Then we can have a sunset reception on the inn's grounds. It'll be so nice, right near the water," she says while her hands touch the top's lacy scalloped edge.

"And the lighting will make for lovely photographs, too," Elsa notes. "I'll have Cliff rope off the beach near the inn."

"Mom and I will decorate your golf cart, Lauren!" Taylor calls out. "We'll tie tin cans to it, and put a *Just Married ... Again* banner on it!"

"What about music?" Maris asks.

"Got that covered," Lauren tells them through the curtain as Amy straightens the top's hem. "We'll head to the inn and use the jukebox in the old Foley's back room. Dancing to spill over on the deck." Lauren looks at her reflection in the dressing room mirror and can just envision the night of her nuptials. "Might as well add some *new* memories to that old hangout room. And to do that, all we need is to play that funky old jukebox." With that, she gives a languorous spin in the dressing room. "Oh, I can't *wait*!"

Meanwhile, Amy moves to the curtain and sets her hand on the edge. "Ready to show the ladies?" she asks.

Still looking at her reflection, Lauren skims her hands along the skirt's delicate lace.

"Lauren?" Amy whispers.

"I'm feeling nervous," Lauren admits first, then nods. "But okay."

When Amy sweeps open the curtain, Lauren sees it all like a snapshot. First there is the sight of the women sitting on two velvet settees. Beyond, white lights twinkle around the bridal shop's display window. Gold chains and gemstones glimmer on a bracelet holder on the store's countertop. To the side, a cupcake dress with a full skirt of lace and tulle hangs on a black dress form.

But Lauren's teary smile comes from the sight of her friends. They all turn to her at the very same time, and with the same collective gasp as Lauren steps out.

Then the silent nods begin, with hands pressed to mouths, followed by instant tears, tears, tears.

Which is when Lauren knows. Yes, *this is it*.

Elsa jumps up first. "Oh, Lauren! How perfect for a night on the beach! I cannot wait to officiate for you and Kyle," she says into her embrace.

"And it fits beautifully," Eva tells her as she touches the lace skirt, lightly lifting the fabric. "What are you, anyway? A size *two*?"

"You look like a model," Taylor says. "Can I wear it next year to prom?"

Before Lauren can answer, Celia puts Aria in Maris' arms. It's obvious Celia is choked up, and Lauren gets it. She's sure Celia believed *she* would be the next Stony Point bride, wearing a wedding dress for her own beach wedding to Sal ... a wedding that was never to be. Celia walks over and hugs Lauren tightly. In a moment, Celia's words are murmured in her ear.

"You are absolutely *gorgeous*, Lauren. And I am so happy for you." As she says it, though, a tremble in her voice belies other emotions.

"I know, hon," Lauren whispers as she wipes a tear from her friend's face. "Shh."

Celia gives her the most gentle smile then, before turning to Maris and taking Aria in her arms again. When she does, Lauren looks in the three-way mirror, lightly lifts the long skirt, and gives another spin. When she stops, Amy is holding a pair of flat silver sandals and a satin headband.

But it's once she's dressed in the full ensemble that the good times really kick in—especially when Lauren announces that Celia will be her maid of honor. So the dress-hunting resumes. Still wearing her two-piece lace gown, Lauren browses the vintage bridal shop with the ladies and finally finds a stunning fitted silver dress for Celia. It'll coordinate just right with Lauren's.

And as though a bit of stardust dropped over these few hours in Wedding Wishes, the afternoon turns into simply this: the sweetest time.

Yes, these days before marrying Kyle *again* have been nothing *but* sweet ... starting from the moment she found her happiness jar on the beach when he proposed. Everything—from the small beach party celebrating her second engagement; to announcing it at the diner; to event planning; to, yes, even to tempting Kyle to break his vow of celibacy—it's all been sweet. She wouldn't trade a minute of it.

Second time, second chance.

While chatting, and laughing, and picking out last-minute touches from a basket of hair clips, and trying on bracelets, and choosing a sash for Celia, everyone around Lauren shares the love, too. The smiles and fussing and hugs don't stop.

The moment is so touching that it gives Lauren an idea. It's daring—that's for sure. More daring than anything she might have ever done before. But yes, as soon as she finds some free time later, she'll do it.

Secretly, but she'll do it.

Second time, second chance, she reminds herself.

twenty-eight

THERE'S NO DISTINGUISHING ONE DAY from the next—it's been that kind of summer. Every morning, the sun rises just as hot. Its rays pulse down the same. Shade provides little relief. The unwavering New England heat is especially noticeable on the boardwalk, in the direct path of that August sun.

Early Sunday, that's where Jason sits and sips a fresh coffee—on the boardwalk bench. He wears a tee, cargo shorts and hiking shoes. His prosthetic limb is covered with a protective sleeve as well. Though his day will be the furthest thing from typical, it's obvious it *will* be a typical day on the beach. Already, empty sand chairs line the water's edge, reserving spots for families and their weekend guests. Beside those chairs, closed umbrellas wait to be flipped up and settled beneath. An early swimmer manages a few laps across the roped swimming area, his arms slowly but rhythmically lifting out of the water, then dropping back in.

As he watches, Jason hears a *thump-thump-thump*. He lowers his sunglasses and looks over the top of the frames to see Kyle on the far end of the boardwalk. He's wheeling along his jam-packed beach cart overflowing with the Bradford gear: umbrella, sand chairs, pails and shovels, floaties and towels.

"Family day on the beach?" Jason asks.

"Finally." Kyle parks his cart and sits with a long sigh, then adjusts his faded *Gone Fishing* cap against the sunshine. "Busiest day yet at the diner yesterday, that patio is crazy-hoppin'. Rob's covering so I can have the day off. I'll catch some rays with the fam." He elbows Jason beside him. "How about you?"

"Lauren tell you we found the Fenwicks' old rowboat yesterday?"

"Hell, yeah."

"Once we made out the boat's name in really faded paint, *Kate*, there was no doubt."

"Kate. That was Carol's mother, right?"

"Yep. Gordon's daughter, too. She was just a kid when he died."

"Man, what a find."

"It truly is. But it's really buried deep in the sand, so today a few guys from the station are helping to unearth the old vessel. Even got a camera crew coming. We're hoping to grab footage to use in some of the episodes."

"How will you get it out of there?" Kyle asks. "Wheel it on some kind of trailer?"

"No, the boat's too fragile after all these years. You know, being abandoned out in the elements, it looks to be in bad shape. Really can't risk jostling it. So we'll be carrying it nice and easy, down the path through the woods. It's the only way, really."

"No shit. Need a hand?"

"The more the better."

Kyle nudges his overloaded beach cart. "I'll drop off this gear and then you've got solid muscle at your service."

"Awesome. It'll be tough to maneuver out of there, but I think we can do it."

Just then, Kyle looks beyond Jason at someone approaching. "Sup, Matt," he says with a wave.

Matt approaches in a slow trot. He wears a fitted compression tee over navy running shorts with gray stripes on the side. "Out for a jog," he says, stopping and setting a knee on the boardwalk bench, then extending his other leg behind him to stretch the hamstring.

"Looking trim there, dude," Jason tells him.

"Little hot for jogging, no?" Kyle asks. "With this sun?"

"Not bad. My shirt's got a back mesh panel," Matt says, turning to show them. "Keeps me ventilated. Got to stay fit for work," he adds while checking his watch. "And now I'm off to cut the grass."

Kyle leans his elbows on his knees and looks over at Matt. "What kind of machine do you have?"

"Bought me a sweet new rider this year."

"Me, too," Jason says. "Gets the lawn cut in no time."

"No kidding." Kyle runs a hand back through his hair. "I've still got my old push mower."

This time, it's Jason who elbows Kyle. "It's good exercise for you, bro. Walking laps around that Bradford property will burn those calories. Keep you in shape for that wedding suit of yours."

Kyle leans back looking a little defeated. "Yeah, I guess."

"So what's going on here with you two?" Matt asks as he finally sits beside them. "Especially at this early hour. Jesus, Barlow. We *never* see you out on a Sunday morning."

"Jason's got quite an operation planned up at Little Beach. His crew's salvaging an old rowboat belonging to the Fenwicks." Kyle points to the lone cottage on the beach. "Folks that own that place."

"They lost a family member in this particular boat, about fifty years ago, back in the sixties. Guy was taken out to sea in a hurricane one summer," Jason tells Matt.

"No kidding. And you found his boat? After all this time?" Matt asks.

"Lauren remembered seeing it deserted, actually," Kyle explains. "Years ago, when she was painting up at Little Beach. She and Barlow checked it out yesterday, and it seems to be the one."

"Wow. That's legit. Mind if I tag along?" Matt asks right as Nick walks up in full security uniform—khaki button-down shirt with black shorts—for his morning patrol duty.

"Tag along where?" Nick asks.

And when Jason explains the salvage operation once more, Nick sits too—squeezing in between Jason and Matt. "I'm coming," he tells Jason, right before getting Cliff on his walkie-talkie. "Changing my post, boss," Nick says into the radio. "Monitoring vessel excavation at Little Beach." When Cliff starts to argue, Nick interrupts. "Ensuring no ordinances are violated," he insists, while also giving a shrug to Jason. "Over," he says before clicking off.

If Jason had given it any thought, he would've put money on what happens next. It goes down within minutes. Cliff rolls into the parking lot behind the boat basin. It's his skidding golf cart that gets Jason's attention. Turning to look, he can't miss the backseat piled high with orange safety cones. Cliff grabs two and hefts them across the boardwalk in their direction.

"I'm glad I caught you, Jason. Because I need to interrogate you," Cliff says while setting down the two orange cones and sitting on the bench beside Kyle.

"About what?"

"Your *unauthorized* excavation."

Jason can't miss it then, how the guys lean forward from their bench seats to watch Cliff's tense grilling. Before Jason can even defend the excavation, Cliff continues.

"I don't believe you petitioned the Board of Governors for approval of your crew's mining the beach," he says while nudging the cones aside with his foot.

"Mining? Are you kidding me, Raines? We're pulling a rowboat from the sand—a boat I just found yesterday! There was no time for your policies and procedures."

"Now you're wrong there. There's *always* time to follow protocol, Jason. You ought to know that more than anyone here, especially with your position of authority on a popular television show."

"Sheesh," one of the guys mutters. "Surprised he didn't bring his gavel."

Heads turn to Jason, then to Cliff—who continues on with, "The rules *are* the rules."

"He's really throwing the book at you, Barlow," Kyle says under his breath.

Which is enough to bring Jason to his feet as he approaches Cliff sitting beyond Kyle. His silent friends watch his every step. "Little Beach is *out* of Stony Point's jurisdiction, and you know it, Judge."

"Okay." Cliff turns up his hands. "Okay, I'll give you that."

"So what's your beef with my boat excavation?" Jason asks as he, yes, as he picks *up* an orange cone and deposits it right in Cliff's lap.

"Oh, for crying out loud." Cliff sets the orange cone on the boardwalk bench and leans his arm on it. "You'll be *accessing* Little Beach via Stony Point property. So I'll make a concession. Warning cones will be out along the main beach, near the path through the woods. *And* I'll accompany the excavation, too. To monitor that precautions are being sufficiently taken to protect everyone's safety."

"Fine." Jason sits again and picks up his coffee cup. "So you basically want to watch."

"Well." Cliff shrugs. "I prefer to call it safety protocol. I'd think you'd appreciate that."

"Jeez, Commish," Matt adds while standing, gripping the top rail of the boardwalk bench and bending to stretch his back muscles. "You're all wound up today."

"Eh, this damn heat's not helping." Cliff whips off his gold-stitched black COMMISSIONER cap and presses his arm to his forehead. "So we're in agreement then, Jason? Nicholas and I will set out these orange cones to block off the path from any Stony Point onlookers." Cliff tips his face up to the sun. "In a minute, anyway," he adds, his voice vague.

Chalking up Cliff's tension to the heat, Jason leans over and simply salutes him. Seems everyone wants a piece of this salvage action today. Even Trent, who sends Jason a text message right then, saying he'll be at the beach in fifteen minutes.

"Good," Jason tells no one in particular as he puts his phone back in his pocket. "I can at *least* finish my coffee now."

"I'll text Eva," Matt says while doing a lunge stretch. "Let her know I'll be home for a quick change of clothes, then I'm off to Little Beach with your crew. The mowing can wait."

"Me, too." Kyle digs out a cell phone from his overloaded beach cart. "I'll tell Lauren. She's home, busy sending out invitations before bringing the kids here for some fun in the sun."

"Invitations?" Nick asks, leaning forward and eyeing Kyle on the other side of Jason. He tips up the brim of his SECURITY cap. "A little late for invitations, no? Isn't the vow renewal next weekend?"

CASTAWAY COTTAGE

"*Email* invitations," Kyle says while his fingers move over the phone keyboard. "We're keeping things low-key. So check your inboxes, fellas."

Jason lifts his take-out coffee and sips it then, relishing the few quiet minutes before Trent's arrival. In the boat basin behind him, the subtle pull of the current gets the moored boats creaking against the pilings. *Boat talk*, they've always called it. In front of him, the pulsing sun casts thousands of sparkles on the blue water. Something about this in-between time lulls *all* the guys, who finally just quietly sit side by side, looking out at the Sound and soaking in the sun's August rays.

⁓

Until footsteps approach. Especially when they're light, flip-flopping footsteps accompanied by soft female voices.

The guys' lazy summer trance is broken, just like that.

Jason can't help but notice how each of them discreetly watches from behind sunglasses. In unison, their heads steadily turn as two women in their twenties approach. One wears a floppy straw sunhat, the other has a canvas tote slung over her shoulder. Tanned and in bikinis, the women animatedly chat while breezing by.

Flip-flop, flip-flop.

As if the sunglass-camouflaged ogling wasn't bad enough, doesn't someone beside Jason actually let out a low whistle then? Surprisingly the women take it in stride, with one of them simply giving a flirty, over-her-shoulder wave. The thing is, she does so right as Nick jumps to his feet, fists pressed against his hips while glaring at the guys.

"What the hell was that? You're all *married men*," he says, whipping off his sunglasses. "All of you!" When he glances at Cliff, he adds, "Practically, anyway."

Still, everyone remains quiet. Everyone except Nick, who paces the boardwalk. "Really, Bradford? A *wolf* whistle?" He stops directly in front of Kyle. "When you're about to renew your vows to Lauren?"

"Who said it was me?" Kyle asks, turning up his hands.

"Wasn't me," Cliff puts in, still leaning back on the bench with his COMMISSIONER cap tipped up, his face raised to the sun.

"One of you two?" Nick asks, waggling his finger between Matt and Jason.

Jason simply shrugs, then shakes his head.

"Matt? *Really?*" Nick leans over and clips his shoulder. "A state trooper with a reputation to uphold?"

"Hey, don't look at me, punk. And hands off," Matt warns him.

"Well, who was it?" Nick asks once more, after tossing a glance at the women still flip-flopping along, their feet softly thudding on the boardwalk's wooden planks. "Who here is our … whistler?"

They all settle back, sunglasses donned, poker faces on.

"Well, I'm *watching* you. All of you." Nick points two fingers to his own eyes, then to all of them before sitting again.

That's not all Nick does, though. Oh, no. Jason catches him in the act—and raises an eyebrow at him, too—when Nick leans forward to steal one more glimpse of the wolf-whistle-worthy departing view before it's gone for good.

twenty-nine

An hour later, the mood's changed. It's somber now.

The setting's changed, too.

The hike along the winding path through the woods was quiet. Carol and Mitch Fenwick joined up with them at the trail's opening, just past their cottage. Trent and his crew were there, too. A few low voices commented along the way; overhanging twigs and brush were pushed past; feet snapped twigs on the rutted trail.

Finally they all turned onto the more untamed Little Beach—which is like passing through a fairy-tale portal—stepping out of the grim, dark wooded world onto the bright and wild beach. Here, silver flecks of mica glimmer in the hard-packed sand near the water. Still quiet, this crew of men carrying backpacks and shovels and digging gear crosses the beach. They round a boulder-strewn bend in the coast, pass tree-limb-sized driftwood lying twisted on the beach, and eventually get to the area where sand and dune grasses nestle up against the rocks.

When Jason stops, everyone listens up.

"This is the place." He walks to where only a portion of the rowboat protrudes from the sand; it's buried that deep. It doesn't escape him that the boat seems to be more in a grave than anything else. Because there is a distinct possibility that while unearthing this boat, skeletal remains might also be uncovered.

Kyle must have the same thought when he sees Mitch pick up a shovel, ready to help dig. "Oh, man," Kyle says when he hurries across the sand to Mitch. "I can't have you do that."

"Why not?" Mitch asks from beneath the brim of his sun-faded safari hat.

Kyle glances back at Jason, then turns to Mitch again. He extends his hand. "I'm Kyle, Mitch. Kyle Bradford. Good friend of Jason's."

Mitch shakes his hand, then looks past Kyle to Jason, who nods to Mitch.

That's all Jason does, though. If his gut is right, he's very much aware of what Kyle's about to say to Mitch; Jason had the same thought, but Kyle beat him to it.

"Listen, Mitch. And Carol?" he asks when he looks beyond to where Mitch's daughter stands. She wears a fitted white tank top over some kind of cropped black jeans with a shredded hem, her big sunglasses as black as her tattered jeans. When Carol steps closer, Kyle shakes her hand, too. "Good to meet you."

"Everything okay?" Trent asks as he approaches Kyle and the others.

"Sure, man." Kyle turns to Mitch and Carol again. "Mitch, why don't you let me use that shovel while you wait on the sidelines. You know. Because it could be a sensitive situation," he says, motioning to the distressed rowboat nearly buried beneath the sand. "And you're *family*, so, well ... Let *us* respectfully have the honor here, as you keep watch over your relative's boat."

"Dad?" Carol asks, touching her father's arm.

Mitch nods and hands Kyle his shovel. "That's awfully

thoughtful of you, Kyle. I'll be glad to stand by with my daughter."

"Okay, that's good," Kyle says, shaking his hand once more.

"But please," Carol tells Kyle, and Jason too, just beyond him. "If you see *anything* as you dig, or have any questions, just say the word."

Jason walks to them. "Will do. Mitch," he says, patting his shoulder. "Carol," he adds, giving her a brief hug. "Are we good to go here?"

With Mitch's slight nod, Jason turns to his crew and the excavation begins.

Carefully, the tips of shovels are pressed into the sand surrounding the rowboat. The men inch closer, scooping sand away as the digging continues. It's hot beneath the morning sun, and the men perspire, pressing an arm to a face, swigging from bottled water. They move slowly, working their way around the boat. Dune grass had taken root in some of the sand covering the boat, and that's carefully removed, too.

"Jason," Carol calls out as she approaches the excavation site. "I'd actually like some of that."

"The beach grass?" he asks while wiping his brow.

"Yes, if it's possible." Carol lifts her sunglasses to the top of her head and nudges a pile of the grass blades with her sandaled foot. "Because it grew from my grandfather's rowboat here. Maybe you could set aside a few clumps for me to plant at the cottage?"

"Sure thing. I'll see if I can get a few large pails or boxes to transport them to your place."

"Thanks," Carol tells him. "Really." She reaches forward and clasps his gloved hand. "Thank you so much."

"I'm on it, Jason," Nick says then. "There's spare buckets in the beach storage shed. You've got enough manpower here, so I'll run back for them."

Jason agrees and the digging resumes. The camera crew maneuvers around, capturing different images of spades being pressed into the sand; images of more and more of the worn and beaten boat emerging; images of one man or another pausing, head momentarily bowed while leaning against a shovel handle; images of the faded, dingy wood on the stern, bearing the boat's name *Kate*; the miraculous image of one oar, unbroken and still clamped in an oarlock.

As the filming quietly rolls, the only sounds are that of the gritty shovels pressing through sand, as well as occasional grunts as the men exert all the muscle they can muster in shoveling the earth away from the boat—all beneath August's pulsing rays of sun.

Once the boat is just about fully exposed, Jason stops any further digging. Witnessing this wooden vessel emerge from beneath the beach is sobering. Because the humble rowboat was used in a heroic attempt to save a life fifty years ago. But when the boat was set in the storm waters then, it also brought an *end* to a life. In the ensuing decades, the boat's white-painted sides have faded to nearly silver, with brown grains of wood showing through. One of the benches is missing; a few narrow planks are rotten at the top; large flakes of white paint peel off.

Yet somehow, the boat is intact.

As Matt, Kyle and the CT-TV crew step back, Jason motions Mitch and Carol closer. They walk to the rowboat, where Carol actually kneels in the sand, tenderly reaches out and glides her fingers over the curved wooden side of the vessel. When she looks up at her father, he crouches beside her.

"I never would've believed it if I didn't see it with my own eyes." Mitch looks back at Jason. "This is beyond incredible."

Jason nods, watching as Carol and Mitch take in the reality of the situation.

Gordon's boat has been found.

Mitch stands and walks around the vessel. Shaking his head, he bends and touches the dried-out wood. When he then moves the oar, it creaks as it scrapes against the rusted oarlock.

Jason's not sure there's a dry eye among them. Because that one sound carries fifty years of grief. Hearing that creaking oar, every valiant effort Gordon made to stay alive in that hurricane comes to mind. Every wave washing over the boat's bow; every heartbreaking haul of the oars; every rise and fall of the vessel is captured in that one ancient oar sound, brought back to life at the hand of Mitch.

He seems to know it, too, as he steps back, removes his hat and presses it to his chest while bowing his head.

Kyle's the first to crouch, then, and do the same.

The rest of the crew follows suit in one of the saddest moments of silence Jason's ever witnessed. The men all pay homage to Gordon the only way they can—on their knees in the sand. A few of the men swipe at their eyes. Even staid, rule-enforcing Cliff is backing away, discreetly blowing his nose into his handkerchief before kneeling, too.

The silence lasts only until Carol walks to her father and puts her arm around him.

"It's a pretty special moment," she quietly says. "Isn't it, Dad?"

"Oh, you bet."

Kyle stands then. "We'll do our best to get this vessel safely home to you now, where it belongs."

"We appreciate that, Kyle," Mitch says with a slight salute.

With the silence over and the talking starting up, Trent motions the cameraman closer to the Fenwicks. "Carol," Trent says. "Can you share what you're feeling? You know, seeing your grandfather's boat here, still intact? And knowing now that it was here all along?"

Pausing to collect her thoughts, Carol begins. "I am *so* very grateful. This is a day none of us ever saw coming." She walks to Jason and takes both his hands in hers. "It's like you're bringing my grandfather *home*. Do you know what that means?"

A thousand answers swirl in his mind. A thousand visions of Neil. Of bringing his brother home in so many ways. In the sandy, salty journals Jason's found. In bringing Neil to every cottage design he pencils onto tracing paper. In the way he had Neil's dilapidated fishing shack towed on a barge, and delivered to his own backyard. All of these his attempt to get Neil—a *comrade*, his father would've said—off the field, and home again.

Oh, Jason knows *exactly* what this day means to the Fenwicks. But he only tells her one thing. "I'm glad to be a part of it all."

"If only my mother could see this," Carol says when she turns back to the camera. "If she could see how we found her *father's* boat. She was only a little girl when he died, a young man himself."

Mitch comes up beside her. "It's a monumental day for us," he says into the camera. "Sad, but so significant."

The camera pans to the nearly unearthed rowboat, capturing every bit of fifty years of weather, and sand, and wind on its every wooden plank—silvered and grayed, rutted and rotted, weakened but intact, still.

With Carol by his side, Mitch heads to Jason. "I'm going back down to the cottage. I want to be sure everything's cleared for the boat's arrival so the crew can safely get it home."

"Okay, Mitch. That's a good idea. Maris should be meeting up with you about now, too. And don't worry," Jason says with a glance back at the boat. "We've got everything covered here."

"You sure?" Mitch asks.

Kyle, who'd been standing close by, reassures the Fenwicks. "That boat's in the best hands now. Trust me," he says, then whistles for the crew to join him at the vessel. "We won't let you down."

As the men circle around the boat, Mitch, Carol and Jason watch. Kyle directs Matt and Trent first, then stops to wave Nick over when he rounds the corner holding three large pails to transport the beach grass plants. The rest of the CT-TV crew takes their place, too.

"It'll be a while still, Mitch. They're first going to lift the boat completely out of the sand," Jason explains. "Inspect it, get some photographs. Some of the guys will stay behind and dig further to see if anything else can be found ... maybe any of Gordon's things. But we shouldn't be too long with the boat."

"I'll stay here, Dad," Carol says. "To be with the boat through all this and keep watch. You go ahead and I'll meet you later."

"Okay, that gives me a little time to clear a spot for it." Mitch turns away, then turns back to Jason. "Thanks again, Jason. For everything."

"Of course."

Mitch hurries over to the others standing near the boat. He gives a final salute before putting on his faded safari hat and leaving for the path back through the woods.

All the while, Jason knows that behind them, the camera is rolling.

Behind them, Carol keeps a lookout for some essence of her long-lost grandfather.

Behind them, Cliff also heads to the wooded path. He'd volunteered to hold overhanging branches out of the way, ensuring a safe and clear trek for this very last leg of the rowboat's final journey.

"On three," Jason tells the crew as he takes his position with them at that old rowboat. Today, the sun is shining, the sea is calm. A salty breeze hitches. A long-overdue rescue operation is finally underway.

Jason looks at the men surrounding the boat. When Kyle nods to him, he begins.

"One." Jason drops his head for a second, then scans the faces. "Two." They all bend and get a secure hold of the rowboat. "Three."

Standing on the upper deck of the last-standing cottage on the beach, Maris braces herself for what's to come. It's only a matter of time before a sad procession will round the curve in the wooded path connecting the hidden Little Beach to Stony Point's main beach. She'd already helped Mitch clear out a large space beneath the elevated cottage. The rescued boat will be safe and secure there now.

After a quiet minute, the slider scrapes open behind her. "Thank you for having me here today," she tells Mitch when he gives her a glass of ice water.

"Since you're finishing Neil's book," he says when he leans on the railing beside her, "I thought seeing all this could be helpful to his story."

"Maybe." Maris sips her water. "But really, Mitch. Something about this feels even too personal for that. I'm just glad to be here for you and Carol, both."

Castaway Cottage

Mitch keeps an eye on the path, too. "Gordon was my wife's father, and would've been my father-in-law. Kate spoke so fondly of him, of the brief years he was a part of her life. So I'm thinking of her today, too. She's been gone five years now, but this would've meant the world to her."

"Oh, I'm sure of that. What a story your cottage has been holding onto, Mitch. I'm so happy that Jason is bringing it to life." When Mitch glances back at her, she tells him, "Thanks for trusting him."

Mitch nods, and then, together, they vigilantly watch the path. To passersby, it can easily be missed. The path begins at the very far end of Stony Point Beach, near the rocky outcropping. The sand there is surprisingly fine and soft. The closer you get to the patch of woods, small beach plants and clumps of dune grass dot the area—almost camouflaging the secret entrance. But if you look closely, the sand clearly extends from the beach and up a slight slope into the woods, narrowing the further in you look. Low groundcover—leafy plants and grasses—edge the little path as it curves deeper in among old pine trees and tall oaks. That path veers to the left at first, then beneath dappled shade from the tall trees, it swerves right. Sunlight falling through leaves plays tricks on the eye, though, so that it's hard to tell if it's the rutted, rising path that winds right then, or if it's just shadows moving over the ground.

But Maris knows. She knows from years of hiking that secret path for quiet walks on Little Beach. Or from the times she trekked it with her summer friends to illicit beach parties late at night—when the liquor flowed around a roaring campfire on the wild beach, and the laughs and dancing and good times grew wild, too.

Today is different.

Today is the day the secret wooded path seems intended for. This one day.

"Oh, look!" Maris says. "Here it comes."

She and Mitch both squint toward the woods to see six men stoically carrying the old rowboat along the path. There's Jason, and Matt. Kyle, Nick, Trent and another CT-TV crew member.

But it's Cliff she sees first. He rounds the final bend, then steps off the path into low brush. From there, he grabs hold of a low-slung tree branch blocking the way of the men carrying the boat. Somehow Cliff manages to swing the branch completely aside as the procession approaches.

The sight is striking. All of the men are silent. Almost like pallbearers, three walk on each side of the boat, which they've flipped upside down. This way, their hands are better able to hold onto the decaying edges of the vessel as they maneuver the twisting, tree-root rutted trail. The procession moves silently, the men's faces as solemn as if it were a casket in their hands—which that boat very well may have been, one tragic day decades ago.

Slowly, to keep their footing sure, they descend the sloping path and emerge from the shadows of the woods. Carol follows behind them. She pauses when the men navigate the final curve together—carrying the rowboat onto the actual beach sand of Stony Point.

When they do, it feels utterly real. It feels like Gordon has *truly* been returned home after all this time. The heroic man who set out to save a young boy, little Sailor, has finally been rescued himself.

Seeing the procession, Maris reaches over to squeeze Mitch's hand. From the deck, they watch as the old, decrepit rowboat is finally carried back to the very spot it was taken from beneath the raised cottage … all those years ago.

thirty

FOR THE FIRST TIME SINCE they've moved into their house on the bay, Lauren enjoys sitting in her dining room. It doesn't matter that the walls are stripped of all wallpaper. It matters even less that most of the room has been rebuilt with brand-new, mold-free drywall. She couldn't care less that no pictures hang on those new walls.

All that matters is that their home is safe to live in now. No mold spores will be breathed. No black stains will creep down the wall. Life is good, again. And this time, she intends to do everything possible to keep it that way.

Starting with celebrating her marriage. At the dining room table, she moves her ruler down one name on her guest list, then turns to her laptop to email the next invitation. She whispers the words appearing on the screen, imagining the recipients' surprise to read them, too. "We *still* do," she murmurs with a smile. "Join us as we renew our wedding vows in celebration of ten years of marriage. Kyle and Lauren Bradford." After adding the August date, and the Stony Point Beach location, she whispers one more word. "Perfect."

Scrolling down on the screen, all that's left are lodging details for her out-of-town guests. "For overnight accommodations,"

Lauren says while typing, "please contact either Eva Gallagher at By the Sea Realty for a cottage rental, or Elsa DeLuca at the Ocean Star Inn. Though the inn is not officially open, Mrs. DeLuca will accommodate vow renewal guests."

The only thing left is to verify each recipient's email address and hit *Send*.

"Next?" Lauren whispers again, then moves her ruler down one line space on her typed list of guests.

"Mommy," Hailey says when she comes into the dining room. "We want a dog."

"What, honey?"

Hailey reaches into her bag of plastic farm animals and pulls out a dog, which she sets on the dining room table. "Maddy liked it when I blew bubbles at her house. She ate them!"

"That's nice, Hay." Lauren pats Hailey's arm. "She was your doggie friend."

"Well, can *we* get a dog?" Evan asks. He's standing in the dining room doorway. "I'll take care of it, I promise. And I can train it, too."

"Oh, Ev." Lauren looks from Hailey to Evan, whose hair is getting thick and moppy in the salty summer air. "It's a really busy time right now. Which is *not* good for getting a dog because they need a lot of attention. And you'll be back in school in a few more weeks."

"No fair," Evan mutters.

"But I'm sure Jason and Maris will let you visit Maddy any time you want to." While she talks, Lauren's cell phone dings with a new email. It's from her Addison friends Brooke and Vera, who *instantly* responded to their e-invitation with an enthusiastic *Yes!*

"But Mommy," Hailey begins as she marches her toy dog across the table. "We really—"

"Listen, kiddos. I have to send just a *couple* more invitations, then we're off to the beach. Daddy got all our chairs and umbrella set up already. So Evan, put Hailey's toys in my straw tote in the kitchen, okay?"

When Hailey and Evan walk to the kitchen, Lauren hears their whispers devising a way to get a dog of their own. She glances after them, then aligns her ruler beneath the next guest on her list. It's Nick, so she sends off his email quickly, knowing he won't miss the event.

Then? Then she does it.

Does what's been on her mind ever since her eyes opened this morning. Since even before that, actually ... Since she said yes to her dress.

She lowers her ruler to the final name on her vow-renewal guest list. It's a name she penciled in at the last minute ... with trepidation. But with hope, too.

Still, her hand hovers over the keyboard as the blank invitation is on the screen. The painted driftwood rowboat from Eva's cottage is her paperweight today, holding down guest lists and itineraries. Lauren picks up the driftwood and runs her thumb over the painted boat. Right about now, Kyle and the guys must be carrying that old rowboat along the shaded trail in the woods. The day she painted this driftwood piece, she was only sixteen years old. But still, it was so obvious that the half-buried boat nestled in the dune grasses back *then* had a story to tell. It was a story she tried to capture in her painting.

And now, she can see something of that story on the driftwood. A sadness comes through in her raw depiction of the abandoned rowboat. And in its faded white paint and weathered wood. But there's something more, too. There's a resilience captured in her paint strokes. A determination for that boat to have a second chance—be it simply on her driftwood painting, or in reality, one day. That day being today.

Second chances. Salvatore DeLuca, dear Sal. He believed second chances were *molto speciale*, he'd say in Italian. Very special.

Having a second chance to say her wedding vows to Kyle, after their first time was so emotionally wrought, Lauren knows the truth of Sal's sentiment. Planning her second vows with Kyle feels all the more special this time around. Maybe it's just the wisdom and life experience you get to bring to a second chance. Naiveté is long gone; hopes have been replaced with gratitude.

So she summons the courage to extend one more second chance. A long, shaky breath comes first as she studies that final name on her guest list. But if her hunch is right, this second chance could be just as beautiful as her second vows with Kyle.

Typing in the recipient's email address—which she's not even certain is current—Lauren pauses to reread the invitation. In that pause, she's actually trying to convince herself to do it, to hit the damn *Send* key already. With a glance at her painted rowboat on a piece of driftwood, she finds her answer there. That boat meant for bobbing and drifting on Long Island Sound did even more. It faced down a stormy sea's wrath and after all these years, it's coming home.

Yes, of course. Today's the day of the *ultimate* second chance. Gordon's rowboat is being brought home after going missing for *fifty* long years. That old boat has a second chance now. Now, it will honor and commemorate Stony Point's forgotten hero—the man who tried only to save little Sailor.

That story—Gordon taking a risky chance to save little lost Sailor—is Lauren's inspiration. She'll take a chance today, too, in honor of the abandoned rowboat she painted so many years ago.

But before she takes her chance, she adds a very personal, but brief, message to the bottom of her vow renewal invitation: *It's time for a truce. Please come.*

Leaning back, her finger hovers over the keyboard. Not everyone gets a second chance. Sal wanted only a second chance to live and didn't get it. Those chances are doled out sparingly, by fate. By destiny. By the powers that be.

Whether it's a rowboat getting a second chance, a marriage getting a second chance, or a person getting a second chance with one secret invitation, there's no denying one thing: Every fleeting second chance is *very* special, indeed.

With that thought, Lauren's finger drops and hits *Send.*

thirty-one

THE NOISE STARTS EARLY MONDAY morning when Maris is standing at her dresser. She's deciding which earrings to wear, and which bracelet, too. Lifting one gold chain, then a bangle, she finally sets both down—distracted by what she's hearing. In the kitchen, cabinet doors are being shut too loudly. Water from the tap splashes; a coffee cup clatters; the silverware drawer rattles when it's impatiently opened.

Too distracted to decide on her jewelry, Maris scoops up a handful of pieces and heads downstairs. As she descends, there's more noise: the printer is whirring on the kitchen counter; Jason's voice—monotone—leaves a voicemail for some contractor, or client, or whoever. Pity the person on the receiving end, Maris thinks, listening to that clip, no-nonsense tone.

"Here we go again," she whispers while walking through the living room to the kitchen. When she gets there, she drops her bracelets and earrings on the table and sits to brush through them.

"Getting ready to write?" Jason asks from where he stands, leaning on his forearm crutches at the printer. Asks without even a glance over his shoulder. Without a *Good morning, sweetheart.*

"No." Maris picks up a gold sailor's knot earring and presses it on her ear. "I'm having coffee with Eva this morning."

"Again?"

Now—*now*—comes his glance. His annoyance is obvious as Maris puts on the second earring.

"Are you working on the book at *all* today?" Jason asks while leaning over the countertop and flicking the screen of his dinging phone.

"Jason, yes." Maris slips on a mesh watchband. "You know that I quit my job to be more present in everybody's lives here. So first I'm having my weekly coffee visit with my sister, *okay*?"

Her *okay* does it. That one exaggerated word gets him to push his phone away and toss her another look—this time with a raised eyebrow.

"I'm making time for people." Maris walks to the coffeepot and pours two coffees. "Something you might consider trying," she says under her breath, *and* while looking at Jason's flashing phone that just dinged—*again*. "What about you? Slacking today?" she asks with a small smile as she sets their coffee cups on the kitchen table.

It's back to his phone as Jason snatches it up and brings it over, where his hot coffee waits and his prosthetic leg leans against a chair. After sitting and leaning his crutches against the table edge, he manages a sip of the brew, then reads from the planner on his phone screen. "Here's my *slacker* schedule, darling: Site analysis. Zoning issue with contractor requiring a design adjustment. But first stop? Beach Box."

"What's happening there?" Maris asks as she puts a cinnamon-chip muffin in the microwave.

"The owner wants to run something by me in their kitchen design. They want to somehow make the room look bigger."

"Hmm." Maris brings her warmed muffin to the table, slices it in half and drops a tab of butter in the center. "Paint it white?"

"Yeah, but nothing really unique there. Glass cabinet fronts help, too. But that's not architectural." Jason reaches over and rips off a hunk from one of her muffin pieces. "I'm thinking bigger windows. And I might be able to take down a half-wall to give an illusion of size. Maybe add recessed shelving." He snags another piece of her muffin and stuffs it in his mouth.

"Hey!" Maris motions to her nearly empty plate. "Hands off my muffin."

"I don't know," he adds while chewing. "We'll see what I can design there."

As he washes down the muffin with a gulp of coffee, Maris slides her plate to him and gets up to heat another muffin for herself. When Jason's phone dings again, she looks over her shoulder right as he looks at the phone, then slides it in his pocket, whispering, "*Later.*"

"Who was that?"

"Kyle. We need to pick up our suits *tomorrow*. For the vow renewal." Jason breaks off another piece of muffin, holding it aloft as he adds, "As if I have time."

Maris squints at him, then brings her second warmed muffin to the table. "Jeez, Jason. *Somebody* woke up on the wrong side of the bed this morning. Anyway, just do what I do," she begins while sitting. "Like I said, you have to *make* time, babe."

Again he throws her another look, all while shaking his head. Once his pilfered muffin's gone, he turns and pulls his silicone liner onto his leg, straightens it over his knee and fusses for a few seconds. Glancing at her, he says, "I might not be able to answer my text messages today," right before pressing his stump into his prosthetic limb.

"No. Oh, no." She's quiet until he looks across the table at her. "You answer *mine*."

He gives her the slightest nod. But when his phone dings in his cargo shorts pocket, he closes his eyes for a long second. Closes his eyes and exhales a long breath.

Which is when Maris knows. He's got so much going on in his head, and today? Today most of it has nothing to do with work. Her suspicion is that the approaching ten-year mark of Neil's death *and* the bike accident is rolling into view on his own *emotional* planner. So she stands and walks around the table to him. "You look tired." Her fingers toy with a lock of his overgrown hair. "Feeling okay? Your leg all right?"

"It's fine, sweetheart. I've just got to watch it, maybe get some rest." He stands and slightly bounces on his prosthetic leg. "I'm seriously losing my footing with Kyle's vow renewal. I'll have to reschedule work commitments just to pick up our suits." When he turns to leave, he pulls his phone from his pocket.

"Jason." Maris crosses her arms and watches him as he roughly zips up his duffel on the countertop. "The vow renewal is for one day. One day!"

He hefts his duffel off the counter, gives her a wave and heads out through the slider, all while saying, "And it's one day too much."

Kyle notices something different about Lauren this morning. He's not sure what it is. Her hair is in a topknot, and her face looks worried. Maybe she's just tense with the fast-approaching vow renewal ceremony. Lord knows their nerves have been on edge, especially since the mold fiasco. So from behind the big stove, he keeps an eye on her as she zips around the diner, filling in for an absent waitress. The place is jumping, and lots of breakfasts are being served. Eggs scramble; bacon sizzles; toast pops. Lauren hurries in and out of the kitchen area with her order pad, putting new orders on his carousel and grabbing overloaded plates to deliver.

But she keeps doing something else, too. She keeps reaching into her apron pocket for her cell phone, then checks the screen. Sometimes she'll just stop in her tracks, hit a few buttons, flick the screen, and put the phone back in her apron.

"What do you keep checking there?" Kyle asks the next time she drops off an order.

"RSVPs. They're still dribbling in," Lauren says while putting her pencil behind an ear. "I need to know how many driftwood place cards to paint for Elsa's table." She checks the time on her phone and sneaks another look at her email, too. "I'm going to leave after the lunch crowd to pick up the kids from Parks and Rec. Then I'll get started painting at home. Elsa needs those place cards soon."

"Okay, fine." Kyle plucks a new order off the carousel and cracks open a few eggs on the stovetop. "It'll quiet down by then."

In a minute or two, when he flips his over-easy eggs, Jerry comes in—ready to cook, too. He passes Lauren as she grabs another plate, this one heaped with fluffy pancakes topped with a thick slab of butter.

"How're the two lovebirds today?" Jerry asks while slipping on his chef apron.

"Fluttering and flitting around!" Lauren gives him a wink as she breezes off into the diner.

"You sure about not being open here on Saturday?" Jerry asks as he mans the stove near Kyle's. "Because I can cover for you."

"No way. I'm closing up shop and want you at the ceremony." Kyle slides the over-easy eggs off his spatula and onto a white plate. Using tongs, he adds a few sausage links beside them. "It'll be a day for the books."

"Okay, boss," Jerry says with a salute. "I wouldn't miss it."

"You're still good to cover for me next week, though, right? Sunday through Wednesday?"

"Absolutely. You two enjoy your honeymoon, with no worries." Jerry grabs two orders from the carousel and squints to read them.

"It should be pretty sweet. We're staying in a lakeside cabin in Addison, not too far from here. Maybe forty minutes away. *Chickadee Shanty*, it's called." Kyle picks up his spatula and scrapes a bit of egg off the griddle. "Celia recommended the place, said it's a really nice spot near a small lake, with lots of hiking trails in the woods." He gives the griddle another scraping, taps off the spatula on the stove edge. "I'll be back to work Wednesday, noontime."

"You're leaving the diner in good hands, Captain," Jerry tells him while ladling out pancake batter.

Kyle throws a quick glance toward the doorway, then wipes his hands on a towel and walks out to the front counter. "Hey, there's the man. How you doing, Barlow?" he asks, shaking Jason's free hand as his other holds a cell phone to his ear. "I'll get your coffee and cruller," Kyle tells him.

Which is precisely when Jason pauses his phone conversation. "Just coffee today," he calls to Kyle while sitting on a red-cushioned stool. "I'm running late."

Kyle shakes his head, then lifts the glass dome of the pastry case right as Jason's telling some poor S.O.B who wants a piece of his time that he's booked solid today.

"I can maybe squeeze you in for a prelim at four forty-five. Where are you?" Jason asks. "White Sands Beach?" A pause, then, "Yeah, I know the place."

Kyle grabs a cinnamon cruller and sets it on a small dish in front of Jason.

Problem is, Jason promptly slides it back across the counter, all while telling his sorry caller, "Call back this number and leave your address on my voicemail. I'll see you this afternoon."

"You're looking gaunt." Kyle pushes the cruller dish back to Jason. "You been eating?"

While flicking through his emails, Jason silently waves Kyle off.

Okay, so Kyle does what he has to. He leans across the counter and roughly rubs Jason's whiskered jaw. "You've got circles beneath your eyes, too. Looking like shit, dude. So *mangia*, would you?" he asks while giving Jason's cheek a firm slap. After that, he turns and pours him a hot coffee in a take-out cup.

Wordlessly, Jason grabs the coffee, pulls a five-dollar bill from his wallet and sets it on the counter. Right as he sips his coffee then, his phone rings. "Yo, Kyle," he says, standing to leave. "I'll see you when I see you."

"Wait." Before Jason can get to the damn door, Kyle calls after him. "Tomorrow, Barlow! And don't you forget. We're picking up our suits at lunchtime." He watches Jason go, leaning to the side to see his friend hurrying across the parking lot—coffee in one hand, phone in the other. Kyle shakes his head, then reaches for the untouched cinnamon cruller and stuffs a bite into his mouth ... still watching Jason drive off.

It's one of Elsa's favorite hours—the one right after lunch. In the heat of the day, life quiets. Few birds sing; bees bumble lazily; folks stroll slowly, flip-flops flipping, on their way back to the beach after grabbing a quick sandwich. They give a friendly wave hello as they pass Elsa outside her inn. Life seems to be in a sweet lull at this hour.

That afternoon, Celia joins her outside. With Aria strapped to her chest, Celia holds the crinkled garden hose and gives the hydrangea bushes a spraying. She's doing something else, too, which Elsa is so glad to hear. Because she wants only happiness for Celia, after all the heartache she's been through. On this warm, sunny Monday, Elsa hears Celia humming. The sound must be soothing to little Aria, too, hearing her mother at peace like that.

What it does, seeing mother and daughter so at ease, is this: It makes Elsa smile. And *that* has her think of her dear son and his favorite mantra. It's during these peaceful lulls in her days that she swears she sometimes hears his whisper in the breeze, *Sorridi, Ma. Smile.*

Quiet minutes pass. Elsa deadheads flowers while Celia waters the plants. Elsa yanks a few weeds while Celia sits on a slatted wood bench and chats quietly with her. When Elsa's cell phone dings, she sits on the bench, too, and pulls the phone from her garden apron pocket.

"Who is it?" Celia asks, leaning close and looking at the text message.

"Aria's godmother!" Elsa brushes a finger across Aria's warm cheek. "Lauren's painting her driftwood place cards this afternoon, and let's see ... She says she'll have them to me soon."

"Oh, good! I'll be able to plan the table décor, then."

When Elsa puts her phone back in her apron, she grabs a straw broom and sweeps sand from the front walkway leading to the inn's main entrance. It's August now, and the ornamental beach grasses are lush, their green blades arching and swaying in a light sea breeze. It's hard to believe the Ocean Star Inn formally opens just next month. Celia follows her around to the front and sits with Aria on the porch swing while Elsa lightly sweeps. It's so quiet out, Elsa can't miss the putter of an approaching golf cart.

Can't miss that it slows and comes to a stop, too, right at her inn. So she squints to see Cliff sitting in the driver's seat, waving to her.

"Looking lovely, Mrs. DeLuca," he calls out. "Good day to you."

Then? Well, heavens! Then he actually blows her a kiss. Leaving Elsa no choice but to raise her hand and catch that kiss.

"Dinner at my place?" Cliff asks as he leans across the passenger seat. "Tonight at five?"

"Oh, you're nothing but a flirt, Commissioner," Elsa says while lifting her sunglasses to get a better look at him. Even from here, she sees the dimple in his small smile as he waits for her answer. "Shoo. Shoo, now!" she says, waving him off and returning to her sweeping.

"Oh, no you don't. Not again." He inches his golf cart along the curb to keep pace with her sweeping path. "Wedding-dress shopping. Grandchild day. Inn business. You're always shooing me away."

So Elsa stops and simply leans on her propped-up broom, smiling and waiting to see what he'll say next.

"Now for once, relax. And have dinner with me tonight."

"Fine, then. But you pick me up."

With a toot of his horn, Cliff peels out, chirping those golf cart tires as he goes on his merry way.

"You two," Celia says from her shaded spot on the big front porch. "I swear that man's smitten with you, Elsa. I take it he's still wooing?"

"Absolutely." Elsa sweeps off the porch steps now, giving a

CASTAWAY COTTAGE

glance back at Cliff's departing golf cart. "Thus the trailer dinner. I've been so busy getting things ready for the inn's grand opening, we haven't seen much of each other lately. But Cliff tries, that's for sure." Elsa glances out to the street again. "Here's the real question though: Is it me Cliff's taken by? Or is it just the dance of romance? Is he simply in love with the *idea* of being in love?"

"With *you*! And it's so sweet," Celia says, bouncing her baby on her lap.

"It is." Elsa can't fight her own smile. "He'll have that tin-can trailer nicely decorated, rest assured, with a red-and-white checked tablecloth over his bistro table. Some candles, maybe. And *definitely* Dean Martin crooning on his record player."

"Is Cliff a good cook?"

"Well. There's not much you can do with a toaster oven. But he surprises me." Elsa thinks of his chicken quesadillas, and mini pizzas made on English muffins, and amazing tuna melts. Why, he's even baked peanut butter cookies in that little oven! There's something so charming about that trailer's back room. Maybe some of it is the meals Cliff whips up. And some of it is the clandestine feel to their being together there, dining and lingering long into the night. Many times, she's spent the *entire* night, waking early the next day on that futon of his.

But their trailer dates always start with Cliff's toaster-oven dinners eloquently served at a meticulously set bistro table—complete with candles, and cloth napkins, and easy conversation. The thought of it has Elsa smile again. And she knows just what she has to do next.

First she leans her broom on the porch railing, then skips down the steps and hurries to her inn-spiration walkway. Picking up a fat piece of chalk, she throws another quick glance toward the street in the direction of that departing golf cart, then writes

245

the day's message across the walkway in her finest, grandest cursive: *Life's a treat ... on a sandy beach street!*

After waitressing all morning at the diner, it's the perfect lazy afternoon for painting. The day is warm and quiet, the sun bright, the waves lapping across the street on the bay. Lauren set out her driftwood pieces on a long table on the front porch, where she sees this all through the window screens. What she likes about the day is the sense of calm to it, a contented calm. It's the same calm she wants to bring to her vow renewal ceremony. Because let's face it, she and Kyle are no strangers to the opposite. To upheaval and turmoil.

But this year? They've finally moved beyond that, into a comfortable place in their marriage.

So she's painting her driftwood place cards with that same calmness. Hailey sits beside her, swinging her little legs as she paints driftwood, too. Lauren set her up with her own paint, and now her daughter dabs her brush and swirls colors onto extra wood pieces. Outside, Evan is riding his bicycle up and down the street, dinging his bell whenever he passes the house.

Yes, Lauren thinks. All is good right now.

Finally.

She and Kyle are settled in at their new house at the beach. The diner's busy. The kids are making new friends here. Life's in a nice groove.

"Honey," Lauren says to her daughter. "Why don't you paint *your* name on one driftwood, and your brother's name on another?" She sets two small pieces of driftwood in front of Hailey. "Then Mommy will put them in the finished pile for my wedding redo day."

"I'll paint mine first," Hailey whispers, very intent on her artwork. She scoots up on her knees and leans well over her work area.

"Decorate it, too," Lauren tells her. "Put little stars on it. Or look," Lauren says while leaning close and holding Hailey's hand. "Let's dip your brush in blue paint," she says, while together they dab blue, "and now we'll paint a wave." Lauren guides her daughter's small hand in a curving motion so that they paint a gentle wave across the bottom of a piece of driftwood. "Okay?" she asks.

When Hailey simply nods, Lauren works on her own place cards. *Maris*, she paints on one driftwood piece. *Jason* on another. Then *Matt*. And *Eva*. She adds paint strokes of waves to some. Dabs stars and seashells on others. And includes a small white starfish on each.

Time passes easily, until finally there is only one name left—the one she never received any RSVP from.

On this last piece of driftwood, Lauren paints a small red lobster along the side. She makes it as realistic as possible, and adds a touch of blue waves. As she does, her body tenses. Just a little, but enough for her to notice, to stretch a bit, and to take a few deep breaths.

Once the images are painted, there's only room for this last guest's name. Glancing first out the window toward the bay, then back at the piece of driftwood, she pauses.

This is her chance. Her *second* chance to change her mind. To toss this piece of driftwood and forget she ever considered doing this.

Or it's her second chance to fix things. To make everything even *more* right than it already is. Because lately, it feels like she and Kyle are on a good roll with their life together. Okay, heck, even with Kyle's vow of celibacy. Because she's having a blast trying to wear him down by flirting, and teasing, and wearing silky nighties—practically every night.

All she wants is to keep the goodness going. To do the right thing.

So after another moment's pause, she takes a decisive breath, dabs her brush in the paint and artfully completes the one last place card. Her hand moves gently over the driftwood as she silently paints each letter of his name. It isn't until it's done that she leans back and for the first time in years, actually *utters* the name, too. Something she's never dared do before this summer.

But somehow, after everything they'd all been through losing Sal, dear Sal—after everything he taught them about living life—she says the word.

Okay, it's a whisper, but still ... it counts.

"*Shane.*"

thirty-two

BEYOND THE FENWICK COTTAGE, A mist hovers like a silver spirit over the lagoon grasses. When Jason caught sight of that foggy view earlier, it didn't surprise him. He'd felt the damp in his leg all morning. He feels it even more so when Mitch and Carol take him to the dank area beneath their stilted, raised cottage to see Gordon's rowboat once more. Fifty years of wind off the sea, fifty years of sand and sunlight have worn it down. What remains of the boat's white paint is streaked and nearly gray; the faded planks of the hull show much of the wood grain now; a bench is broken. But enough is intact—including details like the oarlocks, and the painted stern bearing the vessel's name—to make it worthy of saving.

The entire beaten sight of that boat does something else, too. It makes you want to touch it. To somehow take some of the weary rowboat's fatigue, to know the story that one small vessel tells.

And Jason does. His hand runs along the old, dried-out wood. He touches an oarlock, and *feels* the struggle that Gordon fought with the boat's paddles. Even Madison, who had been veering off toward the sand—no doubt in search of a piece of driftwood—quiets at Jason's side beneath the cottage.

"So. You've got a decision to make today," Jason tells the Fenwicks afterward, when they settle on the cottage's elevated deck. That mist lingers over the Sound, still. Wisps of it look like low, translucent clouds. Jason gives a short whistle for the dog to come sit near him as the television camera crew gets in place. Then he reaches for his duffel, pulls out a large sketchpad and sets it on the patio table. He'd considered presenting his options on a tablet, but prefers the *look* of his actual sketches. They give that same tangible element important to all his work.

Even boat designs.

"I know that rowboat means the world to you both," Jason says to Mitch and Carol.

"You have no idea, Mr. Barlow," Carol agrees from her seat across from him. Her sandy-colored bangs fall over her eyes. "We still can't believe it, that we *really* got back my grandfather's *boat*."

"After all these decades, to have it home again, well it's a comforting feeling," Mitch adds, running a hand along his close beard. He's hatless today, and instead his faded blond-silver hair is pulled back into a tiny, low ponytail. "Every now and then I have to go down below the cottage and take *another* look at it. The boat's in rough shape, and it makes me wonder how much of the damage was from the hurricane, and how much was just time in the sand and sun that wore it out."

"Good question. I'm sure it's a combination of both. But as you can see," Jason says while opening his sketchpad, "it *can* be repaired. We've got a restoration crew ready to roll with it."

"You know, I totally get that," Carol says then, reaching out and clasping Jason's arm with a new insistence. "But I also *don't* want to lose the feeling of what the boat has gone through. And what my grandfather went through, too, looking for Sailor that day. If we restore it to new condition, that will be lost."

"Don't worry. We think alike, Carol." Jason opens his pad and shows her his first sketch. "I've drawn up three options of how you might like the rowboat preserved. Take a look. One would be as a deck planter, right here where I'm sure your family kept a lookout for Gordon that day. Another is to convert it into a bench seat, here on the deck as well. And the third option is to actually stand it on end and turn it into a shelf unit." He flips a page when Mitch leans close for a better view, too.

"I like these," Mitch says.

"The restoration team will strengthen the boat's structure to keep it intact, but they'll also maintain the integrity of time, and that hurricane's effects, on the paint and wood. We'd like to spotlight that restoration on a *Castaway Cottage* episode, too."

"Dad?" Carol asks as she points to the shelf unit. "Are you thinking what I'm thinking?"

Mitch leans back and squints at his daughter, then looks at the drawings. "Could be. Spill it."

"I want the boat indoors, protected and safe from now on. It's struggled enough." Her voice is soft, and her dark eyes never leave her father's as she talks.

"Yep." Mitch nods, squinting at his daughter in the August sunlight. "It's a nice way to bring Gordon home. Your mother would've liked that."

After they all talk further, and decide to arrange framed family photographs on the boat's shelves, Mitch leans back in his chair and motions to Jason. "Question for you."

"Shoot."

"The staff at CT-TV ever dig up any lowdown on the Sailor kid? A name? History of *any* sorts?"

"No." When Jason stands and looks out over the railing toward the rocky ledge where Sailor snuck to that fateful day,

Madison scrambles to her feet and follows. "Nothing," Jason tells Mitch when he turns back to him. "They dug deep into news archives, but there's no mention of Sailor or his family, other than to say that Gordon was searching for a neighborhood boy. It seems the storm was so destructive, and unexpected, that even Gordon's story didn't get much attention, being there was so *much* to cover at the time, including others who'd lost their lives up and down the coast."

Carol joins Jason at the railing. Her cropped faded jeans are ripped in places; her striped blouse is loosely tucked; her feet bare. "Sailor has grown more mythical than even my grandfather. The *mystery* around that kid makes him like a legendary storybook character now."

As often happens, Jason's noticed, everyone quiets when the talk turns to, yes, that *mythical* little boy and his sailor cap—a boy friendly to everyone, known to none. So Jason turns to Trent, watching from the sidelines. "Anything from your people?" he asks his producer. "Any warm trails they're following tracking down Sailor's family?"

"Nothing," Trent tells them. He joins Carol and Mitch at the deck railing and takes a long look out at the nearby rocky ledge. "It's a damn shame. I can just picture the kid hanging out there. Would be something to catch up with him now."

"Doesn't look like it's in the cards," Mitch says. "Like my wife used to say, the family hightailed it right out of here not long afterward."

"And we're talking five decades passing since then," Carol adds.

"I'm sorry we couldn't find more, but we'll stay on it. I'll put out a call to local viewers on the station's website. Maybe some tips will come in," Trent tells them. "In the meantime," he says, shaking their hands now, "*Castaway Cottage* is a wrap for today. Good stuff going on here with that rowboat story."

When Jason moves to help pack the camera gear, Trent stops him. "That's okay, Barlow. I got it," he says over his shoulder before carrying the gear down to the waiting van.

So Jason returns to the deck to collect his own duffel and sketchpad. "I'll be off, then," he tells Mitch and Carol. "Thanks for your time this morning. Now?" he says with a glance at his watch. "Now I've got to pick up a suit for a friend's wedding."

"That must be Kyle?" Mitch asks. He's uncapping a bottled water as he sits on the deck's top step, near the railing.

"That's right. He's renewing his vows Saturday."

"I met him up at Little Beach, the day we salvaged the boat," Mitch mentions. "Nice guy, he seemed really happy about the event. Did he say it's at that new Ocean Star Inn?"

"Yeah, it is. The place Elsa DeLuca owns—I've given her your names, so you can get in touch whenever you have a chance. Especially before demo gets underway here."

Carol looks across the beach, in the direction of the inn set back beyond the dune grasses. "Will Kyle's vow renewal be on the beach?"

"It actually will be. So I'm sure you can catch some of the festivities from right here on your deck. They'll have white chairs all set out on the sand for the ceremony. Dinner will be outside the inn, with a party afterward upstairs, in the turret room."

"Sounds *fantastic*," Mitch says. "A real summer bash."

From the way he says it, Jason gets the feeling this Mitch is a man who's seen a memorable party or two in his day.

"Listen," Mitch continues after swigging his water, then standing at the railing. "Can you do something for me?"

"Name it," Jason says.

"Kyle was a really big help retrieving Gordon's rowboat, and I'm glad to return the favor. I like that guy. So you tell Kyle and his bride to stop by that evening for a photo shoot on the deck here. Wearing their fancy threads, it'll make for some nice shots with the sun setting beyond."

"Will do," Jason tells him. "He'll appreciate that."

Trent rounds the corner of the cottage then, after helping load the camera gear into the van. "Thanks, all," he calls out, climbing the stairs and shaking hands again with Mitch and Carol. "We'll be on our way now. Great job," he says to them, and to Maddy—patting the German shepherd's back while she laps water from a bowl set on the deck. "You too, Jason. Keeping it loose, man."

Loose? Jason thinks it was all he could do to get through this Tuesday morning. Between a bout of phantom pain bothering his leg, and his overloaded itinerary that'll keep him on the road until God knows when, and even the fact he has to stop home to drop off the dog, everything chips away at his time today—and at his regimented schedule.

So after tossing back three aspirins, he grabs a couple of nutrition bars from the kitchen cabinet and eats one while driving to meet Kyle. Surely these bars pack enough carbs and protein and some sort of fruit to keep his energy elevated for the next hour or two. They'll suffice for lunch.

The whole way to the menswear shop, though, all he thinks of is Trent admiring how he kept things loose while filming with Carol and Mitch.

Loose.

Problem is, though he's gotten good at hiding it, he was the farthest from loose that he's been in a long time. His muscles were, and still *are*, tense. A low-grade headache nags at his temples. His cell phone doesn't let up with its dinging. And if one of them is Maris texting him, she's so not going to accept that he just can't answer.

By the time he turns into the store parking lot, he's unwrapping the second nutrition bar. The sun feels even hotter here, beating down on a pavement that sends the heat right back up to Jason on his way to the store entrance. When he walks into the lobby, Kyle's with the tailor headed to the dressing room; two suits are draped over the tailor's arm.

"Jason," Kyle calls when he notices him in the lobby. "Got your suit, man. *Andiamo*. Let's go."

Jason stuffs the last of lunch—okay, he's still not sure you'd call it that—into his mouth. "Really, Kyle," he argues while catching up with him, still chewing. "I don't need to try mine on. I trust it's fine. We can just pick them up and get going."

Kyle stops so suddenly, Jason nearly mows him over. "What?" Kyle asks. "No way. I don't need my best man popping his vest. Come on, this is it!"

When Kyle steps into his dressing room, Jason grabs his own suit from the tailor and goes into the adjoining room. He closes the door, turns to hang the suit on a hook and notices himself in the mirror. "Eh," he says, waving off his own tired reflection before he turns away, takes a long breath, and reluctantly lifts off his shirt.

Kyle figured it would take Jason longer to get dressed, what with messing around with his prosthetic leg and all. So he's first out of the dressing room, and stands on a small pedestal so the tailor can check the fit of his pants. A few minutes pass, with no word from Jason. Silence, until *finally* Kyle hears words that catch him the hell off guard.

"Maybe a vow renewal's not such a great idea," Jason says from behind his door.

"What? What're you talking about? Of course it is," Kyle says. He turns as the tailor checks the side seam on his pant leg.

"I mean," Jason says, "we're just going to end up wearing our fine clothes for the ceremony, but thinking back to ten years ago." Silence—again—as Jason must be zipping and buttoning up. "Some things from that time aren't worth celebrating," he says more under his breath than anything else.

But it doesn't matter. Kyle heard it. Heard every single syllable of it. And what it does is this: It gives him that sick feeling in his gut. The same one he felt yesterday when Jason was so wound up, he wouldn't even sit for a cruller in the diner. Shit, why didn't Kyle do what all the authorities advise and *listen* to his gut?

Because *damn straight*, he realizes now with a sinking dread. This event is too much for his friend.

"You like the fit here?" The tailor's crouched and giving Kyle's pant leg a shake. "Not too loose?" he asks around a couple pins in his mouth.

Kyle, distracted, looks at his reflection. "No. I mean, yes. The fit's good. I don't want them too tight."

"Okay." The tailor stands and directs his attention to Kyle's crisp white shirt.

"Jason." Kyle turns on the pedestal. "It's just a *vow renewal*. Lauren and I made it through some tough times, and we want to acknowledge that."

In a second, Jason's dressing room door opens and he

Castaway Cottage

emerges. He's buttoning his vest, which the tailor motions for him not to do. "Take it off," the tailor says. "I want to check the fit of your shirt, first. I put a couple darts in back to tighten it."

"Really, man," Kyle says when the tailor shifts over to Jason. "Just relax. You're overthinking the situation, that's all. And getting stressed out, too. Which is *my* job," Kyle jokes, trying to keep the vibe chill.

The tailor asks Jason to slightly extend his arms, then checks the fit beneath the arm and down the sleeve length.

"Overthinking? *Don't* tell me what I'm doing, Kyle," Jason says with a glance.

If the tailor wasn't so busy straightening Jason's shoulder seam, then lightly brushing off the shirt fabric, Kyle would argue. But shit, Jason beats him to it, regardless.

"Look," Jason calls over his shoulder to Kyle. "I'm grateful you and Lauren worked things out. I'm grateful you're doing a bang-up job raising Neil's son. But now I'm not sure I need your vow renewal to distract me from the *real* anniversary I'll be thinking about."

"Jesus Christ, Barlow. Where's this coming from, dude?" Kyle asks. "I thought we went over this, and hell, I even scheduled the date *early* so it doesn't coincide with Neil's death, *and* the accident. You *know* that."

Obviously trying his best to ignore the mounting tension, the tailor takes Jason by both shoulders and turns him so that Jason sees the fit of the back of the shirt. "Good?" the tailor asks.

Jason nods, then glances at Kyle patiently watching. "It's just that the closer your big day gets, the more it feels like my father's hourglass. I hear this countdown," he says, his voice low. *"Ten years. Ten years. Ten years.* And it's so *damn* final."

"What is?" Kyle asks.

"A decade without Neil now. A *decade*."

"That's *not* what the day's about, and you know it."

"Sorry, don't mind me," the tailor says when he moves back to Kyle and turns him. "Men have a defined body shape," he interrupts as he pats Kyle's back. "A V-shape, wider at the shoulders, then narrowing. And you, sir, are the groom. So I gave special attention, and think the fit is perfect." He pats Kyle's back, between his shoulders.

But at this point, Kyle can't even focus on his custom, much-anticipated, pale-gray vow renewal suit. All he's seeing, okay, is seething red. "What are you saying?" he asks Jason. "You're *bailing* on being my best man and not coming to the ceremony? And *don't* dick around with me. Not now, man."

After an annoyed glance at the tailor, Jason shakes his head. "I don't know what I'm saying, Kyle. Just have a lot going on right now, I'm so damn busy."

Kyle turns then, when the tailor is handing him his vest to try on.

"Listen," Kyle says to him. "I'm really sorry, but can we have a moment alone here?"

"Absolutely." The tailor adjusts the yellow tape measure looped around his neck. "Give a yell when you're ready, gentlemen."

Now, well now Kyle can't stop himself. He walks closer to Jason and drops his voice low. "So you're saying you don't have time, is that it? Shove it, Barlow." He's just as shocked as Jason is when he gives him a push, enough to nearly throw off Jason's balance. "You know who didn't have time?" Kyle asks, stepping closer. "Sal. Sal didn't have time. Same with your brother." With that, Kyle snaps a sharp flick of his fingers to Jason's shoulder. "Neil didn't have time, either." Before he can do any damage, before he can't stop himself from hauling off and creaming his best man, Kyle turns away and whips off his vest. "Just fucking leave, already," he tells him.

Jason drags his knuckles along his scarred jawline, then waves him off with his open hand, looking frustrated now.

As if he has any reason to be frustrated, Kyle thinks. So he puts an end to all this shit. To all Jason's dredging up of the past ten years. "I said, leave your threads and get the *hell* out of here."

Kyle's aware, too, as he says it. Aware as each word takes shape. There's enough rage in each quiet syllable for Jason to know better than to say *anything* else. Instead, he silently returns to his dressing room and within minutes is leaving the store.

Kyle watches him go, then gives a light whistle to the tailor trying to look busy at the counter—as though he wasn't watching the whole pathetic situation unravel. All Kyle can do is apologize as he approaches, and apologize again when the tailor measures the length of Kyle's buttoned vest, explaining how it needs to cover the waistline.

But everything's a blur to Kyle. The last-minute checking, the way the tailor carries the suits to the counter, the way he asks Kyle if he wants *both* suits today. Kyle assures him he does, pays quickly, apologizes once more for the argument that went down, then walks out onto the broiling parking lot to his junker pickup, where he tosses the suits on the passenger seat. When the ignition whines as he turns the key, he hits the dashboard.

"Damn it," he says, letting the engine idle to warm up. Which gives him just enough time to pull out his cell phone and call Lauren. "It's too much for Jason," he tells her. "*Way* too much. Shit, Barlow's gone AWOL on me."

When the idling truck engine shuts off, Kyle patiently restarts it.

"I really need a new truck," he tells Lauren. "And a new best man, too."

thirty-three

SOMETIMES TIMING IS EVERYTHING. THOUGH Lauren's sure Kyle could quote some statistic or analytical table or psychological study proving that timing is *always* everything. That timing's all tied in with our destiny.

Tuesday afternoon, she thinks that might be true when she stops by Maris' house. This was just going to be a quick visit. She'd deliver a bouquet of flowers along with a restaurant gift card to thank Maris and Jason for opening their home to Lauren and her family. And, as often happens around here, a quick visit turned into an iced lemonade and a bit of chatting. The afternoon is warm; sunshine breaking through a tall maple tree drops golden rays on the deck.

The Barlow deck. Which is where Lauren's comfortably sitting right when Kyle calls her cell phone to complain about Jason.

Ah, yes. Timing.

Because after Kyle abruptly disconnects, saying he needs a new best man, Lauren wastes *no* time telling Maris what just went down.

"A fight, apparently. At the menswear shop. Kyle's pretty upset, Maris," she admits after repeating the things Jason said.

"He cast such doubt on Kyle's decision to renew our vows."

"I am *really* sorry," Maris tells her. She sits there in her sleeveless chambray top with ripped white board shorts, and tucks her hair behind an ear. "But I'm actually not surprised."

"You're not?"

Maris glances out toward the bluff, then back at Lauren. "I've been seeing mood swings with Jason lately. He's been snapping, and tense. And *way* too busy, which is always a clue that something's up. Because he's notorious for using work to keep his problems at bay. But I never dreamt he'd snap at *Kyle*."

"I can get it, that's for sure," Lauren admits. She picks up her lemonade glass and walks to the deck railing where Maddy lies in the shade. "You know, that it's ten years since losing Neil. Believe me," she says while crouching to pat the prone German shepherd, "I've had my share of sad thoughts this summer. It's unavoidable. And I'm sure Jason's memories are hitting him full force. But still." She gives Maris a strained smile. "It's Kyle he's coming down on?"

Maris shakes her head. "Wait till I get my hands on that good-for-nothing husband of mine."

"Do you think he'll still be Kyle's best man on Saturday?"

"If *I* have anything to do with it, he will. Maybe the two of them just need some quiet time right now. Both of them are in a pressure cooker, and they must've went at it like two bulls butting heads in that shop."

"Of all places," Lauren says with a glance at her wristwatch. "While they're trying on suits, no less. Oh, what Kyle's tailor must've thought."

"Listen. Maybe you calm down Kyle, kind of brush it off. And I'll work on Jason?"

"That sounds like a plan, I guess." Lauren walks back to the patio table and grabs another sip of her lemonade. "But listen, the kids are in a basketball tournament at Parks and Rec. I'm running a little late, and promised to watch them."

"Okay." Maris walks with Lauren to her golf cart in the driveway. "Okay, you go, hon. And don't worry. The guys will cool off today, and you can count on Jason being at your house first thing tomorrow morning. *With* an apology." She gives Lauren a hug. "But keep it between you and me. Don't let Kyle think that Jason was *whipped* into an apology. Which … he will be."

Lauren gets into her golf cart, starts it up and slowly heads to the street. "Thanks, Maris," she calls out. "It helped to talk to you."

"Anytime!" Maris yells back with a friendly wave. "We're just up the road now."

Lauren sticks her hand out and waves while backing down the sloping driveway. Her golf cart tires crunch over random twigs and stones, which she tries to swerve around. It's not until she reaches the bottom of the long driveway when, lo and behold, who comes careening in—nearly clipping her with his SUV?

Jason Barlow. He slows up and waves to her, but … oh, no. No way in *hell* is Lauren about to reciprocate. Not after what that jerk just put Kyle through, getting him all tied up in knots days before their vow renewal.

As a matter of fact, she doesn't even look at Jason. Doesn't stop to chat, to wave. Nothing. She simply drops on her sunglasses from the top of her head, sits up even straighter, then burns out onto the sandy street.

⁓

Leave it to Maddy to pick right up on Jason's tension. When he parks his SUV near the deck, the dog scrambles up from her lounging and watches him from the top deck stair. Her tall ears, like radar, follow his every curt sound as he bangs things around, slams doors. It's that tension that keeps the dog from running to him.

"What's Lauren's problem?" Jason yells as soon as he's out of his vehicle.

Maris can't miss that there's no *Hello*, no *Missed you, sweetheart*, no *What a hot day*. Just a glare back down the driveway in the direction of Lauren peeling out—as best she can in a golf cart. But from Jason's annoyance, it's obvious she got her point across.

Jason looks at Maris up on the deck again. "Didn't even wave. Is she bent out of shape about something?"

Maris crosses her arms and squints down at Jason. "Oh, no. No, no, no, Jason. Try rephrasing that question, please."

"What?" he asks while grabbing his black work duffel from the SUV's cargo area.

"More like ... What's *your* problem?"

"Swell."

The word is muttered, but Maris can't miss it. She stands there and watches as he brusquely shuts the cargo door and turns in the direction of his barn studio. This morning he'd put on a plaid short-sleeve button-down over chino shorts for filming with the Fenwicks. The shirt, untucked, looks limp now; the shorts, wrinkled. His day's been long.

"I don't want to hear it," he says then, intentionally under his breath. But intentionally also *loud* enough for her to decipher. "Just about had it today."

"So has everyone else here ... with you!" Maris calls after him. As she does, the dog drops to her belly, her paws hanging off the top step as she still only watches her master. "Lauren tells me you don't want to be Kyle's best man now?"

Jason still crosses the yard to his studio. Silently.

"Really, Jason?" Maris yells, stepping around the dog and descending the deck stairs to the grass. There, she stops and shields her eyes against the sun. "You're going to *ruin* everything for them. *Now?*"

Something about her tone must get to him, because he stops. Stops, drops his duffel, turns around and walks back toward her. "Would you keep your voice down?" he asks. "Really, the *neighbors* can hear you yelling like that."

"If you'd stop walking away from me, I would."

Jason turns up his hand. "Okay, darling. So here I am. Say what you want to say."

As Maris takes a step closer, the dog rushes past and jumps into her plastic kiddie pool, where she laps a mouthful of water before sitting right in it.

"Jason." Maris gives him a quick, disbelieving smile. "Please don't do this."

"Do what?"

"Oh, you know. Walk around with that chip on your shoulder."

He glances at his shoulder, then back at Maris.

"Come on," Maris persists. "It's a ten-year anniversary for *everyone*, not just you. I mean, look at what Kyle and Lauren pushed through ten years ago. They made themselves go through the motions—"

"That was *their* choice. Nobody forced them to the altar, Maris. For crying out loud, Lauren broke *up* with Kyle for Neil—two days before my brother died."

"What are you saying, Jason? That Kyle and Lauren should've gone their separate ways? Because it was either that or stick together. So yes, maybe they went through the motions at their wedding, with sadness. And tension." She steps closer. "But with some hope, too. So if you try to find the silver lining in this, it *can* help."

"Silver lining?" Jason walks to the deck and sits on a lower stair to tighten a leather lace on his boat shoes. "Like what, Maris? Like it's been ten years since I've heard my brother's actual voice? Or ... ten years since I could walk the beach with my *own* two legs?"

"Stop it!" Maris throws the words at him. "Just stop it. How about the silver lining of Kyle and Lauren's marriage? How about the silver lining of Kyle honorably raising *Neil's* son? You need to make this year be about someone *other* than yourself, Jason. *That's* how you'll get through it." She steps closer and drops her voice. "By being a bigger man than what I'm seeing lately."

"*What?*" he asks, standing again.

Maris simply shrugs. But when Jason waves her away and turns toward the barn studio, she grabs hold of his arm. "Kyle's off tomorrow," she tells him when he glares back at her. "And you are going to his house *first* thing in the morning." When he grimaces and twists out of her grip, she gets ahold of that plaid shirt fabric and pulls him closer. "After all he's done for you? You'll knock on his door," she whispers, "and eat a *big* piece of humble pie, begging his forgiveness for what you said today."

"I am not going over there," he whispers back in a way that might scare anyone other than Maris, "*begging*." Then he removes her hand from his shirt and backs up a step. "If he can't handle the way I feel, that's his problem. And *you*, Maris, can quit your meddling. You and the ladies," he says with a sweeping motion to the driveway Lauren skidded out of.

"Ooh, Jason Barlow," Maris answers with a stamp of her foot that gets Madison leaping out of the pool and loping over. "You make me so mad! It's no wonder I get *no* writing done lately."

"That's my fault now, too?"

"Yes. Because I'm too busy fixing *your* messes! If I left things to you, there'd be ... well, let's face it. There'd be *no* TV show, and now there'd be no vow renewal."

When Jason turns back toward his studio, he says under his breath, "Maybe I'd like it better that way."

"*Excuse me?*" Maris asks. Of course she heard him—loud and clear. But her indignation riles her up. "If you have something to say, you say it now, Jason. To my face."

Well. She and her indignation just stand there then, hands on hips. Because Jason keeps going—this time with Madison at his heels. But Maris hears that, too, the whine the dog gives as she licks Jason's hand while walking beside him right up to the studio's double doors, which Jason unlocks and yanks open.

"Fine!" Maris calls after him. But this time, she does walk closer so that only *he* hears what she quietly yells next. "Sit in there alone like you used to before you married me." Another few steps closer, her sandaled feet crunching over twigs in the overgrown lawn. She's got one more line to deliver on this hot summer afternoon before she'll spin around and go back inside the house through the slider there—a slider screen she'll *surely* slam shut. But not before her final blow.

"Sit there and listen to the voices."

As she says it, tears burn her eyes. Lord knows, it's the last thing she wanted to say to Jason.

But it's also time that he make a decision: Either live with the voices in the past, or live in the here and now ... with the people who, damn it, mean the entire world to him. And he knows it, too.

"Son of a bitch, Maddy." Jason looks out through the door to where Maris is walking across the yard to the gabled house, where she slams the slider behind her. "Ah, fuck," he mutters before turning to his work desk. After tossing his duffel beside it, he logs onto his desktop computer to check for any new work emails. "Damn it," he whispers while bending closer to see the full inbox, all while his hand is clicking the computer mouse. There are too many new messages stacked there for him to even *start* reading right now, so he logs out, looks around the cavernous studio space, then rolls out his chair and sits.

Just sits. Behind him, the studio is silent except for the dog's nails clicking on the planked floor as she paces. When Jason's cell phone rings, he checks the caller ID before answering it, wanting to be sure it's not Trent asking why he's ignoring all his emails.

"Paige," he says to his sister on the other end. "Not a good time."

"But I haven't heard from you in a while."

"I'm busy."

"And you usually call at *least* once a week." A pause, then, that Jason does not fill. So Paige finally does. "Everything okay with you and Maris?"

Jason spins his chair toward the studio's double doors and glances to the house across the yard. "Why does everyone think there's a problem with me and Maris?"

"Everyone?"

"Never mind."

"Well, I *hope* you two are good. But now I'm having my doubts," Paige tells him. When he says nothing more, she continues. "Anyway, here's why I'm calling, if you'd even care to know. Vinny and I tacked on an extra vacation week here, so we'll be at what's fondly referred to as Cannoli Cottage a little longer. I thought that on Sunday, the day after Kyle and Lauren's shindig, we could have a beach day with you and Maris. You know, before Vinny has to get back to coaching for the new school year."

"The kids'll be there, too?" Jason asks.

"No. Even though you're their uncle and they *never* even see you, the kids are staying with my in-laws for the weekend. Vinny's parents are babysitting while we're at the vow renewal. So it would just be me and Vinny."

Jason drops his head back and lightly rubs his eyes. "I'll check my schedule, Paige."

"Jason!"

She says it loud enough that he pulls the phone away from his ear, all while still hearing his sister's voice come through. "Make time for family! I just called Mom in Florida. You talk to her lately? She's all excited about going on an Everglades tour with the women's club."

"I'll call her later. Got to go now."

Of course, Paige manages to get in a few more lines about Maris, *and* about Jason's upcoming wedding anniversary.

But that's not what sticks with him as he finally hangs up and moves to his drafting table. Paige's words about his being married to Maris for two *years* now aren't what strike a chord as he works on a blueprint raising the Fenwick cottage to meet flood standards.

Aren't what distract him as he plugs dimensions and computations into his calculator.

Aren't what have him turn on his stool and look out again toward the house across the yard.

Aren't what get him to turn off the swing light over his drafting table, set down his pencil and walk across the wood-planked floor to the double slider, where he stands looking out.

It isn't Paige's words at all, actually, that have him unhinged—

so much so that he can't make any progress on his blueprint, still unrolled on his drafting table.

No, it's *Maris'* words haunting him alone in his silent studio. Even the dog is quiet, watching him from her guard post up in the loft.

Words Maris tossed his way, reminding him of his life before she married him. Reminding him of what so many of his days had been like before the *whirlwind* that is Maris swept into his days, his home, his heart.

Sit there and listen to the voices.

Jason turns around and looks behind him at the empty, L-shaped work desk Maris made him buy when he renovated this barn. He looks at his empty stool at his drafting table. Glances up at Maris' studio in the loft. At the long-ago swiped moose head she pats *every* single time she passes it on the stairs to that loft. Looks at the mighty impressive wall of cottages—framed photographs of his completed renovations. Maris made him put up those, too. Said they should be displayed like an art exhibit for clients to admire.

What it all does, seeing the scope of his life now, is this: It makes him remember, none too fondly, life before Maris. Life working out of his condominium, alone. Life without anyone but his sister checking in on him. Days that ended in a quiet kitchen, over a solitary meal when not even the phone rang.

"Damn it," he whispers as he looks across the yard to his gray-shingled house on the bluff. After whistling for Maddy, he closes up his studio and crosses the unkempt lawn. The sun is setting now; a lone robin chirrups in the tall maple tree, almost as though the chattering bird's scolding him. He can hear a scorn in its persistent song as he climbs the deck stairs. A light is on in the kitchen, and so Jason slowly crosses the deck with the dog at his side.

Outside the slider, he listens for a second. The sounds he hears bring a heartbreaking memory, one that leaves a lump in his throat. Dishes clatter in the sink; water flows from the tap; silverware clinks as the flatware drawer is pulled open.

Yep, they break his heart. Because he remembers hearing those *same* noises while standing on the other side of her screen door three summers ago now. The screen door leading to *Maris'* cottage, before they'd even started dating.

Paradise, he'd thought then. Thought it was as far removed from his life as a ship on the horizon.

And now, paradise is right here, on the other side of *their* door.

He looks inside, seeing some of Maris' manuscript pages on the kitchen table, seeing a starfish leaning against a hurricane lantern beside it, seeing cell phones and tablets being charged on the countertop, and pots and pans on the stove, and mail envelopes and key rings on the cabinet near the door. And he sees Maris, too, barefoot. Casual in her ripped white shorts and chambray top, her long hair pulled back in a low ponytail.

Finally, Jason opens the slider. When he steps inside, Maris looks over her shoulder. She's quiet for a second. And he can't tell if she'd been crying—not that he'd blame her after he'd been such a prick.

But she does it, then, what she always does. Makes things better. She gives him a small smile and says, "Sit down." She hitches her head toward the table. "I made us supper."

Jason hesitates, then closes the slider behind him, walks across the kitchen, sits and lets out the breath it feels like he'd been holding in all day.

No matter what Kyle did the rest of the day, it felt like an out-of-body experience. Working the afternoon shift at the diner; stopping at Maritime Market on his way home; flipping through the mail in the kitchen; pushing his lawn mower across the back lawn. He just hasn't been present since Jason's meltdown. Like a broken record, the memory runs on repeat in his mind as he considers losing his best man days before the ceremony. Over and over again, he hears the tense words, feels his blood pressure rise, sees the image of Jason walking out of the menswear store—alone.

So now, Kyle tries to salvage one of his favorite parts of the day: sitting in front of the TV and watching Connecticut's beloved meteorologist Leo Sterling give the weather forecast.

Until Lauren tries to cheer him up. She sits on the sofa and chats once the kids are in bed.

"Let me just watch the weather now," Kyle tells her, "after the day that Barlow ruined."

"Listen," she says, touching a lock of his hair. "Try to understand, maybe. Just think back to when we got married. Jason was in a wheelchair. I mean, *in a wheelchair*. And completely shot. So give him time to process things. Maybe he didn't count on how he'd feel with a do-over of that day." Her finger lights on Kyle's arm. "But he'll come around."

Kyle looks at Lauren, then back at the TV screen. It's warm in the living room, and he lifts the fabric of his tee to fan his chest. "You didn't hear the fight in that store. Shit, I'm so embarrassed, I can't step foot in there ever again."

"Why would you need to?"

"To get a suit for Jason's *funeral*, after I kill him."

Lauren slaps Kyle's shoulder. "Oh, stop. Don't talk like that. It'll work out. Jason will calm down."

Kyle crosses his arms across his chest now, extends his legs and crosses them at the ankle. "The weather's on. I want to watch."

In a moment, he feels Lauren squeeze his stiff, angry shoulder. His whole body is in knots, for Christ's sake. "I'm going to put on my pajamas," Lauren tells him. "You should, too."

Pajamas, Kyle thinks. Right. As if he'll *ever* be able to sleep tonight.

As soon as she's upstairs, Lauren grabs her cell phone and checks in with Maris. A brief text message should do the trick.

Situation status? she quickly types.

All systems go, comes an equally quick answer. *Jason at your door 7 AM.*

After sending Maris a thumbs-up emoji, Lauren does what she really set out to do. She puts on a short silky nightgown with spaghetti-strap sleeves and goes to the kitchen.

That's right, the kitchen. Because her nightie track history hasn't been working too well in wearing down Kyle's celibacy vow. So this time, she'll add a cookie. A big, fat chocolate-chip cookie warmed up in the microwave. When she finally returns to the living room, she hands Kyle the cookie plate from behind, over his shoulder. He takes it, bites into the gooey cookie, glances back and nearly chokes on his sweet treat after seeing Lauren in her revealing lingerie.

"Pajamas? That's *not* pajamas," he says while sitting upright, still gagging. "And a cookie? What are you doing, Ell?"

"Comforting you." Lauren walks around the sofa and snuggles up beside Kyle. "You're so sad."

"Oh, no you don't." Kyle sets his plate on the end table and crosses his arms over his chest again, still managing to hold onto that cookie, though.

And, Lauren notices, he also can't stop glancing over at her sexy nightie.

"It's been so long, honey," she murmurs, dragging her finger down his arm.

"Yeah. And I'm still saving myself for our wedding night." He takes another bite of the warm cookie. "Best man or not," he continues around the food.

"But it's so close, our vow renewal," Lauren persists. Persists touching him, too. Her gentle fingers land on his neck, his chest, his thigh. "And it's going to be a perfect ceremony. What difference does it make if we fool around, a day or two this way or that?" she purrs while pressing into him, being sure all her right curves land in all his right spots.

"A ton of difference. It'll *jinx* things. You even saying how perfect that day will be is *not* good. Studies show that's the best jinx setup. Acknowledge how *good* things are going and *abracadabra*, a jinx is cast to prove otherwise."

"Kyle! I'm not casting a spell on you ... Unless you *want* me to," Lauren whispers into his ear. "*Come on.*"

When he looks at her beside him, she stands up in her silk nightie and hooks her finger for him to follow her to the bedroom. She walks slowly toward the staircase, never taking her eyes off him, her hand beckoning. "*Kyle,*" she whispers, smiling sweetly.

And never expecting what happens next.

Never expecting Kyle to take a couch pillow, fling it at her, then settle back on the sofa, arms crossed once again.

"*Gesù, Santa Maria.*" Lauren picks up the pillow she'd sidestepped and clutches it close. "Fine, suit yourself," she tells him as she goes upstairs ... alone.

thirty-four

After everything Kyle Bradford's lived through in his entire adult life, not too much surprises him. No, because he's seen it all. Lived it all.

Yes, Kyle's worked hard, and played hard. Fell in love hard, too, before having his heart broken to pieces. Found pure happiness standing behind the big stove at the diner, and seethed with raw anger at people who wronged him. Neil being one, and yes, his forever unspoken-of brother being the other. Kyle's looked death in the face, and marveled at a whispering sea breeze touching his skin. He's fought well, tempted trouble, evaded the authorities. He's ridden the carousel and reached for the brass ring. He's skinny-dipped with his wife. Fished with the guys.

You name it, Kyle figures he's done it—in some way, shape or form. So to *surprise* him, well, you'd have to move a mountain.

Which someone obviously did.

Because Kyle Bradford is nothing less than surprised early Wednesday morning when he sees who's ringing his doorbell.

There's no mistaking who it is when Kyle rounds the corner in his living room and heads to the enclosed porch. On the other side of the screen front door stands a man waiting.

CASTAWAY COTTAGE

Stands Jason Barlow.

But he's not on the doorstep. No. Jason stands on the lawn as though he might be uncertain about this visit; might be about to hightail it back to his parked golf cart.

Kyle stops in the doorway from the living room to the porch and crosses his arms over his chest. "What are you doing here?" he asks.

"Kyle." Jason walks to the step now. "Look," he says through the screen door. "I'm really sorry about yesterday. At the store. A little stress got the best of me."

"A little?" Kyle asks, unmoving.

"Well. That and this damn heat. So. I'm here ... I apologize, guy. You deserve a helluva lot better than the shit I dished out."

Kyle—still not moving, still not uncrossing his T-shirted arms revealing sizable heft—simply eyes Jason through the screen for an uncomfortable second. "I kind of figured something was going on. You know, with the ten-year anniversary of losing your brother and all rearing its head. Christ, that decade mark does funny things."

Jason nods.

"It can really mess with you," Kyle adds.

"No shit."

"So you're telling me you're *good* about being my best man on Saturday? You can get *through* it?" Kyle asks, emphasizing the word as if maybe, just *maybe*, Jason's *not* strong enough.

But hell, of course Kyle knows he is. It's just that his suggestion will get Jason's dander up, and, yeah ... it's payback time. A good opportunity to mess with his friend. Just a little, anyway.

"Definitely." Jason turns up a hand. "Come on, man. Don't make this hard on me."

"Well, the thing is," Kyle says with a glance back into his house. But still, he just stands in the doorway, filling every inch of it. "I've got your suit in my closet and can just as well give it to Matt. Or maybe ..." He pauses, considering what name might piss off Jason. "Nick."

"*Nick?* No way, he's the furthest from best man material. And anyway, that suit's *mine*, Kyle. So I'm telling you, I'm really sorry you had to see me come undone like that. Especially in public."

"Relax, Barlow. I'm just busting your balls," Kyle steps onto the porch now and unlatches the hook on the screen door. "Lord knows you've seen me in a few choice situations." He motions to something Jason's holding. "What's in the bag?"

"Seriously? That's it? You're over it?"

"Eh, that's how I roll. Now what'd you bring for grub?"

"Egg sandwiches."

"The ones Elsa goes gaga over?"

Jason nods. "You got a bench over on that beach on the bay? Sun came up, we can have these near the water."

"No bench. But I've got two sand chairs that'll work just as good." Kyle leans back into the doorway behind him, facing the living room. "Hey, Ell," he calls out. "Back in a half hour."

Lauren rushes out of the kitchen while drying her hands on a dishtowel. "Wait!" she says, squeezing past Kyle to the porch. "Oh, *Jason!* Good to see you ... *today.*"

As Kyle heads out the door and grabs the sand chairs leaning against the side of the house, he hears Jason apologizing to Lauren, too. Something about how he didn't mean what he said yesterday, a full plate got the better of him. By the time Kyle is back in the front yard, though, with a sand chair in each hand, all's forgiven. Lauren hurries out to give Jason a quick hug, then pushes him and Kyle off to eat and make amends.

After a quick stop at Jason's golf cart to snag the take-out coffees he'd also brought, they cross the narrow street to Back Bay's beach. It's just beyond some scrubby bushes and dune grasses. There's a narrow path worn right through by the neighbors' daily treks seaside. Kyle leads the way, chairs in tow.

"So," he says over his shoulder. "Maris give you a piece of her mind to get you here?"

"What? You don't think I came of my own accord?" Jason asks.

Kyle stops to raise his eyebrows at him before walking along the short path that opens onto the sand. Over to the left, running along the far length of Back Bay's beach, a tall, wide embankment rises high off the sand. It's built up with large stones and is topped with the railroad tracks that bring trains by throughout the day.

"Dude." Kyle waits on the sand for Jason to catch up. "I've seen you—before and after, if you get my drift. Before Maris, and now. And heck, there's no *way* she didn't get you here today. You're so henpecked." Kyle starts walking to the shore then, where waves gently lap and the sun is a fireball slowly climbing into the sky.

"Oh, and you're *not* henpecked?" Jason says, walking beside him on the beach, carrying those egg sandwiches in their white bag. "With that *honey-do* list of yours?"

Kyle laughs, just laughs. Well, he also gives his newly restored best man a good shove before opening their chairs right at the water's edge.

⁓

Maris can see it's been a long day for Jason. Starting with fixing things with Kyle, to working on several projects—both in the barn studio and at the Fenwick cottage—to having a quiet barbecue at Matt and Eva's, it all shows on his face. By evening, he looks, if she had to name it ... weary.

It probably doesn't help that this significant ten-year marker of his brother's violent death falls during the summer when Jason's getting a TV show off the ground *and* kicking his architectural name and reputation into high gear. So, she cuts him some slack and tries to lighten his day. Even with small things, like driving the golf cart home from Eva's so he can just sit back and relax.

"It was nice of you and Matt to take Taylor driving while Eva and I cleaned up the kitchen," she says when she's pulling into their own driveway.

"Yeah, she needed some practice parallel parking. A few more times and she'll be good for her driving test."

Helping Maris carry in a few packages, Jason sets them on the kitchen counter as she turns on some lights and gives Maddy a fresh bowl of water. What she notices, the whole time, is that Jason seems a little lost tonight. Like he's unsure of even what to do with himself. Which is something new. Usually some mile-long itinerary has him checking things off right until bedtime.

So did the past couple of days take their toll on him—from pissing off his wife *and* his best friend, to reliving painful memories of a dark date fast approaching?

Maris reaches into one of the bags he set down and pulls out a few plastic containers and a wrapped dish. "Why don't you go sit outside with the dog?" she asks. "I'll bring out wine when I'm finished here."

Jason does, wordlessly. After Maris puts Eva's leftovers in the fridge, turns on their jukebox softly and pours the wine, she glances out to the deck. Jason's lit a couple of tiki torches, the flames flickering in the night. It also looks like he's talking to the dog as he sits there and blows bubbles for her to snap at.

"Hailey must've left those behind?" Maris asks when she comes out with the wine.

"Apparently." Jason holds the bubble wand to his mouth and blows a few large bubbles that the dog leaps for.

The evening is quiet. There's only the sound of the German shepherd's paws clicking on the deck in her bubble quest, along with lazy crickets chirping. Old, familiar jukebox songs make their way out to them, too—slow songs about loving and leaving, waiting and wanting. Maris sits across from Jason at the patio table and slides his wineglass to him.

"Everything okay?" she asks.

"Long day."

"That's it?"

"Honestly, sweetheart?" He takes a swallow of his wine. "It's everything."

"I knew it. Is it too much, then? Kyle and Lauren's celebration at the ten-year mark?"

"No. I'll handle it. Sometimes, though, I can't help thinking how things might have turned out if that accident never happened."

"What do you mean?"

"Like, would it be a ten-year anniversary for *Neil* and Lauren? What would my brother have done with his life? What kind of father would he be to Evan?" Jason looks out to the bluff, to where he sat with Neil and their own father so many times over the years. "I don't know. I've made peace with it, somewhat. But damn. That ten-year mark snuck up on me. Now? Now I just want this month over with."

Maris reaches over and squeezes his hand. "I'll tell you one thing," she says. "Neil would've been so impressed with what you're doing, Jason. He'd be all over it. And then there's his book, almost done now."

"He'd be into it, for sure. All of it. And that helps, I guess. Knowing we're doing him proud."

"Sometimes when I'm alone in his shack working on the manuscript," Maris says, "it feels now more than ever that he's *here*. You know, with his influence on the novel. And on your show, too."

Jason only nods. Nods and sips his wine.

The night is still, like so many of them have been this summer. The flickering tiki torches throw wavering shadows on the deck. From the jukebox, a sad piano melody and slow bluesy drumbeat drift outside—the sound floating on a hint of a sea breeze lifting off the bluff.

"It's just like Foley's, back in the day," Jason finally says. "The way the tunes carry out here to the deck tonight."

Maris sips her wine, then stands and takes his hand. "Come on," she whispers. "Let's dance, then. On the deck, beneath the stars. Just like those old Foley days."

He hesitates, but does it. He gives in.

It's a start, Maris knows, to lifting his spirits. So when he takes her in his arms, she presses close. Because as the record plays, its words about leaving your love behind, well, they have her think of all Jason's been through this past year. It was enough for him to leave *her* behind the night of Sal's funeral. And though Jason often says he fell in love with her dancing on Foley's deck fifteen long years ago, Maris can't help but wonder ... Is she enough?

She rests her head on his shoulder now and feels his fingers touching her hair. Soft violin and strains of saxophone float outside like wisps of fog. Together she and Jason move across the deck in a slow dance that keeps her hips moving against him.

There's no denying he's a man dealt more than most: more blows, more loss. But like the singer insists, she'll be here for him.

It's all that matters.

That he knows he can always bring it home, to her. Bring home his worries, his happiness. His sweet loving.

When his hands slip down from her hair, to her waist, she lets him know that, too. She reaches her own hands behind his neck and kisses him, lightly first. But when he pulls her even closer, she deepens the kiss. Her mouth opens to his, her hands toy with his wavy hair, her body subtly sways.

All while the music plays on, and the tiki torches flicker, and her touch soothes as they dance alone on their deck in the warm, still night.

~

It's funny how regret can almost be a physical sensation. There's no denying it, because later, Jason feels regret coursing through his body. It began on the deck with Maris. After a few dances, they drank another glass of wine and talked quietly before coming inside. The gentleness in her every word, every touch, didn't help. It made him feel even worse about the way he talked to her yesterday, when all that mattered to his son-of-a-bitch soul was his own effin' self-pity. No one else had experienced what he did ten years ago, and he was going to be damn sure they knew it. Maris, and Kyle especially, caught the full brunt of his unrestrained, short-fused emotion.

The thing is, he should be glad, ecstatic even, that the people he loves never *did* experience what he did the day of that motorcycle wreck. He'd subject himself to it all over again before he put it on anyone else.

So, yes. With every murmur, every smile Maris directed at him this evening, he regretted his recent—*dammit*—his recent pity party. A party that had him look like an ass. It had been building ever since Kyle announced his vow renewal, a celebratory ceremony in the anniversary year of the worst day of *Jason's* life.

But two hours of dancing in the moonlight and drinking sweet wine with his beautiful wife put an end to it all. Two hours of a warm summer evening with Maris changed his outlook on this pivotal year.

Life is for celebrating. For loving.

Because let's face it. Loving is forever, Maris had said while sipping her wine. *We never stop loving someone, even after they're gone. So, you know ... Let this be the summer of love, Jason.*

Now, the house is closed up for the night and he stands at his dresser, emptying coins and keys from his pockets, then taking off his watch. When he turns, Maris is sitting on the bed beside his chair. She's wearing that black satin short set he likes, with the lace-trimmed top. The one silky beneath his fingers.

"Come on," she whispers, hitching her head and motioning him over.

When he crosses the room and sits in the chair, she leaves the bed and crouches in front of him. "Let me help," she says, reaching over and touching his leg.

"Maris."

"Shh," she answers, then sets her hands around his prosthetic limb and holds it as he shifts his stump out of it. Carefully, she leans the prosthesis against the nightstand, then turns back to him. "*Let* me," she tells him while tenderly unrolling the silicone liner and sock, too.

It's while she's doing this that regret finally breaks Jason's heart. The feeling—regret—is so palpable, it's almost unbearable.

CASTAWAY COTTAGE

Unaware, Maris' feather-soft touch continues as she removes the liner and sock from his leg, and sets them on the bedside table. Watching her silently, Jason can't believe how mean he actually was to her yesterday, in the backyard. Because if there's one thing he knows more than anything else, it's that he loves this woman he watches. There will never be anyone else for him.

"Maris," he whispers when she draws her hand along his upper leg. Her fingers move aside the fabric of his cargo shorts and trace along his skin there. "I'm sorry," Jason tells her.

"For what?" she asks, drawing those delicate lines down his thigh to where his left leg ends below the knee.

"For yesterday," he says, his voice low. "For the things I said to you."

She stands and bends over him still sitting on the chair. Her long brown hair falls forward; her silky top is loose as one of the spaghetti straps slips off her shoulder. But all that matters is the way she kisses him then. Once, twice. "Don't worry about it," she murmurs before taking his hand and helping him shift over into bed. "Let me forgive you, babe. My way."

And so her forgiveness begins. Those fingers that lightly stroked his leg? They touch his whiskered face now, and his neck, before tracing along the length of chain holding his father's Vietnam dog tags. Jason lies there, an arm crooked behind his head as he listens to her whispers, and hears also the whisper of waves breaking easy out on the bluff. In the dim lamplight, Maris' fingers gently tuck the silver chain back behind his collar before dropping to his tee. There they take the shirt fabric and lift it up and off over his head. She sits up straight then, to toss the shirt on his bedside chair before turning back to Jason.

Before dropping her hands to unbuckle his leather belt, to undo his zipper and slip his shorts off, too.

Before shutting off the lamp and lying with him in darkness now. Salty and damp sea air drifts in through the open windows as he turns to her.

Because it's in that darkness that the moment changes. In the warm heat of the August night, it's *his* hands that reach for her now, that touch the cool satin of her top—his fingers slipping beneath the thin straps and stroking the bare skin of her shoulder. His touch is followed by the trail of kisses he leaves on her skin as she lies on her back beside him. As his kiss moves lower to her breast, her hands tangle in his hair, stroke the scarred skin on his back. When he hears her soft moan, he moves his kiss to her neck, her mouth.

"I love you, Jason," she whispers in the night.

And her words, they get him to stop. To take a breath and lie beside her, stroking her long brown hair, tucking it behind an ear. To look at this woman who won't *let* him be alone, in any way. Even in memory.

Won't let him push her, or Kyle, or *anyone* away.

He traces a finger along her ear, her jaw, while wondering what he *ever* did in his life to deserve her. But when he starts to say he loves her, too, she stops him with a surprisingly insistent kiss— her mouth toying with his as though she's still forgiving him, and all he has to do tonight is take her words, take her touch. Because instead of letting him talk, it's during her kiss that her hands find his and guide them to the satin drawstring of her silky shorts, then leave the rest to him.

Leave him free to tug the drawstring loose, to slide his hands beneath the fabric and touch her there before slipping her shorts off. Leave his hand free to push beneath her back and lift her even closer as he moves on top of her.

And it works, all of what Maris does. Because in this dark

night, alone in their room overlooking Long Island Sound, he knows. Feeling every bit of her body beneath his, hearing her whisper his name in his ear, he knows. Oh, she had her own way of going about it, that's for sure. But she gave him something far more than forgiveness tonight.

In this summer that he'd pretty much written off the map with all the memory and grief it could dredge up, she went and did it.

With grace and love, Maris just gave him his sweet summer back.

thirty-five

THURSDAY MORNING SEEMS STRAIGHT OUT of a dream. It's a crystal-clear, blue-sky beach day. Sunlight reflects thousands of ocean stars on the calm water; the tide is low, bringing small waves lapping on the sand; a seagull's cry carries over and over on the soft sea breeze. And the length of Stony Point Beach is lined with what looks like giant lollipops—beach umbrellas of turquoise-blue and lemon-yellow and cherry-red, some striped, some fringed—rising from the sand.

Sitting on her beach towel, Lauren discreetly does it. Yes, with her arms wrapped around her knees as she takes in the August view, she pinches herself. That's it, one little pinch that proves to her she's not asleep, seeing this in a dream.

It's all real.

"This was the *best* idea for my bachelorette party," she admits while on her towel and feeling the sun's warmth on her skin. "Laying out."

"Utopia," Eva says beside her.

When her party guests all murmur in agreement, Lauren lifts her cell phone and sneaks a fun photo. There they are, each of them lying on a blanket or towel. All are on their backs; none move; some have a leg bent at the knee. Celia's bathing suit straps are lowered off her shoulders; Maris wears a polka-dot tankini; Elsa's gold-chain necklaces glimmer against her jet-black halter-top swimsuit; Eva is propped up on her elbows. All have on sunglasses. Her friends form a perfect line of sunbathing beach girls, laying out at the water's edge. Why, there's even a baby beach girl! Little Aria is sound asleep in her playpen beneath the umbrella.

When Lauren sets her head back down with a long, relaxed breath, there's even more than warmth and chattering voices. There's the comforting scent of suntan lotion that they slathered and sprayed on before hitting the towels.

What it all feels like—the sun, the relaxed voices, that seagull's cry carrying on the salty air—is this: an elixir. It's Thursday, two days before her vow renewal ceremony. And what she feels on the beach is exactly what she feels her life is, finally. Peaceful. Waves lapping easy. Warm. A whisper of a sea breeze brushing her skin.

"I'm really excited for you," Celia says. "You and Kyle are so into this vow renewal." She sits up then and touches Lauren's arm. "Did you ever think you'd marry Kyle again?"

"No. And it's perfect." Lauren sits, too, and sets her wide-brimmed hat low on her head to block the sun's rays. "Now if I could just bottle this sweet morning and keep it forever."

"That's a nice thought," Elsa lets her know. Pushing her cat-eye sunglasses to the top of her head, she sits up, leans back on her hands and tips her face to the sun.

"At least you'll always have the memory," Maris adds, sitting now, too, while straightening her straw cowboy hat.

"Let's add another memory to the day," Elsa says. "A yummy one." She reaches for her insulated tote and pulls out a container. "Because now it's time for my summer specialty," she tells them when she passes the container to Eva. "Blueberry-cheesecake brownies. Made with fresh blueberries from the farmers' market."

"Holy cow, and I thought I was in utopia *before*." Eva takes a brownie and passes them to the others.

Except for a few *mmms* and sighs as everyone bites in, they quiet again beneath the summer sun. As far as Lauren is concerned, all is good with the world.

Until Eva motions toward the approaching security guard. "Uh-oh," she says.

"Quick." Maris is stuffing the last of her brownie into her mouth. "Hide the food."

"Oh, the *last* thing I need is to be issued a fine," Lauren whispers as she drops her sunhat over her brownie.

"Hey, hey, hey." Nick stops in front of them and tips up his black uniform cap to survey the situation. "No food on the beach, ladies." As he says it, he's already pulling out his ticket pad.

"Seriously?" Celia asks. "It was just a snack."

"Food is food. And to quote my boss, *The rules are the rules*." Nick's busy dotting his i's and crossing his t's while explaining. "So whose name should I put on this violation?" He looks at them—pen poised.

"Wait! But we brought one for *you*," Lauren explains, standing at the same time she's finishing her brownie—just in time to grab another and hold it his way.

"Now, I'm sorry to say, but *that* falls under bribery, Lauren." He fills in a number on the ticket, saying aloud, "Ordinance B.3."

Which is all it takes to get Eva to her feet, too. Except she picks up the entire *container* of brownies. "Bribery, schmibery, Nicholas. You want one, and you know it."

Nick lowers his sunglasses and eyes her over.

Wordlessly, Eva steps closer and gives the container a shake.

"Come on," she whispers. "Just rip up that ticket and take *two* brownies, for the love of God."

"Or at least for the love of Lauren and Kyle," Elsa pipes in. "This *is* her bachelorette party after all, before her vow renewal."

"Her what?" Nick asks while helping himself to a brownie before looking at Elsa. "A party?"

"Bachelorette party," Lauren explains, tugging on her sunhat again. "You know. A little fun morning before my *wedding do-over*," she says, air-quoting the words.

He turns to *her* now, mid-chew. "A party on the beach … authorized by the Board of Governors, I'm sure?"

"Oh, for crying out loud," Eva insists while still holding the brownies. "I thought the way to a man's heart was through his stomach."

"Okay, okay. It is," Nick agrees while chewing and looking at his half-written ticket. He manages another bite of the blueberry-cheesecake brownie. "So. I'm just saying. If I tear up your ticket and look the other way, *this* illicit exchange," he says, pausing to take a second brownie, "never happened, ladies. Your brownie bribe is strictly off the record."

"That's better." Eva snags another brownie for herself before returning the container to Elsa, then sitting on her towel again. "Much, *much* better."

Watching this go down, Lauren can't believe it: A bit of brownie bait saves the day. Nick folds shut his ticket pad, drops it in his pocket and continues his beach patrol. "Enjoy your morning," he calls over his shoulder.

⁓

The thing is, with that calamity averted, Lauren can't help wondering if maybe another has been averted, too.

And that would be the Shane calamity. She's silently wavered back and forth on her decision to invite Kyle's brother to the ceremony, and still has heard nothing from him. Problem is, this not knowing is tormenting her. So with Nick off on his merry way down the beach, Lauren returns to her towel and checks her cell phone for any last-minute RSVPs ... for the umpteenth time this week.

And, okay. Though no one knows it, she's specifically checking for *Shane's* RSVP—only to find none. There hasn't been one word from him. Not one in the years and years since his and Kyle's falling-out; not one in the days since she emailed his invitation. Not a *Yes*, nor a *Not-on-your-life no*. Not a *Will be there with pleasure*, nor a *Fuck off*. Nothing.

Now that the ceremony is so close, maybe Lauren's glad, after all. Her attempt to extend an olive branch that might heal the brothers' rift may have been misguided by her, well, her love ... of Kyle. Of Sal, too, and his sentiments about family. If he'd known about it, Sal never would've wanted this breach between brothers to continue.

After another glance at her phone, she then looks at her beach friends, all digging into Elsa's brownies and pouring lemonade from a juice jug. They're perfectly distracted enough for Lauren to grab the tote she'd brought along. It's filled with her painted driftwood place cards for the reception tables. Quickly she digs out the lobster-painted one with Shane's name on it and discreetly drops it into her own beach tote. The whole secret ordeal is done now.

No word from Shane, no driftwood place card, no problem.

"Elsa." With a refreshing relief, Lauren stands and takes the tote to her. "Here are the guest place cards I painted."

"Oh, wonderful!" Elsa lifts out a piece of driftwood, one with

CASTAWAY COTTAGE

Matt's name painted on it. "These will look so coastal on the table."

"Now that those are done, everything's just about set. I only have to finish packing for our honeymoon," Lauren tells them all. "At Chickadee Shanty! A cute little cabin in the woods."

"You guys will *love* it," Celia says. "It's so charming there, right beside a little lake. It's a perfect hideaway in Addison. *And*, a little *love* nest, too."

"Which I'm sure you and Kyle will *fully* utilize," Eva says with a wink.

Lauren lowers her sunglasses and peers over the frame at Eva. "And just what are you getting at?"

"Kyle's vow of celibacy!" Eva answers.

"You *know* about that?" Lauren whips off her sunglasses completely this time. "But that's personal."

"Yup," Maris says, lying back down on her blanket. "It's a real Stony Point secret."

"And we all know what *that* means," Elsa adds as she walks to the baby playpen beneath their beach umbrella.

"Elsa!" Lauren puts her hands on her hips. "*You* know all about my love life, too?"

"Or lack thereof." Elsa shrugs, then lifts little Aria out and holds the baby against her shoulder.

"Swell." Lauren returns to her towel and sits with her arms wrapped around her bent legs. Before her, Long Island Sound sparkles beneath the morning sunlight. The water is calm, nothing but blue, blue, blue unfurling as far as the eye can see. "Well, it'll come as no surprise then," Lauren says, "that I've been *very* frustrated lately. I just can't get any action. For *weeks* now."

"Nothing?" Maris asks.

"Zilch. Once Kyle got this celibacy idea in his head, his mind was made up." Lauren takes a deep breath. "He's saving himself for marriage. Wants our second wedding night to be ... *special*."

"Come on Lauren, you're a bombshell." Eva leans over and lifts her sunglasses to the top of her head. "No sex for *weeks*?" she repeats. "How could Kyle hold out?"

"Believe me, it's not that I haven't tried, Lord help me," Lauren admits. "I mean, I've gone *all* out to seduce that man and get him to break down."

"Well, I hope there aren't any close neighbors at that lakeside shanty," Eva muses. "With all your pent-up sexual tension, who knows what noises might come from the honeymoon suite in the woods."

"It *is* pretty isolated," Celia tells them. "At most, they'll be keeping the deer awake."

"Ooh la la," the women tease Lauren in their singsong voices.

"If the cabin's a-rockin' ..." Maris lightly chants.

"Don't come knockin'," Elsa softly says while putting a sunbonnet on Aria.

"Elsa!" Lauren whips off her own sunhat and gives Elsa a swat. "Really! While you're holding the baby?"

"Now there's an idea," Celia tells Lauren. "Maybe you'll give Aria a beach-baby buddy?"

"That's about enough," Lauren declares before lightly shoving Celia beside her.

The thing is, Lauren loves it all: the laughs, the intimacy, the good-natured teasing. But heck, enough *is* enough. She's not sure she wants her sex life to be this closely scrutinized. So instead, she grabs one of the inflated tubes behind them. "Last one in is a rotten egg!" As they all jump up from their hazy-lazy sun-lounging to race her, Lauren adds one more thing over her shoulder. "Because heck, I haven't *gotten* any in so long, I *need* to cool off!"

Minutes later, when they're all floating in bright tubes on Long Island Sound, and laughing beneath the sparkling morning sunshine, it happens. With her friends chattering around her, and with Elsa wading ankle-deep while dipping Aria's toes in the water, Lauren knows that this ten-year anniversary is one worth celebrating on Saturday.

To be this happy is a rare moment. Ten *years* of working through the intricacies of her marriage with Kyle have finally led to something she wouldn't have imagined a decade ago.

Wouldn't have thought possible kneeling at the altar of Neil's funeral one week, standing at the altar of her wedding to Kyle another.

Wouldn't have fathomed through the tears of loving one man who was gone, and saying *I do* to the one always there.

No. This pure moment of easy happiness is a gift she never saw coming. Oh, if she could, she'd announce it to the world—announce how *exquisite* a feeling it is.

But she doesn't.

Instead, she simply puts her hands in the salty water, gives her tube a good spin, tips her head up to the whirling blue skies, and feels as carefree and light as the buoyant sea beneath her.

thirty-six

IF THERE'S ONE THING JASON Barlow still can't believe, it's this: that former State of Connecticut judge Clifton Raines makes his home in a flat-roofed, modular trailer. It's such a conundrum that every time Jason arrives at the trailer, he has to simply shake his head. It doesn't make any sense, not only that law-enforcing Cliff *sneaks* making his home here, but that the entire beach association's business proceedings transpire there, too. Even though Elsa has tried to dress up the trailer with a summery wreath on the door, and lace curtain toppers on the sliding metal windows, it still defies logic that Cliff lives here.

"Must not be a rule in the handbook forbidding it," Jason says to himself that afternoon as he climbs the four metal stairs and opens the steel entry door. On the other side, Cliff multitasks, wearing black pants and a silvery-gray button-down. He's at his work desk bent over a Stony Point map—which he's diligently marking with large black X's—and at the same time is sending someone text messages. Giving Jason a quick glance, Cliff motions for him to wait.

Jason waits there for a minute, all right. But seeing no sign of Cliff ending his texting and X'ing, he finally drags a metal chair over to the side of Cliff's utilitarian desk, sits and observes firsthand this official beach business transpire.

"What's with the X's?" Jason whispers. When he turns the map for a better look, Cliff turns it back.

"Mosquito spraying," Cliff tells him while adding an X to one of the public scenic pathways. "Any X indicates a problem area that has been officially reported."

"Officially?"

"Via Stony Point's website complaint form."

So Jason leans across the desk to see that apparently the dune grasses surrounding the boat basin are a problem area, as is the perimeter of the public parking lot behind the boardwalk, where overflow seawater tends to pool.

When Cliff's phone dings, Jason turns *that* to read what's happening. He scrolls through the text messages while Cliff administers more X's to his map.

Any mosquito problems at the inn? Cliff had texted Elsa.

No, Elsa texted back. *Only in my secret path through the grasses, to the beach. Very bad there.*

Now Cliff grabs back his phone, and Jason watches as his fingers tap out a response. *Be sure to shut ALL inn windows regardless. Spraying will ensue on the path today.*

"Wait." Jason squints closely at Cliff and motions to his phone. "Did you just send Elsa a heart emoji?"

"I may have."

"What are you implying with that heart, Commissioner?"

"What do you think?"

Jason slides Cliff's phone closer, reads the message, then looks point-blank at Cliff. "I'm thinking you're in love."

At the mere *mention* of love, Cliff snatches his phone back. "Stop looking over my shoulder at my emojis."

"Have you told Elsa you're in love with her?"

"What? *Told* her? Well, no. It's implied ... with the heart." He turns his phone to Jason. "See? And besides, Elsa's busy being a grandmother this summer. She's very happy, which is well deserved."

"Still." Jason leans his arm on the edge of Cliff's metal desk. "Love? You need to up your game in the *wooing* department if it's love, Judge."

Cliff meets Jason's look, then slides his cell phone back. "This is a private matter," he adds before leaning over his X'd map and verifying the X's to a printed list of addresses.

"Anyway, Cliff." Jason sits back in his chair and clasps his hands behind his neck. "The reason I'm here is I need a form."

"For what? Forms are downloadable on the website."

"Yeah, but I was in the area, so just give me one. I've applied for a variance to zoning on the Fenwick job and need the changes to be reviewed at your next BOG meeting."

Cliff pulls open one of his desk drawers, which squeaks on its tracks. After thumbing through folders stacked in the drawer, he tells Jason he doesn't have that form on hand. "I'll print you a couple, it'll only take a minute." He rolls his chair over to his computer and pecks at the keyboard. "Printer's over there," he says, nodding to a small room off to the side.

Jason crosses the little reception area to a space partitioned off the main office. It's a small room, just big enough to house Cliff's printer, a fax machine, photocopier and a lamp.

"Print yet?" Cliff calls out.

"No, the printer's just coming on. Wait." Jason walks to the printer and bends closer to it. "A red light's on. Says it's out of paper."

When Cliff doesn't respond, Jason leans out of the printer cubbyhole to see Cliff cuffing his shirtsleeves while standing at the window.

Castaway Cottage

"Ah, fiddlesticks," Cliff's muttering, all while looking outside completely oblivious to the paper dilemma.

"Raines." Jason knocks on the partition wall. "Where do you keep the printer paper?"

Cliff returns to his desk and snatches up his keys and cell phone. "I have to go," he says, throwing another glance toward the window. "Mosquito Squad's here. Need to direct them to the appropriate problem areas." He grabs his X'd map, then lifts a megaphone off a shelf behind his desk.

"A megaphone?"

"Have to warn folks to shut their cottage windows."

"Wait!" Jason calls as Cliff shoulders the trailer door open—the commissioner juggling keys and phones and papers, with that megaphone shoved beneath his arm. "What about my form?" Jason persists.

Cliff stops halfway out the door and looks back at Jason. "Paper's in the supply closet. In the back," he says with an unclear nod of his head. "Add some to the printer tray and your form will resume its print job." Once he's outside and the door closes behind him, Cliff opens it again. "Leave the completed form on my desk and let yourself out!"

⁓

"*In the back ... in the back,*" Jason whispers while looking for Cliff's supply closet. He pokes his head in the printer room again, but that room is like a closet itself, and has no supplies. "What the hell?" he says to himself, turning back to the trailer's reception area and only seeing Cliff's tanker desk covered with papers and his computer. A few metal chairs are set beside a low table strewn with some old magazines.

There, on the side wall, he finally sees a narrow closet door blending right with the trailer wall. But when he opens it, finds it's just the utility closet filled with brooms, dustpans, paper towels, rags and cleaning supplies. But no office supplies. Not one sheet of blank paper is on its shelves.

Dragging his hand through his hair, Jason eyes the trailer, then walks to the accordion-style door separating the front workroom from the back room in this old hunk of metal. He clatters the door open and there, right behind it, is another closet—this one with a cheap wooden door. So he opens it and figures this must be what Cliff meant when he said the closet is *in the back*.

The thing is, the closet is surprisingly deep. Jason steps back, hand to his chin, and studies Cliff's private lair around him: a kitchenette, sleeping quarters with futon, small living area. For crying out loud, the trailer must have a slide-out room on the back side. A flick of a switch and hidden hydraulics extend the rear wall enough to give Cliff a comfortable apartment—and a deep supply closet.

Moving into the closet now, Jason slides over a hanging rain slicker, and zip sweatshirt, and windbreaker so he can get to the shelves on the side. Up above, several pegs hold baseball caps as well as Cliff's collection of assorted COMMISSIONER caps: some blue, some black, all with gold stitching. And down below, on the side, Jason finally spots the shelf holding reams of printer paper.

"Gotcha," he says, bending low and grabbing one of the reams. But when he straightens, he stops. Stops, turns back and bends low again to peer inside that darn closet.

Reaches in, too. Reaches in for the blue-and-yellow vinyl case that caught his eye. It's tucked on a low shelf in the back. There's no way Jason could miss it; no way he could not recognize it.

He pulls out the vintage Matchbox Collector's Case and wipes a layer of dust off the top. "Holy shit," he whispers as he takes the car case to the bistro table in Cliff's kitchenette. The case looks to be decades old, but is intact. It shows signs of wear, though. The plastic covering has a few wrinkles. And it's worn thin in places from being opened and used often during some long-ago childhood.

During a long-ago childhood on the beach, maybe? The toy die-cast cars zipped around a pop-up city set on a blanket on the sand?

Jason sets the car case on the table, unlatches and opens it to find many tiny compartments—each one holding a Matchbox vehicle. There are metal tow trucks, a dump truck, sedans and station wagons. A police car and farm tractor. A pale-pink camper and a sky-blue speedboat. Forty-eight miniature vehicles that would bring any kid's imagination to life.

But no. It can't be ... Is this the same cherished set of Matchbox cars that was played with on the sandy shores of Stony Point fifty years ago?

He hurries to the closet again and rummages past the jackets and shirts to the rear shelves. Blankets are folded there, as are a couple of sweaters. But nothing that would confirm his suspicions.

Frustrated, Jason backs out of the closet, knuckle to his scarred jaw, and eyes the closet from top to bottom. But it can't be what he's thinking. He brushes through the hung jackets and shirts again, sliding the thin metal hangers to the side.

Little lost Sailor ... He *can't* be Clifton Raines.

Giving the space a closer once-over, Jason lifts one of Cliff's COMMISSIONER caps from a peg, turns it over in his hand and puts it back. He lifts another, then another. Some are plain baseball caps, others uniform caps. And Jason won't leave any unturned. Each one he lifts, then lifts any others beneath it. Over and over again.

Sometimes you just know. Sometimes in life, every detail you're *seeing, feeling, hearing*, comes together like a kaleidoscope spinning into perfect focus. Lifting the caps, knocking down an umbrella, moving aside rain slickers, can't Jason hear the whistling wind of an approaching hurricane? Feel the pelting raindrops? See the young boy on the rocks?

Reaching deeper into that closet, Jason just tosses the visors and caps aside as he manically moves to each peg.

It doesn't take long to find what he's looking for.

To lift the little boy's cap off the farthest peg in the shadowy corner of the closet.

To hold the very blue-and-white sailor cap that hasn't been seen at Stony Point Beach for over fifty years.

Until now.

thirty-seven

"AND SON OF A BITCH. Sailor is *Cliff*."

It's a thought Jason couldn't shake for the rest of the day. But he couldn't give voice to it, couldn't hear it aloud, couldn't convince himself of its truth for hours. Not until he finished drafting a print for a new client looking to add an addition to their cottage; not until he stopped at Beach Box to check on the progress of the reno there; not until he got back from the TV studio in Hartford, where he worked with Trent to plan the Fenwick episodes.

Not until he could walk the beach beneath a quarter moon slung low over the sea. Maris was silent the entire time, riveted to his every detail of Cliff's secret hidden away in a supply closet.

"Oh my God, Jason," she says now. She stops right there—barefoot, her jeans cuffed. "That's *incredible*. Do you think anyone else knows?"

"I'm not sure." They resume walking across the packed sand beneath the driftline, and the Fenwick cottage rises in the night ahead of them. "It's still hard to believe. But all the pieces fit. Even Cliff's age works. He'd have been a kid back in the sixties."

"Did you talk to him about it?"

"No. He left to assist with some Mosquito Squad doing routine spraying today. So I was alone in his trailer, digging in his supply closet for printer paper to get my variance form printed. That's when I found the sailor cap, and his car case."

It's ironic that as they talk about little Sailor, they approach the lone cottage on the beach. The moon casts a faint light on it, and the Sound's waves lap at shore. Jason can almost imagine the family on the deck battening down the hatches during that long-ago hurricane. Can almost hear Gordon and his wife call to Sailor to get off the rocks and get home.

Maris takes Jason's hand in hers as they pass the cottage-on-stilts. "That's so sad," she softly says while looking up at it. "Carol's grandfather, who was such a young man at the time—probably about your age—lost his life in that rowboat. All while looking for *Cliff*."

Jason squints over at the rocks and steers Maris in that direction. "So the question is, what's Cliff doing back here now?"

"You have to talk to him."

"Do I?"

"Jason! I think you do."

Jason leads Maris to a few of the larger boulders facing the beach. He helps her onto one, where she sits with her elbows propped on her knees. It seems a fitting place to consider the right thing to do—right at the scene of the tragedy. Jason hasn't been this conflicted in a long time.

"Don't you think you owe it to the Fenwicks to find out more?" Maris asks then.

"Or owe it to Cliff *not* to, since he's where my allegiance lies," Jason admits while leaning against a boulder. "I mean, the Fenwicks are great people, but they're my clients. Cliff, well ... I can't believe I'm saying this—"

Castaway Cottage

"I get it," Maris finishes. "Cliff's oddly like family, especially since he's with Elsa."

"Exactly. So whether I owe the Fenwicks more, it's hard to say. Because it's *Cliff's* life, after all. And it's *his* choice to keep the matter private." Jason looks out at Long Island Sound. The pale moonlight falls like mist on the water. "I remember something my father once said, years ago, to me and Neil. The three of us were walking the beach when my brother and I were kids, maybe eight and ten years old. This one day, we witnessed a pretty violent act. And the way it all went down was really shocking to watch. But my father, well, he made damn sure we learned a life lesson from what we saw. A lesson we'd *never* forget."

Jason tells Maris that story now.

We walked the beach early that summer morning, Jason begins. *The sun was up, the water all blue ripples. Neil and I were collecting rocks in our pails to use for our 'Nam ammunition, and Dad came along before the day got too hot. It was calm, peaceful—the tide was out, and at the far end of the beach, tidal pools swirled around the lower rocks.*

But as we got close to that rocky ledge, there was a commotion on the beach. So we slowed our step, riveted by what we saw. A big white seagull nervously paced the sand near the water. Back and forth. He was rigid, and alert. At his feet was a crab the gull had caught. A good-sized crab that started walking away—which got the bird to quickly pace around it. Suddenly, that gull grabbed the crab right in its beak and lifted it off the sand.

Well, that crab fought for its life. Its legs were moving, its claws pinching the air. Neil and I were horrified, but relieved when the bird dropped that poor crab in the sand again. It landed on its back, but surely it had a chance to escape then.

"*Look!*" *Neil said, making a move to rush over and rescue it.*

But my father's hand was quicker. He grabbed Neil's shoulder and pulled him back. Right as he did that, the big white bird lifted its mighty head and, with its pointed beak, brutally stabbed the crab's underside. Still fighting, the crab's legs writhed from side to side, its claws opened and closed. But the bird was relentless, and stabbed at it again.

And again.

"*Dad!*" *I said, tugging at my father's arm. "He's hurting the crab. We can help."*

"*No, you can't,*" *my father told us both. He held us back, one of us under either arm, as we continued watching this seagull pluck the crab off the sand, then throw it back down. "You do not interfere with life's natural rhythms," my father quietly, but sternly, explained.*

Sometimes it was hard to actually watch, because we knew we could save that crab a lot of suffering. We argued that it didn't seem fair. Until we quieted but good with what happened next. All we could do was watch this ferocious attack play out.

While on the sand, the crab still valiantly flailed its legs and claws—until the seagull gave it a final blow. Picking up the crab in its beak once more, the gull stretched its head skyward, then gave a wrenching shake that sent the crab's legs thrashing in every direction. And the bird didn't stop shaking the crab until we could see, without a doubt, every single one of its crab legs go utterly limp with death. That bird ultimately shook the life right out of it before taking the dead crab to the rocks to devour it there.

"*Dad,*" *we pleaded. "He killed it!"*

My father nodded, watching the bird peck and stab and fill its belly with the crab carcass. "Yep," he said. "But there's different ways of looking at things, boys. Sure, it's a bad day for the crab … but it's a good day for the seagull." We slowly resumed walking the beach, keeping a wary eye on that killer bird. "And it's not our place to interfere."

CASTAWAY COTTAGE

"So was my father right? Is it my place to interfere now?" Jason asks his wife. He looks through the shadowy night to the beach, and to the lone cottage there. Some of its windows are illuminated, but most are dark. And all hold one huge mystery behind them. It's almost as if the cottage is looking out to sea, looking out to the rocky outcropping where Jason sits with Maris now, looking to the skies over Long Island Sound, seeking an answer to that one looming question: Who is Sailor?

A question that only Jason can answer.

"Should you interfere? I don't know, Jason," Maris says. "You can convince yourself *either* way." She looks to the beach, too, taking in the shadowy sight of the imposing, stilted cottage. "Why do you suppose Cliff even came back to Stony Point, after all these years?" she asks.

After a moment, Jason gives the only answer he can. "We all seem to come back here, don't we?"

thirty-eight

EVEN ON HIS DAYS OFF, Jason multitasks. Like today, on what should be a quiet, restful Friday morning. He stands at the refrigerator, holding the door open and considering breakfast options. But at the same time, he's listening to Maris rustling papers and typing on her laptop. Without looking, he can just picture her at the dining room table, the lantern-chandelier throwing light on her work, a vase of dried marsh grasses nearby for atmosphere. Maris' hair would be pulled back in a big clip, and she'd wear a black tank top with frayed denim shorts. Her fingers might fiddle with the ropy chain of her gold star pendant as she bends over her manuscript.

"*No rest for the weary,*" he whispers at the thought of his wife diligently writing. No rest for him, either. On his one day off, he has to stop at the Ocean Star Inn to help Elsa set up for the vow renewal tomorrow. And he has to check in with Kyle, too.

"Did you say something?" Maris calls from the dining room.

"What?" Jason asks as he leans into the refrigerator and pulls out a plate of Elsa's leftover blueberry-cheesecake brownies.

"Hmm?" Maris answers a moment later. "Never mind."

Jason sits on a stool at the kitchen island, where his phone and tablet are charging. It's warm in the kitchen, so before settling in with a couple of those brownies, he cranks open the window over the sink. Not that it helps much. The August morning outside is hot, the air still. The only thing that comes through the window screen is birdsong from some cardinal serenading the day out in the tall maple.

On the way back to his breakfast, Jason stops at the fridge for the orange juice carton, gives it a shake and pours a frothy glass. "I slept on it," he says when he sits at the island again. "And decided I'm going to see Cliff today. I have to get to the bottom of this Sailor thing."

"You sure?" Maris' voice comes back to him.

Jason bites into the gooey brownie. "It's bothering me. And I have to hear him out, at least." He turns on his stool and briefly stretches out his left leg. "Because if Cliff's really Sailor, that's all tied in to my castaway cottage, too. The Fenwick place. And if I stew on it, my leg will just start acting up, giving me hell."

It's quiet then as Maris ponders a paragraph, or structures a sentence. So Jason stuffs the last of his first brownie into his mouth before washing it down with a swallow of orange juice.

"Well, I hope you're eating a good breakfast in there," Maris vaguely says. "To stay healthy."

"Yeah, I am." A few brownie crumbs dot the island top, so Jason dabs at them with a paper napkin, then picks up another brownie. Fresh blueberries are sunk into the cream-cheese topping. "Having fruit, with lots of antioxidants." As he says it, he plucks off a cheesy blueberry and pops it in his mouth. "And what are you doing in there?"

"Finishing this chapter's notes. The book's almost done, but I have to work in Neil's driftline references. The same way he worked it into that letter you showed me?"

Jason only nods in response, as he's busy devouring the magic that is Elsa's dessert—which somehow suffices for a breakfast, too.

"I'll be so distracted with the vow renewal this weekend," Maris is saying. "I want to clean up my notes so I'll be good to come back to the manuscript on Monday."

"Lord knows we all deserve a weekend off. Been working a lot lately." As if on cue, Jason's charging cell phone dings with a text message.

"Who's that?" Maris asks from the other room.

"My sister, Paige." Jason reads her text. "She and Vinny want us to stop by for lunch later." Jason types an answer, then unplugs the phone from the charger and drops it in his cargo shorts pocket. "I'm going to find Cliff. You need anything while I'm out? Something from the convenience store?"

"No." There's a quiet second as she flips a manuscript page, then, "Just bring me one of those blueberry-cheesecake brownies I hear you scarfing down."

With a shake of his head, Jason grabs the plate knowing nothing gets past his wife. But before delivering the brownies to her, he fusses with his knee and bounces lightly, getting a feel for his prosthesis—which seems bothersome today. When he finally sets the plate beside Maris' papers, she's so busy concentrating on her writing that he bends and only kisses the top of her head.

And is a little surprised when, as he turns to leave, she tugs him back by the hem of his old faded concert tee. Tugs him back and gives him a kiss that counts.

※

Now that he's decided to confront Cliff about being Sailor, Jason can't get to Cliff's pseudo-home in that industrial trailer fast

Castaway Cottage

enough. He hurries there in his golf cart, climbs the four metal steps and knocks quickly at the steel door.

But ... nothing.

No Cliff calling out, no door opening. So he gives the doorknob a jiggle, but the place is locked up tight. If he's not here, there's only one place Cliff Raines would be the day before a significant beach event: at Elsa's.

Jason wastes no time breaking the fifteen-mile-per-hour speed limit to get to the Ocean Star Inn, pronto. Giving a quick knock at that front door, he then walks right in, calling out, "Elsa?"

"Jason? Is that you?"

He can tell by the sound of her voice that she's in the kitchen. And he can tell by the clattering pans and utensils on his way there that she's cooking up something, hopefully with Cliff sitting at her island to keep her company.

But when Jason turns into Elsa's sunny kitchen? Nothing again. No Cliff. Just Elsa at the stove. She's wearing leggings and an olive-green sleeveless tunic, with a hammered gold cuff on her wrist.

"Cliff around, Elsa?"

She looks over her shoulder while stirring a pot of something delicious-smelling. "Nice to see you, too, Jason."

He gets the message. So he walks over, puts his hands on Elsa's shoulders from behind and lightly leaves a kiss on her cheek. "Good morning, Aunt Elsa."

"That's better." She gives his arm an affectionate swat with her wooden spoon. "Now, what do you need Cliff for? I hope it's not business, because Maris said you took the day off to help *me*, here. You're not supposed to be working, for once!"

"No, it's not work. Just had to ask him something. Do you know where he is?"

309

"Oh, yes. It's the sweetest thing, actually." She motions for Jason to sit at the massive island he designed for her.

Okay, if there's one thing Jason's learned about Maris' aunt, it's that sometimes roundabout is the quickest way to an answer. So he caves and sits at her island—which is covered with Lauren's painted driftwood place cards, and a pile of mail, and the day's newspaper, along with a half-filled coffee cup. Okay, and he can't miss it. A coffee cup beside a plate of more of those leftover blueberry-cheesecake brownies.

Which is when Elsa sets down a steaming mug of coffee, right in front of him, and takes away the cold cup.

"Did I tell you?" she asks. "Hmm, I don't think so." She dumps the cold coffee in the sink before turning to the coffeepot and pouring herself a fresh cup. "Lauren will be arriving at her vow renewal ceremony tomorrow in Sal's rowboat! Oh, it'll be *magnifico*." She pauses while adding cream to her coffee, then brings the creamer to Jason, too. Which is when she also sits beside him. "I'm so touched that she wants to honor my son like this. That boat was very special to him."

"It was, I know."

"But it'll be a surprise for the guests waiting for the beach ceremony. They'll all be seated in their white chairs on the sand, and Kyle will be waiting there, too, when Lauren will make her *grand* entrance on the sea."

"Elsa, I'm sorry. That's really nice, but I'm pressed for time. What does this have to do with Cliff?"

"I'm getting to it. *Pazienza*, Jason."

So Jason resigns himself to a nod and a sip of his coffee as Elsa gets to her roundabout point.

A point that apparently requires a visual. She sets down her cup and hurries over to her large garden window. There, she moves aside some of the red pails she uses as herb pots, stretches up on tiptoe and looks out toward the distant water. "I'm not sure if you can see it, but a temporary dock was brought in yesterday." She turns to Jason. "And it's *Cliff* who will be paddling Lauren from the boat basin, out the channel, to the temporary dock."

"Cliff?"

Elsa nods. "Isn't that nice of him? The beach commissioner rowing in the bride. So anyway," she says, checking her thin gold wristwatch, "he wanted to do a practice run and you just missed him. He's headed to the marina, to Sal's rowboat. If you hurry, you can probably find him there."

After tossing down another mouthful of coffee, Jason stands to leave. "Okay, I'll be back later to help you set up chairs and whatnot here. I promise, Elsa. But I've *really* got to catch Cliff now."

With no time to waste except for the two seconds it takes to pilfer a brownie from her covered plate, Jason rushes back to the front door. "Great brownies, by the way," he calls out, just before the door closes behind him.

∼

When there's a knock at the inn's front door ten minutes later, Elsa can assume only one thing: Jason missed Cliff and is back to help her decorate. "You didn't find him, Jason?" she asks while opening the door, surprised that it isn't Jason after all.

Far from it. Instead, a tall man with light brown hair stands there. He's a big guy, with a cotton newsboy cap on his head and overnight duffel in his hand.

"Not Jason," he says right away. "I'm here for the vow renewal?"

"Oh, wonderful!" Elsa sweeps the door wide open and

motions for him to follow her to the inn's front lobby. "This is so exciting," she says over her shoulder. "You are my first official guest. The inn's not formally opening until next month, in time for the autumn foliage season." She steps behind the check-in counter and looks at her ledger first, then flicks on a wall switch. Several Mason jars hanging from a silver barn star mounted on the ceiling illuminate. "So, you must be ... Derek?" She puts on her leopard-print reading glasses, then glances at the ledger again before looking past his shoulder. "Derek and ... Vera?"

"No. No, I should've explained," the man says as he sets down his duffel and takes off his cap. "I don't have a reservation. This is really a last-minute thing. I hope that's okay?"

"It's your lucky day. I have one room left. If you can just fill out this registration card, including your credit card information." Elsa slides the card across the desktop. "Then I'll enter it in the computer."

In a moment, Elsa hears a noise coming from down the hallway. It's the side door opening, in the kitchen. "Elsa?" Celia's voice calls out.

"Over here," Elsa answers, spotting Celia in the hallway. She's wearing cropped white jeans with a navy tank top, and holds Aria in her arms. "Celia! Look, our very first guest."

Celia hurries through the hallway to the check-in desk. "How do you do?" she asks while shifting Aria to her other arm and extending a hand.

"I'm good, thank you. And yourself?" This tall man gives a firm handshake in return before also tapping Aria's hand.

"I'm well!" Again Celia shifts Aria in her arms. "Did you have a long trip here?"

Their guest looks up from the card he's trying to complete. "Just came down the coastline."

"Oh, nice." Elsa glances over the rim of her reading glasses to spot his car through the window. "And did you find the inn okay?"

"No problem," he manages with another glance up.

So Elsa leaves him to his registration and turns to Celia. "Could you check the available room upstairs?"

"Of course! Full house this weekend." As Celia walks back down the hallway, she gives a call over her shoulder. "Nice meeting you!"

Again, their guest looks up. "Same here," he says, then completes the last lines of the registration card.

A few things don't escape Elsa's notice while she waits, like the easy smile her very first guest has. And that his hands filling out the card are working hands—strong and able, with a few faint scars. There's also an intricate sleeve of tattoos covering that writing arm. He's a young man, in his thirties, with the build of someone who knows hard labor. When he slides the card to her, she plucks a glossy brochure from a rack behind the counter. "Now, here's a guide to local spots of interest. You know, restaurants, museums, fishing excursions."

"Thanks," he says while glancing at the brochure, front and back. "But I'm pretty familiar with the area."

"Well, you give that a look. Maybe you'll see something new. *And*," Elsa adds, pulling a sheet of paper from a lower shelf behind the counter, "this is a schedule of meals and guest events, including complimentary rowboat rides. But everything starts tonight with a guys' night out with the groom. Maybe you'll join them?"

"Maybe." The man takes the paper and lifts his duffel, too. "We'll see."

Elsa nudges up those leopard-print glasses and looks at the

registration card to add the particulars to her leather ledger. "Okay, so you'll be staying until Sunday, then?"

"At least."

"Well. It's so nice to have you here." Again her eyes drop to the card. "Shane, is it? Shane *Bradford?*" she asks, looking quickly at him. "Oh …" The inn telephone rings just then, and she turns to it while asking, "Are you a cousin of Kyle's?"

"Something like that," this Shane answers while taking the key Elsa had set on the counter.

"Ocean Star Inn," Elsa says into the phone, all while holding up a finger for Shane to wait. As she talks, he puts on his newsboy cap, then backs up a step and glances down the hallway. "I'm sorry, we won't be open until next month," Elsa tells her caller. "Can you hold please?" She cups the phone's mouthpiece and quietly tells Shane, "Just go up the stairs with the painted beach mural on them. Your room is the third on the right. Last one."

Shane nods. That's it, just nods, tips his hat and walks down the hallway, taking the mural-painted stairs two at a time.

thirty-nine

JASON TROTS ALONG THE BOARDWALK while scanning the boat basin behind it. Most of the boat slips are filled this early in the morning. Little motorboats, and fishing skiffs, and a couple of small cabin cruisers that haven't yet puttered out for a summer cruise are tied to the dock posts. The vessels creak and groan as the tidal current gets them straining against the ropes securing them. When Jason sees someone paddling a rowboat out of its slip, he hooks two fingers in his mouth and gives a sharp whistle.

"Yo, Cliff!" he calls. "Wait up."

As he says it, he rushes down the boardwalk stairs, opens the narrow gate to the boat basin below and hurries down those stairs, too. In the meantime, Cliff has paddled back into his slip and waits as Jason walks past the docked boats and finally steps right into Sal's old rowboat.

"I got your zoning variance form yesterday," Cliff says. "If you're looking for an answer, I'll have to get back to you with the Board's decision."

Jason sits facing Cliff on one of the boat's wooden benches. Out of uniform today, the commissioner wears gray shorts, a dark polo shirt and boat shoes. A navy visor shields the sun from his eyes.

"This isn't about the form." Jason motions for Cliff to begin paddling.

Cliff does, lifting the oars and dipping them into the calm marina water. "You're not going to sway me, Jason. The Board of Governors has to convene on your building matters."

Jason simply waves him off. "It's not that, I said."

Cliff pulls on the oars, getting them creaking against the oarlocks. "Don't be bothering me about that Hammer Law again, either. Vacationing folks need peace and quiet here." He maneuvers the wooden rowboat into the narrow channel leading out to Long Island Sound. "And the rules are the rules."

"*Relax*, Judge." Jason drags a hand back through his hair. "Heard you were doing a practice run in Sal's rowboat for the ceremony tomorrow. Thought I'd catch a leisurely cruise with you."

When Cliff rows the boat into the Sound, he steers it out toward the big rock. Ripples of calm seawater lap at the boat's wooden hull, and the sun beats down warm. Jason sees people setting up for a day on the beach. Colorful umbrellas are being opened, sand chairs lined up. A jogger runs near the water, and a few children float on tubes close to shore.

"Looks like the guest chairs have been delivered." Cliff nods toward the far end of the beach, the area that Elsa's private, sandy footpath leads to. Further back on the sand, stacks of white folding chairs are piled high. "Give me a hand setting them out later?"

"You bet," Jason says. "We'll get them all lined up nice for Kyle and Lauren."

Beyond the chair stacks, back on the Ocean Star Inn's rolling green lawn, a white canopy is visible. Jason's sure some amazing dinner will be served there tomorrow night, beneath the summer stars.

Castaway Cottage

But that's not what's on his mind now. Far from it. He glances out toward the rocky ledge where one particular little boy used to love hanging out. There's got to be a way to broach the subject of Sailor with Cliff. It's the perfect time, as Cliff slowly rows and the boat rises and sways on the gentle waves beneath it. Heck, they're stranded out here together, so there'll be no escaping Jason's difficult questions.

He's distracted, though, when they pass the big rock jutting out of the water. From here, Jason can see the temporary dock Elsa had mentioned. The floating dock's small, with a long ramp for Lauren to walk down to her vow renewal ceremony on the sand.

"Not sure that dock meets Stony Point code, Judge. The BOG approve it?" Jason asks.

"Jeez, you're getting to be as particular as me." Cliff looks over his shoulder in the direction he's rowing. "I can assure you, Barlow, that all safety precautions have been addressed. The dock surface is slip-resistant, and grooves in the ramp ensure that any water will flow off the walking surface and not cause slippery puddles. Not to mention the dock *and* ramp have built-in solar LED deck lights to illuminate it."

"Just checking." Jason leans over and drags his fingers through the salty water. "Leave it to Lauren and Kyle to pull this off. Lauren will make a real grand entrance this way. Nice of you to chauffer her."

"They're good kids." Cliff pulls back on the oars, lifts them and lets them *drip, drip* for a few moments. The rowboat floats there as he turns in his seat and takes in the dock view.

"You know something? Sal would drift out here at night," Jason tells him. "On this very boat."

Cliff turns back to Jason, still resting the oars as the boat does just that ... drifts.

317

"I'd go along sometimes," Jason says, "and he'd tell me shit out on the night water."

"Is that right?" Cliff asks.

"Yeah. Like one time—it was a warm night, a little misty, with a low moon—he told me about his childhood. Mentioned he'd been sick a lot as a boy. When he was feverish and lying in bed, he said he'd dream of floating on the sea." Jason scoops a handful of that seawater and flings it in droplets up toward the bright summer sky. "Hope he's floating up there, now. Somewhere."

"Me, too." Cliff sets the paddles in the rowboat so they drift a little more. Tiny rippling waves lap at the boat's sides, nudging at it, shifting it. "Funny how stories have a way of coming out on the water," he vaguely says.

"They do. You got any stories you want to tell?"

"Me?" Cliff asks. "No. Nothing interesting."

"You sure about that?"

Cliff looks longer at him, then drops the oars back in the water to guide the drifting boat further out, away from the swim rope.

Jason, waiting, lifts his sunglasses to the top of his head and watches Cliff closely. "Got any *sailing* stories you want to tell?"

"What the heck?" Cliff rests the dripping oars in the rowboat again. "Quit beating around the bush. You got something to say? Say it."

Jason sets his hands on the bench and slightly leans back while eyeing Clifton Raines—the persnickety rules-driven beach commissioner; the former law-enforcing judge; the man whose secret roots here date back fifty years to one tragic day when he was just a little boy.

"I do have something to say." Jason pauses then. "Why'd you come back, Sailor?"

Castaway Cottage

Cliff looks at Jason, then away, then back at him again. He tips up his visor and scrutinizes this man sitting across from him on the rowboat bench. But Cliff has no words. Only thoughts that he doesn't dare share. Thoughts like *God damn it*, and *How the hell?*

One thing's for certain: Jason's question blindsided him. Might as well have knocked him overboard, the way it's left him speechless. He's not sure *what* to do as he drags a hand across his whiskered face, looks around. Finally he bends for the anchor and releases it over the edge of the rowboat. For a moment, he looks into the deep water that today is as serene as can be, lapping against the boat's hull.

Ha! Calm waters—why they're nothing but a ruse. He'll *never* be fooled by the sea again.

Never.

The sea can turn in an instant and reach up to grab any life in its path. Grab it and pull it under, no holds barred, no matter what, with no mercy.

Like it *tried* to grab him that long-ago day on the rocks—snatching at him with monstrous waves.

Like it *did* grab an innocent man trying only to save the life of a child ... to save *him*.

Now Cliff looks over at Jason, still waiting for an answer. Ironic that they're sitting here in a drifting rowboat within sight of the Fenwick cottage on the beach, and of the very rocky outcropping where the tragedy happened fifty years ago. So Cliff figures that for Gordon's sake, it's time to come clean. Time to let *one* person—and one person only—know that he's here to make amends for a death he caused.

I begged my mother to let me go to the rocks that day, Cliff begins. *I pleaded and followed her around, not letting up. "But my tackle box is there," I said. "I forgot it this morning."*

She wouldn't give in.

"It's too dangerous, Clifton," my mother insisted while closing the cottage windows, and bringing in folding chairs and beach toys that would otherwise blow away in the storm. "We'll get you another tackle box."

When I'd ask time and again as the wind got stronger, and as spits of rain came and went, she'd tell me the same thing. "You know the rules. We stay off the beach during bad storms. The sea can be treacherous and you could be hurt!" she said while stacking perishable foods in an icy cooler. "No going on the beach." As she rushed outside with a laundry basket to get the whipping clothes off the clothesline, she called back, "The rules are the rules, for a reason!"

But I thought, well, if I ran to the rocks as fast as I could, I'd be back before she'd be done taking down the laundry; before she'd even notice. If I just hurried, and left right now.

So with visions of saving my cherished tackle box, out the door I went.

The storm didn't seem bad when I ran down Champion Road. Even when I cut over behind the Fenwick cottage to the rocks, there wasn't much of a wind. I didn't realize that the berm, the raised dunes and wild grasses, shielded me from it all—until it was too late. I'd made a run for the rocks and got halfway out to my forgotten tackle box before it hit me that things changed. Suddenly there was an urgency to everything: the cutting wind; the seething sea; my tackle-box mission.

Because the waves were making noise now, churning the way they do in a storm. Angry-like, twisting and slapping against the rocks when they'd break. And each time they churned, they inched closer and closer to me. I'd back up a little, but each splashing wave was like some writhing arm of a giant sea monster wanting to take me with it when it madly retreated off the rocks.

Standing back, I heard something—voices from the beach. They came and went, rising and falling on the wind gusts. When I looked over, I saw some older boys surfing in the storm waves. They were hooting and having a grand time. So the way they were laughing, it couldn't be that dangerous out. I figured I'd be okay if I could just grab my tackle box, fast. My favorite smashing rock was in it, and my crabbing line and weights. A netted bait bag. Cripe, I filled that box up all year, waiting to bring it to the beach and go crabbing—especially on weekends, when my dad was off from work. The waves hadn't reached the box yet, and I figured I could run over and grab it before the waves did. Then I'd be back at the cottage, I was sure, before my mother was even done with the clothesline.

With another glance at the surfing boys, I did it. I made a run for it. Just then a wave crashed, close enough to leave a spray of salty water on my face. When I stopped to wipe it off, there was another sound, carried on the wind. A banging noise. That was urgent, too, the way it pounded over and over. Between the hollering surf boys, and the crashing waves, the banging scared me until I saw what it was. Folks were hammering plywood over the deck windows at the cottage on the beach. And that urgent bang-bang-bang echoed over to me.

Well, if they were outside, surely I still had time. So I pulled my hat down low, ducked against the wind and scrabbled over and around the wet, seaweed-covered rocks.

"Sailor!" a woman's vague voice called out. "Saaailor!"

I looked, afraid that it would be my mother. But it wasn't. It was the woman on that cottage deck. Her hands were cupped to her mouth and she leaned my way. Right when I looked from her to my tackle box, a wave broke and flipped it upside down, then pushed it further back on the rocks. Yes! My lucky break. I made a dash for it, slipping and tripping on the wet rocks as the rain really started pelting me then, too.

But that little box was within reach, if I just stretched far enough, and bent closer.

"Sailor!" I heard again as my desperate, wet hands wrapped around that sweet tackle box. "Go home!"

When I turned to leave the rocks, there were two people standing on the deck of the cottage on the beach. Their clothes and hair were whipping in the wind. From where I was on the rocks, I squinted through the sea spray to see them leaning far over the railing. They were madly waving their arms at me, motioning me off the beach.

"Go home, Sailor!" the man's voice called through his cupped hands while the woman kept waving her arm, over and over.

They didn't have to tell me again. Now that I'd retrieved my tackle box, I scrambled off those rocks practically on my hands and feet, all the way to the sand. When I looked over at the Fenwick place, the couple there was back to hammering plywood. So I kept going, rounded the bend in the beach and made it safely to Champion Road, my own cottage within sight.

And as quickly as that, it was gone. Two arms swooped me up right off the ground. I was jostled, my legs flailing—but my arms wrapped around my tackle box—as a woman carrying me ran like the dickens, straight into a cottage a few doors down from mine.

From then on, between the mounting hurricane and the panicked adults, the rest? Well, the rest is all a blur.

A blur that seemed even more ominous than running across the wet rocks. The woman who grabbed me was a friendly neighbor woman. She saw me outside where tree branches were snapping and ran out to get me. Back at her cottage, a dark paneled little bungalow, she set me down, wrapped me in a big dry towel, then right away picked up the phone.

Shivering, I looked around and noticed little things ... like her gold wall phone, and her fingers' rapid tapping of the receiver hook. Again and again, she'd click it, then listen for a dial tone.

And the wind, I can still hear the way it started whistling outside. When I managed a look out the window, all I saw were strewn branches and limbs, the dune grasses flattened, and a telephone pole snapped in half.

But what scared me most was what happened next. The woman's husband came in from outdoors. Water dripped from every inch of him. And his wife rushed over and grabbed his arms, then gave them an urgent shake.

"Get to Sailor's house, please! The phones are down and they don't know their boy is here, and safe." She gasped then, before finishing. "They'll think he's dead, washed out to sea!"

Oh, with that towel wrapped around my drenched body, how I prayed he'd make it. When my mother came in from the clothesline, she wouldn't know where I'd gone! I was an only child, and she'd always been extra protective of me. And now, well now she'd think I was dead! So I watched out the window as the man's yellow rain slicker flapped in the wind. My cottage was close by, and the woman, she huddled close and watched with me. Together, we saw her husband running bent over, dodging sticks and branches, and circling puddles—until he got there. The man in the yellow slicker made it through the debris and the storm to arrive safely at my parents' cottage to deliver the good news.

To tell them I was okay.

Cliff looks at Jason now. Looks him straight on, for the first time in his storytelling.

"But he was too late," Cliff admits. "The good news came too late. My mother was frantic and wasn't even there. She'd run through the pouring rain to the boys surfing on the beach, hoping I was with them. They told her that they'd seen me, but didn't know where I went."

"*Damn,*" Jason whispers.

"Standing on that windblown beach," Cliff continues, "she desperately ran to the Fenwicks' place next, pounding on the door to be heard over the howling wind. Gordon pulled her inside and had to calm her down to understand her, with the way she was crying. When they finally realized she was looking for *me*, her seven-year-old son, they told her what they'd seen. That I was on the rocks, and when they called out to me, urging me home, I headed in that direction. And they said when they looked again and I was gone, they *thought* I had made it okay."

"No, no. And you *were* almost there, which would have prevented the rest."

Cliff nods before continuing. "It got real quiet then. Someone suggested maybe I'd gotten afraid and lost my bearings in the storm. Maybe I went the *other* way over the rocks, around the point toward Little Beach. I guess that's all Gordon had to hear. Maybe he felt responsible, since he didn't do more to get me off the rocks when he was hammering plywood. So he and his brother hauled out his rowboat from beneath the cottage. No one could stop Gordon. It happened in minutes, the way some men helped get the boat in the water, then held it steady as Gordon climbed in. People stood on the beach, watching him paddle away. Further and further out he went, the boat rising and falling ... lost in a cresting wave, then bobbing on top again. People cheered every time they spotted the boat until he finally rounded the rocky bend."

From their own rowboat now, Cliff motions to the rocks and solemnly shakes his head. "That was the last anyone ever saw of Gordon," Cliff goes on. "Ten minutes later, the neighbor's husband showed up at the Fenwicks' and said I was safe. Reported that his wife had brought me in from the storm. But you know ... every domino was already in place sealing poor Gordon's fate." Cliff takes a long breath of that salt air that everyone here says cures what ails you. "My family? They couldn't face it, Gordon's death. We rented that cottage—it was only our second summer here. But my parents packed up a few days later and left. Never came back, either. Felt Gordon's death was on their hands. My father, especially, blamed himself for not being there when the hurricane hit. So they couldn't return knowing that just across the street, a man would never *have* another summer with his family."

"All because of an odd twist of fate," Jason says.

"And he was a young man, Jason. Probably about your age. Gone." Cliff lifts his visor, drags his hand back through his hair, then resettles the visor on his head. "So to answer your question—"

"My question?" Jason asks.

"Yes. Why am I back?" In his pause, seawater splashes gently against the rowboat's hull. As the boat bobs in the current, Cliff dips his hand into the salty water and barely blesses himself— touching his dripping fingers to his forehead and both shoulders. "I came back to repay a debt," he finally explains. "To be sure that kind of useless tragedy is always prevented. To insist that safeguards are always in place. To follow hurricane protocol so that what happened to Gordon never, *ever*, happens here again."

"Cliff." Jason shakes his head. "I'm sorry. I never knew. And that *is* a goddamn tragedy if I ever heard one."

"That's right, it is. And now? Now you can answer *my* question, Barlow."

"What's that?"

"You can tell me how you knew I was Sailor. Because that's one story that had a *lot* of vague loose ends, *none* with my name attached. Only Sailor's."

"*And* Sailor's Matchbox car collection. Mitch told me everything he remembered his wife saying. That'd be Kate. Including how she'd play on the beach with your cars and a pop-up city set up on a big blanket on the sand. All the beach kids did.

And apparently you keep your whole past—including a blue-and-white sailor cap—in a storage closet in that trailer of yours. A closet you sent me to for a ream of paper yesterday."

"Ah, shit."

"That's what I said, when I found your collection. You've got a deep history here, Raines."

"Deep and dark like a stormy sea." Cliff looks out past the point to where Little Beach is on the other side. "That's why when your crew recovered Gordon's boat, I just about lost it. Fifty years erased and it was like I was little Sailor all over again, that day."

"Do you want me to pull the story?"

"What do you mean?"

"From the TV show. *Castaway Cottage*. If it's too painful for you, I'll put a phone call in to my producer to can the Sailor thread. Trent won't be happy, but with a snap of our fingers, we'll find another angle to bring in."

"No. No, Jason. Because he'd want to know why, and you can't tell your producer *anything* about me being Sailor. I need this kept secret. You can't tell *anyone*."

"Oh, Cliff, man ..."

Cliff slowly shakes his head. "You told Maris?"

"Yesterday."

"I figured as much." And Cliff knows. That's all it takes for the story to get out. He reaches over and pulls in the anchor so they can get to paddling again. "Jason," he says then. "My story *has* to stop there. Elsa cannot know. If people knew, it would turn me into someone else—someone to pity. Folks here would look at me differently, and some? Well, some might even resent me. If word got out, I wouldn't belong here anymore."

Jason extends his hand. "You have my word."

"What? Another Stony Point secret?" Cliff asks. "The kind

that no one keeps? I'll do the honorable thing and shake, but know this, too. If this Sailor story gets past you and your wife, I'm out of here." Then and only then does he shake Jason's still-extended hand. "I'm sorry it has to be this way, but if you break your word, my trailer will be empty. And just like fifty years ago, no one will know where I went. Except this time," Cliff adds when he clasps Jason's hand in *both* of his, "this time it'll be on you."

forty

IF THERE'S ONE THING ANYONE who's grown up at the beach knows, it's this: What's told on the water, stays on the water. It's an unspoken, but widely respected, rule. Any man of honor won't break that code.

So when Jason walks into Kyle's bachelor party at The Sand Bar Friday night, it's shoulder slaps and handshakes for everyone, Cliff included, as though nothing went down between them that morning.

If anything, Jason's taken aback at the merriment. And Cliff's right in there, toasting and cheering Kyle with the rest of them. Even more surprising? This party, tonight, isn't in their regular booth. Tonight? It's right at the bar.

"Come on over, Jason." Patrick motions to him from where he stands, pouring drafts. "I've got a stool for each fool: Kyle, Nick, Vinny, Matt, Cliff and—drumroll, please—you, Barlow," he says, pointing to an empty barstool.

On his way, Jason stops behind Kyle and gets him in a headlock before slapping his shoulder and moving to his seat. It's the kind of raucous night Jason hasn't seen in a while. And one he can use, apparently as much as the rest of them. Settling on his stool, he raises his glass of beer to Kyle and takes a long, quick drink.

And the funny thing is, the entire night never lets up. Someone keeps the jukebox well fed with coins so that hard-driving songs keep rolling out of it—songs about summer livin', and cruising the highway, and losing the girl. The warm August air drifting in through the bar's propped-open door only adds to the easygoing mood. And the beach umbrellas illuminated with twinkly lights and propped at either end of the bar? Well, they send the summer fun over the top.

Still, there's one thing Jason's truly surprised to see tonight. Amidst shots and pretzels, laughter and toasts, monster toppling sandwiches and deluxe burgers, a baseball game on the mounted flat-screen TV—Jason's never seen Kyle happier. Ten years have now fallen between the worst summer of Kyle's life and, apparently, the best.

Ten years since Neil Barlow broke Kyle's heart—his life, even—when he stole Kyle's girl.

Ten years since Neil's affair with Lauren suddenly ended with Neil's untimely death.

Ten years since Kyle got his diamond ring back on Lauren's finger.

So hell, if it's true that time heals all wounds, Kyle is living proof. Laughing it up even as the guys poke fun at the sorry state of his sex life, all on the night of his bachelor party.

"How's that vow of celibacy going, Kyle?" Cliff raises an eyebrow with the question, and a twinkle glimmers in his eyes.

"What?" Kyle asks.

Matt leans over to face Kyle. "Come on, big guy. Everybody knows."

"*Gesù, Santa Maria*. I only told one person." Kyle turns to

Jason. "Barlow, can't you keep a secret?"

Jason holds up both hands and leans back. "I've got it on good authority that I *can*. Must've been your *wife* who spilled the beans. Got the ladies chatting it up amongst themselves."

"Oh, man." Kyle takes a long sip of some potent drink Nick bought him for his last kinda-single night out. "Lauren's been slinking around like a little minx. Been having the time of my life, actually, watching her in action. She wears these frayed short-shorts, trying to get me to cave."

"So ... you're a leg man, Bradford?" Nick asks.

"What's that?" Kyle looks over at Nick, sitting past Vinny.

"Mile-long gams do it for you," Matt explains.

"Oh, I get it. Shit, yeah. Legs. And what about you guys?" Kyle raises his drink and motions it toward Cliff. "Judge?"

"I'm all about the smile. When Elsa smiles, it lights up her whole face."

"Eyes do it for me," Matt says, then takes a contemplative sip of his draft beer. "The right look from Eva and I'm gone." He leans past Cliff. "What about you, Barlow?"

Jason sits back, hand to his chin. "There's something about Maris' long hair, if I had to pick." As he says it, Patrick sets another beer in front of him. "Soft, silky."

"Thought you'd be more a shoulder man, guy. No?" Patrick asks.

Jason squints at him, then picks up his glass and takes a long swallow of beer instead of answering.

"Shoulders, legs ... Hell, it all works," Kyle says. "Like I said, these past few weeks, I've had the most self-control I've *ever* needed. Damn." He leans forward and looks to all the guys—first to his left, then to his right. "Hope *you* guys are at least getting some action."

"No kids here until Sunday," Vinny says. "So things are pretty awesome."

"All right, Vincenzo." Kyle walks over to Vinny and punches his shoulder.

And Vinny shoves him right back. "We got that second honeymoon thing going on."

As the ribbing continues, as someone tells Vinny that Cannoli Cottage is more like Carnal Cottage now, as bets are placed on the outcome of a couple of arm-wrestling matches ... easy happiness reigns. The talk doesn't let up until only one thing quiets it.

Food.

Which is a sight of more happiness. Platters heaped with onion rings and fries, burgers and lobster rolls and club sandwiches, pickle spears and coleslaw cups are all set down in front of each guy, in each stool. The waitress moves down the line until she gets to the one empty stool at the end, beside Jason.

"What's up with this one?" Jason asks. He lifts Kyle's *Gone Fishing* cap from the stool. "Saving a seat for someone?"

Kyle somberly looks over. "That seat's reserved for the Italian."

"Sal?" Cliff asks.

Kyle nods. "Damn straight. He would've been here, man. Salvatore was all about love, and family bonds, especially. So I like to think he *is* here, right now. Somehow." Kyle raises his drink high over the bar. "Like to think he's raising *his* glass, to me and Ell tonight."

It's the quietest they've gotten then. Jason suddenly feels Sal's absence in a really sad way. It's so easy—and necessary, actually—to go on without a thought of DeLuca. To have days pass in busyness that prevent any longing. Any sad memories. But tonight, Kyle carved out that moment just for Sal. Just for all of them.

Every glass at the bar is raised high, too, as each of the friends calls out, *Salute!*

⁓

When a knock comes at her front door after the kids are in bed, Lauren's heart skips a beat. And her fear is instant. Her fear that for some godforsaken reason, Shane *did* decide to show up here this weekend. Show up here, at her doorstep.

Shane—who never RSVP'd to her invitation.

Shane—who she hasn't set eyes on in over a decade. Nor said his name aloud.

Shane—whose silence this past week actually set Lauren's mind at ease. Inviting him to the vow renewal ceremony was, well, it was a rash decision. Because the very last thing she or Kyle needs at this happiest time of their lives together is Kyle's estranged brother, Shane Bradford.

But when the knock sounds again and Lauren checks her watch, she sees it's already after nine. And for the life of her, the *only* person she can imagine showing up unannounced at her door this late on a Friday, the night before that vow renewal ceremony, is Shane.

The cottage is still and quiet, still enough for Lauren to strain her ears, listening. She gets up and tiptoes to the front porch, where the lights are shut off. But she can make out the shadow of someone standing on the other side of the door. Shoot. Someone tall, and bulky, and who appears pretty intent on staying there until Lauren opens that damn door.

So she flicks on the light and nearly sobs with relief, then rushes to the porch door and unlatches the lock. "Celia!"

"Lauren," Celia says as she sets down her guitar case. A guitar case that—in the night's shadows—made her look like a bulky man. Far from it. Celia wears a thin cardigan over her cropped skinnies and blue tank top. On her wrist, Lauren can't miss the pale yellow sailor's knot bracelet Sal had bought for her last summer. She also can't miss her friend's teary eyes.

"What are you doing here?" Lauren asks. "Is everything okay?"

Celia shakes her head. "I could tell you I wanted to maybe practice some of my songs for the ceremony tomorrow, and get your feedback. But ... you wouldn't buy that, would you?"

"Oh, hon. Seeing you upset like this? No—"

"Remember when you once said that if I ever feel sad, to come see you?" With a small smile, Celia simply turns up her hands.

Which is all it takes for Lauren to sweep her friend inside, hug her, and get her to a wicker chair on the front porch. As Celia apologizes, Lauren turns on the twinkly lights around the porch windows. And as Lauren tells her *not* to apologize, she pours them each a glass of wine. As Celia mentions she doesn't want to put a damper on tomorrow's ceremony, a train rumbles outside and its whistle lingers in the salt air. And as Lauren leans her elbows on her knees, looks Celia in the eye and asks her what's wrong, Celia lifts her guitar and softly strums.

"It all just hit me tonight," Celia's fingers pluck out a short, sad melody.

"What did?"

"How close Sal and I came to having everything you'll have tomorrow. I stay strong for Aria. I have to, I'm her mother. And for Elsa. She's so special and I love her, too. So I can't come undone in front of them. But tonight? Oh, Lauren. The sadness got the best of me."

"Wait. Where *is* Aria? With Elsa?"

"No. My father's here for the weekend. He's at my cottage with her."

"Okay." Lauren sips her wine. "Okay." Quickly though, she sets her wineglass on a small table and reaches over to clasp Celia's hand. "I'm sorry, Cee. Occasionally I did have that passing thought. You know, of how my day tomorrow might make you feel."

Celia carries her wineglass to a twinkly-light outlined window facing the bay. "It's just that I wanted all this wedding prep so badly with Sal," she says to the night outside. "Oh, after you and I found my sea-glass engagement ring last summer, how I wished that it would be me and Sal getting married. With you as *my* matron of honor!"

"Celia," Lauren says quietly from the shadows. "I want to tell you something."

Celia turns, leans against the open window's sill and sips her wine while waiting.

"You know that Neil Barlow and I were a thing, ten years ago. I'd mentioned it to you before, how we went to the shack together. And, well, it's true. I did leave Kyle for him."

"Lauren," Celia says. "I don't want to dredge that up for you tonight."

"No!" Lauren holds up a hand when she interrupts Celia. "Wait, hear me out."

"Okay." Celia returns to her wicker chair, picks up her guitar and ever so softly strums a couple chords.

"What Neil, Kyle and I had was a very painful love triangle, where everyone got hurt. There was no easy way to unravel it. And when I told the story to Sal one time …"

"Sal?" Celia whispers, her eyes teary.

"Yes. One night when he gave me a ride home. He told me something that really helped me. And maybe it can help you, too."

"What's that?"

"An Italian proverb." Lauren tucks a loose strand of hair up into her topknot, all while remembering the night she took Sal to Neil's abandoned shingled shack. "I can still hear Sal's voice asking me to remember the good moments. The sweet times ... with Neil, too."

"With *Neil?*"

Nodding, Lauren sips her wine. "With the tragic way everything turned out, it's easy to find only sadness in the memories. But Sal? He told me to remember the *good*. To hold on to those special moments. Because here's the kicker, Cee. Sal said to remember the *good* because like that old Italian proverb goes ... You have to tell your life in smiles. Not tears."

"*Sorridi*," Celia whispers while lightly playing another slow tune.

The porch is softly illuminated, with warm August air drifting in the windows. All the while, the slide noise of Celia's fingers moving over the fret sounds like musical tears dropped into the song.

"I miss him so much," Celia admits. "But listen, beach friend. Even though I'm feeling sad tonight, I am *so* happy for you, Lauren. You and Kyle deserve only the best."

Lauren goes to her and gives Celia—guitar and all—a light hug. "And *I'm* so glad you'll be playing your guitar for the guests on the beach tomorrow," Lauren says, sitting again. "Before the ceremony. I know how Sal loved to listen to you play. So maybe somewhere, he'll hear your music carrying on the sea breeze."

While strumming, Celia quickly raises the back of her hand to catch an escaped tear. Then she simply shrugs and sets her guitar on the floor beside her chair. Silently, she stands again and walks to the open porch windows. Her arms are crossed in front of her and she takes a long breath.

"*La dolce aria salata*," she whispers then. "The sweet salt air that I named my daughter after. Oh, Lauren. Sometimes I just can't stop crying." Celia raises her fingers and presses them to her eyes before turning. "But there's salt in *tears*, too, just like in the air. Sometimes it's sweet." She glances out at the night for a long second. "And sometimes ... sometimes it stings."

forty-one

ELSA SITS ALONE AT HER marble-top kitchen island. Sits alone with one thought. How does it happen that a day simply arrives? Especially a long-awaited day that required much planning and preparation? A day that, prior to its arrival, found her busier than she'd been in a long time.

And now? Just like that, Saturday is here.

The Saturday that everyone's been waiting for. It arrived at her doorstep like a gift, delivered special, wrapped in golden sunshine and tied with a ribbon of sweet salt air. The day seems custom-made for Kyle and Lauren. Out on the inn's green lawn, paper lanterns hang beneath a large white tent the caterer set up. And Cliff is on the wraparound porch stringing white globe bulbs. There's a quiet pause at this early afternoon hour as most of the preparations and decorating are done, and everyone waits for the grand event to commence.

Oh, Elsa can just see it—see Lauren arriving by rowboat at a sunset beach.

One thing's for certain: The evening will be magical. Why, Elsa half expects to see fireflies twinkling in the sky like dancing stars, just like they did that night thirty-five years ago. She closes her eyes and remembers being near the lagoon with her sister, June, as the flickering fireflies rose from the swaying grasses ... the fireflies dancing and spinning up to the night sky.

But, back to business. Glass Mason jars wrapped with jute twine line the island. Beside them is a large order of baby's breath the florist delivered. Each flower stem is covered with tiny cloud-like white blossoms. As soon as this task is complete, she'll shower and dress for the ceremony. First, she separates a handful of the baby's breath and fills one of the glass jars. Gently she arranges the flowers, separating and fanning out the blossomed stems. When she's done, Cliff will bring the jars out to the reception tables under the canopy. The jars of baby's breath will be scattered across the tabletops.

If Elsa ever finishes loading the jars. Because a sudden rap at her inn door is followed by merry whistling when the visitor walks right in. The whistling grows louder as this joyous person walks down the hallway toward the kitchen.

"Kyle!" Elsa says when he turns into the kitchen. His hair is freshly cut, and he wears a tee and cargo shorts, with boat shoes, too. Casual as he preps for his big day. "When I heard that whistling, I knew it would be you."

"Hey, Elsa." He bends and gives her a hug. "What a blue-sky day out there. Perfect! Or, *perfetto* ... if I remember correctly from my Italian handbook."

"Ah, yes. And I'm *very* excited to officiate. I've rehearsed my lines and picked out just the right summer jumpsuit."

"Terrific." He reaches into his shorts pocket. "I brought the rings, like you asked. Great idea, by the way. The last thing I need is to forget them later on." He sets two gold bands on the marble island.

"I'll take very good care of them in the meantime. Celia

lacquered a lovely scalloped seashell, and I'll set the rings in it, on the podium where you'll say your vows. It's a special pedestal-podium, actually, to use for beach weddings. It looks like it's made out of driftwood!"

"You think of everything, Elsa."

Suddenly the side door opens and Celia breezes in, carrying little Aria. "Hey, Kyle! Congratulations! It's your big day," she says, leaving a kiss on his cheek.

"Sure is, Celia. I just stopped at Jason's to drop off my suit. Lauren wants the house to herself to get dressed. You know the routine."

"And it's for good reason," Elsa says. "The groom must not see his bride before the ceremony. It's bad luck."

"That's more *tradition* than anything else now," Kyle says. "But back in the day of arranged marriages? The groom seriously couldn't see the bride *at all* before the wedding. Families didn't want him to have the chance to back out, if he didn't like what he saw. Imagine?"

"No way," Celia says.

"It's true. Me? I can't *wait* to see Ell in her gown on the beach. And heck, a little anticipation only makes the moment sweeter." Kyle pulls out a stool at the island and fills one of the Mason jars with flowers.

"Her gown is so beachy, Kyle," Celia says. She picks up the bouncy baby seat Elsa keeps on hand and puts it on the island, then settles Aria in it. "Wait till you see it."

"And how's this cupcake?" Kyle gives Aria's foot a tickle. "We thought of Sal at The Sand Bar last night at my stag. Set aside a stool in his memory."

"That means a lot, Kyle," Celia nearly whispers as she sits at the island, too. She slowly spins one of the Mason jars brimming with baby's breath. "Sal would've loved all this today."

Kyle nods. "Hey, next thing you know, you'll be getting ready for Aria's wedding. Time goes by so fast."

"Whoa!" Celia stands then and pushes in her seat. "I've got a few years still, Kyle. Don't rush things."

"Just sayin'."

"Where are you headed now?" Elsa asks Celia.

"I want to hang more paper lanterns outside. Can I leave Aria with you?"

"Of course!" Elsa slides the baby seat closer to her on the island and touches the baby's face.

"What amazing weather for the ceremony," Celia says when she opens the side door and steps outside. "Not a cloud in the sky."

"Oh! By the way, Kyle." Elsa takes the Mason jar he filled. "One of your relatives checked in here for the vow renewal yesterday. A very nice fellow, he looks a little like you! A cousin, I think he said?"

"Cousin?"

"Yes." She fusses with the baby's breath, fanning them out. "Hmm … *Shane*, I think his name is. Yes, that's it. Shane Bradford."

After a few silent moments, Elsa glances over from her flower-fussing. Kyle merely looks at her, but says nothing. Then he looks to her garden window at the kitchen sink, where the seashell wind chime outside clicks and clatters. Then back to her. What strikes her is the sudden change in him. He's gone from happy-go-lucky chattering, to cat's-got-his-tongue silence.

So Elsa sets aside her twined Mason jar vase and starts to stand. "Would you like me to get him from upstairs? Say hello before the ceremony?"

"No! No, Elsa." Kyle stands quicker than she does, nearly knocking over his stool. He catches it and hurries down the hall toward the front door. "I'm all set," he calls back. "And really very busy, so I have to get going."

When the door opens and closes behind him, Elsa leans over to squint down the hallway, then shrugs and lifts a delicate stem of baby's breath, brushing the soft blossoms across Aria's cheek.

∽

"Look at you, Mr. Barlow," Maris murmurs, her hands pressing against the gray vest Jason wears. "All dressed up with *somewhere* to go, that's for sure."

Jason lifts one of her hands and brings it to his lips. "Definitely a special day for those two," he says.

"Okay, so let's do this." Maris picks up the boutonniere from his dresser top. "I'll get this pinned on for you."

It's a moment Jason relishes. One when he steps closer and simply watches. Watches his beautiful wife align the white rose boutonniere on the left side of his vest before pressing a pin through it. As she does, he reaches over and tucks her brown hair behind an ear.

"Jason," she whispers. "Let me focus. I don't want to prick you!"

"Okay." He stills then, but watches her face as she maneuvers the flower and pin.

"There."

It all seems real now, Kyle and Lauren's big day. Jason steps to his dresser mirror and looks at his reflection. The boutonniere is a white rosebud entwined with dark blue berries and nestled on a sprig of greens. The greens could look like blades of the swaying grass straight from the marsh.

But when Maris steps beside him, it's her that he can't take his eyes off of. She wears a navy sleeveless sheath, with gold zippers curving back and forth down the length of the dress front.

"I've got to get going," she says when she bends to slip on her sandals. "Vinny and Paige are waiting for me downstairs."

"You all headed to Eva's?"

"Mm-hmm. We ladies are going to curl our hair for the big event. And I guess Matt and Vinny will find some game to watch in Matt's man cave."

"Okay." Jason takes her wrist in his hand and pulls her close. "I'll catch up with you at the inn," he says before tucking her long hair behind an ear again, leaving his hand clasped behind her neck and bending to kiss her.

He feels it, too, the way Maris reluctantly pulls away only after sneaking in another few kisses. "Got to go," she whispers. On her way out of their bedroom, though, she stops in front of her own dresser and leans close to examine her makeup.

And all Jason can think is that it's been two years now since it was *them* getting ready for their own wedding.

Two years since he stood at the altar and watched Maris walk down the aisle.

That was the day he knew. Yes, he knew that with Maris in his life, he was a very fortunate man.

Watching her put on a bracelet now, he thinks he's more in love with her today than he was even then. Especially with all her courage—leaving her denim career, taking on the job of finishing Neil's novel. Yes, the best years of his life started with her.

And he's no fool—it's actually Maris who's getting him through this ten-year anniversary of Neil's death, of that horrific motorcycle accident. Ten years since he'd lost his leg. Her unwavering presence is steering him through these difficult days.

Without Maris, he'd be nowhere. Lost.

She gives him a finger-wave as she breezes out of the room to catch up with Vinny and Paige. But halfway down the stairs, she stops and looks back. Somehow she'd sensed that he followed her, watching her leave.

"What?" she asks, a small smile on her face, a clutch gripped in her hand.

"Nothing, sweetheart. Well," he says when she turns away, which stops her again. "I love you. That's all."

forty-two

From the moment Lauren laid eyes on her two-piece wedding gown, she knew there was only one way to wear her hair for her beach ceremony: in waves.

Standing in her tiny en-suite bathroom, she sets down the curling iron and tousles her now-wavy blonde hair, then twists it into a loose chignon. She leaves a few curled wisps framing her face. "Perfect," she whispers while lifting a small mirror to see the back view. "Just perfect."

She hurries out to her dresser then and lifts her bridal flower crown from its box. The headpiece is made of tiny white silk flowers set in a twisted vine. Carefully, she sets the delicate crown on the top of her head, turns to see her reflection, then removes it and gently sets it down until she's ready to leave.

The whole summer's been one of surprises. Moving in to their new house and discovering mold; the Barlows opening their home to them in the interim; Kyle wanting to renew their wedding vows; and, okay, Kyle's recent abstinence—all to make today even more significant.

Which brings the biggest surprise of all: She's truly happy. Lauren has to scrutinize her reflection just to believe this. In the dresser mirror, she watches this woman wearing a high-neck white sleeveless top, her fingers running along its scalloped hem. The white lace is as intricate as a snowflake on this August day. Beneath the cropped lacy top, her midriff is partially exposed. Almost not recognizing this reflected woman looking back at her, Lauren drops her fingers to the fitted, ankle-length lace skirt. Oh, the entire wedding dress is custom-made for her and Kyle's seaside vow renewal ceremony.

Yes, can this really be her—Lauren Bradford—and her actual life? The smile on her face doesn't quit today.

It's a day Lauren never saw coming. No, she'd thought this anniversary would be one to quietly, respectfully get through.

But leave it to Kyle to take this ten-year anniversary of much sadness and turn it around. She's sure he could quote some statistic about outlook, and perception, and changing our fate with sheer insistence.

Which is what he did.

After seeing his name misspelled on their marriage certificate, Kyle muscled happiness right into this day, straight from the get-go. He twisted and wove that happiness into these hours much like the white flowers twisted into the vine of her hairpiece.

Now, after a quick glance at her watch, Lauren picks up her lipstick, bends close to the mirror and lightly applies the mauve shade to her lips. In a minute, she'll call Hailey and dab some on her daughter's lips, too. It's one of Hailey's favorite things to do: get dressed up with Mommy.

So when Lauren's bedroom door swings open, her first thought is that it *is* Hailey—who'd been downstairs as Lauren's mother got her dressed. But when Lauren turns, she's shocked to see Kyle rushing into the room and closing the door behind him.

"Kyle!" Quickly, Lauren snatches up a folded blanket off the end of their bed. She opens it to block his view of her dress. "What are you doing here? You'll see me in my gown, and ... and that's bad luck!"

Kyle only glances at her. Glances at her, then looks around the room as though seeking something—*anything*—that he can smash, or sweep off a dresser, or throw into a wall. "It's all off," he says.

Which gets her to look at him more closely. His skin is pasty. He's sweating. And he's still in his cargo shorts and T-shirt, with no indication he's even showered for the ceremony yet.

"I'm not doing this. I can't do it," he mutters while pacing this way, that way, dragging his hand through his hair, shaking his head. "Jesus *Christ*, Lauren." Finally, he stops. Just stops, clasps his hands behind his neck, looks up to the ceiling, then at her. "Shane is here."

"*What?*" She steps closer, still clutching her blanket. "What are you talking about?"

"He's here!"

Oh, the anger in Kyle's words scares her, actually.

"At *our* beach, *our* community, practically in our home. I don't know *what* brought him here," he says, turning away while dragging both hands through his hair. "But Elsa told me he's staying at the inn."

"So he showed up?"

The room goes silent then. Silent as Kyle turns and squints at her. "Are you *kidding* me?" he asks, unmoving now. "You knew about this?"

"Oh, Kyle." Lauren glances at the blanket she still holds up beneath her chin. Quickly she wraps it around her body like a long shawl. "Please. Don't get mad."

"Lauren."

"No, no. Take a breath and listen." The disbelief is clear in

Kyle's eyes as he slightly shakes his head—no doubt trying to shake out the realization of her involvement in this day's twist. "Wait, wait, wait. Just *listen*, Kyle."

"You can't be serious." His voice drops low. "Tell me," he says, then takes a quick breath. "Tell me you *didn't* invite my brother." He steps closer. "You didn't."

When she reaches for Kyle's hand, the blanket drops to the floor and her white lace, two-piece gown is in full view.

But it doesn't matter.

Nothing matters right now—that's written all over Kyle's face. So it's up to her to fix this, to convince Kyle of her good intentions. "I *did* invite your brother. But I did it because of Sal. When he died, it made me think anything can happen ... to any of us! How would you feel if Shane suddenly died and you never had a chance to make peace?"

"It wouldn't matter, because after what he did? He's already dead to me. Has been for a long time."

"No, you're just saying that! Years have gone by, and we've all changed. Shane is family, Kyle. *Family.* And I listened to Sal talk about *famiglia* all last summer! And listened to him talk about second chances being *molto speciale.* I wanted you and your brother to have that second chance before it's too late."

"But Lauren, you *knew*—"

"Shh! The kids will hear. Listen, Kyle." She takes Kyle's hands in hers. "Listen. If Sal had a brother he was estranged from, he'd have made amends last summer. He would *not* let that relationship go. So ... So I emailed your brother an invitation, that's all. Nothing else, I didn't even talk to him. Maybe it was one of those rash decisions, I don't know. But, but it's *okay*. We're together and happy, right? We have our home, the kids. Shane can't take anything from you. So I invited him, hoping ..."

"And you didn't tell me?"

"Well, no. Because when Shane didn't RSVP, I didn't think he'd ever show up. So no harm done and I let it all go."

Kyle yanks his hands from hers and walks to the bedroom window, where he presses aside the curtain and faces the distant bay view. He talks without looking at her. "I am *so* mad. I cannot *believe* you did this." In a moment, he turns and eyes her. "There's no *way* I can stand on the beach with you and renew our commitment." Again he drags a hand through his disheveled hair and scours the room, desperately. Finally, he looks at only her. "I can't even be in the same room with you right now. I'm leaving."

"Kyle! Wait." Lauren hurries across the bedroom and grabs onto his arm.

The problem is, he instantly twists out of her hold. "I'm leaving, and you're cancelling *everything*," he says as he opens their bedroom door, hurries down the stairs and walks straight out the front door.

"Kyle!" she calls while running through the hallway to the top of the staircase. Downstairs, the house is pin-drop quiet. Not a sound, not a rustle is heard. Nothing. So her kids and parents must've heard them arguing. She's sure her mother's getting Hailey and Evan out to the backyard, or into a distant room, to keep them from hearing even more.

But there will be no more. Nothing at all. Lauren turns and hurries to her bedroom window. She looks down just as Kyle's backing his pickup out of the driveway and taking off. She keeps watching long after he drives out of view.

So that's it.

Pressing back a sob, or telling herself Kyle will change his mind when he cools off, or just finishing up applying her makeup as though none of this happened, well … it's all useless.

Because as quickly as it all began, her sweet happiness just came to one pathetic, painful, screeching halt.

———

If there's one thing Jason Barlow is *not*, nor has he ever been, it's a pacer.

Please. He's too busy to pace. If he can find a blessed minute or two with nothing to do, Lord knows he won't fill it with more walking—which he does enough of as it is.

So finding himself pacing this Saturday afternoon, well, it means only one thing. Something's wrong. Because really, he has no reason to pace on the day of Kyle's vow renewal. Jason's life is as mad-crazy as it always is, but that's normal. And he's already dressed in his pale gray suit—vest in lieu of jacket—boutonniere perfectly pinned, ready to roll.

Ready for the party to begin.

Ready to be at Kyle's side as his best man.

No, it's something else prompting his pacing.

That *something else* being that Kyle's not here. And he should've arrived a long time ago. They were going to have a ham grinder out on the deck, like they did right before Jason got married. And they planned to toast a cold one to Kyle's nuptials redo.

Instead, Jason's pacing, stopping, checking his watch, looking out the window. Being late is so unlike Kyle. He should've breezed in whistling a happy tune over an hour ago now, citing some scientific study about the early bird getting the worm.

Instead, the house is eerily quiet. No bullshitting, no laughing, no back-slapping.

Nothing. No Kyle. Groom AWOL.

And when Jason sends Kyle a text message, his fingers flying over his phone keyboard? More nothing. No answer.

So Jason calls The Dockside. But still, nothing. Just a recorded message stating the diner is closed for the day.

"Okay, okay," Jason quietly says, taking a long look out the front door in case he might spot Kyle's pickup, or golf cart even, wheeling down the sunny street. He gives his friend a few minutes, and cuffs his white shirtsleeves as he does. When he sees more of the same—nothing—he closes the door and pulls out his cell phone again. This time, he finds Lauren's number in his contacts and texts her. *Kyle's not here and not answering his phone. Where is he?*

In less than thirty seconds, Jason's phone dings with Lauren's answer. And the answer is far from the casual, fun response he'd half expected. Certainly Lauren would maybe allude to finally getting her husband to cave on his abstinence commitment—with a few wink emojis tossed in for good measure. Or maybe she'd text something about Kyle having a flat tire on that old junker he rolls around in. Or maybe Lauren's dress zipper is stuck.

Something innocuous and *utterly* Bradford.

Not what he reads instead: *Oh my God, Jason. Please come over.*

"What?" Jason asks, then reads Lauren's message once more. Finally he drops his cell phone in his pocket, calls the dog inside, then hurries out the slider door to his SUV. "*Son of a bitch,*" he whispers as he rushes down the deck stairs to the driveway. "*Son of a bitch.*"

forty-three

THERE'S A KNOCK AT HER bedroom door, though Lauren knows it's not Kyle. She's been standing at her window all this time, keeping an eye on the street, an eye on her cell phone. Kyle's nowhere to be seen, and hasn't been heard from. Even though she knows it's not Kyle, Lauren can't bring herself to even open the door.

Another quiet knock, then, "Lauren, honey?" her mother asks as she comes in the room. "Kyle stormed out of here and seemed really tense. Is everything okay?"

"Oh, Mom." Lauren still looks outside from the window of her house on the bay. Their dream house where she strung twinkly lights around the porch windows and swore she'd turn them on every night, like it's always Christmas here. They were that happy. "We got into a terrible fight," she says, still only looking outside.

"Well."

In her mother's pause, can't Lauren just picture her wringing her hands, forcing a gentle smile to lighten the mood. Especially seeing her daughter wearing her two-piece lace wedding dress ... devastated.

"I'm sure Kyle's nerves got the best of him," her mother

assures her. "People get stressed in social situations like this one, today. Maybe he just overreacted and we can smooth things over?"

As she talks, her voice gets closer. Lauren knows her mother only wants to comfort her, maybe hug her and pat her back. Get Lauren to see that things aren't *that* bad.

"No," Lauren whispers instead as she turns to her mother. And watching her mother's expression drop upon seeing Lauren's tear-streaked face, well, there's no denying how bad things are. "I think I made a huge mistake, Mom."

"No. No, hon. We can fix things."

Lauren's shaking her head. "It's about Shane," she admits. "He's here."

"What?"

Lauren only nods.

"Shane Bradford?" her mother asks.

"Kyle's brother, yes. You have to get the kids out of here."

As she's talking, Lauren can't believe that the day's come to this. *No, no, no.* Her head throbs; her heart pounds; her breathing is difficult. The worst thing that could happen, has. Why, oh why didn't she listen to her gut, like Kyle always says? The gut doesn't lie. But that damn heart does. One thing she's learned today is to *never* listen to her temperamental, conniving, swindling heart. The same heart that convinced her to reunite family has effectively invited the blackest, baddest sheep right back into the flock.

But she doesn't say any of that to her mother. Her mother, who's wearing a metallic-gold off-the-shoulder dress she couldn't *wait* to show Lauren.

A mother-of-the-bride dress to wear for a happy evening celebrating her daughter's ten-year marriage at a seaside inn.

A dress her mother would dance in at a nuptial event that

doesn't follow a funeral; doesn't follow a friend losing his leg; doesn't follow an upheaval of the groom and bride breaking up, then getting back together in some pathetic, emotionally charged frame of mind.

Lauren manages a small smile at her mother in her lovely dress and again tells her, "You really have to get the kids out of here."

"It's that bad?"

"Yes," Lauren whispers. "It's bad." She takes her mother's hands and squeezes them. "Take the kids somewhere. Any place where they won't hear Kyle and me so upset."

"Like where?"

"I don't know. The carousel at Sound View, maybe? Or to that movie theater next town over?"

"But they were so excited to see their parents get married again!"

Lauren only shakes her head. Any words would be so garbled with a painful sob, it's not worth even trying.

"That's it?" her mother asks. "The ceremony's *really* off? But Hailey," she says, looking over her shoulder to the door. A door where Hailey waits on the other side, downstairs somewhere with her grandpa and Evan. "Hailey was going to scatter hydrangea petals down the sand aisle."

"It's all off." Lauren presses the back of her hand to her face to stem the tears. "It's done, Mom. Just you and Dad take the kids, okay? Jason's on his way over to help me here. I'll call you later."

⁓

Nothing prepares Jason Barlow for what he sees when he stands outside Lauren's front porch and gives a loud knock.

"Jason," she whispers as she rushes to unlock the door.

She's wearing a stunning two-piece white wedding gown—the midriff-baring top fitted with a scalloped hem, the ankle-length skirt also fitted, with a small train. Her hair is in a loose chignon. And her face? Well. If ever he's seen panic, literally, on someone's face, it's right now. Her vow renewal day has clearly been brought to ruin by some unfathomable event.

"Lauren, what's going on?" he asks. "Is Kyle okay?"

"Yes. Well, no. Oh, please come inside and I'll explain," she tells him as she hurries through the living room to the kitchen.

They sit at the table, where a flower arrangement is pushed aside—a bouquet Jason's sure Kyle must've sent his bride this special morning. Beside the flowers, there's a lace shawl, likely for Lauren to wear on her rowboat ride. And a tiny floral wreath headpiece is on the table, too, obviously meant for her daughter, Hailey.

"I'm not sure what to do," Lauren says as she pulls out a chair and sits at the old kitchen table. Her fingers clutch a balled-up tissue; her chignon is more undone than done, hanging loose behind her head. Makeup smears the skin beneath her eyes.

"Wait." Jason sets his arms on the table and leans close. "What about Kyle? Where is he?"

"Don't know."

"What in God's name happened?"

"Shane's here," she says, after a long, pointed look.

"What? Shane?"

"I invited him," she admits.

Now? Well, now Jason sits back with a low groan. "You didn't."

"I did. But *listen*. Please hear me out, Jason."

Jason simply looks across the table at his longtime beach friend—today a devastated bride. He nods then, and motions for her to explain.

Of course, whatever went down, it's too big, too bad, to easily repeat. Lauren gives a small smile, then presses an open hand to her mouth before beginning. "Your brother is dead," she says. "Sal's dead. We never know what can happen in life, and Shane? Shane, like it or not, *is* Kyle's family."

"But Lauren—"

"No." She reaches over and briefly squeezes Jason's hand. "Let me finish. Because you and Sal, well, neither one of you would ever let this continue, this brother rift. And don't you deny it."

Jason gives her that, with another slight nod.

"And it was time to fix things," she continues while tucking a fallen strand of hair into her chignon. As she does, tiny sequins sparkle within her lacy cropped top. "The vow renewal was the perfect opportunity to extend an olive branch, which I did. Because after listening to Sal last year, well ... he convinced us all that second chances were *molto speciale*. Very special." She pauses then, with a sharp gasp from some painful sob that she can't keep down. "So I was trying to do the right thing, and only wanted Kyle and Shane to have a second chance, too."

"Oh, man." Jason shakes his head. "I don't know if it's possible with Kyle and Shane." And as much as Jason wants to, it's not his place to get mad at Lauren, to judge her for going behind Kyle's back and attempting this painful reconciliation. One that could have been avoided. Should never have been considered.

Quickly, Lauren stands and fills a glass of water from the tap. She quaffs half the glass, then brings it to the table. As she does, Jason sees that she's barefoot—toes freshly painted, silver anklet glimmering.

But it's when she sits that Jason sees a change. Lauren trembles as though she's cold, even though it has to be nearly ninety degrees out. Her shaking is enough to get her to wrap her arms around herself, around that bared midriff and lace top.

The thing is, Jason remembers that kind of tremble. He'd felt it shortly after he was tossed to the roadside in that bike accident a decade ago. In and out of consciousness, his entire body shook in waves. There was no controlling it, and so that shivering was just another sense of the *loss* of control that day. A doctor later explained that the repeated shaking that came even long afterward was triggered by adrenaline. A rush of adrenaline prepared him for a fight-or-flight response in the heat of the violent crash. But that energy had nowhere to go as he lay on the pavement, on the stretcher, the hospital bed, so his body expelled it by trembling.

And that feeling is one he never wants to experience again, because it means, basically, you're too late. You can't flee, can't fight, and the damage is done.

Which he's sure from the looks of Lauren, it is. And he's sure her heart is pounding, her hands sweating, as she desperately seeks a way out of this, well, this wreck, too. So he takes her lace shawl from the table, gets up and wraps it around her bare shoulders to stop her trembling. "It'll be okay," he says while patting her arm.

"After all these years and everything that came our way, Jason," she says between tears, "I love Kyle so much."

"I know you do. And he loves you, too. But you also know how Kyle feels about his brother. After that stunt Shane pulled?"

"But we're all *different* now. Ten years ago, I was going to be with Neil. Now? Now I'm so committed to Kyle. And to our family."

When her crying grows uncontrollable, Jason walks around the table and drags a chair beside hers. It breaks his heart to see this; Lauren and Kyle both wanted this day—*so* badly. All Jason can do now is reach over and take her hand in his.

"Lauren. Maybe there's still time," he says, leaning close. From here, he sees every stitch of lace in her dress, even as she gasps in a breath. "We'll find Kyle, and ... and delay the guests," he tries to assure her.

She looks at him, sitting so close. "No, don't," she says, her voice low now. "There's nothing you can do."

"We still have time, though," Jason insists with a glance at his watch. "I can get Shane out of the picture. Where is he?"

It's slight, but he sees how Lauren shakes her head.

"No?" Jason asks.

"No. No, don't bother, Jason. It won't work. You didn't see Kyle."

"Oh, boy." After blowing out a long breath, Jason tries again. "Okay. But listen. *You* have to get it together, Lauren. You *have* to handle your guests. They're all arriving, or will be very shortly, and are expecting a grand night out. You can, well ... you can come undone *afterward*."

Not surprisingly, Lauren comes through for him. Because let's face it, she's been around the block with emotional upheavals, too. So she gets a grip, swallows another breath, grabs a paper towel and blots her face, squares her shoulders. "Let's go, then," she whispers.

"No, Lauren." Jason stands and takes both her hands in his, then touches a wisp of her utterly fallen hair. "No. You can't wear your dress. Not now." He shakes his head and gives her a sad smile. "You have to change into something else."

∼

Before it even began, it's over.

Lauren steps out of the sweetest white lace skirt she's ever donned and sets it on her bed. In its place, she steps into a pair of faded denim shorts with a frayed hem.

And in place of the perfect, white-lace top, she puts on a black lace-up silky shirt.

As she fusses with the crisscross laces at the neckline, her phone dings with a text message. It has to be Kyle, it just has to be. She rushes to her dresser—*hoping, praying, pleading* with the powers that be that it is.

It's not. It's a message from Maris and Eva. A sis-pic showing how they'd curled their hair. But what Lauren really sees more than that is the excitement on their faces. Their eyes sparkle; their lips are glossed; their mouths smile.

Lauren looks closely, because she has to face *them* next. Has to tell them her vow renewal ceremony is off.

Cancelled.

Done.

Buying time to, well, to breathe, and to calm her shaking nerves, she slips her wedding skirt and top on its hanger, lifts the outfit up, then hooks it on her closet door—in the exact spot it hung this morning when she'd woken, and it was the very first magical thing her eyes opened to see.

forty-four

IN NO TIME, JASON GETS Lauren to the Ocean Star Inn. Beyond the inn, on the rolling green lawn, a uniformed catering staff sets up their equipment. Paper lanterns glow beneath a large white tent. And the wraparound porch is strung with white globe bulbs. They glimmer in the late-afternoon light; by evening, they'll look like heavy, lazy stars there.

He sees all this as he loops his arm through Lauren's and guides her inside, away from any excited guests wanting to congratulate her. That's the last thing they need right now. Instead, the two of them stop at the inn's door, where Jason knocks, then opens it and calls out for Elsa.

"In here, Jason," he hears in return. "In the kitchen!"

When Jason walks Lauren down the inn's hallway, he knows. This is the very last quiet moment—before all hell really breaks loose. They turn into Elsa's kitchen, where Celia and Elsa are at the marble island fussing with lace-wrapped Mason jars. They're setting tea-light candles into each.

Both women look up from their task and with unexpected surprise, they look quickly again.

"Lauren?" Elsa asks as she sets down a tea-light candle.

"Listen, ladies." Jason pulls out a stool at the island for Lauren. "I'm sorry, but we have some bad news. The event is off."

"*What?*" Celia asks, looking to Lauren then.

"Cancelled," Lauren sobs as tears stream down her face.

"What*ever* happened, hon?" Celia, in a fitted silver dress, leans over and clasps her arm. "Oh my God, is Kyle okay?"

With a slight nod, Lauren looks from Celia to Elsa. "But I invited Kyle's brother to the ceremony, and I *never* should have. They have a bad history."

"His brother?" Elsa asks.

"Shane," Lauren softly says. "I wasn't thinking straight, and I never should have done it." She grabs a napkin off the table and presses it to her eyes. "It broke Kyle's heart, and he's so mad at me now."

"Wait. Shane, you say? Well, he's staying *here*." Elsa leans close to Lauren and touches her damp cheek. "You mean to tell me that Shane is Kyle's *brother?*"

Lauren barely nods.

"Well, we thought …" Elsa begins. "I mean, I thought he was a cousin, for some reason."

"No. He's Kyle's brother." Jason had been leaning against the grand marble island. But now he motions Elsa aside and together they meet up in the dining room. "So Shane's really staying *here,* then?"

"Yes! But I had no idea, Jason." Elsa sits in one of her blue-painted chairs. She's clearly ready to officiate: dressed in her black jumpsuit with fitted lace sleeves, gold mesh bracelet on, star pendant around her neck.

"Is he still here now?" Jason asks.

"Well he *was* around earlier, so unless he's gone out …" She glances through the doorway, toward the staircase leading upstairs. "Are things really *that* bad?"

"Let me give you just a hint." Jason sits, too. Beside them, floor-to-ceiling windows open to a view of the after-ceremony dinner and reception area. It all looks straight out of a magazine, the way the inn's grounds are meticulously decorated. On the green lawn, there are tiki torches and lanterns. A white canopy stretches over a table sparkling with crystal glasses and china dishes. Beyond, the secret path winds through dune grasses to the beach.

And as beautiful a sight as it is, it's also just as sad now. Damn it, why couldn't Kyle and Lauren have the night they deserve?

"A hint?" Elsa asks.

"Yeah. A hint of how bad it is that Shane Bradford is actually here. You might as well say that a powder keg just went off in poor Kyle's life. Everything, and I mean *everything*, is done. Shane obliterated the whole day—the vow renewal and possibly even more ..."

"What are you implying, Jason?" Elsa leans closer and whispers, "Kyle and Lauren's marriage, too? This won't all just blow over?"

"Too soon to say."

"But we're all dressed, the decorations ... and food. Everyone's ready for this," she insists, pointing to Jason's pale gray vest and suit pants. "It's really off? The whole vow renewal?"

"Seems to be."

"Even *you* can't fix this one, Jason? I know how persuasive you can be."

"No, not this time. I mean, I did everything I could with Lauren. But we don't even know where Kyle took off to." Jason stands and goes to the large windows, where he looks out at the festivities hanging in the balance. That's right, everything is stuck in some eerie limbo. "There's no way those two will be standing on the sand, recommitting their love to each other," Jason explains. "And even if we could convince them," he continues, turning to Elsa now, "it's not fair for them to just go through the motions again, like they did ten years ago."

Elsa's voice drops low. "It's really that bad? Because I find it so hard to believe!"

"You have no idea. This Shane? Well, something happened way before your time here. It was years ago. We can talk later," Jason says, giving Elsa a quick hug. "Because right now I've got to find the groom."

Elsa follows him back to the kitchen, where Celia's pouring a cup of tea for Lauren.

"Any word from Kyle?" Lauren asks Jason. "A text message, maybe?"

Jason shakes his head and clasps her shoulder. "I'll call you, Lauren," he says. "Elsa and Celia will help you explain things to the guests."

After Lauren squeezes his hand on her shoulder, he heads out—tugging his vest straight while wondering where the hell to look first. But it isn't until he's halfway down the hall that he hears it.

Hears someone say his name.

"Well, well. If it isn't Jason Barlow."

The words stop him cold. He turns and backtracks to the staircase. The gorgeous staircase covered in Lauren's seaside mural. When he looks up, at first he thinks it's Kyle there. But shit, it isn't. It's Shane standing on the upper landing, leaning on the banister and looking just like his brother in stature, hair color, build. In silhouette, the two could be twins.

"*You*," Jason says in a restrained voice before rushing out the door, "need to get the *hell* out of here. *Now*."

Castaway Cottage

⁓

Not sure where to go, Jason drives home to his cottage on the bluff again. Maybe there's a chance Kyle will show up there.

When he turns his SUV into the driveway, the tires snap small twigs as he drives up around back. Before he even gets out, Jason calls Maris at Eva's, filling his wife in on everything that went down. He explains how he's got to find Kyle, and isn't sure when he'll be back.

All the while, Jason's thinking that the last time something this devastating happened was, yes, ten years ago—when Lauren broke up with Kyle a month before their wedding. Left him to be with Neil, who then went and died.

As Jason gets out of his vehicle, he hears the seagulls cawing out over the bluff. Their cries carry on a hitching sea breeze this afternoon. Hearing the gulls, he heads out to the stone bench his father made after the war and sits there, facing the sea. Being out here on the bluff reminds him of another hot day, many years ago. They were all in their twenties then, the day Jason actually confronted Neil about messing around with Lauren.

That summer afternoon, he and his brother just wrapped up work in a tiny cottage they were planning to flip. In that sweltering hotbox of a cottage, the two of them had swung hammers; they crowbarred walls; they sledgehammered kitchen cabinets.

At day's end, sweaty and dusty, there was no better place to cool off than right here on the bluff—each of the brothers in faded jeans, sweaty tees, construction boots and with an ice-cold beer in hand. A sea breeze lifted off the water, sometimes carrying a faint spray from the breaking waves below.

All afternoon while demolishing the old cottage, they'd gone back and forth talking about Kyle and Lauren—Jason pushing his brother to break things off with Lauren, Neil pushing right back. Something about the whole love triangle had Jason press the issue. It didn't seem right, nor fair. And if all it took was his interference to set things straight, he'd be damned if he wouldn't try.

Sitting here now, doesn't a faint sea spray reach up over the bluff? That familiar cool sensation on his warm skin brings him right back to that day he sat here with Neil, ten years long gone by now.

Neil walked close to the edge of the bluff, took a long breath of cool salt air, then held his ice-cold beer can to his face.

"Shit, it was a hot one today, bro."

"Yeah. And you still haven't said what you're going to do about Lauren," Jason told him.

Which got Neil to turn and squint at him. His wavy hair lifted in a breeze; his soiled tee clung in perspiration. Finally, he raised his beer can in a pseudo toast. "I'm doing nothing."

"Nothing?"

Neil shook his head. "Nothing more than taking a shower and seeing if I can find Lauren around anywhere."

"But I told you already. You're really making it hell for me with Kyle, man. He suspects something's going on with you and Lauren, and keeps bringing it up."

Neil walked to the stone bench and sat beside Jason beneath the late afternoon's hot sun. "Listen, it's not like I did it on purpose, Jay. I wasn't out to get Kyle." As he talked, he looked at the sea spread before them. "Lauren and I'd see each other here and there, lots of times on the beach when she was painting. We'd get to talking, and I don't know. We hit it off." He took a long swallow of his beer. "She's really something special," Neil vaguely said. "And I'm in love with her."

"Bullshit," Jason countered. *"You're in love with the chase. And come on already, those two have been together for years now."* Jason gave his brother a shove, nearly knocking him off the bench. *"Not to mention, Kyle's been your friend forever. Do the honorable thing, Neil. The right thing."*

"The right thing?" Neil stood again and finished his beer in one long quaff. When he was done, he dragged a hand back through his wavy hair. *"Remember that day, a long time ago? The time we saw the seagull kill that crab? Man, that was sick. Damn bird shook the life right out of it."*

"Yeah, I remember."

"But do you remember what Dad told us? When we wanted to stop the attack and save that poor crab?"

"How can I forget?" Jason asked. *"Said it was a bad day for the crab, but a good day for the seagull."*

"And not to interfere. He wanted us to leave the rhythm of life alone."

"So what?"

"So I'm telling you it's the same with me and Lauren, unfortunately. Because, can I change things? Shit, yeah. Can you get involved? Of course. But we're not doing either. I'm not going to change my mind. And you're not going to interfere, Jay, but instead have to accept it."

"Accept what, for Christ's sake?"

"That it's a good day for me, but a bad day for Kyle."

With that, Neil got up, slapped Jason's shoulder and headed toward the house. Leaving Jason alone on the bluff, he called back one thing—repeating their father's harsh words. *"Don't interfere."*

It was one of the last talks they'd had. Days later, Neil was dead on the hot August pavement, having been flung over Jason's back and into the summer air, getting the life shook right out of him much like that crab. Neil's body was as limp and lifeless on the pavement as the crab's on the beach.

Well, shit. So maybe Neil was wrong, Jason thinks now. He sits on the very same stone bench, dressed in an outfit as far from dirty construction clothes as you can get.

Dressed in nice threads: a best man summer suit for Kyle.

And he thinks, yeah, Neil *was* probably wrong. Which means, hell, so was their father. Don't interfere? Well, why not? Then his interference would simply be a part of the natural order of things.

Because, damn. Jason *listened* to Neil that day. Waved him off, finished his beer and let the topic go. He didn't interfere with Lauren, Kyle or Neil again back then.

He let things play out.

And to this day, he wishes he *had* interfered. If he did, maybe Neil would be *alive* today.

Maybe his interference would've changed the course of the ensuing days, and he and Neil would never have been on that Harley-Davidson, idling at a traffic light.

Maybe Jason would never have been driving the bike, with Neil hitched behind him.

Maybe Neil would never have pointed to the rearview mirror while saying over the sound of the idling engine, "*Jay. Hey, Jay,*" before he was plucked from the motorcycle and essentially shaken to his death.

If only Jason had interfered. If only he'd broken up a relationship he questioned from the start. So *what* if it pissed anyone off? So *what* if it caused a little turmoil that would one day settle down.

A little turmoil would've been better than his brother Neil being limp, lifeless and gone.

"That's it," Jason says now, getting up from the bench and heading back to the house. This time, he's *not* letting things go.

No, because this time, he's mad. Mad that he didn't interfere ten years ago and *change* the natural order of things.

This time, he's interfering. Because damn it—Shane being here or not, Lauren overstepping a line with her private invitation or not—one thing's certain. Kyle was *always* so right for Lauren. And Jason has to get him to see that.

If he only knew where the hell his friend went.

forty-five

Rows of folding chairs are arranged on the sand, facing Long Island Sound ... white chair after white chair after white chair. Cliff and Jason set them out earlier today. Sprays of blue beach hydrangeas are attached to decorative piers behind them.

Lauren looks at the empty white chairs, then back at the inn. On Elsa's kitchen island, she knows lace-wrapped Mason jars filled with golden sand and twinkling tea-light candles are also lined up. Elsa and Celia planned to hang one jar on the end chair in each row. Those dancing flames would illuminate the center aisle as she and Kyle walked down it after renewing their vows. Lauren would've held her bouquet of roses, beach grass and white seashells. And Kyle? Kyle would've been smiling that big smile of his. Maybe he'd punch the air, or stop to shake a few guests' hands as they strolled the sand.

Out on the water, the temporary floating dock has a spray of hydrangeas set on it, too. The flowers are illuminated, because as the sun sinks lower in the sky, solar deck lights start to glimmer along the dock's edge. Even the rowboat Lauren was going to arrive in is decorated. Elsa mentioned that the florist wrapped a large arrangement of white roses nestled in greens all around the bow of the boat. Delicate vines hang over the edge, long enough to skim the sea.

Everyone pitched in for this day. Everyone wanted it to happen. It seemed a new beginning, somehow, coming a year after Sal's death.

Now the sights do nothing more than mock Lauren. Everything she sees leaves a painful lump in her throat as she holds back her sorrow. Oh, the stinging regret she feels at sending one foolish invitation.

Because just like that, *snap*, it's done.

Maris and Celia helped her send all the guests on their way: Vera and Derek; Brooke and her husband; waitresses from the diner; old neighbors from Eastfield; all her friends here. Though Lauren didn't share the personal details, she received lots of long hugs, sad smiles, whispered reassurances.

It wasn't an easy afternoon.

But when she told *Jerry* the ceremony was cancelled, she felt a different kind of pain. Kyle's worked with Jerry for a long time—starting when Kyle was a part-time cook back when he was laid off from union shipbuilding work. He and Jerry have stood at their beloved big stoves, side by side, through much of Kyle's adult life. Through Kyle and Lauren's wedding, and the birth of Evan and Hailey, more layoffs and marital problems, good times and bad ... Jerry was always there to listen and guide Kyle. To talk and laugh. Through all these years, Jerry's been more like a father to Kyle than anything else. So telling him the news hurt especially.

After the guests have left, Lauren wonders how she'll ever wake up in the morning and get back to normal.

Celia comes over now, still wearing her silver maid-of-honor dress. Together they sit in a rear row of white chairs. When Lauren turns to give a last wave to Jerry as he heads for his car, she notices Cliff stepping off the inn's wraparound porch and heading her way.

"Elsa filled me in on the details, Lauren. And I can't help but feel that this is all some terrible misunderstanding," he says when he sits in a chair beside her.

"No, Cliff." She gives him a small smile. "It's a terrible *mistake* is what it is. And it's all mine. I *never* should've invited Shane."

"But you have a good heart! Kyle will come around."

"What difference does it make now?" When Cliff pulls a folded handkerchief from his pocket, she takes it and dabs her eyes. "We'll never have our vow renewal. It's over. I don't know how we'll ever get past even this day."

It just feels then like she's out of words. Really, what more is there to say? To anyone? So Lauren stands and folds one of the white guest chairs.

"Lauren!" Maris calls out as she rushes over from the inn. Eva is behind her. "No, no." They both take the chair from her hands, open it again and set it down. "You leave those be."

"I'll get them later," Cliff assures Lauren. "Don't you worry."

"You need to get home, hon. Have some food, rest." Maris tucks back a wisp of Lauren's utterly fallen chignon. "Wait for Kyle," she whispers.

"I'm just so devastated," Lauren admits, sitting again. "And mortified that *everyone* saw this."

Celia leans close and hugs her. "Shh. I'm going home with you so you're not alone. We'll get things settled there together."

Lauren nods, but still sits and faces the evening beach. The sand is streaked gold and pink as the setting sun paints pastel colors on it. Lazy waves lap at the shore. "We would've taken pictures. Look at the gorgeous lighting."

In a moment, she notices Elsa crossing the lawn now. Lauren's heart breaks all over again when she sees Elsa's wearing her favorite black fitted jumpsuit. With its sheer lace neckline and lacy sleeves, Elsa looks stunning and wore the jumpsuit special for her very first Justice of the Peace event. She sits beside Lauren and quietly takes her hand in hers.

"I'm bringing Lauren home now," Celia tells Elsa.

Elsa leans forward to talk to Celia on the other side of Lauren. "That's good. I'll help your father with Aria. We'll check in with you."

"Okay," Celia says. "The baby's asleep, so she should be all set. And thank you, Elsa." Celia leans over and clasps Elsa's hand that's clasping Lauren's. "I appreciate it."

Lauren notices, too, how Celia simply leaves her hand clasped there.

"Is Shane still around?" Celia asks Elsa.

But somehow, just asking the question does something to Lauren. This whole catastrophe all becomes *real* with the thought of Shane's presence. A real nightmare. Everything around her swirls in some sort of dream sequence. The faces of everyone here that she loves move in close, whisper, smile ... all at the mention of Shane's name.

Shane left for a bit, but his bags are here. He hasn't checked out yet.

Eva breezes in front of them and waves her hand toward the sea. Oh, never mind him.

Where are Hailey and Evan?

With her parents for the night. Celia squeezes Lauren's hand. Isn't that right?

Eva again. So hopefully you and Kyle can privately talk this out.

Maris sits in a chair behind Lauren's and pats her shoulder.

Has anyone heard from Kyle?

No, Jason is out looking for him.
Cliff paces in the sandy aisle.
Matt and Nick are searching, too.
What about all this food?
I'll package some up and drop it off at your house, Lauren.
Lauren.
Lauren.
Lauren.

Don't they get it? Lauren can't *do* this anymore. It's too much. When she drops her face into her hands, concerned touches begin—Elsa hugging her, Maris fixing a strand of her hair, Celia stroking her hand. And there are hushes, and shushes, as Lauren's sure they're all giving each other secret, worried looks.

But what, really, can anyone do?

One thing, Lauren decides. One person can do one thing. It might be Lauren's only hope. She dabs her eyes with Cliff's hanky again and turns to Maris behind her.

"Maris, can I ask you a favor?" she asks.

"Of course!" Maris hurries around and crouches down in front of her. "Anything to help."

"If you see Shane, try to get him to leave? Elsa says his bags are still here, but really? He needs to go now."

Maris nods as they all listen to Lauren draw some invisible, deep line between Maris and Shane. Between goodness and evil.

"I'm not sure he ever got over you, so I bet he'll listen to you, of all people," Lauren insists. "Shane always did *anything* for you, Maris."

Silently Maris squeezes Lauren's hand, and that's when Lauren knows she's done. There's nothing more to do here. She has to get home and wait for Kyle.

"Come on," Celia stands. "I'll go with you now."

When Celia heads toward the inn, though, Lauren stops her. "Can we walk, Cee? It'll be good to work off some of this emotion."

And they do. Together they cross the beach instead of the lawn. The horizon is violet; a few early stars glimmer in the sky. A salty breeze brushes Lauren's face as they walk near the easy breaking waves. A lingering seagull swoops low over the dark water, the gull's plaintive cry echoing across the sand.

Celia doesn't say much; she's just there for Lauren. A true beach friend.

They leave the inn and beach behind, and what happens is this: Like those waves, the night recedes. The celebration recedes. The memories recede. Hope recedes.

There's only darkness, lapping, lapping over Lauren as everything slips further and further away.

forty-six

K YLE BRADFORD KNEELS IN THE dimly lit St. Bernard's Church. His elbows are propped on the back of the pew in front of him, his head bowed. He needed a quiet space and somehow ended up here, of all places. But there was nowhere else to turn. Anywhere else—be it the diner or The Sand Bar, the Stony Point boardwalk or home—it would all be the same. Someone would be at him, bothering him, asking questions, talking, talking, *talking*.

And what he needs to do is *think*.

Cruising down Shore Road, he considered stopping in a couple of honky-tonk beach bars, or at a roadside take-out seafood joint. Nearly drove past this low-slung church with its shingles weathered the same dusty gray as Long Island Sound. With its stained glass windows still tipped open to let any cooling salt air drift in off the sea. Got practically rear-ended when he slammed on his pickup's brakes and veered into the church parking lot. Waved off the long blare of the enraged driver who swerved around him.

Finally, Kyle pushed open the church's double doors and dropped into a pew halfway to the altar—not long after the Saturday vigil mass let out. Above him now, ceiling fans slowly paddle the air. A few low lights still glow over the altar. And in the side alcove, blue and cream candles flicker on a tiered candle stand.

Seeing all the hushed details, he's reminded of why he and Lauren decided *not* to have their vow renewal here. Closing his eyes and bowing his head again, he visualizes those reasons.

First is Neil's casket being carried out of this very church ten years ago. Hearts were heavy then, on one of the bleakest days of their lives.

He sees, too, in the darkness behind his closed eyes, his own wedding day with Lauren not long after Neil's funeral. Jason's father pushed his ravaged son down the aisle in a wheelchair, so that Jason could be Kyle's best man. Could sit in a formal suit beside Kyle at the altar. Still scarred from the accident and still without a prosthesis, Jason's left leg was kept prone on an amputee board attached to his wheelchair. Kyle had the passing thought at the time that Jason might not actually survive all he'd been through.

And, still kneeling, Kyle sees as recently as last summer, another funeral. This one? Sal's. The Italian. The man who heard *all* their secrets while keeping the biggest secret to himself: that he was living on borrowed time.

Without a doubt, many memories here at St. Bernard's Church are too dark. So Kyle and Lauren decided on an easy-breezy vow renewal ceremony on the beach, instead. To start the next ten years with a carefree celebration.

A lot of good it did them.

With that thought, Kyle pushes up from the kneeler, walks to the candle stand in the alcove and drops a few dollars in the offering box. He lifts a taper, touches it to a flickering flame to light the tip, then stops, uncertain.

The only person Kyle's ever lit a candle for is his brother, Shane.

About to light a church candle now, it strikes him that he's never lowered the burning tip of a taper to the wick of a candle for anyone else. Not his wife; not his children; not a friend. He's never done this for others in his life—loved or not, alive or not. Not for Neil, after his death. Not for Jason when he'd lost half his leg. Not for Evan, once Kyle discovered his son was actually Neil's boy.

No. Only Shane Bradford has been at the receiving end of any lit taper Kyle's lowered. Even a few weeks ago, at Aria's christening, he felt compelled to do so.

As his taper ember burns down now, Kyle chooses a blue candle in the back row. He dips the taper low, hesitates, then lights the damn candle.

For who, or for what ... this time, he's not really sure.

forty-seven

It's a perfect night. *PERFECT.*

Jason walks up the boardwalk steps, sits on the bench and feels a scarce sea breeze on his face. Behind the boardwalk, boats in the marina rise and fall with the gentle tide. The vessels creak and groan as they pull against the pilings to which they're secured, and that comforting boat-talk sound floats in the night air. Further down the boardwalk, strung twinkling lights cast a misty glow beneath the shade pavilion.

Yes, it's the perfect summer night for a vow-renewal shindig.

And the heavy, nearly full moon rising over Long Island Sound makes it something more. Makes it magical.

Which makes the whole damn sight a crying shame.

He's exhausted all options looking for Kyle. Couldn't find hide nor hair of his six-foot-two friend, anywhere. Hell, Jason stopped in every drinking establishment—squinted into the dark clubs, walked past each barstool, heard bluesy jukebox tunes and the sharp crack of pool sticks. He cupped his hands around his eyes and peered into the Dockside Diner's locked-up-tight glass door—looking for a glimmer of light from Kyle's office, or for a shadow of his friend sitting alone in a booth, nursing a coffee. He rattled the front door at Kyle's empty house, then swung by there again and talked to Lauren. Finally, he walked the dark beach at Back Bay.

Every sandy crevice of Stony Point has been scoured.

Now all Jason's got is fatigue, worry, and an aching leg. So he stands, tugs at his suit vest, cuffs his shirtsleeves and hurries along the planked boardwalk. A walk on the hard-packed sand below the driftline might help some phantom pain nagging at him. But first, he has to check in with Maris, so he pulls out his cell phone and calls her.

"I've looked everywhere for Kyle."

"No sign of him, babe?"

"Nothing." Jason looks out at the beach. In the distance, the white folding chairs are still arranged in rows; the floating dock glimmers on the water; decorative wooden piers and lanterns dot the sand. "I'm going to clean up the beach now. Stack the chairs, take down decorations."

"Okay, good," Maris quietly says. "I'm with Eva at home. I gave the dog her kibble and let her out for a few minutes. Now we're on our way to Lauren's with some food."

"What a mess."

"We'll keep an eye out for Kyle. Got to go, love you."

"Love you, too, sweetheart."

Jason double-checks for any messages from Kyle, then heads down the boardwalk. He can't get to that packed sand soon enough, to walk a stretch of it and soothe his gait. As he nears the opposite end of the boardwalk, though, a man in suit pants and a button-down shirt climbs the steps. On the top step, he removes a wooden vow-renewal pointer sign. Lauren had made the sign from old boardwalk planks to aim guests in the right direction for the ceremony.

Jason squints through the darkness. "Cliff?" he calls out.

Cliff squints right back at him. "Jason," he says, walking closer. "Did you find Kyle?"

"No. All the guys are out looking. Matt and Vinny just texted me from the casinos. They can't find Kyle anywhere there. Any word on your end?"

"Nick went out in his Whaler to check the local fishing spots. You know, out on the rocky outcropping, around at Little Beach. But nothing, Barlow. Nick even gave a look out on the swim raft. I guess Kyle's been known to do some night laps?"

"He has. No sign of him?"

"No."

"Shit," Jason says under his breath. "I checked the diner, the local watering holes. He's just gone, man."

Cliff sits on the boardwalk bench and leans the vow-renewal sign against it. "Hope he's okay, poor guy." When Jason sits beside him, Cliff quietly asks, "You don't think he'd harm himself, or do anything foolish like that?"

"I don't think so, Raines." Jason remembers the time he saved Kyle's life, right here, and mentions it to Cliff. "He was in a bad way that night, three years ago now. It was before he bought the diner and was at the end of his rope. No money, no work, afraid he and Lauren weren't going to make it. Got himself in a situation," Jason explains as he stands and turns toward the boat basin behind the boardwalk. He puts a knee on the bench and rests his arms on the top of the seat back. "Somehow, when no one was looking, Kyle climbed up on this top rail here."

"You mean he *sat* on the rail?"

"No. Shit, no. He hauled himself up on his bare feet and walked that top rail like a tightrope. It was dark, late at night. And he was liquored up and unsteady already, then lost his balance when he got distracted by a swan paddling through the boat basin. Somehow, through the good grace of God, I ran up and managed to grab hold of his arm and yank him to the beach." Jason looks over the top rail to the concrete landing surrounding the docked boats twenty feet below. "Kyle came so *damn* close to falling in the wrong direction and hitting concrete."

"Holy smokes." Cliff stands to look over the railing at the little marina's cement walkway.

"Kyle was pretty wasted that night," Jason tells Cliff. "Calmed down, got a grip, and he and Lauren have come a long way since then. So I think he's safe. But still, he didn't deserve this mess today."

Cliff turns to face the beach and the dark Sound beyond. "Well, folks don't need to wake up tomorrow and see all these decorations. Thought I'd help out in some way and clean things up here."

"My thoughts exactly. So let me give you a hand, Cliff."

"Thanks. I could use the help." Again, he picks up the vow-renewal pointer sign and heads down the boardwalk.

"How's Elsa?" Jason asks, walking beside him.

"Not that good. This vow renewal was supposed to be her first major event at the inn and it imploded. She spent the afternoon trying to gently inform the guests *and* evade their personal questions. So, Elsa's kind of upset, too. You know, she really had high hopes and was trying to make her son proud of all she's accomplished with the inn today. But that's done now."

"Is Celia with her?" Jason asks. He steps off the boardwalk and picks up a silver bucket filled with flip-flops. Just like he and Maris had at their wedding, Lauren packed the bucket for guests wanting to kick off their fancy shoes in the sand.

"No. Celia's at Lauren's place."

Holding the flip-flop bucket, Jason steps back onto the boardwalk. "Listen, Cliff. Why don't you go help Elsa clean up her patio and kitchen, so she's not alone."

"Oh, she's not alone. She just put on a pot of coffee." Cliff drags a hand back through his salt-and-pepper hair. "Wants to get to the bottom of this situation with that Shane fellow."

"*What?* Are you *kidding* me?" Jason stops still. "Shane's still *here?*"

Cliff leans over and plucks another pointer sign from the sand. "Apparently," he says. "I guess he went out for a while, but came back. You know, his room's booked through the weekend."

"No, no. Elsa is *not* to play intermediary. Not this time, Cliff. You go tell her to pour that coffee down the fucking *drain* and get that Shane out of there." He gives Cliff's shoulder a push. "Now!"

"Sheesh, Barlow. What's up with this guy? He sounds like serious bad news, because I haven't seen you this riled in some time."

Jason sits on the boardwalk itself, his legs dropped over the edge, feet in sand. The nearly full moon sits low over the water, painting a gold streak across it. In its light, he sees the silhouette of the floating swim raft and the big rock beyond it. Stars twinkle high in the vast sky beyond. He sees it all as his pulse races enough for him to take a long breath, to lean his elbows on his legs and drop his head. Finally he clasps his hands behind his neck, stretches out a knotted muscle, then looks over at Cliff. Commissioner Cliff Raines, standing there holding two pointer signs ... and utterly clueless.

"Listen. You have to decide where your loyalties lie," Jason says in a low voice. A couple out for an evening stroll walks past, briefly nodding hello. "I've got your Sailor story buttoned up tight. Gave you my word, my loyalty is to *you*," Jason continues once the couple passes.

"I get it. And I appreciate it."

"And tonight, *your* loyalty needs to be to Kyle. There's no time to rehash the Shane story, but you can trust me on this one," Jason insists. "We'll talk later. But now? You're the commissioner of this beach community. For God's sake, throw your weight around and get that Shane the hell out of here. Make something up if you have to."

"Like what?"

Jason looks out at the water, then drags his hand across his scarred jaw. "Tell him the inn's not allowed to be open with guests. Elsa's violating a code. Anything."

"Okay, I'll do what I can." Cliff sets the two wooden pointers beside the flip-flop bucket, then pulls a key ring from his pocket. "These are to my golf cart and the supply shed. Put any decorations in the shed." He points down the beach where tiki torches glow in the night. "Plenty of orange cones on the sand, too, blocking off the event area. You'll need to grab those. Might have to make two trips, but everything should fit in my golf cart. Afterward, leave the shed key under the doormat at my trailer."

No sooner does Jason grab the keys than Cliff hurries off in the direction of the Ocean Star Inn. Watching him go, Jason also sees Elsa's grand inn set far back off the beach, behind the dune grasses. The turret is illuminated, and he can make out the old Foley's back room—decorated for the vow renewal reception. The large deck off the hangout room is strung with hanging lanterns.

"Damn it," he whispers before grabbing up the flip-flop bucket and pointer signs on this night that just won't quit.

forty-eight

LATER, THE BEACH IS STRANGELY empty, though it's early still—just past nine. It's as though people sense something bad went down. Plenty of vacationers must've been secretly keeping an eye on the white guest chairs, on the illuminated floating dock. Couples must've planned evening strolls to get a glimpse of the gala festivities hinted at in the flickering tiki torches in the sand; in the twinkling paper lanterns hanging beneath the white canopy on the inn's manicured grounds. Families maybe lingered late on the beach, hoping to see the bride in her white gown; see the groomsmen in their summer suits. See the teary guests watching an emotional ceremony. See fists pumping the air, the groom dipping his bride in a romantic kiss, guests clapping and whistling afterward.

Everybody loves a celebration.

Now, everyone stays away—like there's some bad juju associated with the ghost town left behind on the far end of the beach. In the sea breeze, haunting echoes of laughter and music that never came to pass might whisper in the night.

"You out there, Neil?" Jason asks from where he stands on the packed sand beneath the driftline. He stops and picks up a stone, joggles it and waits at the water's edge.

What happened tonight? he hears as a small wave rolls onshore.

"A blast from the past is what happened." Jason gives a side-arm throw and skims the stone across the dark water. In the glow of that heavy moon, the stone skips across the ripples. "And it's bad."

Seriously? Been waiting for this night, bro, comes Neil's voice when the dune grasses further back on the beach sway in a salty, hitching breeze. *Was hoping to see the old friends together.*

Jason walks a few steps to work the ache from his leg, then plucks the white-rose boutonniere off his vest. His fingers rub a few petals off the flower before he flings the whole thing out to sea. "Shane's what happened, man. The whole situation fucked with Kyle's head." Again, Jason walks the beach, heading to all those white chairs neatly and precisely set out in rows. That low-slung moon casts an unreal glow on them. The way the chairs glimmer in the dark, you'd almost expect to see spirits arriving, taking seats, dancing on the beach—women's translucent dresses floating around them as they twirl on the sand.

Jason picks up three orange safety cones on his way to the chairs.

Shit, that dude's had his share of hard knocks, he hears his brother admit about Kyle, right as Jason slides those cones one on top of the other.

"Yeah," Jason says under his breath. "And he deserved none of them."

The thing is, Jason knows that *one* of those hard knocks—maybe the worst—was dealt by Neil himself. By Neil stealing Lauren from right beneath Kyle's eyes ten years ago. From right beneath Kyle's engagement ring and upcoming wedding. Neil just swooped right in and whisked Lauren away from him.

Walking along the shore, Jason breathes the salty air. Breathes in, then out. Focuses on *that* instead of his problematic leg acting up with the day's stress. Ahead, those white guest chairs come into clear view. He drags a hand through his hair while taking in the sad sight, then walks to the far end of the first row. When he snaps a chair shut, there's nothing. No more whispers from Neil, no words about Kyle, or Lauren, floating on the breeze.

Not until he sets the folded chair down and there's only the sound of lapping waves in the night.

But in the end, Kyle got the girl, Jason swears he hears his brother's voice admit. *Didn't he.*

~

Jason jumps, then, when he hears something else. It's someone snapping shut a chair behind him ... in the back row, on the other end. His blood pressure spikes when he makes out, in the misty moonlight, Shane. He's lifting a folded chair and tossing it in the sand, then reaching for another.

If Jason has any say in the matter, that's the *last* chair that asshole will toss. When he feels a slight shove from behind, he glances back. *Look again, Jay,* he swears is whispered right as another chair is snapped closed. So Jason leans forward while squinting through shadows.

Son of a bitch. It's *Kyle* he sees closing chairs, *not* Shane.

Kyle, who he *expected* would be wearing his light gray suit pants and the vest perfectly fitted to a man's V-shaped body—to hear his tailor explain it. Not wearing the same wrinkled cargo shorts and tee he must've been in all day. Must've never even taken off for his big, cancelled event.

Kyle, who *damn it*, from a distance looks exactly—in size and stature—like his brother, Shane Bradford.

"Jesus Christ, Kyle," Jason says as he hurries around the chairs to his friend. "Everybody's looking for you. You all right, guy?"

"I've had better days," Kyle answers as he drops another folded chair onto the sand.

"Where've you been?"

"You never came." Kyle, with a beer in one hand—wait, a beer *and* a cigarette—somehow manages to snap shut another white chair. "Never showed up."

Jason picks up a chair near Kyle and folds it closed. "What are you talking about? Showed up where?"

Kyle looks at him, raises his beer can and takes a long swig. "You know, your brother told me once that the sea speaks to you, man. Said that when shit goes down …" Kyle says, stopping to take a drag of his cigarette now. "When big shit goes down in life, listen to the sea. If you sit still enough in front of it, it answers your questions."

Jason drops his folded chair in the pile and picks up the next.

"Doesn't fucking work," Kyle says then, the words slurring. "Because I sat and listened to the sea tonight, out on the bluff. Listened for some explanation from the effin' waves breaking on the rocks. Sat on your old man's bench."

"At *my* place?"

"That's right. Looked out at that God damn sea. You know what it told me? Nothing. My life still sucks." Kyle picks up a chair and manages to close it with a loud clatter. "Waited for the past hour, thought you'd show up."

Well, it's a good thing all these opened chairs are here, Jason thinks. Because folding them one at a time gives him a chance to gauge his friend. How far gone is Kyle? It's hard to tell. He looks tired, and a bead of perspiration trickles down the side of his face. And he's holding that beer. So did he have a *few* drinks, or a few too many? Jason watches as Kyle pulls a vow-renewal pointer sign out of the sand and tosses it aside.

"Did I do the right thing cancelling all this?" Kyle asks over his shoulder, raising his voice right when a few teenagers pass them on the beach. "Or did my brother get the best of me again?"

The last thing Kyle needs is to draw any more attention to this fiasco of a day. So Jason hurries closer, but keeps his voice low as the kids move past. "I can't answer for you, Kyle."

Kyle looks at him, then walks toward the water. That's when Jason notices how he stays close to the chairs. Close enough to grab hold of the top of one here, another one there, all to keep his balance on unsteady feet. Once he gets near the water, Kyle flicks his lit cigarette butt into it.

Okay, so the question's answered. Kyle's had a few too many. Maybe more than a few.

Because he stumbles as he makes his way back to those chairs. And if there's anything Kyle Bradford—former steelworker climbing the gridwork around ships being built—is, it's this: steady on his feet. He grabs another white chair and carries it to the folded-up pile.

"Hey, man," Jason says, taking the beer can and chair from Kyle's hands. "Let's walk down the beach. We'll go to the rocks, talk about things there." He folds the white chair closed and drops the empty can and chair in the sand. "We'll listen to the sea together."

Kyle, as though he doesn't hear him, picks up another chair, snaps it closed and tosses it aside. Then another. "Shit, Barlow," he says when he picks up a third. "You're more a brother to me than anyone ever was. In my whole pathetic life." Another snap of a chair, another thud as it hits the sand.

So Jason does the same. Works beside Kyle, lifting and snapping shut the white chairs. Snapping and thudding, over and over again. Giving his friend time to blow off steam. To cool down. To breathe that salt air that cures what ails you.

When they've finished a row and a half of chairs, Jason hits Kyle's shoulder. "Hey, got an extra smoke, guy?"

Kyle reaches into one of his cargo shorts pockets and pulls out a crumpled pack of cigarettes. He shakes one out for Jason, who takes it and grabs another for Kyle, too.

"Give me a light," Jason tells him, then cups the flame when Kyle's shaking hand manages to strike a match on the third try. Taking a long drag, Jason walks to the water. Just leaves the scene of what *feels* like a crime—behind. Maybe Kyle will do better by not seeing all the memories that *never* happened today. The ones that were supposed to fill another photo album he'd page through from time to time.

The images of his and Lauren's first dance on the sand, Lauren in her white two-piece gown, her hair in a loose chignon, her body pressed against Kyle's as Celia strums a romantic tune on her guitar.

The image of Kyle cupping his bride's face and deeply kissing her before scooping her up in his sizable arms and spinning her around in the shallows.

The image of a multitude of crystal glasses being raised in a toast.

The image of a beaming Elsa, so very proud to be the officiant of Kyle and Lauren's vow renewal in her first Justice of the Peace gig.

The image of the guys in their dress pants and vests, horsing around and grabbing up Kyle together as though they're about to throw him in the water.

Castaway Cottage

The image of the whole gang gathered in the Foley's hangout room in the turret—old booths and jukebox and pinball machine still intact—as they party and dance their stompin' feet on the refurbished wooden floor there once again.

Jason leads Kyle in the direction away from all those missed memories.

If he can just get him to the rocks, they'll sit there. The Gull Island Lighthouse beam will pass over the sea; the water will swish with some badass bluefish chasing in a school of minnows in a feeding frenzy; Kyle will no doubt toss a few handfuls of cold water on his face.

"So now what?" Kyle asks when he takes a drag of his own smoke. "I can't even picture tomorrow."

"I'll *tell* you what," Jason says. "Don't picture tomorrow. Just get through tonight first."

With his cigarette hanging from his lips, Kyle pulls off his boat shoes and sloshes in the small, breaking waves. "So is that it for me and Ell? Shit, we never should have come back here to Stony Point. I *knew* it, Barlow. What a mistake." He stops and takes another drag of that smoke. "You can't go back," he says, his words slurring again. "We're done now."

"No, you're not."

They walk down the beach, leaving the chairs behind as they head to the rocky ledge beyond the Fenwick cottage.

"Yeah, we are. Finished." Kyle looks over at Jason, nearly stumbling when he does. "You were right in that shop the day we got our suits. What was I trying to do? My wedding was a nightmare then, and it was a nightmare today. You can't fucking change history."

Kyle kicks at the water, then picks up a rock. Standing there, he twists back and gives it his all, heaving that rock out into the water as though he's trying to throw the whole day with it. Tie up these twenty-four hours with that rock and sink them in the sea. As he does, he almost falls—but catches his balance when he reaches his hand into the water and touches bottom.

Shit. Jason's big, six-foot-two hulking friend, brought to his knees by one day, one person. Shane.

"Kyle." Jason takes a last drag of his cigarette, then flicks it into the waves. He puts his arm around Kyle's shoulder and steers him onto the sand. "Get it together, man. It's all right. You and Lauren are still together."

"But she never even told me what she did. Went behind my *back* and invited Shane."

The problem now, Jason sees, is the way Kyle's weaving in and out of the water. Because Jason doesn't need to mess around with his prosthesis, just to keep hauling Kyle to dry land. They really need to get down the beach to those rocks, where they can sit in the shadows and Kyle can calm down, once and for all.

Where he can listen to the sea. Can breathe. And breathe some more.

forty-nine

GROWING UP AT THE BEACH, Jason and Neil learned the rules of the sea from their father. He taught them things like how to escape a riptide. That's right. *Escape.* Even the sea had parallels to their father's Vietnam War days. Because you had to *escape* a riptide like you would escape an enemy. Don't fight it; don't let it exhaust you. Relax and go with it. Stay afloat and see where the rip's taking you. A moment will come when it'll loosen its hold, and that's when you make your move. Swim *parallel* to shore to escape. Though common sense wouldn't dictate that. Common sense would urge you to swim directly toward shore—a potentially deadly move. *So common sense doesn't always work with an enemy*, their father said.

Or there were rules about navigation. At sea, sometimes you can't tell where you're going. There's only vast water, everywhere, to be crossed carefully. Or there's fog. Or tossing waves. You just have to stick to your course, through calm seas and rough. You'll get there. *I knew to navigate that damn jungle the same way I'd navigate the sea*, their father told them. *Very carefully. Warily. Fight when I had to. Move quietly, too. Patiently. And I always made it out alive.*

So walking beside the sea now, that's what Jason's thinking. If his father were still alive, what would he tell Jason tonight? How can the sea help him?

Up ahead, the lone cottage on the beach rises like a black silhouette from the sand. Only a few lights are on inside, casting vague illumination on its white wraparound deck. "Kyle, man," Jason calls after his friend in a hoarse whisper. He passes the cottage-on-stilts to catch up with him. "Let's get to the rocks and sit down. It's just a terrible day, but that's all it is."

"*Another* one." Kyle mutters, veering toward the lazy breaking waves again.

Jason sticks to the hard-packed sand, within easy-enough distance of Kyle in case he has to haul him away from drowning himself.

"Jason?" a man's voice suddenly calls out in the night.

The sound of it surprises Jason. He looks over to the Fenwicks' deck, where he can make out a shadow standing there, leaning on the railing.

"That you, Jason?" the voice carries.

"Yeah, Mitch." Jason trots to Kyle and quietly orders him to wait right there, then turns toward Mitch.

"Been waiting for that vow renewal." Mitch motions to the roped-off beach where the chairs are only half stacked. "Was hoping to see the festivities."

"The thing of it is," Jason begins with a glance toward the roped-off area, too. "Hell. It's all been called off."

"Seriously?" Mitch asks, shielding his eyes as he squints over in Jason's direction.

"Unfortunately."

"Everything okay?"

Jason walks closer to the deck so he can keep his voice low. "Actually, Mitch? No. It's really not." He motions toward Kyle near the water. "You met Kyle. And, well, he's in a bad way tonight. And kind of lit."

"Ah, this cruel life." Mitch walks along the deck railing, taking in the sight of Kyle near the water's edge. "Tell you what. Why don't you two come in out of the damp? Get off the beach and get your bearings inside." He pauses a second. "It's just me and Carol here."

The slider scrapes open on its rusted track then. "Dad?" Carol asks, stepping outside. She wears a long, gauzy kimono over her tank top and ripped jeans. "What's going on?"

"It's Jason," Mitch tells her. "Having a little problem on the beach."

"Mitch, Carol." Jason walks to the deck stairs and looks up at them. "I don't want to impose, really." But when he looks back at his distraught friend sloshing through a breaking wave, it's obvious that imposing might be his best option.

"Anything we can do to help?" Carol calls down to Jason from the deck.

Jason looks at her, then crosses the sand to get to Kyle. "Yeah," he calls over his shoulder. "Think I'm going to take you up on that offer to come inside."

"That's good," he hears Mitch say. "Calm your friend down."

But Jason's jogging now, while loosening a few buttons on his gray vest. *Damn*, he thinks while sloshing into the shallows. Not only is his prosthesis wet, but his suit pants are as ruined as the day now, too. From behind, he puts his arm around Kyle in a faux headlock. "Come on, you big lug." He turns Kyle back onto the beach, not letting go of him this time as he drops his arm around his friend's shoulders. "You'll be okay, guy. Let's go inside now."

Kyle says nothing. And Jason can figure there's nothing much left to say. By calling off the vow renewal today, either Kyle did the right thing, or he didn't.

Who knows? Maybe it *was* a mistake. But Jason wasn't there when it happened. Didn't *see* Kyle face the return of a brother he'd evicted from his life years ago. The brother who'd done him wrong. The brother Kyle had sworn off with all the beach friends when they sat around a bonfire up on Little Beach one summer night. As the flames flickered and rose to the sky, Shane Bradford was written off as good as dead. By all of them.

And today? Well, today feels pretty much like a storm washing Shane right back.

⁓

In the dark night, Jason snatches up Kyle's boat shoes and leads him to the deck stairs of the last-standing cottage on the beach. They climb the wooden steps, and once inside, Mitch brings Kyle to a seat on the porch facing the water. Hooks his arm around Kyle's shoulder and talks to him, calms him right down. Mitch has that way about him. It's all there in his low-key voice, his chill mannerisms. So how many times did Mitch, back in *his* day, talk someone down? Get someone through, like he's getting Kyle through tonight. Yeah, if Jason had to say so, Mitch actually has a bit of hippie soul in him.

So Kyle's in good hands here.

Jason follows them onto the enclosed porch. He walks to the paned windows overlooking the Sound and the rocky outcropping. That low moon casts a swath of pale light on the water, while leaving the rocks in shadow. Jason drags his hand along the splintery windowsill, and he feels peeling paint on the dried-out wood. A steady dose of sunshine and salt air will do that, in no time. The furniture in this dimly lit room is sparse, too. Sparse as the weathered window frames. There are graying lobster-trap end tables; faded wicker chairs; dusty table lamps; a chipped blue lantern—its glass casing filled with seashells rather than a candle.

Ordinarily, his architect mind would be filing away these nighttime details. But Jason can barely even think straight—let alone imagine resuming work here in this castaway cottage in the coming days.

All the while, Carol is turning on lights in the adjoining living room, while Mitch sits beside Kyle. Mitch leans forward, elbows on his knees, face turned to Kyle as he talks.

But something else draws Jason's attention. He'd never noticed it before: a framed photograph hanging on the wall over one of those lobster-trap end tables. He steps closer, cuffs his damp shirtsleeves, and studies the photo. Mitch had mentioned weeks ago that he had an actual picture of Hurricane Carol crashing into this cottage in the 1950s. This must be it. The camera caught a towering wave rising over Stony Point Beach. Several cottages on the sand, including the Fenwick cottage, are in that furious wave's direct path. The storm surge in the photograph is violent—a mountain of churning sea reaching right up and over the stately two-story beach homes like some mythical sea creature.

Running his knuckles along his scarred jawline, Jason glances over at Kyle. He's quiet, sitting with his head bowed down, his hands clasped behind his neck.

Overtaken by the day.

Overtaken by the way Shane surged back into their lives, as threatening as the ocean wave washing over the cottages in the black-and-white photograph.

And just like in that grainy photo, something's going down with today's wave. Jason can feel it. Maybe that's why his leg's been acting up. He's been sensing the ominous reach of Shane Bradford since this afternoon.

Standing in a room where the salt-coated cottage windows never let the sea out of his sight, Jason knows *exactly* what rule of the sea his father would tell him. He'd stand beside Jason, look out at the water, and be sure his son fully understood this rule. Understood the dire consequences of not obeying it.

Never turn your back on the sea, boys, his father often said. *As beautiful and peaceful as it is, don't trust it. Because as soon as you're not looking, it'll change. It'll rise up behind you and do its best to take you down, to pull you right into its depths and even end your life.*

Like it did to those cottages on the beach. The sea rose up and claimed them.

Like it did to Gordon, too, in his rowboat while searching for little lost Sailor.

Jason watches Kyle sitting in shadow now, sipping from a glass of water Carol gave him. Kyle wasn't looking, and today? The sea turned right behind his back. The same way it did in the mounted photograph, some frothing seawater in Kyle's life reaches as high as those weather-beaten cottage rooftops on the beach.

There's no denying that Shane Bradford's arrived. Everyone here has felt that blow today. And there's no telling who or what will remain intact, once this godawful day recedes.

Never turn your back on the sea. That warning couldn't be more fitting. Because Jason gets it now, as surely as if his father were standing beside him. It's instinct, really, the way Jason tugs at the Vietnam dog tags hanging around his neck.

Tonight, the one thing Jason Barlow knows, and it scares him as much as it angers him, is this: As long as Shane Bradford is in town, Jason will never—not for one single, treacherous moment—turn his back on that man.

The beach friends' journey continues in

NIGHT BEACH

The next novel in The Seaside Saga from New York Times Bestselling Author

JOANNE DEMAIO

Also by Joanne DeMaio

The Seaside Saga
(In order)
1) Blue Jeans and Coffee Beans
2) The Denim Blue Sea
3) Beach Blues
4) Beach Breeze
5) The Beach Inn
6) Beach Bliss
7) Castaway Cottage
8) Night Beach
9) Little Beach Bungalow
10) Every Summer
—And More Seaside Saga Books—

Summer Standalone Novels
True Blend
Whole Latte Life

Winter Novels
Eighteen Winters
First Flurries
Cardinal Cabin
Snow Deer and Cocoa Cheer
Snowflakes and Coffee Cakes

For a complete list of books by *New York Times* bestselling author Joanne DeMaio, visit:

Joannedemaio.com

About the Author

JOANNE DEMAIO is a *New York Times* and *USA Today* bestselling author of contemporary fiction. The novels of her ongoing and groundbreaking Seaside Saga journey with a group of beach friends, much the way a TV series does, continuing with the same cast of characters from book-to-book. In addition, she writes winter novels set in a quaint New England town. Joanne lives with her family in Connecticut.

For a complete list of books and for news on upcoming releases, please visit Joanne's website. She also enjoys hearing from readers on Facebook.

Author Website:
Joannedemaio.com

Facebook:
Facebook.com/JoanneDeMaioAuthor

Made in the USA
Middletown, DE
15 May 2023